Books by Cheryl Holt

*My True Love**

*Mountain Dreams**

*My Only Love**

*The Way of the Heart**

Double Fantasy

Forbidden Fantasy

Secret Fantasy

Too Wicked to Wed

Too Tempting to Touch

Too Hot to Handle

Further Than Passion

More Than Seduction

Deeper Than Desire

Complete Abandon

Absolute Pleasure

Total Surrender

Love Lessons

*Published by Kensington Publishing Corporation

MY TRUE LOVE

CHERYL HOLT

ZEBRA BOOKS
Kensington Publishing Corp.
www.kensingtonbooks.com

ZEBRA BOOKS are published by

Kensington Publishing Corp.
850 Third Avenue
New York, NY 10022

All Kensington titles, imprints, and distributed lines are available at special quantity discounts for bulk purchases for sales promotion, premiums, fund-raising, educational, or institutional use.

Special book excerpts or customized printings can also be created to fit specific needs. For details, write or phone the office of the Kensington Special Sales Manager: Attn. Special Sales Department. Kensington Publishing Corp., 850 Third Avenue, New York, NY 10022. Phone: 1-800-221-2647.

Zebra and the Z logo Reg. U.S. Pat. & TM Off.

ISBN-13: 978-0-8217-7872-2
ISBN-10: 0-8217-7872-2

First Printing: March 2001
10 9 8 7 6 5 4 3 2

Printed in the United States of America

CHAPTER ONE

Lucas Pendleton hurried quietly down the long corridor, counting the doors he passed, looking for movement and checking for hiding places in case a servant came wandering by. Luckily he'd not seen another living soul since sneaking inside.

Laughter came from somewhere far off in the grand house. A handful of silver clanged on china, and he paused, listening for footsteps, but none came in his direction. He took a deep breath, let it out, then started off again.

So far, the hastily drawn map he'd coaxed from the tavern maid, Peggy, had proved to be surprisingly accurate. The alley, the mews, the unlocked back gate, the concealing hedges, the open entrance off the terrace, all had been located in exactly the spots she'd indicated. According to her calculations, the library would be just ahead on the right. Very soon he'd be inside, where, according to Peggy, he would not have long to wait for the duke to make an appearance, as he purportedly did after each evening's meal.

He hoped the girl was as well-informed about the exalted man's personal habits as she was about his house. If she was mistaken and the duke didn't show his face, Lucas was prepared to wait hours, or even days, if that's how long it took to force a confrontation.

As he thought of Peggy, the plump, friendly young woman he'd cajoled and seduced in order to obtain the necessary information about Harold Westmoreland, the Duke of Roswell, he felt double stabs of guilt and regret. A bag of coins was being delivered to her just about then, along with his carefully penned good-bye note, and the combination would ease some of her upset. Although Peg was hardly an innocent, he still hated using her as he had, but he hadn't been able to find anyone else who possessed the knowledge he needed to get him safely in and out of the manor.

His dispute with the Duke of Roswell was a family matter, and where Lucas's family was concerned, he would take any risk, shoulder any task, carry any burden in his efforts to protect them. His parents had died when he was a young boy, causing him and his brother and sister to endure the hardest of childhoods. Lucas had grown up knowing that he would eventually assume the care of his two younger siblings, and that's exactly what he'd done. For years their lives and happiness had been all he cared about, and if he had to deceive a kind person such as Peggy in order to discharge his responsibilities to one of them, so be it. There was no other choice.

In all the weeks he'd been in London, trying and failing to arrange a valid appointment with Harold Westmoreland, it had quickly become apparent that he was going to have to use alternate methods to obtain his meeting. Westmoreland was too wealthy, too powerful for a man such as himself to gain an audience if the duke wasn't willing to grant it.

Lucas had knocked on the duke's door numerous times without being admitted. He'd written a dozen unanswered letters and finally taken to watching the duke and tracking his movements, attempting to find a means by which their paths would cross, but Westmoreland never went anywhere alone. He was always surrounded by armed servants, fit and serious-looking, who appeared to know their jobs and understand their duties, the main one apparently to prevent the rabble from approaching their distinguished employer.

If they had been on more equal terms, if Lucas had brought along a cadre of his own men instead of just his brother, Matthew, he might have been successful in arranging a showdown. As it was, he was an American, an outsider, highly visible because of his clothing and accent. He couldn't infiltrate the duke's world by himself.

Before coming to England, he and Matthew had agreed that they would try to keep the affair as quiet as possible. The duke was married, had two grown children, and Lucas and his brother had no desire to embarrass them or to cause any sort of public uproar. They had simply intended to resolve the problem with a minimum of fuss and bother.

What they hadn't counted on was that the duke could not have cared less that a pair of upstart Americans wanted to speak with him. In the times they'd rapped on Westmoreland's door, politely requesting a meeting and having it denied, it wasn't as though Lucas could blurt out to a doorman the important reason for his solicitation, not unless he wanted all of London to know their business. They had eventually decided to resort to more effective measures, but it would certainly have been prudent to have brought along a few more hands to set to the job.

While Matthew was highly competent in carrying out any kind of dubious enterprise, and exactly the type of man you wanted protecting your backside, there were only the two of them. They hardly had the forces to overwhelm the duke's guards, so Lucas hadn't been able to do more than catch an occasional glimpse of Westmoreland as he went to and from his carriage.

"But that's about to change," he murmured to himself.

Stopping short, he looked up and down the hall, then slipped into the library. A hasty scan indicated that no one was there. A fire burned in the grate, a brandy had been poured and awaited the duke's pleasure, sitting as it was in the center of the large desk. Lucas thought about downing the amber liquid himself and leaving the empty glass for the duke to discover, but he didn't. Much as he relished the idea of committing that one small, rude act, he dared not. He wanted no trace of alcohol dulling his senses.

He walked to the end of the room in order to hide behind the heavy velvet drapes, but as he passed, he couldn't help but observe the opulence of the surroundings. With each step he'd taken through the vast structure, his eyes had lingered on costly objects. The place was quiet and cold as a tomb and seemed much like a museum, packed as it was with treasures and valuables—artifacts, knickknacks, paintings, rugs. The wallpaper shimmered with gold inlay, the brass fittings glimmered in the dim lights. Everything was dusted, polished, expensive, and displayed with the obvious intent of letting others perceive just how large a fortune the man enjoyed, how supreme and omnipotent he was because of it.

The luxurious ambiance only strengthened Lucas's resolve. The man could pay. The man *would* pay. If it was the last thing Lucas ever did in his life, he would see to it that the Duke of Roswell lived up to the obligations he had incurred to Lucas's family.

His wait was not long. In minutes the library door opened, and footsteps crossed the floor, coming around the desk. Wanting to be certain it was Westmoreland and not a servant, Lucas glanced out from his clandestine location just in time to observe the back of the duke's head as he settled himself in the large chair. Sighing wearily as if he were carrying a huge weight on his shoulders, he leaned against the soft leather, closed his eyes, and relaxed for a moment before reaching for the glass of liquor.

Lucas watched furtively as the infusion of drink visibly caused the tension to leave the duke's body. Lucas waited while Westmoreland sampled the beverage a few more times, then set the heavy crystal on the desk. Only after he'd steepled his fingers over his stomach did Lucas make his move.

With a silent tread he was away from the curtain and behind the other man, the barrel of his pistol dug hard into the duke's neck. "Don't move," he warned, "or I'll blow your head off." Westmoreland shifted slightly, and Lucas pressed the barrel deeper into his throat. "I mean it. I'll kill you without a thought."

"I believe you," Westmoreland responded, instantly growing still as a statue. "What do you want?"

"Put your hands where I can see them." Westmoreland didn't budge, so Lucas ordered, "On the desk! Now!" The man leaned forward as much as he could with the gun hovering so intimately against his skin, and obeyed by resting his palms against the dark mahogany.

"If it's coin you're seeking," Westmoreland said carefully, "I don't keep any in here. . . ."

"Be silent!" Lucas advised. "I want you to look upon my face"—the duke's brows rose at this—"so I'm coming around the desk. Keep your hands in plain sight and keep your mouth closed unless I ask you to speak." Westmoreland's gaze flew to the door, and he wondered at his chances if he called for help. "Don't even think about it," Lucas threatened. "I'll kill you before anyone can make it through. It matters not what happens to me after that, and it won't matter to you much either. You'll be long dead before they arrive."

"All right," Westmoreland said with a hint of a nod. "Please explain yourself."

Slowly Lucas removed the pistol, then tucked it into the waist of his trousers. In his thirty years he'd used a weapon numerous times and knew he could retrieve it in an instant if need be, but he truly hoped he wouldn't be required to shoot the despicable swine. Much as he would like to see Westmoreland cold and in the ground, Lucas would much rather have him alive and repenting his sins.

Keeping a wary eye on the duke, he took one step, then another, until they were face-to-face for the very first time. To his great surprise, Westmoreland wasn't anything like he'd expected. Certainly he appeared wealthy and refined, dressed as he was for supper in a dark blue velvet jacket. Set against it, the white of his shirt was dazzling, the knot at his neck intricate and perfectly tied. But he was a much younger man than Lucas had imagined him to be.

Although he had heard the man was only forty-five, for some reason he'd gotten it into his head that Westmoreland was decrepit and elderly. While Lucas had wanted him to be old and disgusting, the duke seemed active and actually quite handsome. Lucas had fed his anger and outrage off visions of an ancient, experienced lecher who pleasured his sick physical appetite at the expense of innocent young women, but this man seemed capable of nothing of the sort. He was the absolute representation of an English gentleman.

Slender and roguish, he was one of those lucky fellows who grew better-looking with age. Obviously of aristocratic blood, with high cheekbones and a patrician nose, he was the type of comely devil over whom women swooned. His full head of white-blond hair just going to silver was tied back in a short tail. His eyes were a deep sapphire, the shade enhanced by the blue of his jacket. They showed evidence of a keen, shrewd intelligence, taking in all the details and nuances of the situation and missing nothing.

There was an aura of command and strength about him, indicating he was comfortable with his position in life. Most likely he'd have been enormously successful at any endeavor, even if he'd been born without all the trappings afforded by his fortune and pedigree. A powerful individual, he was clearly used to giving orders and getting his own way. He would be a tough adversary, but then, Lucas had suspected he would be, and he was not daunted by the idea.

In his struggles as a boy, unwillingly conscripted to the hard life of a sailor, and later as a young man starting and running his own shipping business, he'd repeatedly gone up against the worst class of villains, brutes who were a thousand times more ruthless and vicious than this highborn man could ever be.

Nothing scared Lucas anymore, especially not the rich, pampered nobleman sitting before him.

"I apologize for all this drama," Lucas asserted, "but I have been trying to arrange an appointment with you for weeks."

Westmoreland shrugged. "I am a busy man."

"My name is Lucas Pendleton," he said tersely. If his identity meant anything at all to Westmoreland, he didn't indicate it by so much as a blink. Deep down Lucas had been hoping that the duke was afraid to meet because he knew who Lucas was, why he'd crossed an ocean to seek an audience, what kinds of demands he would make, but Westmoreland showed no reaction.

"How do you do?" the duke said, nodding his head in polite recognition of the introduction.

"My sister was Caroline Pendleton," Lucas declared, but still the bastard didn't move a muscle, and Lucas's anger came to a quick boil. "Before you have time to think of some inane response, let me tell you that if you pretend you don't know who she was, I shall come around this immaculate desk, wrap my two hands about your throat, and squeeze until there is not a single breath left in your body."

Harold Westmoreland glared into the eyes of the enraged man before him, and all he could wonder was why the fates had conspired to bring about such a dreadful encounter at just that moment. Hadn't the family supper he'd just survived, attended by his daughter Penelope's new and extremely horrid fiancé, been quite enough torture for the evening? Would his torment never cease? How much emotional upheaval could one man be expected to endure in a single night?

He hated the fact that he was sitting while his foe was standing, because their positions put him at too much of a disadvantage, yet he didn't think rising to face Pendleton would be a good idea. Harold liked to flaunt his rank in order to keep others cowed, but Pendleton clearly placed no importance on titles or position. If he had, he would never have dared commit so outrageous an act as breaking into Harold's home. No,

Harold's usual haughty attitude would hardly work, but his height wouldn't intimidate either.

Pendleton was over six feet tall, Harold three inches or more shorter, so he couldn't overawe the knave with excessive size. Even if they were of the same build, he had none of the younger man's impressive, lithe, predatory grace. Pendleton moved like a stalking cat, tanned, lanky, and fit, with the type of solid torso that comes only from a lifetime of strenuous employment. Given those broad shoulders, long, muscled arms, and strong fingers, Harold felt quite certain that Pendleton could easily carry out the threat he had just made about strangulation.

The scoundrel's nerve and physique were just two of the reasons Harold stayed seated. There was a third: Pendleton was filled with righteous indignation. The man was like a lethal keg of gunpowder ready to blow, and Harold couldn't expect to avoid an explosion except by remaining cool and calm.

"I know Caroline," he admitted cautiously. "A lovely young woman. An American, I believe. I met her several years ago when she was here visiting her English cousins."

"Yes," Lucas said, filled with relief that Westmoreland had admitted the acquaintance. There'd be no cause to beat it out of him.

"I haven't seen her in a very long time," Harold said, stalling, trying to recall everything he could about her. There had been so many women in his life that sometimes it was difficult to distinguish one from the next, but not in this case. Upon seeing the brother with all his long, dark hair and those intense brown eyes, the sister was easily remembered. Beautiful and graceful, in her early twenties, she was thin and tall, having no similarities to the pale blond English beauties with whom he typically consorted. She'd had a quiet, interesting manner about her, a good sense of humor, was easy to talk with and easy to like. All in all, she was exactly the kind of female he often wished he'd been allowed to marry.

Unbidden, a smile flickered and, as rapidly as it came, he suppressed it. Once Caroline Pendleton had learned the ways of intimate affairs, she'd become a passionate, involved mistress—although he hardly intended to mention such a tidbit to her outraged male family member.

Ah, Caroline, what a sweetheart she had been! How joyously their pretty summer had passed. And how quickly! Pulling himself back from his hasty, delicious reverie, he queried, "How is she?"

"She's dead."

"You have my sympathies," Harold said, trying to show little sentiment himself. "My condolences to your family."

"We don't want your condolences," Lucas said hotly. "Wouldn't you like to know how she died?"

"If you would like to tell me," Harold responded, hesitant now, beginning to fear where this might be leading.

"She died in childbirth," Lucas said, finally getting the reaction for which he'd been waiting. The duke went completely still, not breathing, not flinching, simply processing. Lucas could almost hear the wheels spinning inside Westmoreland's head as he added, "Approximately six months after leaving England."

"Isn't that interesting?" Harold said weakly, not meaning it, and suddenly feeling as though he might become ill. Swallowing, he asked, "How long ago was that?"

"Almost five years."

"Then, I must beg your pardon," he blustered, "but I'm extremely confused about what brings you here. I assume it has something to do with Caroline's death, but I fail to see what any of it has to do with me. . . ."

"Shut your lying mouth," Lucas barked, wishing he had the fortitude to kill Westmoreland then and there for what had happened to Caroline. Sarcastic, and intentionally wanting to goad, he used Westmoreland's given name. "It's a *boy*, Harold. Congratulations." Before the duke could comment, Lucas retrieved his pistol once again and aimed it directly at the man's chest. "He's four years old now, almost five, and if you say that he is not yours, I will put a ball through your heart before you can draw your next breath.''

Harold ran his tongue over his bottom lip, his mind briskly calculating whether it was possible. Could he have left her with a bastard child?

Their affair had been exactly the kind he liked best: short and sweet, with no chance for lingering affection and no opportunity for hanging on after he was ready for the woman to be gone. Rarely had he been alone with Caroline, their handful of assignations so risky, their time together curtailed by her return to America. There had been so much more he could have taught her, so much more he had wanted her to experience.

But a child? No, it simply couldn't be. He refused to accept it.

If such a disastrous event had occurred, why would she not have written once she became aware of her condition? Just as abruptly, he realized that perhaps she had, but with the vagaries of ocean travel he had never received her message. Which was just as well. What could he have done anyway?

Staring down the barrel of a loaded pistol cast a definite pall over his usual assuredness. Prudently he began, ''I'm not saying I'm not the lad's father—''

''Harry,'' Lucas interjected. ''His name is Harry. She asked us to name him after you,'' although that wasn't entirely true. Caroline had never admitted who the father had been. Lucas had used a variety of threats in attempting to learn the answer, but she'd refused to tell, correctly assuming that Lucas would want to exact revenge against the man who had compromised her while she had been so far from home and away from the protection of her two older brothers.

On her deathbed, with practically her last breath, she had requested that her male babe be named Harold and referred to as Harry, but she had not explained why. It was only years later, when Lucas had come across the letter she'd written but never sent, that he had discovered his nephew's paternity.

''Well . . .'' Harold murmured, for once at a loss for words.

They glared at each other angrily, neither willing to be the first to look away, and Harold had to suppress a surge of admiration for the reckless American. Few men of his acquaintance were brave enough to challenge him in such a fashion.

Pendleton was either immensely courageous or completely mad. Perhaps it was a combination of both.

Finally Harold asked, "What is it you want from me?"

One utterance described all that Lucas required. "Recognition."

Harold snorted in disbelief. "You can't mean it!"

"I am serious." Lucas's finger flexed on the trigger. "Deadly serious."

"I have no intention of claiming the child," Harold insisted, suddenly feeling more bold. A chap like Pendleton, who was seeking a father's declaration for his illegitimate nephew, couldn't get it from a dead man. No matter how much Pendleton swaggered or prognosticated, he wouldn't kill the only person who could confirm or deny the allegation, and Harold wasn't about to confirm anything.

As far as he was aware, he had sired one other bastard child, a grown daughter named Maggie. Despite their rocky past, they managed to lump along rather well, but he still hadn't publicly declared himself to be her father, even though she was now an accepted member of society and married to the Marquis of Belmont. She'd been born years earlier to a mistress before Harold had wed, and if he hadn't gifted *her* with paternal identification, he was hardly about to take such a drastic step on behalf of this foreign upstart over a boy he'd never met and who hadn't existed for him until the past few minutes.

"And I think I've heard enough," he said, confidently coming to his feet. "It's time for you to go. I will *never* acknowledge the boy. Despite what you say or how fervently you press, you will never convince me that I am the bastard's father."

Lucas let pass the slight over Harry's birth. There were other, bigger issues to address, and the facts clearly indicated that Harry *was* a bastard. But Westmoreland was going to ease the lad's way. Lucas would see to it if it took every last breath, his very last penny. He reached into the pocket of his vest and pulled out a miniature that had been painted a few months earlier, just before they'd set sail from Virginia, headed for London.

"Look at that boy's face," Lucas said. He tossed the likeness onto the desk, where it landed with a damning thunk. "Look into those blue eyes and then have the gall to tell me he is not your son."

Tentatively Harold picked up the gold frame and perused the rendering. It might have been a portrait of himself at the same age. Still, he felt compelled to assert, "No one will ever believe you."

"We'll see, won't we?" Lucas said, trusting that the unpleasantness would never become public gossip, that it could be resolved peacefully and privately. "I realize you would not wish to embarrass your wife and family with the details of Harry's birth. I understand your concerns. Therefore, I have no need for you to make any general announcements. I'm happy to handle it confidentially, just between us."

"You are mad!" Harold sneered, thinking now that the American was insane after all. He'd listened to enough nonsense and wanted only that the blowhard be dispatched without delay.

"Jensen!" he shouted at the top of his lungs, calling for his butler, but the man was probably far away, in another part of the house, and unlikely to have heard his summons. Harold yelled again, hoping in vain that someone, *anyone,* might come to his aid, but chances were remote. As per his standing order, he wasn't to be disturbed for any reason during this regular respite of quiet in the evening. No servant would be lurking outside the door.

To summon assistance he needed to reach the bellpull on the other side of the room, but Pendleton would never allow that. Harold knew he was already pushing his luck by bellowing for Jensen, but he hadn't been shot outright for his bald action, so he was greatly encouraged. Pendleton wasn't quite as ruthless as he was trying to appear, but he was foolhardy. He couldn't know how isolated they were, that rescue was improbable; at any moment footmen might burst into the room, yet he stood there, calm as you please.

"All I require," Lucas said, completely ignoring Westmoreland's outburst, "is your signature on papers I've prepared." His eyes narrowed in disgust. How he ached to kill the man that very second! But he had sense enough to know he couldn't, not when he had yet to obtain what he had come for. Later he could call out Westmoreland, exacting his final retribution, but only after the entire impasse was successfully concluded.

He continued. "You will admit that you are the boy's father. You will put funds into a trust account for him that will remain sealed until his twenty-first birthday. You will also pay the start-up costs of whatever business he chooses to undertake as an adult. Other than that, you will never hear from us."

"Why don't I believe you?" Harold scoffed. "You're nothing but a bloodsucking blackmailer."

Westmoreland's volume was rising with each word. Lucas listened carefully, and off in the distance he could hear people rushing down the cavernous hall. Only seconds remained. "If you refuse to comply with my terms, I shall exact my revenge publicly." He leaned closer, pressing his thighs into the edge of the desk and adding quietly, "On your family."

"You wouldn't dare!"

"Wouldn't I?" Lucas asked. "I have not killed you today, but I don't think you should question my resolve." He turned toward the fireplace. It took up a good share of one wall. Above it hung a portrait of the woman Lucas knew to be the duke's wife. Lucas aimed and fired, hitting the posed duchess right in the heart. Westmoreland was so shocked that he gasped and fell back into his chair. From out in the hall came clamoring and noises, but Lucas didn't mind, for he was ready to depart. Reaching behind his back, he pulled out a second pistol and pointed it at the duke.

"I'll give you three days to consider your answer," he said, then walked to the door and opened it as though he hadn't a care in the world. Casually glancing out, he saw two maids huddled on the stairs, a third hurrying down. "I'll kill anyone who follows me," he pronounced loudly, tipping his head toward the cowering women and causing all three to jump. Over his shoulder he glared at Westmoreland a final time. "I'll send word on how you can reach me with your decision."

With that he was off and running, disappearing from the enormous house as quickly and easily as he'd come.

Frozen in his chair, Harold watched the blackguard go, but he didn't give chase as he supposed he should have. The room was filled with smoke, and his ears were ringing from the sound of the blast. He didn't know why the exhibition had left him so shaken. Pendleton had only shot at a harmless painting— one of which Harold had never been fond—but there was something extremely disturbing and violent about the act. Yet, Pendleton hadn't batted an eye while committing it, hadn't so much as flinched when the pistol banged and jerked so loudly.

Harold's knees had turned to jelly, and he couldn't seem to raise the alarm so that others would attempt to catch the lunatic, which was probably just as well. Pendleton was deranged, and heaven forbid that any of the servants come face-to-face with the madman. There was no telling what he might do.

All Harold could accomplish was to sit speechlessly, steadying his breathing. Many minutes later Jensen appeared, his supper interrupted by recent events, a napkin still dangling from his collar. Several curious footmen and maids fluttered behind him in the doorway, trying to see what had occurred.

On seeing that the duke was alive and in one piece, the short, squat, unflappable butler calmed himself, instantly halting while straightening his jacket by tugging at its hem.

"Your Grace," he said with a slight bow, his usual reserve firmly in place, "may I inquire, are you all right?"

"Yes, Jensen."

"May I get you anything?"

"A brandy, please."

"Very good, Your Grace." He flashed a menacing glance to those peeking around him, and they scattered like leaves in the wind, then he went to the sideboard and poured, filling the glass nearly to the rim.

Harold took a long gulp, draining the drink in a single swallow, letting the burn sizzle though his stomach and instantly go to work on his shattered nerves. Severely frazzled, he rested his head in his hands.

Another bastard child! he raged, bemoaning his luck. *Would they now start coming out of the woodwork?*

What had been the Good Lord's reasoning to create mortal man with such overpowering physical needs and drives, only to leave unwanted children as the result? Harold was only human after all. How could he be expected to resist the luscious temptation offered by the Caroline Pendletons of the world?

He looked up, found the butler waiting patiently for orders. "We've had an unwelcome visitor, Jensen."

"I surmised as much," the butler affirmed, his eyes straying to the ruined portrait and back again without betraying a flicker of curiosity.

"Send word around to my man, Purdy. I absolutely must consult with him this evening. I need him to find information on an American. He goes by the name of Lucas Pendleton."

"I'll have the message delivered immediately."

Harold stared at the man's napkin, still immaculately folded under his chin. "That will be all," he said. "You may return to your meal."

"Thank you, milord." Jensen took a step toward the hallway before looking back at Harold with no hint of any emotion showing on his worn face. "And the painting, milord, of Her Grace. Should I have it removed?"

"Later."

"Very good, sir. I bid you good evening."

He walked out and the door clicked shut, leaving Harold alone with his calamitous, guilty introspection.

CHAPTER TWO

Penelope Westmoreland strolled along the rear wall of her father's dark garden. The air was moist and cool, and she suppressed a shiver—one that was not entirely from the cold—and pulled her black sable cloak more tightly about her shoulders. It was an exotic piece of fur given to her as a gift by a Russian countess, and she ran her hand across the soft nap, thinking how perfectly it contrasted with her virginal white gown and long, blond hair, making her flawless skin appear pale and translucent.

The meal she'd just eaten in her parents' lavish dining room had been a tedious affair, as she'd known it would be, so she wasn't certain why she'd gone to so much trouble with her appearance. Habit, she supposed, and she had to admit that she'd looked beautiful with her hair swept up on her head, the two ringlets dangling on her bare shoulders exactly as they were supposed to. She'd worn a new dress that had been expertly tailored by the finest French modiste in London, and it was styled to show off the newer, trimmer figure she'd acquired; her personal debacles of the past three years had caused her to lose weight.

Even her jewelry had been dazzling, all those strings and

bangles and combs of pearls. The very finest, most exquisite pieces had been taken from the family vault just for that evening's special engagement supper.

No doubt about it, she had looked exceptional. Custom of a lifetime had required that she not appear at her father's table unless she was magnificently turned out. She had always been the wealthiest, the prettiest, the most sought after girl in the world, but not any longer, so adorning herself meticulously hardly seemed worth the effort.

At age twenty, and quickly marching toward twenty-one, she was well past her prime, far beyond those first heady days of her debut three years earlier, where the only thing that had mattered was what gown she would wear to what event. Those times of innocent flirtation and romance were gone, but how she wished she could recapture some of the excitement they had engendered!

As the only daughter of the Duke of Roswell, she had been fawned over wherever she went. Hostesses had begged her to attend their soirees, other girls jealously regarded her across crowded ballrooms, wondering which of the men they wanted for themselves might be considering Penny instead. And there had been so many.

The gentlemen had lined up, making marriage offers to her father, while she in return had passed her leisurely hours doing nothing more strenuous than having her skin creamed and her body perfumed, reviewing invitations with her mother, orchestrating her fate, and setting the standard in appearance and affluence that others could only blindly follow.

But that thrilling era was behind her.

She rarely went out anymore, because when she did, people laughed at her behind her back, pointing and sniggering over her plight. The women she'd grown up around, whom she'd always considered friends and admirers, weren't that at all. They were married, most having already produced the heirs expected of them, and they were ready to gloat, happy to rejoice over how far Penny had fallen from her lofty beginnings. A vicious lot, their malice was frightening to see, their words painful to hear, their dislike palpable.

Where once on a Saturday evening she would have passed from ball to supper to ball and danced till dawn, now she was merely tired, distressed, and wished only to be left alone while she figured out what course of action she could take to keep the future from rushing toward her. With the ferocity of an approaching storm, her destiny was bearing down, and very like a force of nature, she could deduce no method for steering it in another direction.

Even though it was March, her mother had had lamps lit along the walkways so that guests could enjoy an evening stroll, but Penny had been the only one to slip outside. Many of the tapers had burned down, and they gave off just enough light to mark the path but were dim enough to provide her with privacy. An added benefit, the multiple shrubs and hedges shielded her from view from the back of the house. Still, she cautiously glanced toward it. If Edward, her current fiancé, saw her and came out into the garden, she wasn't certain she could be responsible for her actions.

"Oh, Father," she murmured, shaking her head as she recalled how unperturbed the duke had appeared throughout the wretched meal they'd just endured. "How could you do this to me?"

If he had his way, she would be wed in June, at last. After all the cancellations, the machinations, the plotting and planning, it would finally happen. Once upon a time she had truly believed that marriage to a gentleman of their social class was the one and only occurrence that could make her happy. Now she shuddered at the thought.

It would be her third attempt at making a trip to the altar. On the first occasion, she had been betrothed to Adam St. Clair, the Marquis of Belmont, the man she had dreamed of having as her husband from the time she was a child. Adam was more than a decade older, sophisticated, and worldly in every manner she was not. The proposed union had been a typical arrangement, but she'd believed herself to be madly in love, and she'd naively assumed Adam would grow to love her in return.

During those marvelous months of their engagement she'd been deliriously ecstatic, certain she had made the grandest match in history, reveling in the envy of others, flaunting her good luck wherever she went.

But to her mortification, Adam cried off at the last moment, deciding instead to commit the unspeakable act of marrying his mistress. Just a week before what would have been the most splendid wedding ever held in London, she'd been jilted.

Although her father had spread the appropriate stories, saying Penny had decided they didn't suit, everyone knew the truth: Adam preferred someone else, and Penny's life had never been the same since. For months she hid in her rooms, refusing to venture out, unwilling to suffer the stares, finger-pointing, and crude remarks made just on the edge of her hearing, remarks that never failed to cut like the sharpest sword.

Then her father had come up with an excellent solution. Another man was willing to have her despite the embarrassment of what had happened with Adam. The candidate was a viscount who would become an earl someday, and he was close to her own age. Penny had been exhilarated, convinced that a good marriage would end her ongoing humiliation. Her husband-to-be lived and worked on his family's properties in Jamaica, and Penny decided that if nothing else, she could return to Jamaica with him and remove herself from the taunting, hateful eyes of Polite Society.

However, her second union was not to be either. Her swain was supposedly killed in an accident before he could make it to England for the nuptials. Her parents insisted that his carriage had overturned on a slick road, but after the furor had died down, she began to hear shocking stories about him. That he had been a gambler, a drunkard, a womanizer and wastrel, sent abroad by his London relatives because they couldn't abide his behavior. He had not been killed in an accident at all but had met his death while dueling over a woman—another man's wife.

While she'd never confessed as much to a single soul, she was relieved to have narrowly escaped being joined to the ne'er-do-well. She refused to accept her mother's type of existence, one of painfully whiling away the years in silent torment and pretending not to notice or care that her husband dallied with every lightskirted woman who caught his eye. Penny would rather be dead than suffer such a circumstance.

Finally, for the third attempt, her father had chosen Edward Simpson. He had just turned sixty-three the previous month. A widower three times over, he was bald and obese but also a wealthy and powerful earl, his fortune said to be equal to that of her father. At a more innocent time in her life, and despite his advanced age, she might have been excited and impressed by the prospect of becoming his countess. No longer.

Now she simply wanted to run away in order to avoid the coming calamity. After her second engagement had fallen through, she had begged the duke to secure another with someone who could quell the whispers and gossip, but she never imagined Edward would be the kind of man her father would select. On one melancholic occasion she had dared ask why, and he had answered honestly and brutally, as was his usual style.

No one else would have her.

The duke insisted that she wed a man of sufficient rank and prosperity, but in any given year there were not many marriageable men who met his exacting standards. Of those who were available, who were younger and would make her an appropriate husband, none was interested. For an unattached noble son seeking matrimony, there was a large assemblage of acceptable, unencumbered females from which to choose a bride, and Penny was no longer part of that group.

For the past three years she couldn't help but hear what people were saying about her: that she was jinxed, that she was bad luck, that she was a pompous, demanding shrew who was only getting what she deserved. Some even whispered that she'd been compromised, and that's why the duke couldn't find her a husband. The very idea made her laugh aloud, as she sometimes wondered if she wasn't perhaps the oldest living virgin in England. Gads, she was almost twenty-one, and she'd never even been properly kissed.

The wind rustled the trees, sending a blast of frigid air swirling through the garden, and she looked up at the sky, fearing the rain that had threatened all day would finally fall. How she hoped not! Foul weather would force her inside—to where Edward would be waiting. If she ran into him, she'd have to plead a headache and make an attempt for her room, but her mother would never allow her to escape the small party. The gathering was for the two of them, a signal to family and friends that the prenuptial festivities were about to officially begin.

Just then a shadow came down the path, and she hesitated, a bit unnerved. Who else might be out in the yard? When the form took shape, to her great dismay, she saw Edward approaching.

From the time she was still in the nursery, she had been acquainted with him as a colleague of her father's, though she'd not really known much about him. But with the engagement, he had been spending time in their home, and she was disheartened to discover that he was a drunkard, a glutton, a man of strong opinions and short temper who seemed to be always undressing her with his eyes and muttering sexual comments under his breath. On the few occasions he'd managed to get her alone, he'd taken physical advantage, attempting to kiss and paw at her. Just the thought of his touch started her shivering anew.

Had her father understood the kind of man Edward was when he arranged the marriage? Had he known of the drinking, the lewd language, the bouts of temperament? Had he known and, having no regard for Penny, gone ahead anyway? She wanted to hope that the duke was just learning, as she was, what her fiancé was truly like. After passing three hours at the supper table with Edward, she wanted the duke to be as miserable as she, but she was only fooling herself. Her father was perfectly content to have the entire affair proceed as planned.

The previous month, when she'd first been informed of her father's decision, no amount of pleading or arguing could change his mind. She'd stoically accepted Edward's proposal, sitting silent and graceful through the whole nightmare, letting Edward kiss her briefly on the mouth after she'd said yes, trying to smile while drinking sherry with the family to celebrate the news.

Edward had stood next to her through the ordeal, holding her hand or touching her shoulder, back, or waist, as though their arrangement had immediately given him special authority over her person. The afternoon had dragged on for an eternity, and once he'd departed, she'd run to her room, vomited again and again into the chamber pot, cried for hours, then remained in bed for two days, until the duke appeared and threatened to beat her if she didn't rise and carry on.

After all the scheming her father had instigated, after all the orders he'd forced her to obey, after all the paths he'd led her down while she'd blindly followed, here came her final reward: This man with the foul breath, body stench, lack of hair, and rotund figure, this elderly, obnoxious gentleman, was her father's idea of a suitable husband. And as Penny watched him approach, a drink in hand, the odor of alcohol lingering strongly, she couldn't help wondering if perhaps her father hated her. If perhaps he always had. If perhaps he'd never cared for her one whit.

"There you are, my little ducky," Edward said, slurring his words, stumbling and staggering. "I asked about you, but no one seemed to know where you'd gone."

"I needed some fresh air," she said, meaning it.

"You should have asked me to join you. I would have been more than happy to accompany you out of doors."

"Thank you," she murmured. "Next time I'll remember to invite you."

She wasn't certain how to deal with him. Although she'd never heard any whispers about him being abusive with his previous wives, she suspected that his temper could be formidable. He scared her, and she always felt the need to be on guard.

In his presence she never knew what to say or how to act. He constantly turned the conversation to physical topics, about her looks or size or some such. The manner in which he regarded her made her queasy, as though he were evaluating her for their wedding night, wishing he could find the opportunity to hurry things along.

"You misunderstand," he said, suddenly seeming more menacing. "I'll not have you walking about in the dark by yourself. Even on your father's property."

"All right," she said, thinking it best to agree. "I'll not do it again."

"That's my girl," he chided, his hulking figure blocking out the lights from the house. Her sense of unease grew in direct proportion to his nearness. "I like a child who knows how to do as she's told. Do you know how to do as you're told, my darling little Penny?"

"Of course," she said, smiling hesitantly.

She took a step back, and he moved with her. They were at the far end of the garden. Behind her there was a large expanse of high brick wall. The mansion was too distant for anyone to hear if she called out, and the only avenue for evasion was to slip by Edward and run in the direction from which he'd come.

"You'll be a fast learner, won't you, Penelope?" he asked.

His question sounded mean and frightening, and she couldn't help remembering how much he'd drunk during supper, how long the men had been at their port after the women had left the dining room. He had to be deep in his cups.

Feigning a chill, she pulled her cloak tighter. "It's getting rather cool, isn't it? Would you escort me back to the party?"

He laughed low in his throat, then reached out and twirled one of her ringlets around his finger, winding it tighter to the point where it started to hurt. Using it as leverage, he drew her close, until the flare of her skirt tangled around his thighs. "I don't want us to go just yet."

"I do," she insisted, feeling outright afraid.

"I think I'll steal a little kiss while we're here. You don't mind, do you, dearie? I've had so few opportunities to get you by yourself, and I've been eager to sample a little taste of what I'm buying."

The crudeness of his comment set her temper flaring, and she shook off her trepidation and tried to shove past, but he grabbed her arm. "Good night, Edward," she said in her fiercest tone, the one that always set others to trembling, but it had no effect on him.

"I'm not ready for you to leave," he said, his eyes glittering with a sickening carnal desire.

"You're drunk," was her reply.

"Not as drunk as I intend to be," he snickered.

"And you're being rude. Good night," she repeated more forcefully, trying to jerk away, but he only strengthened his grip, his fingers digging in hard. "Let go of me!" she demanded. "You're hurting my arm."

"Then do as I say," he ordered, "and I won't have to hold you so tightly." Instantly she relaxed, and his grasp lessened too. "See? You're learning already."

She bolted, but for an intoxicated man he reacted swiftly. There was a bench next to them, and he wrestled her onto it, forcing her down, then stretching out on top of her. Their bodies were on the smooth stone, their legs off on the grass. Before she realized what he intended, his mouth descended on hers, and she was invaded by his tongue working back and forth in a vulgar rhythm. He tasted like rancid tobacco, stale liquor, and unclean teeth, and by the time he pulled his lips away and began painfully biting and sucking against her neck, she was gagging and choking with disgust.

"Help me," she cried. "Please . . . someone . . ." But his large, fleshy hand covered her mouth, and she was silenced. Between her legs he was rocking his hips, and she could feel the hard ridge in his trousers that her French maid, Colette, was always yammering on about.

"What a wildcat you are." He breathed heavily, the putrid smell of his breath wafting over her face with each exhale. "We shall have many lovely hours of bed play between us. I can hardly wait."

The man was revolting! To think he dared treat her this way! He imagined he could steal a bit of her virtue on a garden bench as if she were some lowborn serving girl!

Completely outraged, she struggled in earnest but made little headway. He was too heavy to dislodge. She kicked with her legs and turned her head back and forth, finally managing to bite his hand. He angrily yanked it away, and she was able to call out. "Help! Someone!"

Suddenly Edward vanished. One moment he was there, the next he wasn't. Shakily she rose onto her elbow, only to behold another man picking him up by the lapels of his jacket. The force of it popped the fine stitching along the seams.

"What the bloody hell . . ." Edward muttered just as a fist connected with his stomach. The blow doubled him over, and the unknown attacker struck again, a severe right to the chin that sent Edward flying into the shrubbery.

The stranger was dressed all in black, from shirt to trousers to knee-high boots. His long hair looked black as well and was tied back with a black ribbon. His eyes were two dark pools gleaming with outrage and threat. With his high forehead, strong cheekbones, and aristocratic nose, he was very likely the most handsome man she'd ever seen.

Tall and broad-shouldered, his muscles thoroughly defined, he towered over Edward, protecting her and shielding her from further harm. Although he didn't know her or anything about her, and had absolutely no reason to intervene on her behalf, there he stood—her protector and savior. He was a magnificent specimen of potent male fury, shaking slightly, poised on the balls of his feet, and ready to pounce again at any second.

"Are you all right, miss?" he asked in an accented voice,

probably American. It was a deep, rich baritone that floated on the night air and skidded across her frazzled nerve endings in a soothing way.

"Yes . . . no . . ." She shook her head, unable to assemble a coherent thought. "I mean, he didn't have time to hurt me. I was just frightened . . . very frightened. . . ." Holding her terror at bay, she shuddered violently. "If you hadn't come along, I don't know what might have happened."

He turned his attention back to Edward, who was still cowering in the bushes. Crisp with affront, he kicked out with the toe of his boot, landing a hard thump against Edward's side, causing the other man to wince and recoil further.

"Wait! Stop!" Edward complained, holding up both hands in surrender. "It was just a bit of love play . . . I didn't mean any harm by it. . . ."

The foreigner reached down, grabbed him by the center of his shirt, and with one hand lifted him up until they were eye to eye.

"Apologize to the lady," he commanded in a manner that brooked no refusal.

Edward swallowed firmly, glanced her way, then mumbled, "I apologize."

The stranger lowered him until his feet touched the ground. "Bloody, drunken sot," he growled. "Get back to the house."

Edward tried to bluster, tugging at the bottom of his vest, patting at his thin, mussed hair. "How dare you lay a hand on me! Don't you know who I am?"

"No," the American said between clenched teeth, "and I don't give a rat's ass." He tipped his head slightly in Penny's direction. "Begging your pardon, miss."

"I say," Edward whined, "you can't just come up to me and do whatever you please!"

"I just did," the foreigner said dangerously, "and I'll not be responsible for my future actions if you don't immediately depart. I'm sickened by the sight of you."

Edward hesitated, glaring at her as if his comeuppance were

all her fault. The malice in his stare caused her to shift back
as though he'd slapped her. He made a move toward her, but
the stranger stepped in front of him, blocking his view and his
advance.

"This is your last warning," the interloper asserted. "If I
see your face again this night, you're a dead man!"

Apparently Edward believed the warning, for he started backing down the path, keeping a wary eye on his tormentor. The
American hurried him along by giving him a shove that sent
him floundering, but he regained his balance and lumbered
away, finally realizing he would be greatly out of his league
in trying to do battle with a sober, much younger man.

Lucas watched him go, every muscle primed and ready for
a fight, every sense prepared and alert for the possibility that
the coward might return, but apparently the windbag was tough
only when roughing up young women. He scurried toward the
grand domicile, slinking away like a whipped dog.

Once Lucas ascertained that the other man posed no further
threat, he turned his attention to the victim. She remained sitting,
shivering, a hand to her mouth, her eyes wide and fearful.

"Are you all right?" he asked again more softly. He took
a step closer, not wanting to frighten her any more than she
already had been, and when she didn't shy away, he seated
himself next to her.

"Yes, just terribly shaken," she admitted, unable to meet
his gaze, as though she had somehow been to blame for what
had happened.

Although he knew he should make good his escape from
Harold Westmoreland, he couldn't abandon her until he was
absolutely convinced that she was unharmed. He'd always been
a pushover for damsels in distress, having made a fool of
himself on numerous occasions for various women who found
themselves in dire straits. This instance seemed no different.
Cursing himself for the idiot he appeared to be, he stayed
despite every instinct telling him to flee.

For the time being he felt secure enough. As far as he could

surmise, after his dramatic exit Westmoreland had not raised
the alarm, so he had a few moments to spare. Refuge was a
mere leap away, his route to safety carefully planned and ready
to be executed. At the first sign of threat, he'd be over the wall
and swallowed up by the night.

He wondered about the fetching girl he'd chanced upon.
From her clothing, jewelry, and demeanor, she was obviously
from a wealthy family. Her fur cloak alone was probably worth
more than he'd earn in his entire life. Very likely she was a
supper guest of the Westmorelands. But who was she?

She was young, too young to be by herself with such an older
man. Had the cad lured her outside? Had she come willingly,
innocently unaware of his dubious intentions? Had she run into
him by accident and the knave taken drunken advantage? He
couldn't help speculating as to who her parents might be, and
what kind of people they were that they had allowed such a
dastardly misadventure to occur practically under their noses.

"Would you like me to walk you to the house?" The offer
was perilous, but he could hardly leave her huddled up and
anxious in the dark.

"No," she said, refusing with a shake of her head. "I'll be
fine. I just need a moment to gather myself together."

"But someone should know what happened," he said. "Is
your father about?"

"He wouldn't care, I shouldn't think."

"You must be joking."

"No, I'm not. Unfortunately." Her eyes glistened with
unshed tears. "That man you chased off is my fiancé. My father
selected him for me."

"Now I know you're joking," he insisted.

"I'm not. They're longtime acquaintances. My father knows
exactly the sort of man Edward is, yet he arranged a marriage
anyway."

Just then the clouds decided to part, and a sliver of moon
broke through. Its brilliant glow shone down on her, and he
felt his breath catch. In the shadows her beauty had been hinted

at, but in the fuller light she was spectacular. Her face was perfectly formed, heart-shaped, and lovely, with creamy skin, high cheekbones, a small nose upturned at the end, and generous pouting lips, the kind meant for kissing and no other task.

Her hair had come loose during the skirmish, and it hung long and free, so blond that it looked silver, and she seemed to shimmer with an unearthly luminescence. Though the moon was bright, he could not distinguish the color of her eyes, but he suspected they would be blue, a deep, dark sapphire that would only add to her allure. She stared at him, courageously fighting the tears that clung to her lashes.

"Oh, dear Lord," she exhaled softly, "what am I going to do?" Leaning forward, she rested her arms on her thighs, her shoulders sagging, her head down. "The wedding is in three months. I don't see how I shall be able to carry on until then. And after . . . oh, I can't bear to think about after. . . ."

"Is there anyone you can talk to?" he asked. "Anyone you can turn to for help?"

"No. There's no one," she said, and the admission was the last straw. The tears she'd so carefully held at bay began to fall, looking like tiny diamonds as they splashed down her cheeks. There was only a pair at first, then another and another, until it was a raging torrent of despair.

She even cries prettily, he thought, completely touched. He knew he should leave her to her own devices. A woman's tears always made him feel helpless and out of his element, but he couldn't forsake her during this private moment of sorrow.

"Here now, love," he said quietly, "it's not as bad as all that."

"It's worse," she said. "It's so much worse."

It appeared that her heart was breaking, that she'd been carrying the weight of the world on her shoulders and had finally collapsed from the strain of it. "Have a good cry, then," he advised. "You'll feel better."

He dug around in his clothing, surprised to discover that he actually had a kerchief. Tugging it out, he gave it a shake, then tucked it into her hand. She pressed it to her face and wept for a time, making no sound, as though sobbing were an indignity far beneath her position. Without thinking, he rested his palm on her back, stroking up and down, comforting her as one might a small child who's had a terrible upset. After a lengthy time the emotional upheaval began to wane, and he could sense her relaxation.

"I'm sorry," she said, giving him a somber half-smile. "I didn't mean to make such a scene." She dabbed at her eyes, willing her tears to return to the reservoir from which they'd sprung.

"What's your name, lass?" he queried, deciding that she was without a doubt the most enchanting woman he'd ever met, and that he'd have to see her again.

"Penelope," she said. "Penelope Westmoreland."

The name hit him in the center of his chest like a physical blow. His heart skipped several beats, and he had to force the air out of his lungs. Striving to remain calm, he asked, "Harold is your father?"

"Yes," she said, obviously not finding it odd that he would know her father's name. Most people did. The duke was famous and infamous.

She straightened, fiddling with her skirts, and finally turned to look at him. As she shifted, he couldn't help but notice what should have been apparent from the beginning of the encounter. Of course she was a Westmoreland! His young nephew, Harry, was her double. In her face, hair, and eyes he could see how the boy would look when he was grown, but that was hardly surprising. Miss Westmoreland was, after all, Harry's half sister.

Just then, a commotion erupted from the house, and he stared over his shoulder. Several figures were milling about on the terrace. One of them was the duke, and he was flanked by several men who looked armed and determined. Immediately he jumped to his feet. "I have to go," he announced.

"What?" she asked as she stood, confused by the sudden change of circumstance. They'd been conversing so pleasantly, and she couldn't remember the last time she'd felt so uninhibited in the company of another. In a few short minutes she'd admitted secrets to the stranger that she'd never disclosed to anyone.

"I have to go," he repeated, peeking warily through the hedges.

From a distance she heard the duke's voice calling, "Penny? Are you out there?"

"That's my father," she explained, gazing up in consternation at her handsome protector. "He can't be looking for you! Edward wouldn't have had the audacity to say anything about what happened."

"I doubt if it was anything your Edward might have said or done," Lucas responded, flashing her the jaunty smile that had never failed to melt a female heart, "but your father and his men *are* looking for me." He gauged the brick wall and the leap he'd be required to make, then smiled at her again. "I need a head start in order to be safely away. Please don't tell anyone you saw me."

"I won't," she vowed, not knowing what he was doing in their garden, where he'd come from, or where he was going, but in a world where no one cared about her, he'd become a fast friend. She'd protect him no matter the cost, despite the risk to herself.

He bent down, reached into his boot, and retrieved a knife. "Keep this," he urged, handing it to her. "Bring it with you the next time you come out to the yard alone. If that scoundrel dares to accost you a second time, don't be afraid to use it!"

Her eyes widened in surprise, but she gladly latched on to it. The weapon was small and deadly-looking, with a sharp blade, and an ivory handle that exactly fit the curve of her hand.

"I'll keep it at the ready," she promised, smiling too, while glancing to the house. The duke remained on the terrace, leaning against the balustrade and scanning the property, but his men were rushing down the steps onto the pathways, and her visitor's urgency became her own.

"What's your name?" she asked hurriedly.

"Lucas," he said. "Lucas Pendleton. But don't tell anyone we've met."

She shook her head, liking this bit of intrigue they shared. "May I see you again?"

"Yes," he said without hesitating. "Tomorrow night. Right here."

"Midnight," she agreed, not in the least apprehensive or concerned about arranging a rendezvous. There was something about him that made her feel secure in his presence.

Footsteps were quickly approaching. "Remember," he cautioned, "not a word to anyone!" He grasped her by the shoulders and placed a light kiss on her forehead. "Until tomorrow night," he whispered, and in an instant he'd vanished.

Penny looked at the spot in front of her where he'd been standing only moments before, and blinked several times. Mr. Pendleton had come into her life, then disappeared so rapidly that she could barely believe he was real and not a dream. Still . . . she held the knife and his kerchief—definite proof of his existence. She raised the kerchief toward the light and saw his initials, *L.P.*, embroidered in the corner.

"Penny!" her father shouted again.

Others were calling, "Lady Penelope!"

Relieved that she was allowed to keep those articles, she carefully tucked the blade and linen square under her cloak, then started down the walkway. "Father!" she answered. "I'm here. What is it?"

One of his men came charging up, his eyes searching the yard even as he made his bows. "Are you all right, my lady?" he asked.

"Quite," she said calmly. "Why wouldn't I be?"

Her father bustled to her side, saying, "How long have you been out here?"

"Goodness . . ." she mused, acting as casual as possible in the face of their alarm and anxiety. Whatever could Mr. Pendleton have done to create all this furor? "I suppose it's been nearly an hour."

"Begging your pardon, my Lady," the other man said, "but did you happen to notice a darkly clad gentleman dashing across the grounds?"

"My heavens, no," she lied. "I've been walking for quite a spell, and I've seen no one. Although I did hear a dog barking next door, in Lord Wessington's yard. . . ." She pointed to the house that sat on the adjacent lot, far away from the route Mr. Pendleton had taken. The duke's men needed no other encouragement; they simply took off in the direction she'd indicated.

Satisfied with her night's work, she turned to go in, but her father stopped her. "Where are you off to now?"

"Is Edward lurking about?"

"No," he answered. "Your mother mentioned that he left in a hurry. After he returned from talking to you, he seemed somewhat agitated."

"Really?" she asked, sounding as bored as she could manage.

The duke looked at her in that stern, fierce way he had, waiting, then waiting some more, for her to comment on why Edward had departed so abruptly, but age had made her more wise in their dealings. Let him wonder. Let him stew.

"I believe I shall be off to my room," she said, refusing to tarry and be interrogated. "Make my apologies to anyone who feels they are necessary."

She walked away, leaving her father in the deserted garden while his minions scaled the wrong wall, looking in vain for Lucas Pendleton. Pausing once, she offered up a prayer of God-speed for the American, and she rubbed her fingertips over the place on her forehead where he'd kissed her. It tingled and burned as though afire.

By the time she reached the stairs, Lucas was many streets away. He casually strolled into a noisy tavern and blended with the throng, pretending he hadn't a care in the world. His brother, Matthew, lingered with false patience for him to arrive. Their eyes met the second Lucas stepped through the door. They possessed the same tall, broad-shouldered physique, so Matthew stood a head above most of the other men in the establishment, making him easy to locate.

On seeing Lucas, Matthew signaled the barkeeper, and an extra glass was prepared by the time Lucas worked his way through the crowd.

"What did the bastard say?" Matthew asked, foregoing any light conversation.

"He refused."

"What a surprise," Matthew said, shaking his head. "How did you leave it?"

"As we planned. I told him he had three days in which to reach a better decision, and that we'd be in contact for a different answer." Lucas sipped at the frothy brew, letting it slide down his throat. "I think he'll end up agreeing."

"Really? You never thought so before. What makes you think so now?"

Lucas paused, considering the sweet turn of events and how he could best put them to beneficial use. "You won't believe this—"

"What?"

"I've chanced upon his daughter, Penelope."

"No." Matthew gasped, then laughed. "Don't tell me that's what took you so bloody long to get back here."

"It seems she fancies me," he said, his eyes full of mischief and plotting.

"You always did have the devil's own luck with women."

Lucas shrugged, knowing it was true. "Westmoreland has made an outrageous wedding arrangement on her behalf to a drunken pervert, and I can believe he did it only because he stands to gain a fortune through the match."

"Which means she's worth her weight in gold," Matthew deduced sagely.

"Exactly what I was contemplating," Lucas agreed. Pensively, ominously he asserted, "I'd say Harold Westmoreland is going to be more than happy to meet our demands. No doubt his pretty Penelope will prove extremely beneficial in changing his mind."

CHAPTER THREE

As Penelope waited for her coming tryst with Lucas Pendleton, the next twenty-four hours were the longest she'd ever endured. After leaving the garden and retiring to her room, the night had proved endless as she'd tossed and turned, unable to sleep. She kept recalling the incident with Edward, reliving all that he had said and done, and what his behavior would mean for the future.

Interspersed with memories of him were those of Mr. Pendleton. She couldn't seem to think of one man without immediately thinking of the other, so back and forth she went. When she closed her eyes, she repeatedly heard Mr. Pendleton's fist as it collided with Edward's stomach, with his jaw. There was such a sweet ring to it. Her fearless American had been tense and ready to continue the fight, able and confident in his ability to send Edward packing.

Who was this mysterious stranger who had come to her aid without a thought as to the consequences? As Edward had intimated, he was very powerful, an equal to her father in nearly every way, a nobleman who could commit any despicable act and never be held accountable. Yet, Mr. Pendleton hadn't blinked an eye at confronting him. If anything, he seemed to relish the idea of taking the brawl to the next level. He'd actually threatened to kill Edward! And Penelope had the feeling that it was the kind of caveat upon which he'd be more than able to carry through.

In her entire life she'd never met anyone like him. There was certainly not another who equaled him in looks, and no gentleman of her acquaintance could hope to match him in bravery, daring, or chivalrous comportment. He was like a prince out of a fairy tale, and he had rushed to her rescue like a knight in shining armor, just as it had always happened in those make-believe stories of her childhood.

As a girl she'd read them voraciously, always imagining that the same sort of handsome, bold, adventurous hero would sweep her off her feet someday, that she would fall madly in love and be whisked away to live happily ever after.

Over the past three years, though, her eyes had been opened to reality, and she'd had to put aside her fanciful dreams with their idyllic endings. There were no dashing princes or courageous knights waiting to deliver her from her plight. She was frightened and overwhelmed, and her meeting with Mr. Pendleton had only underscored how desperately she needed to devise a plan in order to survive the coming months. If she didn't develop a strategy, she had no idea how she would make it through her wedding day—or her wedding night.

Although she was supposed to be an innocent on conduct of men and women in the marital bed, she wasn't. Her personal maid, Colette, never passed a chance to regale her with stories of what went on in the bedchamber, so while Penelope still had a few questions about the details, she had a fairly clear notion of what would be required once she spoke her vows. After Edward's mauling, she didn't see how she could perform her wifely duties. Indeed, so great was her despair that several times it had crossed her mind that she would rather kill herself than submit to him, but as quickly as the thought came, she hastily pushed it away.

Her life had been one long, interminable lesson about duty.

Her responsibilities had been drilled into her until it was difficult to fathom acting of her own accord. Her father had found her a husband; he had ordered her to marry. In her small, structured society there was no alternative but to obey. In fact, so carefully had she been groomed that she couldn't consider the possibility of doing anything but following his lead.

Occasionally she liked to fantasize that she was a braver person, the sort who had no qualms about running off and starting over. Infrequently she imagined herself finding a place of her own where no one recognized her or had any expectations of her. But where? Where would she go, and how would she survive?

She had no illusions regarding her condition: She was completely dependent on her father. While it was amusing at times to picture herself just walking away, she never would. There were women of the lower classes who worked to support themselves, but she was hardly one of them. She had no skills that were particularly valuable, having been raised to be competent at only those tasks that would be essential for the countess or duchess she would eventually become.

She knew all there was to know about such topics as planning a huge dinner party, what servants were necessary to the smooth running of a large household, and how to appropriately seat guests around the supper table, but there were no calls for those abilities out on the streets of London.

The other option would be to ask a relative to take her in. Only a handful of acquaintances might initially welcome her if she fled her father's house, but none of them would be willing to let her stay. They'd never go against the duke by shielding his errant daughter. Indeed, most of them would perceive her refusal to marry Edward as immature and uncalled for.

In her world a daughter did as her father commanded. No one would think twice about the actuality that the marriage had been arranged and wasn't to her liking. Such a happenstance occurred often, and it wasn't for the daughter to question her father's motives. In fact, she could imagine seeking shelter from distant relations, only to be turned back at their door and sent home to where they would feel she belonged.

How she wished her father had found her a husband such as Mr. Pendleton—one who was strong and tough yet who could be gentle and supportive. He was exactly the type of man she always imagined she might someday marry. What would it be like to build a family with one such as he? She couldn't even begin to envision it.

All she could hope for was that he would meet with her in the garden as they'd planned. If she was fortunate, perhaps he would visit on a few added occasions so that she would have a handful of marvelous memories to carry with her as she went down the road toward matrimony.

Just then Colette entered. She was a thin beauty, several years older than Penny, who had been employed for her expertise in coiffeur technique and wardrobe management when Penny entered her teen years. Her hair was long and black, and she had dark eyes. Her skin was dark too, a strange sort of olive color that made her look as if she'd spent too many hours in the sun without a bonnet. An exotic woman, she was full of chatter about the people Penny knew—Penny's family members or the servants. Usually her tales highlighted their romantic woes, and it was from her that Penny had learned all she knew about physical love.

As an unmarried female Colette was an endless source of information on numerous topics about which she shouldn't have known. She'd filled Penny's head with stories about male conquests and lovers, and she'd provided detailed insight and guidance concerning the masculine animal—with much of her wisdom apparently gleaned from personal experience. Whether Colette's copious adventures were true was a matter for debate, but she certainly told a good yarn and she absolutely adored scandal and intrigue. With her penchant for gossip, she could definitely put the women of the *ton* to shame.

"Tell me!" Penny started to say impatiently the moment Colette stepped through the door. "What did you learn?"

"No one, they do not know anything"—her French accent was still strong, and *anything* came out as *anyteeng*—"but what His Grace has told them."

"What is that?" Penny asked. Being desperate to know all, she had sent Colette on a mission to find out all about Mr. Pendleton: what he'd been doing in the house, how he'd caused such an enormous ruckus, why the duke's men were chasing him. She hated to think that the resourceful woman had returned empty-handed.

"The *monsieur* was visiting His Grace on a matter of business."

"But what about the gunshot?" Penny exclaimed. "I thought you said everyone heard a gunshot. That Jensen saw the hole and smelled the smoke."

"*Oui! Oui!*" Colette responded, waving animatedly. "Did I not tell you this is so?"

"And?"

"Your father, he says this was an *accidente*. That Monsieur Pendleton did not mean to do this harm to your mother's portrait. It was a problem with the pistol." She raised her hands in the air, gesturing and saying, "Poof! It explode."

"If it was an accident," Penny reflected, trying to make sense of the little Colette had related, "why were they chasing him off the grounds?"

Colette shrugged. "No one knows this"—*thees*—"answer."

They spent a good portion of the morning pondering Mr. Pendleton. As usual, Colette proved herself a worthy companion when it came to obsessing about the previous night's events. While Mr. Pendleton had asked Penny not to reveal his identity, she could hardly keep him a secret from her abigail, and she didn't intend to. Colette was a trusted confidante, and Penny never had to worry about her. Though Colette could talk herself blue in the face, she also had an uncanny knack for understanding when to be silent. She could be as tight-lipped as a jar of preserves when the circumstances warranted.

Mr. Pendleton's auspicious entrance into Penny's life was

extremely exciting, and she wasn't about to let his coming pass unheeded, not when she had someone like Colette with whom to share it. Plus, there was the next assignation, and Penny needed Colette's stealthy assistance in order to attend the midnight rendezvous.

Throughout the day Penny repeated everything that had happened in the garden, every punch that was thrown, every threat that was made, every kind word spoken. With the analytical skills of Bow Street investigators, they tore it apart and delved into each nuance of the entire situation.

Why had Mr. Pendleton surfaced when he did? What did it mean?

They ruminated until the afternoon's light faded into evening. By the time they went through Penny's closets, searching for the appropriate dark-colored dress for her to wear to her appointment, they had become convinced that there were great forces at work.

Colette was constantly reading such things as tea leaves and the stars, looking for signs and omens, and surely his arrival had to be significant. Perhaps fate had lent Penny a hand.

What else could Mr. Pendleton's appearance possibly portend?

Lucas paced the deck of his moored ship, the *Sea Wind*. It was one of five that he owned and used for transporting goods along the eastern seaboard of the United States with an occasional trip between the New World and the Old. The vessels were his pride and joy, accumulated through a lifetime of toil and struggle.

As a lad of only five, he'd been kidnapped from the harbor near his parents' home in Virginia and forced onto a merchant ship. In the years he'd been lawlessly indentured, he'd sustained himself with his memories of the loving family from which he'd been wrongfully stolen. Upon his return as a young man, he'd been heartbroken and outraged to discover that the home of which he'd often dreamed was gone, and he couldn't bring it back. His parents were long-dead from influenza, and his brother and sister had been farmed out to neighbors, growing up lost, confused, and abused.

Though not much more than a boy himself, on seeing their condition, he'd vowed to work and fight until he was a man in his own right, one who did not need to rely on others, and one who could care for the two younger siblings his parents had left behind.

When he thought back to those terrible days, it was difficult to remember that he had ever been that determined child, and he wasn't certain where he'd found the drive that pushed him to succeed. He had lied and cheated and stolen, doing anything and everything necessary in order to provide for the three of them.

By age fifteen he'd won his first ship at a turn of the cards. It hadn't been much to speak of or look at—a rusted-out, worm-eaten schooner that barely floated—but standing at the bow as it cut through the waves, he'd felt like the king of the oceans. By age twenty he owned two ships. By age twenty-five he possessed five first-class sailing vessels and a small estate outside Jamestown that grew plenty of valuable tobacco. They lived in a fine house, filled with servants and the best items to be found on that side of the Atlantic.

His sister, Caroline, had blossomed as she'd matured, becoming a rare beauty. She'd organized their home and managed their affairs during the long weeks he and Matthew were away. Then the opportunity had arisen for her to visit England. The invitation had come from some distant cousins, a baron's family who had a daughter Caroline's age who would be making her come-out.

Initially Caroline had raised the idea and, unable to refuse her even the smallest request, he had reluctantly assented to her suggestion that it would be fun to go to London for a season of balls and parties. He had truly believed that she deserved the exotic escapade and, reasoning that she would be appropriately supervised by her hosts, he hadn't worried that they were making a bad decision.

When she'd returned, all grown-up and developed in ways he couldn't quite define, the explanation hastily became clear. He could still vividly recall the morning one of the serving women had whispered her suspicions in his ear. During the confrontation that followed, Caroline had happily pronounced the news, stubbornly refused to name the father, and joyfully accepted the chance to bear the man's bastard.

After her death Lucas could never move beyond the unwavering conviction that her passing had been his fault. The regrets piled high: if only he hadn't let her visit England . . . if only he'd traveled with her to act as chaperon . . . if only he'd forced the name of her paramour from her lips before she'd died . . .

He never stopped wondering about the lover who had been able to seduce such a levelheaded woman as Caroline. While the cad was obviously the type who could callously commit his dastardly deed, then send her home to Virginia once he was finished, he was also the sort of man who could instill strong ardor and devotion long after the time for loyalty and silence had passed. Relentlessly Lucas had obsessed over who it could have been.

To learn, in the end, that it was Harold Westmoreland!

Westmoreland had a reputation for regularly beguiling women, with one beautiful female after the next linked to him romantically for decades. The handsome blackguard was a master at seduction, and Caroline hadn't stood a chance against his wily charms.

Well, this time Westmoreland had ruined the wrong girl. By setting his sights on Caroline, he had pompously underestimated the gravity of the sin he'd committed. He had no way of knowing the strength of Lucas's commitment to his family or the lengths to which Lucas would go to avenge his sister. Westmoreland *would* make good on the debt he owed Caroline Pendleton. Lucas intended to see to it. Nothing and no one would stand in his way.

He paced to the stern, then back toward the bow, looking

out across the busy docks, trying to see Matthew coming through the crowd of people, but his brother was nowhere in sight. For a while he lost himself in watching the hustle and bustle on the surrounding ships. In contrast, his own was quiet. The sailors who'd accompanied them from Virginia had been given extended shore leave, and the coin to enjoy it, until the two Pendleton brothers concluded their private English business and were ready to head for home once again. He didn't like the deserted feeling on the deck, but it couldn't be helped.

Soft footsteps sounded behind him, and he stiffened, biting against the smile that threatened to break out as he felt a small toy sword pressed against his waist. In mock play he raised his hands, saying gruffly, "Who goes there?"

" 'Tis I, Blackbeard," a young boy's voice said in return, trying to sound vicious. "Your money or your life!"

"Hmmm ..." Lucas pretended to think it over. "And if I don't have any money to give, what then, my bloodthirsty pirate?"

"I'll throw you to the sharks!" the boy declared.

Lucas spun around and grabbed him, swinging him off his feet and into a tight hug. "What a ferocious lad you are."

"Were you scared?" Harry asked.

"I was terrified," Lucas lied.

"Really?"

"Really," Lucas insisted as he sat the boy on top of a barrel.

As always when he looked at Harry, he couldn't quite fathom the depth of emotion the boy always managed to stir. From the moment Caroline had died, Lucas had loved him unfailingly. It was impossible not to.

He was pretty, if such a comment could be made about a male child. His eyes were bright blue, his cheeks rosy red, his hair white-blond and just starting to turn dark underneath the top layer.

The Pendletons were all dark-haired, so Lucas had often suspected that Harry's father had been blond, and he'd been proved right. In fact, he'd made several interesting discoveries during his brief foray into Westmoreland territory: Little Harry looked just like Harold and Penelope. Now that Lucas had seen the other bloodline from which Harry had sprung, he was forced to admit that the Westmoreland ancestry was probably more strongly conveyed in Harry's features than the Pendletons'.

Another peculiar finding, one he didn't like to admit, was that Harry had the Westmoreland temperament. Since Caroline had been a softhearted soul, Lucas had convinced himself that Harry's strength of character, his determination, and his ability to act like a pampered, royal babe had all come from the dominant men in the Pendleton family.

To his dismay, his visit to the Westmorelands had changed his mind. Harry was a perfect match with the mighty, endowed family. With his stalwart opinions and excess of will, he was such an exact fit that he could be plopped down in the middle of them, and he'd fit right in without needing any opportunity to assimilate. The observation was disheartening and one Lucas didn't intend to dwell upon.

Young Harry was a Pendleton born and raised, so what did it matter if he shared a few common traits with the Westmorelands?

"What have you been doing, lad?" he asked.

"I've been helping Master Fogarty."

Lucas liked hearing that the wizened old sailor had taken the boy under his wing. "How have you been helping him?"

"We've been working on my sewing, but he says I need some extra practice with my stitches."

"Well, stitching is an important skill for a seafaring man."

"That's what Master Fogarty told me," Harry responded, appearing much too mature for his age.

As they conversed, Lucas spied Matthew coming in their direction, and hope flared that his brother had been able to make the arrangements they'd discussed after talking stridently most of the night.

"Uncle Matt has returned," he pointed out to Harry. They

could see him weaving his way around several large carts that were loaded down with produce.

Harry jumped off the barrel and ran to the rail, waving and shouting, "Uncle Matt! Uncle Matt!" Despite the din of noise, Matthew managed to hear his cries. His head swung up, and he smiled and waved to his merry nephew.

Lucas walked to the rail as well and rested a hand on Harry's head. "I need to talk to Matt alone," he instructed. "Why don't you go below. I'm sure Master Fogarty could use some more of your valuable assistance."

"Oh, Uncle Luke," he grumbled, but he didn't argue. He was a good boy when he wasn't causing mischief.

"I'll call you when we're finished. We'll go have supper at that pub you enjoy." The promise of food lit up his face, and he disappeared down the hatch before Matthew stepped onto the gangplank.

From the confident gleam in Matthew's eye, Lucas instantly ascertained that they'd met with success, and he couldn't help but think that the ease with which they'd resolved their main problem was a sign they were proceeding correctly.

"I've found us a house," Matthew said without preamble.

"Well done." Lucas nodded.

"I think it will fit nicely with what we've planned."

"How so?" Lucas asked, although he didn't need to inquire as to the details. He and Matthew had always been of similar mind in their devious pursuits, and his younger sibling would very probably pick exactly what Lucas himself would have selected.

"It's less than an hour from the city," Matthew explained.

"So, we'll be able to ride in easily to complete our business."

"Exactly," Matthew said. "It's on the edge of the village, close enough to walk to the marketplace but far enough out so that nosy neighbors won't be stopping by to see the goings-on."

"And the accommodations?"

"It's hardly a ducal palace"—Matthew shrugged off the

type of luxury to which their pending guest was accustomed—
"but it will suffice for our purposes. The place is owned by a
local merchant. He's out of the country just now, attending to
his foreign commerce."

"Due back when?"

"Not for months."

"So, it's completely furnished?" Lucas questioned, painting
a mental picture of the dwelling he'd be calling home for the
next short while.

"Right down to the bedding."

"Good work."

"I thought you'd be pleased," Matthew said. His brother
could hardly have been anything but. Cautiously he added,
"There's one other issue we need to address."

"What?"

"It comes with a wonderful yard. There's a small orchard
with apple trees that would be great for climbing, and a slow-
running stream just made for swimming—if the situation goes
on that long and we get into summer."

"Oh, Lord, let's hope it's completed before then," Lucas
said fervently, and they both laughed. "I don't think my nerves
could take that much intrigue."

"Harry would love it," Matthew insisted, but Lucas hesitated. In their hours of scheming about how Lady Penelope
Westmoreland was to help them achieve their goal regarding
her father, this had been the only sticking point.

Harry had been trapped on the ship for all the weeks of the
frigid crossing of the North Atlantic. Then he'd languished at
the London docks while Lucas had frantically tried to find an
opening with the duke. With the spring weather upon them,
the lad needed to be where he could roam and play before they
began the long journey back to America, but the two brothers
had other, more pressing concerns about where the boy should
be situated.

As they put their strategy into action, they weren't sure of
the best location to keep him safe. Leaving him aboard with

Fogarty wasn't an option. They couldn't risk the possibility that Harold Westmoreland might chance upon the boy by accident and then end up abusing him in some fashion in order to get back at Lucas for what was about to happen to Lady Penelope.

Yet, did they dare expose Harry to what would be occurring at the country house?

"I can't decide," Lucas finally said. "Let's see how the rest of the week shapes up. We'll discuss the matter again when the time is closer."

"Fair enough," Matthew said. "Other than that, we're set to proceed."

"I'm glad. It's a load off my shoulders to know we're ready." He turned toward the hatch in order to ask Harry to join them. "All this plotting has left me famished. Let's go eat."

"A grand idea." Matthew clapped him on the back. "And after we've finished dining, are you prepared for this evening?"

"More than prepared," Lucas answered, thinking of his skills with the ladies, and of all the charms at his disposal that he used regularly to get them to do whatever he wanted. "My darling Penelope won't know what hit her."

CHAPTER FOUR

Lucas perched on the top of the wall, letting his eyes adjust to the darkness, but he saw no guards roaming the fancy garden. He had to stifle a laugh at how complacent—and foolish—Westmoreland was. From the duke's lofty view of the world, it had probably never occurred to him that Lucas might return intent on doing something as diabolical as stealing Westmoreland's most prized possession right from under his very nose.

Lucas's bold act, committed in the duke's own library, went so contrary to what a common English person would dare against a peer of the realm that the duke could never comprehend what a foreigner of Lucas's background and determination might do. The duke's inability to judge Lucas's resolve was exactly what Lucas was counting on, and why he felt so confident that his scheme would succeed.

He gazed about for several minutes. Once he was convinced there'd be no surprises, he slid to the ground and, quiet as a snake, worked his way around a hedge until he was standing a few feet from the bench where he and Lady Penelope had met.

At first he couldn't locate her, and he suffered an instant of panic that perhaps he'd misjudged the woman and she'd changed her mind about their assignation. Then his eyes settled on her. She was sitting quietly, dressed in black clothing and wrapped in her sable cloak. Moonlight reflected off her in silvery waves, and he realized that she didn't look like a proper gentlewoman at all, but one who was waiting for her secret lover to appear.

His heart skipped a beat. The situation was proceeding much better than he could have hoped.

She'd worn her hair down, and it was loosely restrained with a dark-colored ribbon. Like a shimmering waterfall, it flowed down her back until the curled ends brushed against her hips and nearly touched the seat of the bench whenever she shifted.

There was probably an innocent explanation for why she'd styled it in such a fashion—perhaps her maid was abed and not able to offer assistance—but he couldn't suppress the thrill he received upon considering that she'd done it just for him, that she'd wanted him to see her in a state of dishabille, which meant she already fancied him much more than she ought. Such a circumstance would certainly make his job easier.

Still, as he stood silently watching her, it gradually occurred to him that, given their predicament, he was too excited by the sight of her provocative locks. He was becoming fixated on her for extremely male, utterly base purposes, the likes of which weren't appropriate and wouldn't do at all. Now was not the time to be intrigued by her comeliness. It was imperative that he regard her as an object, a person to be manipulated in order to bring about the fortuitous completion of his plans. In no way, shape, or form should he consider her a *woman*.

Nevertheless, he couldn't alter the direction of his eyes or the direction of his thoughts. The long strands of her hair were smooth and radiant, and he wanted to find out how it would feel to run his hands through the heavy mass. If he pulled her close and rubbed it across his cheek, he imagined it would be soft and luxurious.

Scandalously his fingers tingled at the idea of touching her. So alluring was the prospect that he caught himself wishing he could abandon his carefully drafted scheme. Obviously he was reasoning with a part of his anatomy much lower than his brain, because at that moment he would have given anything for the opportunity of an uninhibited rendezvous where they could discover just how close two people could grow in a very short time.

Dismayed by his carnal fantasies, he shook off the unwanted temptation and acknowledged it for what it was: His masculine senses always came to full alert whenever a beautiful woman crossed his path. He had a second instinct for ferreting them out—the prettier, the better—so he chose to recognize this initial enchantment for what it was and to move on.

Penelope Westmoreland was a mark. Yes, a lovely one, pleasing to the eye and the spirit, but a mark nonetheless. And he had every intention of keeping her as one and nothing more.

Not wanting to scare her, he moved from the shadows and onto the walkway. "Hello, my pretty Penny," he said, remaining still and letting her adjust to the idea that it was he and no other.

"Hello," she said, smiling and rising to face him.

"I'm sorry I'm late," he offered.

"I was beginning to think you weren't coming."

"I wouldn't have missed this for the world," he declared, but his words carried an interpretation entirely different from what she heard.

He took one step toward her, then another, until they balanced toe to toe and there were only a few inches separating them. Her skirts swirled around his calves and feet, the bottoms brushing his boots. To her credit, she didn't shy away to put distance between them. If anything, she welcomed his nearness, behavior he wouldn't have conceived possible given the short, odd nature of their acquaintance.

She was calm and self-assured, and he noticed to his chagrin that there was an abundance of sexual energy flowing between them. It was so strong that he was surprised he couldn't see shooting sparks. The hair on his arms and the back of his neck stood up as though he were outdoors in a lightning storm.

As a man who was vastly accomplished with women, he knew this sensation for what it was: a hot, wild, physical attraction that meant he desired her. From his past sensual adventures, he'd come to realize that it was beyond his control, a potent, magnetic allure that caused him to react to a certain female as he never would with another.

She gave off an invisible signal, and his senses were instantly and carefully attuned to her, almost as though he were an animal searching his herd for the finest female of the bunch. He was aware of everything about her: The manner in which she moved. The amount of space her body occupied. The warm temperature of her skin. The shiver that passed across her shoulders at his approach.

Mostly he was conscious of her scent. It tickled his nostrils and set his muscles to quivering. An earthy, lusty odor unlike any he'd ever experienced, it was a kind of chemical emanation that only he could distinguish and appreciate. If he'd been blindfolded in a room of a hundred women, he could have picked her out by that distinctive scent alone. They were made for mating, her body calling to his like a beacon in the dark. Down to the tips of his toes he felt ready and able, in a thoroughly male fashion, to indulge her in whatever stimulating exploit her untried flesh might crave.

Of all the luck!

Why had this happened now, when he needed all his faculties concentrating on the task at hand? And why hadn't he perceived it the previous evening? If he had, he might have decided on another course of action. As it was, the enterprise had been set in motion, and there was no turning back. Lady Penelope had a part to play in the resolution, just as he had one himself.

Having neither the time nor the inclination to become involved with the ducal prize standing before him, he vowed he would fight this sexual enticement till his last breath. Too much was at stake to risk it by dallying, but he was near enough so that he might have run a finger across her full bottom lip. The moon took that instant to shine down ferociously, haloing her in golden light, her superb face perfectly outlined, and he felt a hitch in his breathing.

Gad, but he'd forgotten how magnificent she was!

Very likely she was the most ravishing creature he'd ever laid eyes upon, and he had to bite back a groan. Despite his firm determination, how was he going to manage to keep from sampling just a taste of the delights she offered?

"I'm so glad you're here," she said, tentatively reaching out and resting her open palm against the center of his chest. Before he knew what he was about, he snatched it up, raised it to his lips, and placed a lingering kiss on the back. Her skin was as soft and silky as he'd imagined it would be.

"So am I," he said gently. Gazing into those blue eyes, he experienced a flash of absolute alarm. He was in deep. And he was in trouble.

As a distant clock had chimed midnight, Penny had been sitting on the bench for nearly an hour, terribly frightened that Mr. Pendleton might arrive early and she would miss him. At the stroke of twelve she'd made the decision that she would tarry all night if need be, and she didn't know what she might have done if he hadn't come.

In some ways she felt she had been waiting for him her entire life, although she didn't comprehend why. After all, they'd spoken only a handful of words, and had passed only a few precious minutes in each other's company. Yet, with a certainty she'd never possessed about any other topic, she sensed that they shared a destiny.

For some reason she felt connected to him as she never had been with another. She could tell him things, important things; she could share her worries and fears and he would listen and understand. And help.

She knew his positive characteristics, though she hadn't any reason to do so. He was brave and strong and kind, a true and loyal friend to those he deemed worthy. Never would he let her down, disappoint her, or leave her in time of need.

While she had to admit it was entirely possible that dire necessity had caused her to conjure this remarkable image, she didn't think so. There was something about his calm, collected demeanor that made her hope he would turn out to be the answer to her prayers, a dream fulfilled, a wish granted, a problem solved.

"Let's sit, shall we?" he said, motioning toward the bench.

"I'd like that very much," she replied, eager and elated when he laced his fingers through hers and kept them there. She'd never held hands with a man before, and it was extremely fulfilling. They sat side by side, touching pleasantly from shoulder to thigh, and a shiver ran down her spine and prickled the skin on the backs of her arms.

Once they were comfortable, he shifted slightly, turning toward her and dazzling her anew with the full force of his attention. No doubt about it, her memories of his beautiful face hadn't been distorted by events. He was every bit as handsome as she recalled.

"I have a confession to make," he said.

"What's that?" she asked, smiling, liking the timbre of his voice, his heat warming the air around her.

"I thought about you all day."

"Really?" she asked, thrilled at the news. "How very sweet. Then, I have a confession as well."

"What might that be?"

"I was thinking about you, too."

"All day?" he asked.

"Well . . . there may have been a few seconds here or there when I lapsed." He chuckled, and the resonance made little butterflies dance in her stomach. "Truly, I'm embarrassed to say that you crossed my mind nearly every minute."

"I'm glad."

"I've always been such a levelheaded person. I don't have any idea what's come over me."

I do, Lucas thought to himself. She was encountering the definite affinity that existed between them. There was neither rhyme nor reason behind it, but the sensations it caused were real. Luckily he was practiced in the loving arts, recognized the impulses she stirred, and knew how to control them, but he pitied her. In her naïveté she would feel confused and out of sorts and never understand why.

"How are you?" he asked, deftly changing the subject before they had a chance to delve into it. "I trust you weren't overly upset by what happened last evening."

"No," she admitted.

"Did you meet with your fiancé today?"

"No," she said again. "I had no appointments scheduled with him, nor would I have kept one if it had already been arranged. I had always suspected that the man was a swine. Now I'm certain of it. He'll get no forgiveness from me for his disgusting behavior."

With her back stiffened, her head tilted just so, she appeared assured, tough, unbending, not at all like the spoiled, immature girl he heard talked about on the streets of London. He almost felt sorry for the drunkard to whom she was engaged. She looked every inch the daughter of the Duke of Roswell, and her bumbling betrothed had no clue what he was up against. He had met his match and hadn't even realized it.

"May I ask you an intimate question?" he inquired. "Please let me know if you don't wish to answer."

"It's all right. You can ask me anything," she said. Usually her engagement foibles were painful to discuss, but they wouldn't be with him. He would understand her anguish and despair, and his empathy would make the telling easier.

"How did you come to be affianced to such a disgusting man?"

"It's a long story."

"He just seems so . . . so . . ." Lucas was surprised to feel himself tremble. Picturing her with the inebriated sot was disquieting.

"It's difficult to believe, I know. I'd always thought I would marry someone—" She caught herself before blurting out *someone just like you,* and she was glad she hadn't given him such a startling glimpse into her heart.

As a girl who had spent her life being coddled, pampered, and assured through word and deed that anything she desired was hers for the asking, she'd grown up expecting to marry the most wonderful man in the world. She had anticipated that he would be exactly like Lucas Pendleton, that they would wed for duty but live for love, and they would enjoy the kind of idyllic marriage of which other women could only jealously dream.

She paused, sighed, then continued. "I thought I would marry someone closer in age. In temperament. But my chosen fiancé had to be of sufficient rank, and there are so few men who my father deems suitable."

Lucas frowned. As an American, it was difficult to fathom all the attention these British paid to their elite positions in the order of society. "Is rank all that matters to him, then?"

"There are other considerations, I suppose." She mulled it over, then added, "Increased wealth, certainly. The property to be exchanged during the contracts. Plus, Father has several bills before Parliament that interest him. Edward is an earl and will be a powerful ally in accomplishing his goals."

Lucas wanted to shake his fist in the air. Her value to the duke had to be immense and was growing by the moment. Carefully he said, "Still, even with all that to be gained, I can't imagine a father marrying his only daughter off to such a scoundrel."

Penelope had too much pride to admit what the duke had told her—that after all her betrothment debacles, Edward was the only man who'd have her—so instead, she said what she wished to be true. "I think my father is as surprised as anyone in learning what Edward is really like. Especially with his drinking, and . . . well . . . his temper. Before Father entered into the arrangement, they were casual acquaintances who had not socialized extensively. Now that the wedding is approaching, we're all forced to spend more time in his company, and it's been quite . . ."

She hesitated, searching for the appropriate word to describe how awful he actually was, but there didn't seem to be one that was vivid enough. Swallowing, she shivered away a wave of disgust at the way in which Edward occasionally looked at her, and finished with ". . . quite dreadful."

Suddenly her burden seemed too heavy. Tears flooded to her eyes, although she was too proud to ever allow Mr. Pendleton to see them fall a second time, and she pressed the tips of her fingers below her eyelids, needing the extra pressure to hold them inside. "Oh, what am I going to do?" she asked aloud, not really expecting an answer but needing to give voice to her constant worry. "The wedding is in three months."

Lucas couldn't believe how stirred he was by her declaration. He had every intention of being unmoved by her plight and unconcerned for her welfare. To carry out his strategy, he had to be unaffected by her personal problems, but to his consternation, it was impossible to remain impassive. Just as he was attracted to her physically, he was attracted to her emotionally as well.

He hardly knew her, yet for some bizarre reason he felt better in her company. From the moment they'd sat down on the bench, he'd felt superb. More relaxed. More content. Her presence worked magic on his frazzled nerves and simmering impatience. He enjoyed holding her hand, sitting close, and watching the changes that passed over her face as they discussed one ardent topic after the next. If he spent much time with her, he would turn into an awkward, lovesick fool who did nothing but moon after her like an inexperienced boy.

Horrid as it sounded, he was going to have to help her. He'd seen and heard Edward in action, and he couldn't imagine abandoning her to the dreadful man and his deviant habits.

That's simply the kind of man Lucas was and always had been. So, despite how he proposed to use her in accomplishing his goals with the duke, in the end he would see her free and unharmed.

Quietly he made the vow to himself: No matter what, he wouldn't forsake her to her father's machinations.

"Have you thought about what you might do as an alternative?" he asked. "There must be somewhere you could go. Somewhere you could stay."

"No," she said, shaking her head. "There's no place. There's no one who would come to my aid. They're all too afraid of Father and the power he holds."

Lucas nodded. No one would dare cross the duke on behalf of his daughter. "Perhaps you could go off on your own. Do you have any funds?"

"No. Not a farthing to my name," she admitted. "I had given some thought to having my maid pawn some of my jewelry, but many of the pieces are quite valuable, and I was afraid that someone would take notice and my attempts would be discovered. I really don't know what my father might do if he thought I was planning to run away."

She shuddered, but not from the cold, and Lucas couldn't prevent himself from reaching for her. He enfolded her in the circle of his arms, and she came willingly, nestling close and stretching out, and he wasn't surprised to find that she fit perfectly.

Although he tried to convince himself that it was only a gentle embrace meant to reassure, he couldn't get beyond the impression that he was surrounding her with his protection and offering her refuge. He felt as though she'd always found sanctuary from her worries by snuggling up against him, and their intimate position was nothing new because she'd rested in just such a fashion a hundred times before.

Penny pressed her cheek to his chest, listening to the strong and steady pounding of his heart. His proximity was soothing and exciting. She could have lain there, unmoving, for the remainder of her days and died a completely happy woman.

"I won't let the duke do this to you," he assured her, the sound of his baritone rumbling from deep within and tickling against her face. "We'll find a way to make sure you're sheltered from harm."

The promise was so heartfelt that she pulled back, needing to witness the look in his eyes when he made such a pledge. Though she hardly knew him and couldn't have put into words why she felt as she did, his steady gaze made her decide that she could put her life in his hands and it would be safe in his keeping.

"I know you will," she agreed.

There were many more words that could have been exchanged, more subjects discussed, more information traded, but from the first, theirs had been a different type of relationship. Because of how Lucas had thrust himself into her problems, and because of the pressures facing her, they had skipped the introductory steps that normally occurred when two people were just getting to know each other.

A strange hurdle had been jumped, a sort of speeding-up of the present, that put them far past the preliminaries. Their friendship was established, their bond unbreakable, and it was as though they had been acquainted for years instead of hours. For the first time in a long time she faced the future and saw a faint glimmer of hope on the horizon that events might work out after all.

His eyes were glittering, and he was smiling down at her with an easy, confident expression, and she couldn't help thinking he was the most phenomenal, exotic person she had ever met. With a fierce conviction she vowed that he would never regret his decision to offer her assistance. If it took the rest of her life, she would gladly spend it showing him how grateful she was. She would do whatever he asked, go wherever he requested, complete any task he required, be whoever and whatever he needed her to be, and she would do everything in her power to make him very, very happy.

Lucas paused. As though there had been a subtle shift in the temperature or the wind, he could tell that something had changed between them. In the soft glow of the moonlight she was gazing at him with an unwavering regard that made his pulse increase. From any other woman he would have recognized the look for what it was, one of love or, at least, deep affection. Coming from Lady Penelope, it had arrived too early on to be love, but what else could it be?

Realistically he should be secretly celebrating how well things were progressing. *Fondness* on Lady Penelope's part was precisely the type of emotion he hoped to cultivate. Events were unfolding just as he'd hoped, giving him the chance to play on her innocence and inexperience in order to gain her trust.

However, despite his best intentions regarding his dubious motives, he couldn't prevent the leap of joy he received from the simple idea that she might be developing a fancy for him. Where it came from he couldn't say, but it was as real and as definite as it was terrifying.

She was the one who was supposed to develop tender sentiments—not him. From his perspective, toying with her was part of his strategy, a business matter, a means to an end. *He* wasn't to sustain any feelings for her at all other than relief that meeting her had helped to resolve his situation.

Still, there was something perfectly lovely about the manner in which she was looking up at him, as though he were the bravest, truest man she'd ever encountered, the world revolved around him, and the sun might not rise if he didn't give the appropriate command.

His overt interest was going to create serious problems. The tangles they would eventually end up unraveling because of the ways she stirred his untoward, uncontrollable desires didn't bear contemplation. Yet, he hardly cared. All he knew was that he suddenly felt ten feet tall, a hero and savior, and he liked the perception very much—and wanted it to continue.

Some sort of demon appeared to be leading him to his doom, and he couldn't prevent himself from moving to the next level, to where kissing her was the only possible option. As he leaned forward, he couldn't dull the observation that he was someone else, watching another unknown, idiotic man commit this grievous, critical error in judgment. Then his lips brushed lightly against hers, and none of his misgivings mattered one whit.

There was only Penelope.

He closed his eyes and let himself be filled by her. Her lips were warm and soft, her breath honeyed as scrumptious candy. She was wearing a light, flowery perfume that was unnoticeable until he was so near that nothing separated them.

He made no attempt to deepen the kiss. He didn't press himself against her or run his fingers through her hair or massage his hands along her back. He simply enjoyed the experience of having her lips melded to his own.

They sat unmoving, as though they were two statues posed just so. He couldn't have said how long he kissed her, but by the time he finished, his ears were ringing, his heart was pounding, his fingers tingling, and, most shocking of all, his knees were weak and he was terribly glad he was sitting down so she wouldn't know how deeply he'd been affected. The kiss had been chaste, probably the most harmless he'd ever shared with a woman, yet he felt he'd encountered the most erotic embrace of his life.

The eeriest impression swept over him, that he had stumbled upon something rare and wondrous. Until that moment he hadn't realized he'd been missing her, but in fact he had been searching for her all his life.

A severe discernment of dread began at the tips of his toes and worked its way up his legs, spreading through his body until it made him shiver with the realization that he was in way over his head, probably about to drown, and there was no one available to toss him a rope. He needed to get back to solid ground. Fast! To where he could cogitate and gather himself together, or else he'd remain exactly where he was and commit many other disturbing blunders.

Penelope's eyes fluttered open. All her life she'd imagined receiving a kiss like the one they'd shared. It had been just as romantic as she'd always assumed it could be. Her pulse was racing, her breathing labored, and her lips were warm and prickling, as though a spark of energy had passed from him to her, and she wanted to do it again, for as long as possible.

Nothing else mattered. Not Edward, not her father. She wouldn't have cared if they had been discovered in the midst of their torrid embrace. The kiss had left her strangely elated, and she would have risked any hazard to have it continue. However, as she looked at Mr. Pendleton, she suffered an instant of panic.

Where before he had appeared affectionate, now there was an unreadable expression in his eye, and she couldn't move beyond the impression that he hadn't enjoyed the occasion at all. She blushed, happy for the shadows so that he couldn't notice her embarrassment. Obviously he was a man who'd had extensive interaction with women, and while she'd sat there, imagining the moment was the most fabulous of developments, he'd probably been dreading every second.

She felt like a fool!

"What it is?" she asked softly.

Lucas was surprised that she seemed to know him well enough to realize that something was amiss. It was disconcerting that she could peer so deeply into his lagging conscience. "Nothing," he lied. "We've tarried for quite some time. I need to be off."

"So soon?" she asked, mentally kicking herself because the query came out sounding so desperate.

"Yes," he insisted. "It's late, and the longer we linger, the greater the likelihood that you might be missed."

She wasn't concerned about discovery; she only wanted him to remain, but he stood quickly, as though intending to disappear that very second, so she rose too, trying to find the means by which she could convince him to dawdle. "Are you sure you must go? I hardly know anything about you, and I have so many questions. I haven't had the chance to ask any of them."

"I have many questions as well," he said. "We can give each other our answers tomorrow night, if you would like to meet again?"

She felt like a dying woman who'd just been given hope of a cure. "I would like that," she said forthrightly, knowing there wasn't time to play the coquette as she'd been taught to do with men. "At midnight, then?"

"Yes," he agreed. "At midnight."

Lucas bent to kiss her good-bye, but at the last second he realized his folly. If his lips touched hers, the pleasure would be indescribable, and he might end up in a situation he didn't want the two of them to experience, so he hastily moved away, grazing her forehead with a quick, light peck.

"Until tomorrow," he said in a voice full of promise.

Years of practice had schooled Penny's emotions, so she carefully hid her disappointment that he had not kissed her on the mouth. She started to make her farewells, looked around, and realized he was already gone, vanished a second time.

"Until tomorrow," she said to the cool night air, then turned and headed to her father's dark, lonely house.

CHAPTER FIVE

Harold Westmoreland, Duke of Roswell, sat behind the massive desk in his library, trying to find the comfort he usually enjoyed in that room. Regretfully the tranquillity of the place eluded him, and he wasn't certain how to regain it. His private domain had been thoroughly invaded by that brash American, Lucas Pendleton.

Though it was a mad supposition, he no longer felt safe in his own home. In his own library! The peace and serenity of his sanctuary had been destroyed. Whenever he entered, he experienced a small twinge of fear that someone might be lurking in the shadows. His eyes would cast about furtively, looking for movement or change. He had always sought refuge behind the heavy oak door, but not any more. Now he had to force himself across the threshold and the floor, and he caught himself timidly reaching for his brandy and chair.

How he hated feeling so displaced!

Over the years he'd always chosen to hold his private conferences in this room as opposed to any other because it had the best ambiance in which to work out important deals or to whisper over momentous confidences. The potent atmosphere brought others to heel, made them hesitate, give in, or give up.

When haggling over an extremely delicate matter, he gave his opponents just the right look at just the right moment, letting the effective milieu wear them down as gradually and as surely as the weight and authority of his presence.

But, somehow, Pendleton's brief appearance had sucked out the power.

Harold would never admit as much in a thousand years, but he couldn't get over the sensation that the space had been altered by the man's unexpected arrival and climactic exit. There had been a definite shift, leaving him with the feeling that he was no longer in control and no longer in charge, which he hated. It remained a mystery as to how Harold was going to exorcise the scoundrel so that he could once again enjoy the beneficial attributes of his special haven.

He hoped conditions would improve once the wall over the fireplace was repaired. Pendleton's pistol shot had passed through the portrait of the duchess and lodged in the plaster behind it. The large painting had been removed, leaving faded wallpaper, a hole, and black powder marks, so it was impossible to glance around and *not* be immediately reminded of what had happened.

Every time he looked in that direction, he could see and smell the smoke that had erupted from the gun. Every time he sat down, there was a coating of barely perceptible powder on his belongings. Despite how thoroughly the staff cleaned, flakes of white from the damaged wall continued drifting down onto the rug and furniture like fine bits of beach sand, a constant reminder of Pendleton and his brazenness.

Crazy as it seemed, Harold felt the falling particles were a sort of magic dust cast about by Pendleton as a memento of his dastardly deed, one that made it impossible for Harold to forget or to forge ahead. While he was used to retiring to his library for a good part of each day so that he could ruminate and make plans, since his encounter with his unwanted visitor he couldn't accomplish a single task.

All he could think about was Pendleton, his pretty sister,

Caroline, and her bastard son, little Harry. How was a man supposed to concentrate when his home had been invaded by such a crew?

For years his memory had not strayed to Caroline. She'd been just another in an unending string of women. Prettier, certainly, and more charming than most. But one of many. Now, as irritating as a bad toothache, her brother had completely insinuated himself into Harold's life, and he couldn't put any of the Pendletons aside. Especially the child. A male child! What man worth his salt wouldn't be intrigued by the idea of having another son? Bastard though he may be, how was a man supposed to move ahead with images of such a boy lingering on the fringes?

Harold already had a son, his legitimate get and heir. By any standard, William was a handsome, strong lad possessed of all Harold's best and worst attributes, which combined to make him a worthy friend or foe. He was smart and tough and, in the exalted tradition of the Westmoreland family, he would one day be an excellent eighth Duke of Roswell.

But still, another boy!

A second son had been his greatest wish in life. After years of visiting his wife's bed, trying to create another, the duchess had never conceived again, and he'd long ago abandoned the idea of increasing his number of children. So . . . to learn of this son, this child, and in such a shocking fashion!

He had no intention of doing as Pendleton had asked—wild horses couldn't drag a paternity agreement from his lips— but he couldn't prevent his musings from wandering to this newfound son. Unable to tamp down his curiosity, he unlocked the top drawer of his desk and pulled out the miniature that Pendleton had left behind. His eyes searched the lad's face while his finger traced over the fine features, committing them to memory.

What a good-looking child he was!

Footsteps sounded in the hall, and to his dismay he jumped even though he instantly realized they belonged to Penny. The awareness of how fainthearted he'd become set his temper to flaring anew, and he braced for the coming encounter that he knew would be entirely unpleasant.

Lest someone see the treasure he cradled so carefully in his hand, he prudently pushed it to the back of the drawer, then locked it just as Penny entered. As always, she was perfectly turned out, her face tranquil and composed, her blond hair swept up and neatly coiffed. Her light blue gown was expertly tailored, fitting immaculately on her trim figure.

However, as he looked at her standing there with her head held high and her emotions carefully guarded, he experienced the strangest perturbation that she had recently undergone a profound transformation. She appeared older, wiser, as though she were someone entirely different from whom she'd been the week before.

It was eerie, but he couldn't get past the impression that she was someone he didn't know at all, which was madness. This was Penny, his demanding, self-centered daughter who had never had to do anything more strenuous than decide what to wear each morning. She wasn't the most interesting of creatures, and because she was a girl, and a difficult one at that, he'd never felt the necessity of spending much time with her. He'd certainly never given her much thought other than to contemplate how he could use her to further his interests.

After two decades of manipulating her, ordering her about, and directing her actions, he knew how to handle her. At least, he always had in the past, until Pendleton had burst into his life. The blasted man had him questioning everything, including his ability to interact with his daughter.

Another crime to lay at the rogue's feet!

Over the years he and Penny had had many meetings such as the coming appointment. In fact, it suddenly occurred to him that they'd hardly ever spoken anywhere else. As a girl, she had been allowed to visit him once a day, and he would ask her about her lessons. As a young lady, she'd still visit once a day, but the topic had become her marriage prospects.

Who, how, and *when* had occupied their thinking for so long that he couldn't remember when they'd talked of any other subject.

As she moved toward her marriage to that disgusting boor, Edward Simpson, a man whom Harold couldn't abide, they all had to grit their teeth. Harold felt badly about this third engagement. At the time he'd initiated the agreement, he'd absolutely believed he was making the correct decision. While the age difference had initially given him pause, he'd encouraged the man's attentions because he'd felt that an older husband would be good for Penny.

She'd always needed a firmer hand than the one he'd provided in raising her, and he'd anticipated that Edward would afford her guidance and management. However, he'd truly had no idea how obnoxious the lout was, how offensive, how drunken! The choice had turned out to be horrendous, but he'd never let her know. The damage was done, the contracts signed, and there was nothing for any of them to do but move forward with the inevitable. The sooner she came to terms with it, the better.

"Yes, Father," she said tensely. "You wanted to see me?"

The manner in which she said the word *Father* brought his head swinging up. There was a challenging tone in her voice that he wouldn't tolerate. It caused him to wonder if, perhaps, the balance of authority in their relationship was shifting. Shaking off the absurd notion, he decided it was simply more of the unease created by that arrogant American intruder.

"I did," he said, nodding toward a chair. "Sit." She complied, looking bored and put out.

Taking an overly long time adjusting her skirts, she finally asked, "Well?"

He continued silently to assess her, and he couldn't get over the feeling that he shouldn't take his eyes off her, that she was about to do something outrageous, dangerous even, and he squinted, trying to bring her into clearer focus. She stared back with a steely gaze so much like his own that he was startled. He'd always despaired over the fact that she'd never gotten any of his resoluteness, that she hadn't grown up clever and strong-willed like her brother.

But, as he carefully regarded her, sensing all sorts of changes he couldn't begin to specify, he realized she'd gotten more of his dominant nature than he'd imagined. The idea frightened him. If she was no longer the Penelope he'd so carefully fashioned, who was she? And what might she do? How was he to deal effectively with such a complete unknown?

"Well?" she asked again, annoyed and impertinent.

"Your mother informs me"—for some ridiculous reason he decided that he should proceed very cautiously—"that you have canceled your evening engagement with Edward."

"That's correct."

"May I ask why?"

"No, you may not."

Her response was so out of character and so unexpected, he was confounded into silence. He gave her the irate glare that never failed to instill fear in the recipient. Yet, she was thoroughly unmoved. In the tone he'd always used with her—the one that said argument was useless because he couldn't be swayed—he ordered, "You will attend the evening soiree with him."

"I won't," she retorted. "As a matter of fact, I doubt that Edward will ever again have the pleasure of my company." Rising, she said, "Now, if that is all you wished to discuss, I have better things to do."

He was so shocked by her insolence that he rose as well. "You will not depart until I give you leave."

"My apologies, Your Grace," she said, emphasizing his title in a rude fashion, her voice mocking and disrespectful, "but I find that I have no stomach for listening to another of your diatribes, and I would ask that you not summon me further. I don't believe I shall obey." With a dismissive nod of her head she turned toward the door. "Good day."

Stunned by her blatant disregard for his position—as her father, as her duke, as her lord and master—he could barely think of a reply. His cheeks flushed red, his pulse raced. For the first time in her twenty years she'd defied him, and he was at a complete loss as to how to progress.

Sneering, he asked, "What should I tell your betrothed?"

She stopped and glanced over her shoulder. "You may tell him," she said, frightening in her calm, "that I had my maid purchase a small knife. I shall carry it with me wherever I go. If he ever comes near me, I intend to use it."

In a swirl of skirts she exited the room, magnificent in her fury, royal in her bearing, absolutely her father's daughter, and he was terrified at witnessing the change. Who was this person? And what about the threat directed at her fiancé? Did she mean to stab him at their next encounter? What kind of insanity had overtaken her? Did she think to call off the wedding too?

Obviously Edward had exceeded his bounds, but with the wedding so close, Harold felt it didn't matter. At age twenty Penny was certainly ready to have some idea of what animals men could become when aroused. Harold had been remiss in that respect, telling himself it was best to keep her virtuous and unsuspecting, but if she'd had a taste of male desire and found it distressing, he hardly considered her distaste to be a reason for female hysterics or for her refusing to go through with her duty.

The wedding would go forward whether she wanted it to or not, and if she thought she had any say in the decision, she was in for a surprise. Harold would see her turned out in the streets before he'd let her embarrass the family in such an immature fashion.

Seething, he barely had time to take a breath before his next visitor arrived. He would be forced to deal with her later, and deal he would.

Purdy, his private man, stepped through the door just as Penelope departed, so Harold struggled for composure. The underling must never suspect that Harold had just engaged in a major battle with his daughter, or that he was suffering from the strong impression that his daughter had made.

"What did you learn?" Harold asked, reining in his temper.

Purdy, a short, thin, balding man, had been one of Wellington's most trusted aides before injury brought him home. He was discreet, reliable, persistent, and the person Harold counted on whenever he dare not trust another. Purdy competently carried out investigations, obtained sensitive information, and paid bribes. Whatever Harold needed to have accomplished, Purdy was more than willing to do, and he always did it well. While he certainly wasn't the brightest star in the sky, he was as tenacious as hell, a trait Harold counted on and paid well to enjoy.

The man opened a notebook and began to read. "Lucas Pendleton is an American—"

"I know that, you idiot," Harold growled. "I'm the one who told you as much."

"Well, yes . . ." Purdy grumbled, distracted by the outburst. "He's from Virginia." Harold started to interrupt a second time—this was also information he'd provided—but Purdy forged ahead without pausing. "He owns a shipping company that services mostly the East Coast of the United States and the Caribbean, with occasional trips to Europe. Four or five vessels running at the current time."

"A family enterprise?"

"No, apparently he's built it up himself from scratch."

"Ah," Harold mused, "a self-made man." Exactly the kind he loathed. There was nothing more exasperating than a fellow who had earned his wealth. "So, he must have come to England on one of his own ships."

If they could find the ship, they could find the American, and Harold wanted him seized immediately. Pendleton was going to suffer extensively for the effrontery he'd shown by invading Harold's domain.

"That's what I'm thinking," Purdy responded, "nevertheless, we haven't yet been able to locate it."

"That seems a simple enough matter," Harold cut in, irritated by the delay, even though it hadn't been forty-eight hours since the event. However, Pendleton had given him three days in which to meet his demands regarding young Harry's paternity, and two of them were already gone.

With Pendleton's threat to the duke's family, who could guess what unscrupulous exploit he might commit if Harold didn't do as he'd asked? They needed to move quickly; Pendleton had to be located before any more time had elapsed. Of course, Harold hadn't shared any of Pendleton's true purpose with Purdy, so Purdy didn't understand the necessity for haste. He had simply been told that Pendleton was dangerous, unstable, and needed to be found. After seeing the hole in the duke's wall, Purdy hadn't had to hear any other particulars before setting out on his mission.

"Not actually, Your Grace." Purdy cut into his reverie. "He might have docked in a distant town and come to London by carriage or horse. He might have arranged to anchor the ship in the Thames farther out and used another boat to bring him ashore."

"I see," Harold said. "So, he's not stupid enough to pull up to the public docks, where all of London can find him?"

"Absolutely not, Your Grace. From what we've learned, he's definitely not stupid."

Just foolish, and very, very brave. "Keep looking."

"We are," Purdy insisted. "We'll find the ship. And him."

"Good," Harold accepted, knowing the man would be true to his word. "Now, tell me about the scoundrel. Everything you know."

"There's not much so far," Purdy said, "but we're asking about. He's thirty years old. His parents are deceased. He's been the guardian for a younger brother and sister since they were all quite young. I believe the sister may be deceased as well. We're still trying to confirm."

Harold pondered the disclosure for a few moments, knowing that Caroline was dead but deciding not to reveal as much to Purdy. If Harold started providing intimate history, he'd give

Purdy unnecessary ideas about Harold and his relationship with Caroline, ideas that weren't any of Purdy's business.

Harold thought about how lovely Caroline had been, how gently reared, fresh and unspoiled, generous and kind, and he was forced to admit that Pendleton had done a good job with her. He had obviously cared for her deeply too, enough so that he would sail across an ocean, years after the occurrence, in order to demand satisfaction on her behalf.

Methodically he began mentally to catalogue the characteristics that described Pendleton, knowing he had to understand every detail about his adversary in order to bring him down. He appeared to have many admirable qualities. On the one hand, he was bold, courageous, loyal, smart, hardworking. On the other, he was conniving, imprudent, impetuous, and a risk taker who would dash into any situation without regard to the consequences.

After all, what if Harold had been armed when Pendleton had accosted him? What if Pendleton had been seen in the house and the alarm raised before he could make his getaway? What if Harold hadn't been alone but accompanied by one of his guards? What then?

Pendleton's lack of fear over the outcome was disturbing. He was willing to advance despite the obvious peril, so Harold adjudged him to be an unstable individual, one who had little consideration for his own safety or that of others, and one who had no qualms about carrying out any action, despite the odds.

He was rash, emotionally charged, embarking on what he felt was a moral mission, and certain he was in the right. All combined, he was a lethal antagonist who could and would do anything.

"I want him found," Harold said. "By tomorrow morning."

"You can count on me," Purdy declared, bowing himself out of the room.

* * *

Lucas stood, watching the crowd on the busy street. His eyes appeared to be on the wealthy customers entering and leaving the elegant shops, but he wasn't really seeing them. He was focused on the quiet interplay behind the scenes. Small hands and small bodies wound their way through the throng, and that was where his attention remained.

As a child, during the years he'd been conscripted at sea, he'd spent a great deal of time working the busy docks, slipping in and out between the adults as he'd stealthily searched for unexpected gain. He'd gotten quite proficient at thievery, but he was still caught now and again. Once, he'd nearly lost a hand as punishment for his pickpocketing, but fortunately he'd managed to escape the backwoods jail before any justice had been meted out.

Hunger and poverty were conditions he understood well, although anyone looking at him now would never suspect his humble, desperate beginnings. Yet, he'd committed extreme acts in order to survive, so he made no judgments about the boys and girls he saw canvassing the area. Besides, those who were about to lose their money to the little brigands could afford to part with a few coins.

He wasn't exactly clear on what type of boy he was seeking to assist in his scheme against Harold and Penelope Westmoreland, but he assumed he'd know when the appropriate one caught his eye. Neither too young so as to be easily frightened nor too old so as to be easily noticed or remembered. Not too timid, not too brash. But smart. He needed a child with brains and an ability to think on his feet. How he was supposed to ascertain these glowing traits merely by looking was a mystery, but he was certain his problem would be solved soon and with a minimum of fuss. For a change, events were going his way, and he was feeling extremely lucky.

The pair struck swiftly. One boy ran down the street in a trained move, jostling an older woman who had just exited a carriage. Before she could quite get her bearings, another stepped out of the swarm to help. With one hand he took her elbow and steadied her. With the other he smoothly and efficiently reached into her bag and removed a valuable which was hastily stuffed inside his trousers.

By accident Lucas made eye contact with the boy, and Lucas realized instantly that he'd found the child for whom he'd been searching. He was small, which made him seem to be only seven or eight, but in reality he was closer to twelve. He had dark hair and eyes, appearing very much as Lucas himself had looked at that age and time in his life.

They were standing so close to each other that he had to appreciate that Lucas had seen his furtive maneuver, but he didn't give himself away by so much as the blink of an eye. As though he had all the time in the world to dally, he calmly helped the elderly woman to the door of the shop she'd been intending to enter, all the while acting the part of a virtuous choirboy. With his mark safely sent on her way, he turned to vanish into the mob of people, never making a hurried move, never glancing back, never engaging in any out of the ordinary conduct that might be observed by casual passersby.

Unfortunately for him, there wasn't anything casual about Lucas's assessment, so when he finally turned to dash down an alley, Lucas was already there waiting, having previously scoped the various getaways the children were using after committing their petty crimes. He easily blocked the boy's route, surprising him so that Lucas was able to grab him before he could disappear.

"Let go of me, or I'll scream me bloody lungs out," he insisted as he struggled against Lucas's restraint. He was wiry, agile, and tough as nails, just as Lucas had hoped and foreseen he'd be.

Lucas stepped farther into the shadows.

"Go ahead and scream," he declared. "If anyone dares come to your aid, I'll tell them about the little purse you stole and have crammed in your trousers." The boy's struggles increased. "That bit of knowledge should be worth a trip to Newgate.

Maybe deportation. Would you like that? Starving to death on a rat-infested boat bound for Australia?''

"What do you want?" the boy asked, relaxing slightly, but Lucas wasn't foolish enough to loosen his grip, as the boy was obviously expecting that.

"I have a proposition for you," Lucas said calmly, but the instant he spoke he could discern that considering their location and circumstance, his overture had come out sounding dreadfully unnatural. But it also told him he'd picked the appropriate child. The lad was furious but not so frightened that he'd fail to find the means to escape as soon as he was able.

"You've got the wrong boy," he gibed. "Best keep looking till you find someone more your style."

"That's not what I meant," Lucas contended. He was handling himself badly, which was foolish, for better than anyone he understood this kind of child and knew what it was like to exist on the streets. All kinds of horrible atrocities had probably been committed against him in his short life.

Lucas retrieved a gold coin from his pocket and waved it in front of the boy's nose. "I'm willing to pay you. . . ."

"I won't do it for money either, ya bloody pervert," the boy spit out.

Lucas rolled his eyes, feeling like an idiot. "I don't want anything like that," he said. "I'm involved in a secret enterprise, and I want to hire you to carry out a task for me."

"Right!" the boy scoffed.

"I am looking for someone who is brave and smart," he said, allowing the compliments to sink in. "Yet, he must be tough and loyal too. I was watching you go about your business, and I knew right away that you were exactly the man I needed." Shrugging, he lightened his grasp. "But if you're not interested, well . . ." Letting go completely, he waved toward the dark end of the alley, encouraging the youngster to depart as if Lucas didn't care one way or another about the lad's decision.

The boy took a step back, then one more, until there was room to flee, but he kept his gaze on the coin Lucas dangled.

"How much money are we talking about?" he finally asked, and Lucas knew he was hooked. The lure of easy cash was too hard to resist.

"Quite a bit, actually," Lucas said, increasing the bait. "And the work would be simple."

"What would I have to do?" he asked, continuing to eye the coin.

"I need you to convey a letter to a gentleman's house. A *wealthy* gentleman," he added with emphasis, "and you'd have to run off after you delivered it. You couldn't allow yourself to be caught."

"Why?"

"Because he'd probably want to know where I am. And he might be rather nasty in the methods he'd use in getting you to divulge my whereabouts."

"I'd never tell. He couldn't make me," the boy proclaimed with a razor-sharp determination that was frightening to witness in one so young.

"I realize that," Lucas agreed. "That's why I picked you." The boy straightened with pride at being singled out for perhaps the only time in his life.

He queried, "How much are you willing to pay?"

"Twenty pounds," Lucas offered. The amount was a fortune for someone in the lad's condition. "There might be two or three deliveries. Maybe even more. I'm not certain." With a flick of his wrist he tossed the coin, and the boy moved so quickly to catch it that his body movements were hardly visible.

"How do I know this is real and not some trick?"

"You don't," Lucas responded. "Do you know the Boar's Head tavern?"

"Down by the docks?"

"Yes," Lucas said, nodding. "Go there and ask the barmaid named Peg about me. If I sound all right, meet me back here at noon. I'll tell you then what I'll need you to do."

"For how long?"

"A few days," he said. He and his brother had argued often

and hard, trying to figure the length of time it would take Harold Westmoreland to capitulate. "A week at the most."

"If I don't come back at noon?"

"Then I'll find another boy. One who wants my money more than you do." He shifted, putting more space between them. "What's your name?"

"Paulie."

"Your real name."

"Paulie," he said defensively. "What's yours?"

"Lucas. Lucas Pendleton." He nodded toward the boy's escape route, urging him on. "Go ask Peg about me," he ordered. Turning, he stepped out to the thoroughfare, not looking back until he was certain the boy had disappeared.

CHAPTER SIX

Penelope stood next to the bench in her father's garden, listening. As she was alone and it was late, she should have been frightened, but she wasn't scared in the least. The leaves rustled, and she knew Mr. Pendleton had arrived. For the past forty-eight hours he had filled her world, and she could sense his presence without actually laying eyes on him.

She'd become so attuned to him that she easily pictured how he moved, smelled, sounded, and carried himself. While she was forced to consider that her overt fascination might be caused by the fact that she wanted him to be her savior, she was perceptive enough to realize that it was more complicated than that. He had invaded her life, her imaginings, and her dreams, and she couldn't think, eat, or sleep without mentally keeping him by her side.

Smiling, she turned, and there he was. Standing tall and straight, he was outlined against the night sky, and her heart fluttered in her chest. He was more handsome than she remembered, which was saying a great deal, because she thought he was the most beautiful creature she'd ever seen.

"Hello, Mr. Pendleton," she said softly. His dark eyes glittered with an emotion she couldn't describe, but the way he was looking at her made her feel coveted and cherished.

"Hello, my pretty Penny," he said in that low voice she loved so much. "And you must call me Lucas."

"I'd like that."

He didn't move, so she did, taking one step toward him. She detected the tang of soap from his hair, the freshness of the cool night air on his skin, and she breathed deeply, relishing the chance to inhale the manly scents of horses and tobacco and whiskey. Underneath, she detected a musky aroma that she understood, on some primal level, to be the very essence of him. It called to her unceasingly and mercilessly, and she couldn't remain separated from him.

When he was close by, her body cried out with an overwhelming desire to touch and be touched. She'd never experienced such a physical reaction around a man before, so she wasn't quite certain how to behave in his presence, but it was impossible to stay detached, and with so much at stake she refused to be timid. They were meant to be joined, and she extended a hand, hoping he would take hold of it.

Lucas watched her approaching. After the previous night, when he'd recognized his attraction to her, he'd spent the day convincing himself that he could resist the natural force that drew them together. He was a grown, experienced man; she was a young woman, an innocent who could be readily led astray by passion. His plans for her were ominously unfair, so trying to enjoy anything more than a surface relationship would be foolhardy and reckless. And cruel.

Despite his aim not to like her, he did. He felt sorry for her, and he wanted desperately to help her find a good end to her situation, but he could never act on the depth of his feelings. He knew better than to start a dalliance, and the wiser course was so clear, he could have traced it on a map, but as she neared, all his good intentions flew out the window. She reached out to him, he reached for her in return, and then she was in his arms, and he was overcome by the strongest sensation that she was right where she belonged.

His hands slipped under the weight of her luxurious cloak, circled her small waist, and held her, but while they begged to roam higher to cup her breasts, or lower to encircle her hips, he refused to let them. He battled an inner war, wanting to pull her tight, but he didn't dare. As she leaned into him, ready for their bodies to meld, he balanced her precariously, unwilling to allow the contact, yet not wishing to keep her at bay.

Her aroma was tart and sweet at the same time, like lemons mixed with flowers. It was a luscious ambrosia, and he'd already learned that it was a dangerous siren song, appealing loudly to his basest animal instincts. His pulse pounded, his blood rushed through his veins. To his horror, it flooded to his groin, and he hardened, desiring her with an abrupt and fierce erection that almost doubled him over.

Needing more but knowing he oughtn't, he leaned down and pressed his lips to her forehead, giving her the same type of chaste kiss he'd offered upon his retreat the prior night.

Penny was surrounded by his height and warmth. His hands were at her waist, causing a strange ache that began in the center of her stomach and flowed out from there, making her weak, uncomfortable, twitchy, as though her skin were suddenly too small to cover her torso. His proximity heated the woman's spot between her legs, made her breasts swell and her nipples harden to where they rubbed in an irritating fashion against the lace of her chemise. It was the very first time she'd noticed her body in such a physical way, and it made her feel feminine and alluring.

Barely able to breathe, she raised her face, ready to receive his kiss, when he again pressed his lips to her forehead. Gravely disappointed, she was having none of it.

"No, Lucas," she said, tensing just as his mouth made contact. She grabbed the front of his shirt and rose up on her toes. "Kiss me," she ordered quietly, more brave than she ever imagined she could be with a man, but she craved this so much.

Too much. It was all she'd contemplated for hours, for days, for so long that she felt quite mad.

"Penny," he said, placing another light kiss to her brow, to her cheek, "I can't."

"You can!" she insisted. "Kiss me. As you started to last night. As though you mean it." Nibbling the bottom of his chin, she rose farther and found his mouth with her own. If he wouldn't kiss her, she'd kiss him! She was far past the point where she was content to wait for him to get on with it. Time was wasting.

Lucas suffered the fleeting notion that if someone had chanced to see the two of them at that moment, their positions would have seemed extremely hilarious. He, Lucas Pendleton, who imagined himself to be the ultimate ladies' man, was standing in a dark garden, utterly alone with the most beautiful woman he'd ever seen, a female who was amenable and interested, untried and eager to learn all that he might teach, and he was fighting her off.

If he'd had a long stick, he'd probably be waving it at her, trying to propel her away. Their predicament was ludicrous. It was laughable. It was incomprehensible. Then her lips brushed against his, and it was wonderful, and there was no longer any valid reason for resisting.

She was exquisite. Everything about her called to him, and he couldn't prevent himself from kissing her back. He didn't even try. After the horrid events that had shaped the beginnings of his young life, he'd sworn never to deny himself what he truly yearned for, and he wanted her as he never had anything, or anyone else.

Besides, he told himself in a particularly convoluted bit of logic—which made him realize that he was definitely thinking with a body part other than his brain—he was going to commit so many despicable iniquities where she was concerned. What was one more?

He intended to win her confidence, her favor, her friendship and loyalty, all for nefarious, outrageous purposes, and simply to further his own ends. In the process, he would confuse her, hurt her, abuse her trust, and when he was finished, she would hate him and rue the day they'd met.

So . . . what did it matter? After all, it was only one little kiss, one small sin in what would eventually be a huge pile of sins.

He let his hands leave the safety of her waist. One came to rest on the center of her back, the other lowered to her rounded bottom. He urged her closer, until she was pressed against him from mouth to breasts to thighs. Her tight nipples rubbed against his broad chest, the softness of her stomach cushioned his hardened phallus, the mound of her sex stroked his leg.

The intensity of the contact was unexpected; he'd never encountered anything like it. Alive, on fire, as though she'd invaded every pore, he was acutely aroused to the peak of anguish, and he needed to relieve some of the pressure by flexing his hips, but he restrained himself. She was a virgin, one who'd nearly been raped two nights earlier by another man who was out of control, and she hardly needed a second groping, offensive male thrusting and fumbling with her person.

He had to exercise some discipline, but he couldn't imagine how, so he dropped his grip on her backside, instead circling his arms around the outside of her cloak, hoping to use the sumptuous sable as a barrier. But the instant he buried his hands in the elegant fur, he knew the move had been a mistake. All he could think about was what it would be like to lie down with her on the rich pile, and how creamy and pale her delicate, white—naked!—skin would look against the black coat.

Lest he perpetrate an act even more grievous than those he'd already contemplated, he linked his fingers tightly together behind her back so they couldn't linger or stray. He did not flex, he did not caress, he did not explore, he did not digress. In fact, he hardly stirred, turned to stone by his terror at the level of his burgeoning passion.

When she playfully nipped his bottom lip again, an agonized groan escaped, then he dipped under her chin to nuzzle her neck, thinking it to be a safe spot, but his lips encountered a hot, smooth nape and shoulder, and he groaned even more.

"What is it?" she asked breathlessly. "Are you all right?"

"Yes," he managed to answer, "but we have to stop."

"I don't want to," she asserted.

"We have to," he declared. Even in the darkness he could see how her hair was mussed, her lips wet and swollen. She was staring up at him with such affection, an icy barricade against emotion melted in the center of his chest. Her tender regard made him want to blubber like a schoolboy, to babble, to blush, to do any asinine, insane thing she asked.

He inhaled deeply, reining in his impulses, and explained gently. "If we don't stop now, I don't think we'll be able to stop at all."

"I don't care," she said, taking him in, loving how she felt safe and secure in his arms.

Colette had often explained to her what it could be like, but she hadn't understood until then. He was hard where she was soft, lean where she was rounded, rough where she was smooth. And he wanted her. He was hard and ready and pushing against her abdomen. It made her reckless and agitated, ready to complete any mad deed. Her stomach rippled, full of butterflies, her heart pounded, her skin was feverish. All combined, the moment was so joyful that she didn't want it ever to end.

"I want to know what it's like," she said. "With you."

"I realize you do." He chuckled at her freshness, her verve, her desire to go forward at any cost. "But you don't understand what you're really saying."

"I *do* know," she insisted. "I'm not as naive as you think." She recalled the discussions she'd had with Colette. Although she'd never had the chance to put any of her maid's advice into practice, she comprehended what would happen if they continued. She was filled with an overabundance of unmanageable longing, her body dangerously craving his. Colette had said it would be like this if the man was right, if the time was right.

Lucas gazed down at her and couldn't help wondering if perhaps she did fathom more than he'd guessed, but he still couldn't go forward. "I don't think you're naive," he answered honestly, "but I do think you're untried, which means you could not possibly know all the consequences. And you offer me a generous gift, but it's one I won't accept. Especially not here, on a cold bench in your father's garden."

Finally feeling more in control, he unclasped his hands from behind her back and rested a palm against her cheek. "Your first time should be special. You deserve a large bed and a deep mattress. Soft sheets and candlelight. Not a quick tumble in the dark with your skirts thrown up and grass in your hair." At the mention of her beautiful blond locks, he reached for a handful and pulled it to his face, inhaling the smell of her shampoo.

Penny sighed at the sweet sentiment, and she couldn't help imagining the picture he'd painted—of the room and the bed— as she said flirtatiously, "I wouldn't mind a little grass in my hair."

He laughed, a rich, full sound that made her stomach tickle anew as he let go of the long strands he was holding. "Will you sit with me? Just for a while?"

"Yes," she said, thinking that she'd do anything he asked.

He moved to the bench, and she came with him, but as he began to ease her down beside him, she refused to cooperate. She didn't know how long he intended to stay, when he might jump up and be over the fence before she could object, and she wasn't about to spend the rest of their time chatting politely as though they were sitting across from each other at supper. These were desperate times, and desperate times called for desperate measures.

Do not play the shy one, Colette had advised as she'd left the house, and she could hear the Frenchwoman's voice as though she were standing off to the side and giving directions. *Show him that you are not afraid. Let him take you as far as he dares, to the point where he cannot bear to leave you behind.*

Penny crawled onto his lap, a feat she couldn't have imagined performing a week earlier, but since she'd met him, she seemed to have become a different person. The manner in which she conducted herself was so altered that no one in the grand house knew what to make of her. Servants whispered among themselves and scurried out of her way. Her parents took surreptitious glances, trying to see what had changed, or understand what had come over her, but they were not quite bold enough to ask.

If they had, she'd have told them that she was no longer the same biddable girl she'd been previously. In a scant matter of hours she'd turned into a mature woman. Her unexpected rendezvous with Lucas Pendleton had given her an overflowing supply of courage, and she was determined to put it to good use. With a clarity she'd never thought possible, she knew what she wanted, and she had a fair idea of how to go about getting it.

Colette had dressed her in a simple dark gown that had an excessively low-cut bodice and required a minimum of petticoats. She rucked up the hem, holding it just so, and straddled his thighs. Then she tugged the edges of her fur cloak around them both, shielding them in a heated cocoon.

"This is a very bad idea," Lucas announced as Penny snuggled near and wrapped her arms around his neck. Her chest rested against his, rubbing erotically with each breath she took. To his surprise, she wasn't wearing a corset, so there were no stiff encumbrances between them. Only a few thin layers of fabric separated flesh, making physical contact achingly precise.

Lucas was in misery. He was able to feel the exact shape and size of her two full breasts, the valley in between, the poke of each pert nipple. They were hard peaks, swollen and aroused, and begging for attention. Her legs were open and relaxed so that her sex hovered precariously above his groin, causing his erection to increase to an astonishing size. It took every ounce of fortitude he possessed to keep from pulling her tight and grinding himself against her sizzling, welcoming center, where he knew he would find some relief.

He repeated, "A very, very bad idea."

"Do you think so?" she asked, looking wide-eyed and innocent.

"I *know* so."

"But it's cozy to sit close," she said, "and it's dreadfully chilly out this evening. It's much warmer with you near."

"Yes . . . well . . ." She shifted again, her firm breasts moving in a slow circle across his chest. This was not good. Definitely not good. "But I need to talk with you, and—"

"We are talking," she said, her voice husky and brimming with sexual promise. Her mouth floated mere inches from his, ready for another kiss that he definitely was not going to give her, when her tongue flicked out and wet her bottom lip, making it glisten. If he hadn't been convinced of her virtuous state, he'd have sworn it was a practiced move.

Penny was having the time of her life, although events weren't proceeding exactly as Colette had explained. Her maid insisted that the only route to a man's brain was through his lap, so Penny was right where she needed to be. Her entire body was stretched out against his, but he wasn't participating, and she wasn't certain how to bring about an increase in the level of his ardor. To accomplish the goal she'd set for herself, she needed to make him so enamored of her that he'd do whatever she asked without question or hesitation.

Frantic to hurry matters along, she reached for the clasp at the neck of her cloak.

Lucas wanted to steer the conversation back to solid ground, but she committed the unthinkable, unfastening her fur wrap and letting it fall just as he made the uncorrectable mistake of glancing down. The dress she was wearing was hardly there at all, and as she leaned forward, both her breasts dangled in his face. He could see the tops as well as the ridges of the aureoles, and her nipples pressed against the edge, waiting to burst out. A simple joggle of the fabric would have them bare and free. She'd be in his hands, in his mouth. He'd be able to judge the weight, mold the shape, thumb the nipples, manipulate the cleavage. . . .

This is my penance, he told himself, *for every bad deed I'm ever going to do to her.*

"Is something wrong?" she asked.

"No," he lied. "Why would you think anything was wrong?"

"You just look like you're . . . in pain," she said as she reached behind his head and removed the ribbon that had been holding his hair. The long locks fell about his shoulders, and she laced her fingers through it.

"I'm not," he insisted, powerless to say more, incapable of thinking beyond the pleasure of feeling her hands in his hair. He couldn't move. He couldn't remember what he was supposed to be about. What mortal man could? After all, he was only human. He needed space, distance, a chance to gather his wits, so he tried to find purchase in order to lift her away.

Unfortunately her skirts were bunched up around her legs, so he discovered naked skin instead, along with soft lace, silky undergarments, and a frilly tied garter. His palm came to rest against a bit of exposed leg, just above the knee, and he couldn't resist running the tips of his fingers in small circles.

"Oh, Lord," he exhaled.

"What?" she asked, looking innocent again. *Too* innocent, he realized, and he wondered fleetingly if perhaps there weren't many things going on here of which he was completely unaware.

Who was using whom? And for what? But just as quickly as the thoughts had formed, they disappeared into sensation.

"Tell me what you did to my father," she said, moaning softly over the feeling of his warm, searching fingers.

"Your father?" he asked, and his voice came out in a near squeak. He cleared his throat. "Oh, yes . . . your father. Ah . . . he and I had some business. Ah . . . he owes me money."

He absolutely had to remove her from his lap, away from his tense thighs and raging phallus, before he did something they'd both regret, but his wretched body wouldn't behave as he commanded. Before he realized what he was doing, he'd transferred his other hand under her skirt and both were stroking her. The expensive lace of her undergarments kept catching on the calluses of his work-roughened hands.

"Did you truly try to murder the duke in his own library?" Penny asked the question to which everyone in the house was dying to hear the answer. No one knew exactly what had happened, and her father certainly wasn't saying.

"No," he said, "I just fired my pistol. Trying to make a point."

"To get his attention?" she inquired, squirming slightly against the blistering heat of his palms at such a naughty spot on the backs of her legs.

"Yes," he answered, completely distracted, barely cognizant of what they were discussing.

"That can be difficult."

"You sound as though you speak from experience."

"I do," she said, her hands leaving his hair in order to massage the rigid muscles of his shoulders and neck. "Although I must admit that I've recently discovered the way to help him focus completely."

"How did you do that?" He couldn't decide where he liked her hands more—on his shoulders or in his hair—and he caught himself holding his breath, wishing she'd caress his chest.

"I've told him that I'm not marrying Edward. In fact, I may have mentioned that if I ever see the lout again, I plan to murder him." She wiggled her brows suggestively. "With my new knife."

"Bravo, my little beauty," he congratulated her. He loved to see her taking charge and fighting back. In all the stories he'd heard about her, no one had ever mentioned that she was tough as nails. Perhaps it was a trait she'd always enjoyed, one that had been hidden, but it had now risen to the fore, and he imagined the men who were manipulating her life weren't certain what to do with her. ''And what did the duke have to say to that bit of news?''

She stopped moving, stopped her roving hands, stopped her shifting hips. This was the moment to risk all, to take what she wanted and needed more than anything in the world. She could do it too, and she would prevail. There could be no other conclusion than success.

''He said that he's going to reschedule the date of the wedding and that I can't get out of it. Despite what Edward's done, or how I feel about him, it's too late to call a halt to the proceedings.'' She swallowed hard. ''We're going to skip the fanfare that would have made it a grand social event and have a private ceremony, without all the balls and parties. The wedding is coming. It's in three weeks.''

Lucas's first impulse was to tamp down a surge of excitement—if Westmoreland was so determined to marry her off, her value had just increased tenfold—but he was hastily shaking his head in disbelief, wondering how a father could be so cruel to his own flesh and blood. If he would commit such a craven act against his legitimate daughter, what chance did any of them have for getting little Harry his due?

''What is the matter with that man?'' he asked, not expecting an answer. There couldn't possibly be one that would adequately explain his reasoning or his behavior.

''I can't go through with it, Lucas,'' she said adamantly. ''I can't.''

''No, no,'' he said, shaking his head again. ''You're right; you can't. I'll not let him do this to you,'' he vowed, thinking that he now had two of Harold Westmoreland's children in his care.

He could never abandon her to the fate the duke had planned. The very idea was impossible to contemplate, and the more time he passed in her company, the stronger he felt that spiriting her away was the proper thing to do. Notwithstanding how he'd initially arrived at his decision, the steps he'd arranged would keep her safe and out of her father's clutches.

Her stunning pronouncement had the blessed effect of cutting the cord of physical desire that had held them together, and he was able to find the strength he needed to plunge ahead, down a different road from the one they'd been on since they'd first entered the garden. He located her waist and lifted her to the side, sitting her on the cold stone of the bench. Kneeling in front of her, he took both her hands in his.

"Will you come away with me?" he asked. He went on quickly before she could say no. All subsequent events depended on her answer. "I realize that you hardly know me, that we've spent very little time together, but I am an honorable man." He gritted his teeth in order to get past such an absolute fabrication. "I'm not rich by any means, not by your father's standard anyway, but I'm well off after a fashion, and I have a fine house and my shipping business makes a substantial, steady income and—"

"Yes," she said, cutting him short. Though she'd come to the garden dreaming that their rendezvous might lead to this moment, she hadn't realized how deeply his capitulation would impress her, and she was unable to prevent the swell of tears that flooded to her eyes. His proposal had lifted the weight of the entire world from her shoulders. Suddenly she could hope again. "Yes," she repeated, "I will come with you."

"We would need to go soon—"

"Now?" she asked, perfectly willing to comply.

"Not tonight," he said, unable to explain that he wasn't yet ready to make off with her, that he had too many final errands to complete.

"Tomorrow night?"

"That would be best," he agreed. "There's very little moon. It will aid in our getaway."

"I can be ready by then." She nodded, her mind already racing a thousand miles ahead to the furtive arrangements she would need to make, to the last-minute chores she would need to finish.

In spite of the fact that she didn't want to frighten him in case he hadn't thought this impetuous venture all the way through, she wondered if he truly realized what a risk he was taking by assisting her. He needed to understand the possible consequences before they proceeded. She said, "I think he'll come looking for me."

"I think so too."

"We might be in danger."

"Let me worry about that."

What a relief it was to see that he wasn't afraid. Not of the duke. Not of his authority. Not of his power. "Where will we go?" she asked. "How will we be safe?"

"We'll marry. As soon as I can get it arranged," he said, giving voice to the lie that would set everything in motion.

As he'd sat alone on his ship, planning the entire caper down to the last detail, he'd often thought ahead to this occasion. He'd convinced himself that the falsehood would be easy to speak, that it would spring freely from his lips, but as he promised the wedded state to her, one he had no intention they'd ever enter, he felt like the lowest sort of vermin.

The taste of deception was bitter, vile, especially when she was staring up at him with her heart in her eyes. When all of this was ended, she would never forgive him. He knew it as certainly as he knew his own name. There were some betrayals that could never be forgotten. Surely this was one of them, but he continued anyway.

"Once we're married," he said, "the duke won't be able to do us any harm. So . . . will you have me? And mind now . . . before you answer," he cautioned, "think about this: Your life will be very different. I haven't your family's wealth or connections. We will have a comfortable home, plenty to eat, but I could not hope to match all this. . . ." He gazed over his shoulder, across the grounds to the dark mansion. A single lamp burned in an upstairs room. Beyond that it was unlit and quiet.

For one meager instant he wished he could promise her all the grand possessions he could see scattered about, for after they went off together, no other man of her society would ever have her as a wife. The reality of what he was taking from her poked at his conscience like shards of sharp glass, and he was overcome with a vicious urge to put a halt to his preparations, but he forcefully pounded it down.

He was doing it for Caroline. For Harry. He would see them avenged!

"Yes, yes, I will marry you," she said, smiling and thinking he was the most remarkable, exceptional person she'd ever met. "I don't need any of the worldly goods in that great house in order to be happy," she said, looking past her shoulder as well. "I never did. It's a very lonely place."

"As long as you realize what you'll be leaving ..." he cautioned a second time.

And what I'll be getting, she thought to herself. "I'll be a worthy wife to you, Lucas Pendleton. I swear I will."

Her vow was so heartrending, so freely conferred, so strongly made, all he could do was accept it with a slight inclination of his head. He'd have given anything in the world to be able to make such a pledge in return, but he'd told enough untruths for one evening.

He stood, pulling her to her feet with him. "It's time for me to go."

"So soon?"

"Yes," he said, determined to leave so that he could spend the remainder of the night kicking himself for being such a swine, such a horrid excuse for a man. The lengths to which he would go to injure this poor woman were beyond imagining, and he needed to be alone so that he could come to terms with the extent of his folly. "We need to be careful now. If you are caught out here this evening, you'll never be able to get away tomorrow night."

"You're right," she concurred. "What time shall we meet?"

"Midnight, but not here," he said. "By the back gate. Over by the mews. We'll slip through and walk some distance to a carriage. One small bag is all you can bring. We'll buy you more clothes and necessaries later.''

''That sounds fine,'' she agreed. Gaily she added, ''I can't wait.''

''Neither can I.'' Because she appeared so blissful over the turn of events, it seemed appropriate to indulge her with one brief, light kiss, just a touch against her mouth; then he was over the wall and away into the shadows.

''I'll make you a great wife,'' she promised once more to the vacant spot where he'd so recently been. ''Just see if I don't.''

A feeling of freedom coursed through her veins, excitement wracked her nerves. Barely able to keep a leisurely pace, she turned and walked back to her father's house, trying to pretend that nothing was amiss.

CHAPTER SEVEN

Paulie hovered in the shadows across from the exclusive gentlemen's club. His gaze was alert and perceptive, checking out the carriages and the liverymen pulling up in front of the door to drop off or collect their esteemed passengers. Waiting. Patiently. It was a slow time of day, when the members were passing by for an early drink, to read the paper, or chat. For over two hours he'd been watching them come and go.

Then he saw what he was looking for: the immaculate team of four white horses, and the green and gold of the coachmen that belonged to the Duke of Roswell. The moment had arrived, and he knew exactly how he was going to accomplish his goal. Admiringly he looked down at the new set of clothes Lucas had bought for him. The outfit, coupled with the bath Lucas had made him endure, had changed him into someone other than who he had been. He now resembled an apprentice or a shop boy. No one would pay him any mind as he casually made his way about.

He waited a few more minutes until the duke emerged. When Paulie saw the white hair and fancy coat, the immense gold ring on the duke's hand, his fingers tingled at the thought of what kind of fortune he might be able to filch from the older man's pockets, but he quickly pushed the notion aside. He'd promised Lucas that he would behave. Since Lucas was the only adult he'd met in ages whom he deemed worth his salt, the one who, in a short time, had earned his respect and admiration, Paulie wouldn't let him down.

The duke walked out into the cool, wet afternoon. There was another man with him, one who was older, fat, bald, and he also wore the expensive trappings of affluence and authority. The two of them glanced up at the sky, at the puddles in the street, and the duke said something that sent servants scurrying. One approached with a small canopy held high, and the two men walked under it, shielded from the mist, to the duke's carriage.

There was a slight delay as one of the liverymen opened the door and lowered the step, and Paulie made his move. Casually he slipped as close to the duke as he dared and said, "I have a message from Lucas Pendleton." He tossed the missive in front of the duke, and it fluttered to the ground at his feet.

The powerful man turned, impaling Paulie with his fierce blue eyes, just as one of the servants noticed him.

"Off with you, boy!" the servant spit out in warning. "Who are you to think you can speak to your betters!" He pulled his arm back, ready to cuff Paulie about the ears, but Paulie didn't even flinch. He'd been dodging blows all his life and knew just how far away he needed to stand in order to be out of range.

Before the man could proceed, however, the duke made an abrupt gesture with his hand, stopping the attempt. He glared at the envelope lying between them as though it were a venomous snake poised to strike. Finally he pointed toward it, and one of the liverymen retrieved it and handed it to him. He thumbed open the flap and angrily scanned the words.

Paulie was dying to know what the letter said, but he couldn't read, not even his own name, so he hadn't bothered trying to sneak a peek, because the scribbling would have been nonsense. But whatever Lucas had penned, it was obvious that the intent was effective. The duke's face reddened as he read the directive once, then again, and he moved away from his entourage and in Paulie's direction. He had a vicious look about him, but Paulie hardly cared. Grown-ups other than Lucas had never regarded him in any other fashion, and that's why Paulie was so willing to see this task successfully completed. There was something about Captain Pendleton that he liked very much.

If he'd been older or wiser, he might have recognized that Lucas Pendleton was the type of male that lost boys such as himself dreamed about having as a father. As he'd never known a real father, or even an uncle, he couldn't identify the buried wish for what it was. He knew only that Lucas had singled him out, that he enjoyed Lucas's respect, and that he would make Lucas proud by doing his job well.

The duke pulled himself up to an astonishing height, his hands gripped behind his back, and demanded, "What do you want, boy?"

Bravely he answered, "Mr. Pendleton said that I was to give you his note, and he said I was to ask if you had any message in return."

"Do I have a message?" he blurted out, taking a menacing step in Paulie's direction. "Do I have a message!"

"Yes. I've got a good memory. I won't forget a single word." Paulie wisely took one step back, judging the distance. He wasn't afraid. With ease he could outrun this pack of obese, lazy men. As fast as they could snap their chubby, beringed fingers, he would vanish into the back alleys of London, and they'd never see him go.

He pronounced cockily, "If you have no answer, I'm to tell him that as well."

"Does Mr. Pendleton seriously think," the duke said, backing Paulie up a pace at a time, "that I will engage in discourse on a public street with the likes of you?"

"Does that mean you have no response?" Paulie asked. "If you don't, he said I should remind you that he intends to move forward with his plans. That this is the only warning you'll receive.''

"See here!" one of the servants said, shocked by Paulie's outrageous behavior.

The duke waved him off, saying to Paulie, "You miserable little whelp. Do you think you can threaten me and get away with it?"

The pretentious older man trudged forward, straightening a bit of lace at his cuff and asking, "Who is this ruffian, Harold?"

"No one. No one at all," the duke replied with such insult that Paulie couldn't resist tweaking his nose out of joint just a bit further.

"That's what you think, you old bastard," he muttered just loudly enough for everyone to hear, and the servants gasped, for no one could imagine a boy speaking to the duke at all, let alone in a rude manner. He added forcefully, "This is your last chance to answer."

As he'd expected, the duke nodded his head at his underlings, silently ordering three of the liverymen to jump at him, but Paulie was away before any of them had a chance to react. He bounded down one narrow avenue, then another, rounded a corner, hearing their shouts and cries, but he knew where he was going, and in a moment he'd be safe.

Unfortunately he took that second to glance over his shoulder, and when he looked ahead once again, two women were coming out of a shop. He ran into them head on, and their packages scattered. The impact of the collision tossed him to the side, and he was knocked against the cobbles with a hard thump. For a brief instant he lost his wind and his bearings, and it was just long enough for the three men to catch him.

One grabbed a leg, the other an arm, and he started to struggle. The third reached around his neck, and Paulie bit down, tasting blood and causing the man to yelp in surprise. He hit Paulie hard across the face, sending him sprawling.

"I say!" one of the women shouted indignantly.

"Stand aside, miss!" the man ordered, but to Paulie's sur-

prise, she didn't listen. She proceeded into the center of the
fracas, shielding him from his attackers. From his position he
couldn't see much except the expensive fabric of her skirt. She
leaned over and gazed at him with compassion in her blue
eyes. Raindrops dotted her blond hair and sparkled like tiny
diamonds, and he decided she appeared to be a fairy-tale princess, and he fell in love on the spot.

"Are you all right?" she asked firmly.

His ears were ringing, his head ached, his ankle pounded,
but he was too dazzled by her to do anything but nod. Using
his elbow for support, he sat up just as she turned to face his
pursuers.

"Three grown men," she scolded, "accosting a boy. You
ought to be ashamed of yourselves." Her eyes narrowed on
the livery one of them wore. "Why . . . you're John Coachman!
You work for my father! What do you think you're about,
brawling with a child like this in the middle of the streets?"

The irate glare she was flashing had the men snapping to
attention. Respectfully removing his hat, one of them said,
"Beg pardon, Lady Penelope."

"The duke will hear about this, I can promise you!" she
threatened, then she returned her attention to Paulie as the other
woman bent over and helped him to his feet.

"Up you go," the princess said as the other, darker one,
patted the dirt from his trousers while chattering something in
French. Paulie had no idea what she was saying, but the sound
of it soothed something down deep inside, at his very core,
and he decided that he was in love with her too.

The princess slipped a coin into his hand as one of the men
gulped, bowed, and said almost fearfully, "His Grace, the duke,
wanted us to retrieve the boy, milady."

"Well, that's too bad, isn't it?" she said sweetly. "Because
he's going on his way now." There was a hint of steel in her
voice to which the other men responded instantly, and Paulie
breathed a sigh of relief, knowing that he was about to escape,

but just then the duke's coach-and-four rumbled around the corner and jingled to a stop.

With the kind of pomp that only a very wealthy man could call up, he descended, looking as regal and full of himself as the Prince Regent, had he decided to happen by for a chat. Bystanders paused for a glimpse, craning their necks and whispering as to his identity. It wasn't often that one was allowed to view such an exalted figure.

"I didn't do nothin'," Paulie whispered to Lady Penelope's back. "I swear it, miss."

"I know you didn't," she said quietly. "Don't be afraid. He's all bluster. I won't let him harm you."

"Caught him, Your Grace," one of the liverymen mumbled as the duke approached.

"Good work," the duke said, nodding, then he pulled up short when he recognized Penny standing between himself and the boy.

Harold saw red all over again. It was bad enough that he had to put up with the gall of that American. But having a street urchin approach him in front of his very own club! With Edward Simpson and a cadre of servants present as witnesses! Now this!

She looked murderous and determined, characteristics he'd never have attributed to her a week earlier. It was a fine day, he thought, when a man couldn't predict how his own daughter might act. "What are you doing in the middle of this?" he growled.

"I was just standing here," she said, "when your men started beating this boy while onlookers beheld their atrocious course of action. Really, Father, how could you let them?"

"Enough!" he barked, moving close, refusing to argue with her while everyone and his brother hung on their every word. What had come over her, thinking she could challenge him like this at every turn?

"They hit this boy! Look at his face!" she said, stepping

aside so Harold had a better perspective of the swelling on Paulie's cheek. "They said they were only doing your bidding."

"Yes, well . . ." he said, clearing his throat, deeming that the little bastard had gotten exactly what he deserved. "Perhaps they were a little rough," he allowed.

"What do you want with him anyway?" she demanded. "He's just a child. He could have done nothing to you."

People were gathering to watch, and Harold was certain that all of this would be the talk of London before the hour was over. Maliciously he eyed the boy, but the insolent child belligerently showed no fear, as though he'd seen so many horrid things in his young life that nothing frightened him anymore.

"I'm not interested in this boy," he said, suddenly pretending to be gracious. "I think there has been some mistake."

"There! See?" she said, announcing the happy resolution to the crowd. She hovered next to Paulie's ear and whispered, "What's your name?"

"Paulie, miss," he answered.

"You're free to go," she said, smiling the most beautiful smile he'd ever seen. With a knowing wink she added, "And if I were you, I shouldn't dally."

"No," he responded, "I don't believe I will."

She nudged him on his way, and he took a step from her, backing up so that he could keep an eye on all of them while he moved toward the alley. Just as he thought he was safely past the duke, the man seized him by the arm. He painfully crunched his fingers into Paulie's shoulder blade as he hissed, "You tell your Mr. Pendleton that I have a noose with his name on it. Before I'm through, he'll be swinging from the yardarm on one of those ships he loves so much."

"Well, you'll have to find him first, won't ya, guv'na?" Paulie asked. As though he'd become a phantom, he shook off the duke's hand and disappeared like a puff of smoke into the milling crowd.

Harold straightened, then stiffened on seeing the angry and penetrating looks of dismay and disgust he was receiving from those surrounding him. Only wanting the public spectacle to be over, he glared at Penny and ordered, "Get in the carriage, and I'll see you home."

At that moment Edward took the opportunity to peek out the window. With all the excitement, Harold had forgotten about him.

"Harold, did you catch the little twerp?" he asked in that voice that had grown more irritating each time Harold had been forced to spend time in his company.

Penny circled toward the carriage, and the sight of Edward caused her to quiver with abhorrence. She then faced Harold squarely, as though daring him to explain.

In the past he'd never concerned himself with what feelings she might or might not have for him as her father; he'd always accepted that he was held in the highest esteem simply because of who he was. But for the first time in his life, he was able to recognize her true opinion. She loathed him! Her own father! The realization was as shocking as it was disturbing. When had this happened?

"I have my own carriage," she said, "and even if I didn't, I'd walk home—all the way—before I'd join you." Without so much as a *good day* she departed, abandoning him and leaving him alone with her dreadful fiancé.

Refusing to make more of a scene in front of so many, he walked to the carriage and wearily climbed in.

"I say," Edward asked, straining to see through the crowd, "wasn't that Penelope?"

Harold gaped at the other man for a long moment, then sighed. "No, it wasn't," he lied. He tapped on the roof and they were off.

Lucas stared out the window into the yard behind the house Matthew had rented as the secret hideaway that would enable them to carry out their plan. Harry had climbed up into one of the apple trees, and Lucas enjoyed watching him at play. The boy was delighted to finally be off the ship, so he was acting wild and burning up all the excess energy that had built up during their months at sea and the long wait at the docks once they'd arrived in England.

After much deliberation they'd decided to bring Harry to the country. With Harold Westmoreland's men hot on their trail, they weren't about to leave him in the city with any of the crew members. Although Lucas trusted his men, he knew he'd be distracted if Harry wasn't nearby, that he'd constantly be wondering if the child was all right, if he was well cared for, and once the conspiracy was set in motion, he couldn't have distractions occupying his mind. Hence, with few choices available as to what to do with him, they'd finally brought him to the country house. It meant that he would meet Penny, but that wasn't necessarily a bad thing.

If Penny was surprised to find a boy living with them, it wasn't as though they'd had much time to discuss their personal lives. As to the lad's connection to all of them, Lucas intended to tell her part of the truth—that Harry was his nephew, the son of his deceased sister and Lucas's son in every way that mattered. No mention would be made of Harry's relationship to Penny or Harold, but Lucas viewed the boy as a sort of insurance policy against the amount of disdain Penny would harbor once the event was ended.

Penny wouldn't be able to resist growing attached to Harry, and Lucas believed that her fondness would help her to eventually come to terms with why Lucas had committed so many horrible acts. Perhaps someday, though she'd never be able to forgive him, she might at least be able to understand. That was something worth hoping for.

The kitchen door opened, and Matthew came in from the backyard. "He's getting on well," he said, referring to Harry.

"He's a good boy," Lucas said, looking at his brother over his shoulder. He turned back to the window, taking in the isolated grounds. "This place was an excellent choice."

"I thought so the moment I saw it," Matthew agreed.

Simple. Clean. Close to London. Secluded. Perfect in all ways.

"Are you sure you'll be able to keep her here? And keep her happy for as long as it takes us?" Matthew asserted, "It's quite a step down from what she's used to."

They were both worried about Penny, about how she'd cope with the drastic change in her circumstance, because they couldn't afford to have her dashing home in a fit of pique. If they'd been in Virginia at their riverside house with its gentrified social life, large staff of servants, tobacco fields, and stables, they wouldn't have fretted so much about her transition, but this small, quaint cottage was another matter. They'd have a part-time cook and a maid who would come in from the village for a few hours each day, but that was it, and they didn't know how Penelope would adapt.

They couldn't have her grumbling over the lack of servants, then rushing off in a huff before they'd brought Harold to heel, but for some reason Lucas wasn't worried about her ability to persevere. He had only to recall the way she'd gazed up at him in the garden the previous night. She was made of sterner stuff than either of them had suspected. She'd given her word, and Lucas knew she'd never go back on it.

"She'll do fine, Matt" was all he said.

Matthew nodded. "No going back now," he mused pensively, as if taking one last moment to wonder if they should change their minds and walk away.

"No. No going back," Lucas said, sealing their decision and their fate. "Not after what Westmoreland allowed his men to do to Paulie." His temper flared at contemplating what might have happened, what kind of heinous deed the duke could have executed against the boy's person, and it would have been Lucas's fault.

When Paulie had returned to their rendezvous location with a black eye, torn clothing, bumps and bruises and cuts, Lucas had given him a few good shakes for being so reckless. He'd been told to simply deliver the message to a coachman and go;

they'd never suspected he'd do anything so rash as to actually have an encounter with the duke. The boy was lucky to still be alive.

"It's just another crime to add to the ones Westmoreland has already perpetrated," Lucas said, and Matthew dipped his head in agreement. "More reasons he needs to pay."

Matthew walked to the sideboard, poured them both a brandy, and he handed a glass to his brother. "To Caroline," he said, tipping his in Lucas's direction.

"To Caroline," Lucas echoed.

"And to Lady Penelope," Matthew continued, "who will help us to make sure we all get our due."

"To Lady P," Lucas repeated, gesturing with his glass again, but he couldn't add anything to the toast, nor could he feel any joy in proposing it. Penny didn't have any idea of the sacrifice she was about to make, of the ways in which her life was about to be irrevocably altered, and if Lucas could have conceived of any other means of intimidating her father, he'd have used it.

All for Caroline, he told himself. *All for her, and for Harry.*

For a very long time, revenge and retribution had been all that counted, but now that he was about to obtain the recompense for which he'd waited, the thrill of receiving it was greatly faded. He thought of Penny, of the joyful smile she gave him in the evening shadows, how she had kissed him and held him and looked at him as though he were the finest man on earth, and he couldn't find any gladness for what he was about to do.

Taking a long swallow, he knocked back his drink, letting the burn sizzle all the way down, then he stood.

"I'm ready," he said. "Let's finish it."

Penny walked slowly down the magnificent hall, taking it all in as she passed by for the very last time. It was late, her father and brother gone off to a night of parties, and her mother remained cloistered in her room, as she so often was these days. With the exception of the handful of servants awaiting Harold's and Willie's return, everyone else was abed, so she had the monstrous place to herself, which was just as she'd wanted it.

Strolling quietly, she let the flicker of light from her lamp cast shadows and illuminate memories, and she was sad to realize that there were so few happy ones. She and Willie had been raised as though they were a prince and princess, never as children who simply wanted to laugh and play. In fact, she couldn't remember a single occasion she'd rolled in the grass, or soiled her hands and skirts while doing something as pleasant as digging in the yard.

Her eyes scanned the rooms she'd be leaving behind, and it was depressing to think of how much she'd been given, of how much she'd had, how every whim, every wish—no matter how extravagant—had been indulged, but how all of it had brought so little satisfaction.

There was the rug over which she'd once tripped as a girl, resulting in a chipped tooth and a flurry of unusual preoccupation from her parents due only to their anxiety over how the injury might affect her future appearance.

A line of ferns in the solarium brought back the incident when she'd hidden behind them, hoping to surprise her absentee mother, only to find herself the unwitting listener to one of her parents' private arguments about her father's latest in a long line of mistresses, an unmentioned but disturbing cause of constant household tension.

In the kitchen she ran a loving hand over the edge of the table in the corner, where, as a lonely, solitary girl, an elderly cook had slipped her biscuits and told her stories, until the afternoon her mother discovered she'd been tarrying with the servants and had banned her from the room. Penny had never seen the kindly old woman again, had never had the nerve to ask what had happened to her, but she suspected the cook had been let go for being too familiar with the Westmoreland's little darling.

Her meandering took her through the portrait gallery, and she didn't pause until the last painting, which was of her mother and father. It was commissioned when they were newlyweds, and, though they'd aged, they still appeared much as they had in the early years of their marriage. Stern, unsmiling, wealthy, and self-assured, there wasn't a sign of warmth between them, and Penny couldn't remember ever seeing one.

Had they ever been in love? Had they ever been happy?

She didn't think so. Theirs had been a typical arranged union, where the two parties had realized early on that they had little in common, so they had set about building separate lives. Now the situation had deteriorated to the point where they never spoke privately anymore, refusing to pass time in each other's company, coming together only for an occasional social engagement or supper party where their hostesses had the good sense to seat them at opposite ends of the table.

Her father's life was busy; he saw to his vast estates, his clubs, his duties in Parliament, and his women. Always his women. But what about her mother? Efficient servants ran the big house, so there was little to supervise. She had her friends and her correspondence, her regular array of events, which she attended alone for the most part, since Penny rarely went out.

Was she lonely? Did she miss Harold's company? Did she ever crave, as Penny so often did lately, another sort of life, one filled with merriment and friendship? Perhaps the kind of life Penny was hoping to encounter with Lucas Pendleton? Did her mother ever look to the past and wish it had been different?

Penny didn't know and wouldn't ask. She could hardly raise the subject of Harold's indifference or his affairs, of his bastard children or upsetting peccadilloes. Nor would she dare to examine the issue of her and Willie's childhood. What purpose would such a discussion serve?

Their youthful years had passed exactly as those of their peers, with governesses and tutors, the time sprinkled infrequently by a longed-for audience with Mother or Father. Through it all there had been a lack of concern or interaction on the part of their parents. While growing up, it had never occurred to her that this method of child rearing had been quite terrible, but over the last few years, as her personal life had gone from bad to worse, she'd had lengthy moments to ponder her upbringing.

She would have loved the opportunity for a heartfelt discussion with her mother, but talking wasn't something the Westmorelands did. Instead, they lumped along as though no problems existed, as though nothing had changed, when in fact everything had.

Penny didn't want to leave her father's house only to repeat the life she'd passed there. The feel of it, of each day blending into another until they were all a hazy gray, had become so stifling, she could barely breathe, and she wanted to escape, to run for something new and better.

To find joy! That's what she wanted. To find some joy in her life, put there by someone who cared about her.

Staring at the portrait of her parents made her overly melancholy, so she left the gallery and climbed to the nursery. Though it had gone unused for over a decade, the servants still kept it clean, the toys neatly stacked on the shelves, the rocking horse placed just so by the window. It looked very much as it had on the last occasion when Penny had been young enough to feel comfortable spending time there.

Willie's children would play in the room someday, perhaps her own would join them. She closed her eyes and tried to imagine how all those little blond boys and girls would look, but instead, she saw a vision of herself as a youngster, sitting with a doll, while her grumpy nurse stood stoically in the corner.

As she recalled the memory, she sustained a strong wave of emotion as she realized that she hadn't really been playing with her doll. She'd been listening for footsteps, wondering if her mother or father would deign to visit, if she would be allowed to see them that day, and she shook her head at the thought of what had been lost. She didn't really know her parents at all. And never had.

"What a waste," she murmured to the silence. Quietly she closed the door, and as she did, she understood that there was so much she was leaving behind, but at the same time, so little.

Then and there she made a vow to her own children, to the ones she'd have with Lucas: They would never live like this. They would know laughter and happiness, all the cheerful sentiments Penny hadn't realized she'd missed as a girl. They might not receive a new pony every birthday, but they would always be showered with plenty of love and attention. She would expend every bit of her energy and make every necessary sacrifice in order to see that they were content.

On a sigh, she returned to her chamber and slipped inside. As always, Colette was waiting patiently.

"You are ready?" she asked.

"Yes," Penny answered.

"You have made your *au revoir?*" She wrinkled her nose in dismay.

"*Oui,*" Penny said, giving a reassuring smile.

For a change, her usually bold Colette was fretting and stewing about their secret plan. She urged Penny to take more time, make better arrangements, be more cautious.

Although Colette rarely talked about her early years, she'd mentioned enough for Penny to know that her mother had been an aristocrat's mistress during the Terror. His entire family had been murdered, and with Colette only six or seven years old, she and her mother had fled Paris in the middle of the night, running for their lives. They escaped to England with only the clothes on their backs and a handful of coins, and her mother died shortly after they arrived. Colette had known poverty, she'd been hungry and gone without shelter, so she wasn't overly keen on the prospects offered by Penny's decision.

In contrast, Penny hadn't spent a moment worrying about whether she was doing the right thing. She viewed her elopement as a grand adventure, where Colette saw adventure as something frightening and to be avoided at all costs. Colette would take safety and security over adventure anytime.

"Everything will be fine, Colette," she said, patting the woman on the shoulder. "Trust me, please. Mr. Pendleton won't let anything bad happen to either one of us."

She gave a definitive French growl low in her throat. "How can you know this to be true?"

"Wait till you meet him," Penny insisted, "then you'll see what I mean."

It was strange to be in the position of defending her rash behavior. Colette was the romantic, the first to see the possibilities in any arrangement between a man and a woman. Penny was always the more pragmatic of the two, but not in this instance. Although Colette talked a good story, the woman's fears of destitution were too ingrained. She detected nothing engaging about Penny's resolution, but she was extremely faithful and would go along quietly.

"But what kind of man is this one," Colette asked, "that he would take you away from your home and your family?" She gestured about the beautifully appointed room, which housed only the finest things that money could buy. "I cannot feel comfortable about this."

It had been their ongoing quarrel, with Colette certain that they were making a huge mistake and Penny unable to persuade her otherwise. But then, Colette wasn't the one facing marriage to Edward Simpson. Penny was convinced that Lucas was the answer to her prayers, but there would be no swaying Colette. She'd have to see for herself, so continuation of the disagreement was pointless.

Besides, it was quickly nearing midnight. Their opportunity for dispute had ended. "It's too late for arguing, Colette, and you know you can't change my mind."

"This is true, for I have tried my best."

"You can still change yours though," Penny assured her. "You don't need to come with me."

"Bah," Colette said, angrily waving her hand, "as if I would let you go off by yourself with your *American.*" She muttered the word like a vile curse. "Someone must watch out for you."

"Thank you," Penny said, truly appreciating her loyalty and devotion. "I'm glad."

"So am I," Colette said, and she walked to the dressing room and came back with their cloaks and the two rather large portmanteaus she'd packed. While Lucas had advised Penny to bring one small bag, they'd settled on two bigger ones. Penny required some finery for her wedding day, and Colette, ever the adviser *d'amour,* had selected several fancy, sheer undergarments for Penny to use to entice her new husband.

They'd haggled relentlessly about what to take, gradually whittling down their choices, but the amount couldn't be helped. There were some sacrifices a woman of Quality simply couldn't be expected to endure!

Colette set the bags on the floor, then stepped over to Penny and hooked the clasp of her cloak, encircling her in the dark sable. As she smoothed out the fur's swirl, she reached for the hem and laid it in Penny's hand.

"I have sewn coins in the lining. Just in case." She lifted her own cloak, a lighter wool, gave it a hearty shake, and Penny heard it rattle. "I have placed some in my own as well. You must promise not to tell your man."

"Colette . . ." she breathed, exasperated with the woman's caution.

"Promise me!" she demanded sternly. "The coins will be our secret."

"All right," Penny reluctantly agreed.

"A woman can never be too careful," she said. "She can never know what might happen . . ."

"Yes, yes," Penny said irritably. She appreciated Colette's wariness but knew they would never need the covert stash of money.

Her last task was placement of the note she would leave behind, the one that would explain her departure. Her mother would be wondering where she was, so she felt it necessary to allay any undue fears. She'd debated what she should or shouldn't say, finally deciding that she wouldn't mention Mr.

Pendleton or her hasty marriage. The news would only set her father into a frenzy of searching, increasing the risk of discovery, so she'd chosen the simplest explanation she could.

At her writing table she read through the words that had been so carefully written on the slip of parchment.

> *Mother and Father,*
>   *I cannot marry Edward, so I have gone away. I am fine. Please do not worry. I will contact you again after I am established in my new situation.*
>
> *Penny*

She wanted to express more—that she loved them, or would miss them—but it wasn't their way, and she wasn't certain deeper sentiments would be welcomed. She wanted only that her mother not fret. Sealing the note, she placed it on her pillow, where she hoped it wouldn't be discovered for many hours to come.

Suddenly overwhelmed by the moment, Penny leaned forward and gave Colette a tight hug, the first one ever in all the years they'd known each other.

"Are you ready, *mon amie?*" Penny asked, for the initial time calling her maid *friend.*

"*Oui,*" Colette answered, her eyes wet with tears.

They longingly gazed around the room where Penny had spent most of her life. Then, needing the extra support, she slipped her hand into Colette's, and they linked their fingers tightly. Together they walked into the hall, down the back stairs, and out the door, and they disappeared into the gardens, ready to meet the future.

CHAPTER EIGHT

Lucas glanced at his timepiece, but he couldn't see the placement of the hands. It was too dark, and the fog was swirling, creating a perfect atmosphere for clandestine activity. Along the back wall of the Westmoreland property, where he stood silently in his black clothing, nothing moved. Neither people nor animals were willing to brave the thick soup that made it impossible to see or sense direction. Even the rats had gone into hiding. Apparently he was the only being foolish enough to venture out in such conditions.

It was late. Too late, if she was coming. Had he misread her? Had she changed her mind? Or, worse, had she merely been trifling with him, never planning to join him at all?

"No, no," he said to himself. "She gave her word. She meant it!" But even as he attempted to reassure himself, he couldn't prevent the feelings of apprehension from creeping over him. It was the fog, he knew. It had a way of displacing thought and process, prompting a man to doubt the world and his place in it.

Though it took much to unnerve him, the dense cloud in which he was enveloped took on a life of its own, forcing him to question his resolve. Throughout his global travels, he'd never encountered anything like it, and in the weeks he'd been in London, he'd not begun to get used to it. It crept up stealthily, slithering across the ground and reaching out like a ghost's long fingers. It swallowed sound, making the busy London streets unnaturally silent, causing him to leap at shadows and hear too many bumps in the night.

Try as he might, he couldn't put aside the trepidation it stirred. Just as he began to ponder whether he should return to the ship, he heard footsteps, but from two persons instead of one. He stayed where he was, wondering if she'd told their secret, and if the duke's men were, even at that moment, ready to close in.

Holding his breath, he waited. Then two figures, both cloaked in black, halted directly in front of him, so near that he could have touched either one.

"Are you certain this is the correct place?" a woman whispered in a French-accented voice, and he braced.

"Yes, but this blasted fog is so thick. I can't see my hand in front of my face."

Penny. He nearly sagged with relief.

"I am here," he said softly, and even in the dim light he could see both jump at the realization that he was right next to them. He stepped from his hiding place.

"Lucas," Penny said, breathing an audible sigh of relief that it was he and not another.

"I was beginning to think you weren't coming."

"Me? Not come to be with you?" she asked. "Are you mad?"

He could sense her smiling, hear the joy in her words, and before he could stop himself, he was extending his arms and hugging her tightly. She came willingly, fitting so well. The hood on her cloak fell back, exposing all that blond hair. Unfortunately it shone like a flare, and he allowed himself one incredible instant to run his fingers through the silky strands before he shielded her from discovery by covering her head once again.

Unable to resist, he placed a kiss on her forehead, allowing his lips to linger much longer than they should. He knew the modest embrace was subterfuge, that he was horribly in the wrong, but as with the other times he'd been around her, he was physically overwhelmed by her and incapable of keeping his hands to himself.

Then and there he made the decision not to—at least for the time being, and on this harmless level. They were supposed to be eloping. His bride certainly believed they were, so why not play along? Why not act as if they were in love and running off together? What could it hurt to hold her hand, to steal a few kisses on occasion? The gestures would ease her nerves, make it easier to spirit her away, and if it helped to calm some of his own mounting desire, so be it.

He stroked down her back, holding her close, adoring the way she leaned into him and held his waist in return, but his enjoyment was short-lived as he remembered the other woman who had come with Penny. Her quiet regard was so intense that it felt as though her eyes were sharp knives pricking at him.

"Who is this?" he whispered in Penny's ear. The fog did strange things to sound, sometimes swallowing it completely, other times magnifying it so the echo carried forever. They were hardly safe or freely away, so they had to be extremely circumspect.

"My personal maid, Colette," she answered.

Lucas tensed. He'd never imagined that she'd bring another person with her. The idea had never crossed his mind, and he had to stifle a laugh at his own folly, thinking, *That's what happens when you kidnap someone you don't know anything about!*

His mind raced, trying to work through the ways the abigail might be a benefit or a danger, but they were in a precarious spot, time was short, and he couldn't think of all the angles. He didn't want to hold a lengthy debate on the subject, but he understood that a second individual simply meant extra ways in which events could go awry. She'd be one more person to contain, one more person to silence, one more person who could escape and tell all. She had to be left behind. There was no other choice.

"You didn't need to bring a maid," Lucas said. "I have funds. I will hire you one."

Before Penny could respond, the maid stepped closer. On the surface her accent was pleasing, but underneath it was a hint of temper. "You would hire a stranger to care for Lady Penelope?" Aghast, she asked, "Who do you think you are taking with you? This is Penelope Westmoreland, not some merchant's daughter!"

"I realize that," he said, struggling for calm in the face of the servant's fury.

"She must have only the best of care. By me and no one else. I will not allow another to usurp my place at her side! No one else could possibly know how to look after her correctly." She nodded her head. "So, I will accompany you, *oui?*"

"No," Lucas said.

"*Oui,*" Colette insisted, adding slyly, "or I am thinking I will be raising the alarm, eh? I will not let my lady go off alone!"

"Oh, for crying out loud . . ." Lucas muttered.

"Lucas, please?" Penny said, laying the palm of her hand on the center of his chest and rubbing it in an intoxicating circle. "I'm terribly nervous about all of this, and I'd feel so much better if she's with me. Please, let her come."

She asked so prettily that his heart melted. No wonder her father had spoiled her as a child, that she'd grown up being given everything she'd ever wanted. What man could ever say no to that lovely face? "Penny," he said, sighing and trying to refuse even as he knew he'd already conceded the argument. "Having her along will make things much more difficult."

"No, it won't, Lucas," she said. "I swear she won't be any inconvenience."

Lucas knew that wasn't true. Even in the dark he could tell the maid would cause all kinds of trouble. She was too astute, too assertive, and much too devoted and ready to come to Penny's aid.

Penny reached for his hand and slipped her fingers through his, giving a light squeeze. "Please?" she asked once again.

Gazing down into her blue eyes, he knew it was a lost cause. Colette was coming.

"All right," he breathed to Penny, utterly capitulating even as he wondered if this would be the way their entire relationship would go.

He had to find a method of lessening the effect she had on him so that he could be more severe. He needed to exercise more control when he was in her presence. This wasn't an adventure or a lark. It was a kidnapping, for pity's sake, but he was quickly learning she had a style about her that he couldn't resist, and he had no defense against it.

Despite every wicked intention harbored deep in his heart, he wished to make her happy, and therefore, he was completely and dangerously at her mercy. Whatever she wanted, he was apparently willing to do, and he sighed in disgust at himself, acknowledging that this was a dreadful manner in which to begin his career as an abductor.

"But you," he warned, pointing an accusing finger at Colette and trying to pretend that he'd regained some command of the situation, "you'll do as I say. You won't cross my path; you'll see to your duties. If you cause me any trouble, I'll send you packing."

"Thank you," Penny said as she rose on her toes and kissed him sweetly on the lips. "Thank you so much."

It was all he could do to keep from prolonging the moment by kissing her back. As for the maid, she grumbled something in French under her breath, and while he grasped only a handful of words in the foreign language, he was fairly certain that her remark hadn't been a compliment.

Stealing one last hug, he smiled down at Penny and whispered, "Let's be off."

He briskly reached for their two bags, but as he lifted them, he grunted in dismay. Both were so cumbrous that he knew he'd soon be breaking out in a sweat.

Upon hearing his discomfort, Penny asked, "Are they too heavy for you?"

"No," he said through clenched teeth. What was in the blasted things anyway? Rocks?

"They're rather large," Penny apologized. "Would you like us to help you carry them? We could take turns—"

"No, I've got them," he said, managing to sound gallant even as his back was straining against the load.

The three of them tiptoed to the back gate. Well oiled, it opened without making a squeak, and they silently moved into the alley. Without speaking, they walked out to the street, then continued on for several streets. At times the fog was so thick that Lucas had to touch the fences of the houses they passed in order to count the number, lest they miss the turn to where the carriage waited.

As it was, they came upon it so suddenly that they almost ran into it. One of the horses, sensing their approach, shook its withers, causing the harness to jingle and rattle.

"Who goes there?" Matthew's disembodied voice came from the driver's seat, but he didn't bend over to give anyone a better view of his face. Bundled as he was, the women wouldn't be able to see him, which was as he and Lucas had planned it. Because they couldn't predict how circumstances might eventually unfold, Matthew's participation might take on furtive proportions, and they didn't intend to reveal his identity.

" 'Tis I," Lucas responded quietly. "I've brought my lady *and* her maid," he said cryptically, cutting off the curiosity he knew would spark in his brother when Matthew saw three people approaching instead of two. Lucas lowered the step, helping Penny, then the maid, to climb inside.

As he made to close the door, Penny leaned into the opening. She extended her hand, and he automatically took it, enfolding it in his own, and he wanted to kick himself at how quickly and easily his body responded to her.

"Are we off to Scotland?" she queried.

"No," he said, realizing she imagined they were taking the lovers' route to Gretna Green, the village just across the border where couples often went to marry when they needed the matter accomplished in haste.

"Then . . . where are we headed?"

Lucas could hear her hesitation but also her determination to proceed. She was about to embark on a journey with a man she hardly knew, and she was bravely ready to go forward without so much as knowing their destination. The absolute faith he'd managed to instill in her was a wondrous thing, and he felt like the lowest cad for creating such misplaced trust. "I've taken a house in the country through the summer."

"Oh, how marvelous," she said, and he could tell she was smiling again. "I've always enjoyed the country."

"I thought you might," he said, smiling in return.

"But—" She paused.

"But what?" he prodded lightly.

"When will we marry?" she asked, and he vacillated much too long before answering. It was tricky business, lying and deceiving and trying to appear sincere while doing so. Inside the coach he could feel her maid's ears perk up, waiting for his reply. Into the silence Penny added, "I just thought that we agreed we were in a hurry. To wed, I mean."

"We are," he said, patting the back of her hand, "so I've made arrangements for the wedding to be held just soon as we're settled at the house."

"Excellent," she said, greatly relieved. "Will we be traveling far?"

"No, not far." He started to step back, but she tightened her grip.

"Can you ride with us? I'd like the chance to chat a bit. I've many questions I'd like to ask."

Nothing would be more fantastic—or more horrible—than being trapped with her in the small, enclosed space. She'd laugh and talk, luring him with her charms and causing him to like her more and more. Inquiries would arise about where they were going and what they were doing, and there weren't many explanations he was prepared to give.

The less time they spent together, the better. Opportunities to learn about him or his personal affairs gravely increased the risk. It was best for all concerned if he kept his distance, but, oh, it was tempting to say *yes*. On this dreary, moist night, facing nothing but dark, empty streets, he'd have loved nothing more than to snuggle next to her on the plush seat. He would smell her perfume and feel their thighs touching. They would sit with their heads together as they whispered confidences and shared the warmth of the coach's interior.

"We'll have plenty of opportunity to talk once we arrive," he said, "but I think for the moment that I'm going to have to walk with the horses. At least until we're farther from the river." Looking around, and meaning it, he said, "I hope the fog will let up as we proceed out of the city."

"It's awfully thick tonight," she agreed, "and there are so many dangers that could be lurking." Her mouth moved close, she whispered for his ear alone. "Be careful for me."

"I will," he said, and something inside his chest swelled and hurt at her words of concern.

They'd tarried long enough, they had to be off, but he couldn't help wanting to steal a kiss, although he didn't dare. The maid, Colette, would certainly expect to witness such an eventuality, but Matthew wouldn't. He was sitting atop, listening to their every word, and while his brother knew of the ruse Lucas had used to get Penny to come along quietly, he didn't know the extent of Lucas's attraction or the depth to which he was willing to stoop in order to keep her happy.

Best not to go down that road when Matthew might hear.

His younger brother wouldn't hesitate to give him a swift kick in the rear if he decided one was necessary, and Lucas didn't want to have to explain his terrible yearnings for the woman, when he barely understood them himself.

Easing her back into the coach, he regretfully relinquished her hand. "Rest yourself and don't worry about me. I'll be fine." He started to step away, then remembered to add, "There are blankets under the seat to keep the chill away."

"How sweet of you to worry over our comfort," she said.

Longer than he should have, he stood there, unable actually to see her, but nevertheless extremely reluctant to break the minor contact. There was something so enchanting about being close to her. Eventually he forced himself back, closing and latching the door.

As he moved away, he heard Penny whisper to Colette, "What do you think?"

And he winced when he heard Colette answer, "Do not worry, *ma petite*. I shall be watching heem very closely."

It was a slow trip out of London. Lucas led the horses for nearly two hours, and the fog eased somewhat as they traveled farther from the Thames. By the time they approached the outskirts of the city, it had dissipated to where he was able to climb onto the box. Still, it was thick enough to warrant extreme caution. What little moon they could infrequently see was only a tiny sliver and provided hardly any light, so the journey was agonizingly deliberate. Dawn was breaking in the east when they finally pulled into the yard of their new home.

With a few hand gestures and signals, Lucas told Matthew that they needed to rush. He wanted the women inside and Matthew gone before the sky grew any lighter. Matthew pulled up to the front entrance, and Lucas jumped down. They hadn't heard a peep from the two women during the long excursion, and occasionally he'd wondered if they were asleep. Or was it something more sinister? Had they changed their minds? Were they thinking they'd made a grave error? Were they already plotting their escape?

He reached for the door and tugged it open, prepared for anything.

Penny looked out to see Lucas standing there, smiling in welcome. "Have we arrived?" she asked.

"Yes."

She held out her hand, and he grasped it immediately, helping her navigate the two steps. It had been a difficult night, as they'd been jostled and tossed by the rough road in the badly sprung carriage. Her muscles were sore, her back ached, and her head throbbed from listening to Colette's harangue.

The maid had lamented continuously, whispering feverishly about the varying fates that might await them: that they would be robbed and murdered. Robbed and abandoned. Sold into slavery. Used sexually and discarded.

The woman's imagination knew no bounds, and with each passing hour her dire predictions became more grim, until Penny's resolve had begun to weaken and she'd started to distrust her decision. But as Lucas steadied her feet on solid ground, she looked up at the home he'd found for her, the one where they would begin their life together, and all her fears vanished.

Lucas carried a lamp, which gave off only a tiny glow so she couldn't see much, but she could see enough. It was an admirable house, not big or grand in the fashion to which she was accustomed, but fine just the same. Quaint but comfortable-looking, it was made of a grayish stone and was two stories high, with numerous windows and white trim and shutters. There were window boxes with spring flowers just beginning to bloom, and planters on either side of the door, to welcome those who approached.

The drive was circular and brick, the boundary hedged and offering privacy. Although it was still too dark to see much of the area, she sensed open space and lush greenery. From somewhere off in the distance she thought she could hear the delightful sound of a bubbling brook.

The apprehension that had increased during the lengthy coach ride, which had been urged to the fore by Colette, disappeared like ice on a warm summer's day. She turned to her husband-to-be and said, "It lovely, Lucas. Absolutely perfect."

"Do you really like it?"

"Yes," she said, gazing around, taking it in. "It's exactly the kind of dwelling I'd been hoping you would find for us." It was cozy, inviting, a place where she imagined many generations of happy couples had passed their lives. It offered solace and solitude, was small enough to afford close contact, but the outer property would provide space if one of them felt the need of it as they stumbled through the first steps of growing to know each other better.

All in all, it was ideal for a pair of newlyweds who wanted to start their marriage off properly, and she knew then, without a doubt, that she'd made the right choice by joining her future to Lucas's.

Lucas aided Colette as she maneuvered the steps, then he retrieved their bags and set them down. The driver snapped the reins at the horses, and the carriage lumbered off into the darkness. He headed out to the road, closed the gate, and vanished.

"Is that *our* carriage?" Penny asked, wondering how they would get to the village and back.

"No," Lucas said, looking at the entrance that now shielded them from the view of passersby. "I haven't had time to purchase transportation for us yet. But I will," he said. "Actually this has all happened so quickly that there are many matters that remain untended. The house isn't in nearly the shape that I'd wished it to be before you arrived. I hope you'll bear with me through these first few days while I get everything arranged to your liking."

"Everything is already arranged to my liking," she said, patting his arm, "and I'll help you with anything that need doing." One of the few lessons she'd been taught by her mother was how to ensure that a household ran smoothly. For the first time, she'd be able to put her tutoring into practice, although on a much smaller scale than she'd ever supposed.

"I'd appreciate your assistance," Lucas said. "Let's go in, shall we?" Penny slipped her hand into his, and they walked to the door. Colette reached for the two bags, prepared to follow, and he said over his shoulder, "Leave those. I'll come back for them."

Inside, it was cold and dark, the last embers of an evening fire long since burned out. Her first sentiment was one of irritation, that a servant should have kept the room toasty and welcoming for their arrival, that someone should have had the house lit and ready for her inspection. But the minute the notions crossed her mind, she shook them away.

That was her old life. This was her new.

Perhaps Lucas hadn't hired any servants yet. Perhaps he had and they weren't aware they should have been awake for the initial appearance of their new master and mistress. Whatever the situation, there obviously weren't any people about, so they'd have to fend for themselves, which Penny had every intention of doing.

When her first engagement—the one to the marquis—had fallen through, she'd spent months listening to her parents' bombast about how the entire debacle had been *her* fault. They insisted the marquis decided against marrying her, choosing another instead, because he found Penny too immature, too spoiled and demanding, too difficult to please.

Not this time! she vowed to herself. Never for a moment would she let Lucas know that she was dissatisfied. She was so grateful for her rescue from her marriage to Edward that she was never going to let him perceive any emotions but complacency and appreciation.

Besides, she thought brightly, she could build her own fire. She never had before, but how difficult could it be? The very idea of completing such a task for herself only added to the sense of adventure. She could do it! Colette could teach her how, and how to do many other common duties as well. Penny intended to learn everything necessary in order to make their lives enjoyable.

At the end of Lucas's day, when he was finished with business, she wanted him to enter a home that was a snug, agreeable residence, one to which he'd long to hasten each evening. When he came through the door, he'd find her content and happy and excited that he'd finally returned.

"What do you think?" Lucas asked, gesturing with the lamp, and throwing shadows about the walls.

"I think it's charming," she said cooperatively just as Colette stepped in behind her.

"It's cold as the dickens in here," Colette muttered irritably, hastening forward and wrapping Penny's cloak more tightly about her shoulders. "What are the servants thinking of, leaving the place like this for my lady?"

Penny flashed her a quelling look as Lucas responded politely. "There's only one woman here, and I didn't know when we'd arrive, so I told her not to wait up." Ignoring the maid, he looked at Penny and said hopefully, "I think we'll manage just this once, don't you?"

"Of course I do," she answered, sending Colette a glare meant to silence and threaten. To her relief, the maid said nothing further, and Penny was able to inspect the furnishings of the front parlor without interruption.

The room was modest and unpretentious, appointed with a matching couch and chair, a colorful rug, a writing desk, and a cheery hearth. There was a painting of the house and yard, a very pleasant rendering, hanging over the fireplace. There appeared to be two or three other rooms on the main floor, but before she had time to look at them, Lucas was saying, "You must be exhausted. Let's get you upstairs to your room, and you can explore in the morning, after you've rested."

"That would be wonderful," she said affably, glaring over her shoulder at Colette and daring her to disagree.

Holding her hand, Lucas led her up the stairs and into the first room on the right. As with the downstairs, it was small but comfortable, containing hardly more than a bed with a thick mattress and a warm quilt, vanity, and wardrobe. Lucas set his lamp on the stand next to the bed and lit a second one. Momentarily the room was growing more gay. There was a stove in the corner, with chunks of coal in a bucket on the floor, and Colette set about starting a fire as Lucas went to retrieve their bags. By the time he returned, the flames in the grate were already chasing the chill.

Lucas scrutinized the bedchamber, making certain everything appeared in order. "I think you have what you need for the time being. Until morning at least."

"Yes, I do."

"Are you hungry?" he asked almost as an afterthought. "I hadn't considered—"

"I'm not hungry," she said, cutting him off. "I'm fine. Don't worry about me."

Now that they'd arrived and the plan was well and truly in motion, Lucas felt nervous and shy as a schoolboy, and he couldn't resist the comfort he'd find by touching her. He neared and took hold of her hand once more. "I've hired two women from the village. One to cook, one to clean, but they won't be staying at the house. They'll help out during the day but go home to their families at night."

"I'm sure we'll manage," she said, smiling.

"Yes, I'm sure we will. Anyway, there's a servant's room off the kitchen, and they won't be using it, so Miss Colette can have her own room."

"That's very nice," Penny said, "isn't it, Colette?" The maid grumbled something unintelligible, as Penny said by way of clarification, "I imagine she'll stay with me tonight though. Just till we're more familiar with our surroundings."

"I was thinking," Lucas continued, "that if anyone should ask, you might want to say that we've already been married for a time. I don't know how far your father's reach might extend, or where he might search for us, but he'll be looking for a pair of newlyweds."

"An excellent idea," she agreed. "How about if I say we've been married for a year."

"That would be credible. Also, I know that life in the country will be different for you, and you may get bored or lonely, but I don't believe you should go into the village or have callers. At least until we're far enough along that there's no going back. We can't know what your father might be doing."

"I think that's a wise course," she concluded.

He cleared his throat and inhaled deeply. "There's one other matter."

"What is that?"

"There's someone else in the house whom I want you to meet." She stiffened, and he realized that he'd started it badly. His initial words had sent her imagination flying in all directions. "My nephew," he added hastily. "He's just a boy. Almost five."

"A child?" she reflected, extremely surprised. In all her ruminating about their first months together, there hadn't been any children in the picture, and on such short notice, she couldn't seem to get him to fit anywhere.

"Yes," Lucas said, hurrying to dispel the frown he'd brought to her face. "He's a good lad. Respectful and . . . *usually* well behaved, but he can be full of a bit of mischief. He was my sister's boy. She died in childbirth, and I've cared for him ever since. He's my own son in every way, and it would mean ever so much to me if you could be kind to him and perhaps take the time to get to know him."

"Certainly, I will," she assented, thinking that her encounters with children had always been extremely limited, so his faith in her ability to interact with the boy was decidedly undeserved. In her world, children were secluded from adults. In fact, when that street urchin had crashed into her the previous day while fleeing from her father's minions, that had been the first time she'd talked with a child in ages. But Lucas wanted her to try to get along with his nephew, and that's what she'd do.

"What's his name?" she asked.

"Harry," Lucas said. "I know I should have told you before, but there's been so little time for sharing confidences. . . ."

"It's all right. Really," she declared, giving his hand a reassuring squeeze. "And the wedding, Lucas? When will that be?"

"I'm working on it," he said enigmatically. "I'll probably have everything arranged by tomorrow or the next day."

"Wonderful."

"In the morning I have some business matters to attend in the city. We'll talk again when I get home. In the meantime, Harry will be here, and the two local women. They'll be more than able to fill your day."

"I'm sure of it," she said. "Ah, Lucas? What is your business? I've never asked."

"Shipping, Penny," he said. "I earn my income through shipping. I own five vessels. We're based out of my home port in Virginia, and we do quite a bit of commerce up and down the eastern seaboard of the United States."

"Do you have a home there?"

"Yes, in Virginia. A very nice one."

Her heart beat a little quicker at learning this news. "Will we be going there?"

"Eventually," he said after a long pause.

"I can't wait," she declared, more excited than she'd assumed she might be at the prospect. Other than a handful of trips to her father's country estate in Scotland, she'd never been out of England. She'd never considered traveling so far, or voyaging to such an exotic locale. Her escapade with Lucas Pendleton was growing more thrilling by the moment, and she couldn't believe how glad she was that it was so. The view of her old life was fading quicker than she could mark its passing.

"Where will you be staying?" she asked.

"Just across the hall," he said, gesturing, and there was a long, charged hush as Penny thought about the night, very soon, when she would be residing there as well. A flood of heat shot through her body from her head to her toes. If mere musings could bring on such a wave of pleasure, what would the actual event be like? She couldn't wait.

"Good night," she said.

"Yes, good night." But he couldn't seem to make himself leave. For a lengthy time they stood mutely in the center of the room, holding hands and grinning at each other like two love-struck fools. Finally he said, "I'm glad you're here."

"So am I."

"Until tomorrow." He brushed a light kiss across her lips.

Wanting to deepen it so that the feeling would last her through her slumber, she raised her arms to pull him closer, but it was like reaching for smoke. He was out the door and into his own room before she could hold him.

CHAPTER NINE

It was afternoon when Penny woke. She hadn't intended to sleep so long, wanting to be up and about. Considering it was the only place she'd ever lived besides her father's house, she had expected to doze for a few hours, then be ready to face her circumstance head-on. Instead, she'd dropped off completely, and she was ashamed to realize that her two new servants probably thought she was a slugabed. At a previous time in her life she wouldn't have cared, but these were the first attendants of her very own, and she desperately hoped to make a good impression.

When she descended the stairs for her initial entrance, she wanted to look well groomed, so she needed Colette's help, but Colette was already risen and gone out. There was probably some method of calling her, but she didn't see a bellpull or any other means of evoking assistance.

If she rang and Colette wasn't present, one of the new retainers might appear, and she didn't want to meet either of them while in a state of dishabille. At their introductions, she wanted to appear confident and prepared, so she decided to dress herself, something she rarely did.

She walked to the wardrobe and searched through the scant

Cheryl Holt

offering of clothes. Considering the fact that she hadn't known what to expect from her elopement, the trousseau she'd packed was meager simply because any of her more elegant gowns would have taken up too much space in her travel bag. Of the dresses she'd brought, any would be easy to put on by herself, but a corset was out of the question, so she donned a chemise and an unpretentious blue day dress, one that needed only a thin petticoat.

As she smoothed the fabric across her abdomen and down her thigh, she realized that she couldn't ever remember going without a corset. It felt good to be able to take a deep breath, so she took several—just because she could—and the motion caused a friction on her nipples that she hadn't noticed before, except during the brief occasions when Lucas had embraced her.

Minus all that sturdy whalebone holding them up and pushing them together, her breasts shifted and moved, making her feel scantily clad. Walking to the mirror, she stared at her reflection, leaning this way and that, liking how her bosom played against the bodice, how she could see a hint of her nipples against the cloth. She just might have to abandon her corset more often, especially after she was married. Her husband, she was quite certain, would enjoy the sight.

Unable to manage her long hair by herself, she tied it loosely with a blue ribbon, then looked in the mirror again. She was overly pale, so she gave her cheeks several hard pinches in order to bring them some color.

Obviously her clandestine escape from London had been stressful. Even though she'd passed enough hours in her bed to rest fully, she still seemed tired, groggy, and disoriented. Chances were good that she might feel poorly for a few days, or possibly even a few weeks, while she adjusted, but there wasn't any hurry. She'd have plenty of opportunity to learn her roles and her responsibilities, and in no time she'd be pushing ahead with her usual enthusiasm.

Her examination of the upstairs took a matter of minutes. In addition to her own bedchamber, she discovered two others, plus a functional water closet. The rooms were similar to the one in which she'd slept, with sturdy but plain furnishings, colorful wallpapers, rugs, and curtains. She thoroughly explored all the space, but she lingered in Lucas's.

At some point he'd unpacked a bag or two. His clothes were all the same style, workingman's dress, she supposed it would be called. There were several pairs of woollen trousers and leather breeches, cotton and linen shirts, a vest, and an extra pair of boots. In the dresser, one drawer contained what looked to be male unmentionables, and though she was dreadfully curious, she could not find the courage to poke through them.

At the wardrobe she reached for the arm of one of his shirts and pressed the fabric against her nose, inhaling deeply. She probably looked terribly silly, but she couldn't stop herself. His clothing had touched his skin, and his odor was enmeshed in the weave. Despite the strong scent of laundering soap, she conjured an image of him that was so clear, she felt as if he were standing right beside her.

In front of the mirror he'd laid out his shaving equipment, and she picked up each piece individually, handling it, turning it over, smelling the leather of the strap and the soap in its cup, testing the sharpness of the blade with her thumb, rubbing her hand across the soft bristles of the brush. She'd never seen a man's bathing materials before, and she wondered if he might let her watch him use them on occasion after they were married. The thought of being allowed to share such an intimate ritual was thrilling.

There was a secret enjoyment to be had from touching his possessions, but she'd die of embarrassment if he suspected that she'd been investigating him so completely. Her heart was pounding by the time she set the items back down, arranging them exactly as they'd been placed. Then quietly, lest someone detect what she'd been about, she tiptoed out of his room and down the stairs, ready to be welcomed. To her dismay, no one greeted her—no servants, no Lucas—and she couldn't help feeling a bit let down.

While she realized Lucas was a man of commerce whose business dealings had to come first, she couldn't help wishing that just this once he had remained at home in order to spend part of their first day together. There were many topics she wanted to discuss with him, especially after the previous night's hasty revelation that his home was in Virginia and they would be going there to live. She couldn't help wondering what the world was like in such a far-off land, what their ocean crossing would entail, how they would pass their time in America.

For all she knew, this might be her wedding day! If Lucas managed to have the proceedings organized, she could be taking her vows shortly. Tonight might be her wedding night! If so, Lucas would join her in her bed, and while she was certainly ready for such an episode to occur, she was apprehensive about the marital act and the intimacy it would entail. She couldn't help thinking that the coming event might not seem so frightening if she'd gotten to know a little more about him before it happened.

In the kitchen she paused. It was a clean and efficient room, warmed by the smells of baking. Someone had left her a noon meal on the table, a hearty plate of bread, cheese, an apple, and glass of milk. The fare was simple, a far cry from what the French chef at her father's house would have created. As she sat in the chair that awaited her, she noticed a note lying next to the dish. Her heart gave a skip of exhilaration as she recognized it was from Lucas and addressed to her.

So . . . he hadn't forgotten her after all! She couldn't help smiling as she read the words he'd hastily penned.

"Pretty Penny," it said, and the salutation caused those persistent and newly acquired butterflies to shoot through her stomach.

I'm sure yesterday was difficult for you, so I hope you will spend the day relaxing. Ask the two serving women

*if you need anything. I've instructed them to take good
care of you. I won't be back in time for tea, but I'll try
to make it for supper. We'll have a chance to talk more
then, but please don't wait up if I am late.*

Lucas

She read it over so many times that she memorized it, looking
for nuances and hidden meaning but finding none. Her index
finger ran across the dried ink, tracing the lines where his pen
had made its marks, until she finally folded it and slipped it
into the sleeve of her dress. The parchment scratched against
her skin, a constant reminder that his words were with her.

Once again she turned her attention to the table, and surprisingly the sight of food made her realize that she was hungry,
and she couldn't remember the last time she'd eaten. The previous day, as she'd waited for night to fall and Lucas to arrive,
had been fraught with anxiety, so she hadn't taken any meals,
not even any snacks. Suddenly famished, she gobbled down
every bite, glad that no one was around to see her appalling
table manners.

After she'd finished, a silence descended on the house, one
that she didn't care for. She was used to the busy noise in her
father's house, where the servants bustled past in the halls,
coming to and fro from the rooms. To her brother, Willie,
laughing and carrying on just down the hall. To the constant
knocks on the front door, carriages in the drive, and visitors
in the parlor. At this hour there'd have been a flurry of unending
activity.

Forlorn and melancholic, at loose ends, with no responsibilities and nothing to do, she finished her search of the lower
floor. Other than the front parlor and kitchen, there was just
Colette's room, evidence of her recent occupancy apparent by
the fact that her clothes were hanging from the hooks on the
wall. A pantry was situated beside it, the shelves mostly bare,
as though no one had lived in the house for a while and food
was being added for the new tenants.

At the end of the pantry was a door to the back garden, and she stepped outside into a lovely spring afternoon. The grounds had many fruit trees and flower beds, and she could tell that someone had once gone to a great deal of trouble to have the lawns nicely plotted, though it had been some time since the beds had been turned or the leaves raked away. The property looked sad and neglected.

She made a mental note to ask Lucas to hire a gardener to get it back in shape but instantly caught herself, realizing the request called forth their financial situation. Never before had she worried about money. Economy was a topic about which she knew nothing, and she wondered what kind of budget she'd have. If she decided she wanted the garden tended, could they afford it?

With a smile she thought of her dowry, the substantial amount of money and property that would go to her husband once she was wed. It was supposed to have been Edward's, but she felt certain her father would turn it over to Lucas once he saw how happy Penny was with her decision. Even if he refused, there was still her grandmother's trust, scheduled to come to Penny when she turned twenty-one. The duke couldn't do anything to prevent her from receiving it.

Lucas was about to become a very rich man. For the time being she wouldn't mention the fortune that would soon be his, thinking it best to wait until their situation was untangled, but she was gratified to know that she could bring him a gift that would make his life easier. He wouldn't have to work so hard, and he'd be able to spend more time at home, where they would pass their days in companionable pursuits.

She just knew it could happen that way. She just knew it! They were destined to be together.

Stepping down the path, one that needed weeding in order to keep the vines back where they belonged, she walked through the yard. There was a thick wood shielding them from whatever neighbors might be scattered about the area. Where the grass met the trees, a small boy played, swinging on a rope that hung from a large branch. He was short and slender, in functional clothes.

To her surprise, he had white-blond hair very much like her own. It was a bit darker under the top layers, as though it would turn brown as he aged. She approached cautiously, coming as near as she dared, and noticed that he had her blue eyes. A sudden flash of recognition made her feel as though she were watching a scene from her past, when her brother was a child and frolicking in much the same fashion.

This boy's resemblance to Willie was uncanny.

"Halloo," she called, waving, causing him to stop and look at her, and she took a few more steps in his direction. "By any chance, might you be Master Harry?"

"Yes, I am," the boy said, seeming very mature for his age.

"I'm Penny." He made no comment, so she added, "Your uncle Lucas is a very good friend of mine."

"Yes, I know. He told me you'd be here today."

She hardly had any idea how to deal with a child, but she figured that talking was probably the best method for beginning. There was a bench next to the spot where he played, so she went to it and sat. "Lucas isn't here," she said. "He's gone into the city on business."

"I know that too," he replied.

"Well, I'm glad you're here," she said. "It's terribly quiet, and I do believe that I'm quite lonely."

"You don't need to be," he said. "Lucas asked me to look out for you."

"Did he now?" she asked, pleased that Lucas had been thinking about her, had cared enough to discuss her with the lad.

"Yes."

"And will you?"

"Of course. I'm very grown-up."

"I can see that you are," she agreed.

"I'm almost five."

"Really?" He nodded, and she asked, "Have you met my maid, Colette?"

"She went to the village with the other women. They'll be back later."

"I see," she said, leaning against the bench and letting the afternoon sun shine on her face, and hoping, even as she did so, that Colette might chance to purchase her a sunbonnet. While her station in life had fallen, some things were simply too important to abandon. "An afternoon stroll sounds rather enjoyable. How come you didn't go with them?"

"I wanted to stay here to see if Paulie would come," he said, grabbing the rope again and trying to swing, but he couldn't quite do it.

"Is Paulie your friend?"

"Yes, but he comes only when I'm alone. No one can see him but me."

"He must be very special," she said. "Does he live around here?"

"No, he doesn't live anywhere."

"Ah . . ." she said, thinking this Paulie was an imaginary friend, and recalling the days when she'd had a few imaginary friends of her own. Hers had always been invented because she was so lonesome. Could Harry be lonesome as well? Perhaps they were kindred spirits. "Could I meet him?"

"No. Adults can't see him."

"My, he sounds like a magical boy," she said.

"He is," Harry agreed, looking serious. "And he's old too. He's almost thirteen."

"That is old. I met a boy named Paulie once," she said, remembering the lad who had collided with her, though it now seemed to have occurred a lifetime earlier. "He was very nice."

"My Paulie is nice too." He leaned closer and whispered, "He came to me in the night, and he told me a secret about you."

"About me?" she asked, surprised. "What was it?"

"He said you would look like a fairy-tale princess."

"And do you think he was right?"

"Absolutely!" he gushed.

As easy as that, she decided she loved this boy. How could she not? "It's very sweet of you to say so."

"You look just like the picture of a princess I have in a storybook. Lucas gave it to me. He brought it all the way from a town called Boston."

"I'll bet it's your favorite," she said, amused and thoroughly enchanted.

"It is. There's a picture of an angel in it too," he said. "Lucas told me it looks just like my mother. She's an angel. Did you know that?"

"I did," she said. Lucas had mentioned the woman dying in childbirth.

"But my father's not," he said, looking serious again.

"What is he?" Penny asked, unawares.

"He's a cad and a bounder," Harry said, his brow furrowing. "Do you know what that means?"

Penny nearly choked and had to glance off to the trees in order to hide her shocked smile. She bit hard against her lip in order to keep a horrid laugh from bubbling out as she managed to ask, "Where did you hear such a thing?"

"Lucas was talking to Uncle Matthew."

"Ah . . ." she said, struggling to tamp down her mirth, and thinking she hardly required Lucas's presence in order to learn all about the family into which she was marrying. If she needed information, she could just sit in the garden and listen to his nephew babble. "Who is Uncle Matthew?"

"He's . . . Uncle Matthew," Harry said as though she were the thickest person on earth.

"Of course," she responded, speculating on how Matthew was related to Lucas and wondering when she'd ever get to spend enough time around her wayward betrothed to be able to ask.

"I know how to skip stones," the boy said, careening off on another topic, and she was relieved that she wasn't going to be obliged to define the words that had been used to describe his father.

''That sounds like a marvelous skill. Would you like to show me?''

He jumped to her side, and with a show of absolute trust slipped his tiny hand into hers and dragged her off toward the woods and the stream that was hidden there. They played next to the water for over an hour, then went back to the garden and played some more. Penny fed him, talked with him, learned his games, taught him new ones, read books, and told stories.

And she came away amazed. Did all children have this much ceaseless energy?

By the time Colette returned from the village with the cook and a basket of fresh vegetables in tow, Penny was exhausted. Her head was throbbing, her back aching, and though she'd never conceived that such a thing could be possible, her ears hurt from listening to the lad's chatter. Who could ever have imagined that a four-year-old would know so many words? Or that he would speak them all without stopping to take a breath?

Penny rested while the other women fed him and put him to bed, although she had to go in to read him a bedtime story, since he insisted he wouldn't go to sleep if she didn't. The tale he chose was from the book where the princess looked like Penny and the angel looked like his mother. After it ended, she sat with him in a contented quiet, while he instantly fell into a peaceful slumber.

In the calm that followed, she was finally able to talk with the woman Lucas had employed to prepare their meals. The woman explained about country hours, how people usually ate early and went to bed early, and how Lucas had promised she could fix supper, then head home in order to feed her own nine children, who were waiting for her to return.

Penny toyed with the idea of asking her to stay late for the first night so that Lucas would have a warm meal to welcome him home when he returned. But she hadn't any idea what hour it might be, and once she'd learned of the cook's family situation, she hadn't the heart to ask her to remain.

She and Colette dined alone, eating a tasty stew and bread

while chatting about Colette's day and their impressions—of the house, the boy, the village. Colette pleaded fatigue, and Penny ordered her to bed, then relaxed in front of the dying fire and listened to the house settle while she contemplated what to do about heating the food. It was a strange situation not to have a cook available when she wanted one. At her father's house, meals could be had at any hour. If she'd awakened in the middle of the night and demanded a hot snack, a sleepy cook somewhere belowstairs would have lit a stove and hastily complied with her request.

Oh, well, they'd make do, she thought to herself. It had been only one day, and no one had starved yet. Besides, it was all Lucas's fault that he'd missed his evening meal while it was still warm. If he showed up hungry, they'd devise an alternative, and he wouldn't have any reason to complain.

Sighing, she stared into the dim shadows of the quiet room, and she had the most outrageous thought. Perhaps she'd learn about cooking herself. Other women did it. How hard could it be? Cook could show her how to work the stove, how to mix some simple ingredients. Certainly she could master the task if she set her mind to it.

Her life had changed. Not that she was complaining; she wasn't. But it was already painfully obvious that she needed additional and different skills if she was to succeed. Heaven forbid that Lucas perceive her as incompetent or useless. She wanted him to think of her as the kind of woman he could whisk off to America, one who would thrive there despite any circumstance she ended up facing.

More than anything, she wanted Lucas to be proud of her, so she'd do what was necessary to make him happy. If that involved cooking, so be it. She had to admit, there was a definite excitement to be gained by imagining Lucas sitting down at the table to a meal she'd prepared herself. It seemed to be exactly the manner in which newlyweds should pass their time.

She tried to wait up for him, to ask about his day, but dusk turned to night, and one hour passed to another. The clock on the mantel chimed eleven, and her eyelids began to droop. When she caught herself nodding off in the rocker before the hearth, she rose and climbed the stairs, taking a quick detour through Lucas's room and touching his belongings one last time before she went to her own room. She undressed in silence and slipped into her nightgown without assistance. The moment her head hit the pillow, she was fast asleep.

Sometime in the wee hours, she thought she heard him come in, but it might have been a dream. In the morning, when she awoke to Harry's bright chatter coming from downstairs, she descended, only to discover that Lucas had come and gone without so much as a hello or a good-bye. He hadn't even left a note, and her heart sank.

Harold Westmoreland was angry, but his fury was not due to the fact that Penny was gone. Neither was it caused by the fact that Pendleton had taken her. Nor by the fact that he was expected to meet Pendleton's blackmail demands in order to effect her return.

No, what really irritated him was that she had been absent from the large house for nearly two days before anyone had missed her. How could such an event have occurred? After questioning all involved, he'd learned that everyone had simply assumed she was keeping to her rooms, as she was wont to do ever since her latest engagement had been announced.

Embarrassingly it had not been family members or servants who found that she had disappeared. The discovery was made by Harold's secretary, who had been efficiently opening and reading the day's correspondence, when he happened across the ransom note from Pendleton. Apparently Pendleton's street urchin had handed it to a coachman who'd been out doing errands, and the servant had dutifully placed it in the stack of mail upon his return.

The secretary's attention to detail was what had brought the debacle to light, and Harold couldn't help wondering: If the man hadn't been so meticulous at his duties, how long would Penny's departure have gone unnoticed?

Holding the piece of parchment in his hand, he read it for what must have been the hundredth time, and he still couldn't believe his eyes. It said:

> *Westmoreland,*
>
> *I've taken Lady Penelope. Regarding our previous discussion, if you agree to my demands, I will return her immediately, unharmed. If not, I cannot guarantee her safety. The choice is yours. I am waiting for your response.*
>
> *Lucas Pendleton*

The bastard had done it! He'd really and truly done it! Though Pendleton had threatened as much, Harold hadn't wanted to believe that the blackguard would actually make good on his threat to exact revenge against the family.

What kind of man committed such an insane act? And why Penny of all people? She'd done nothing to Pendleton; she had no part in his argument with Harold. It made no sense to attempt vengeance against her at the risk of destroying her reputation— and thus her life—by absconding with her when the disagreement was with her father. If word got out that she'd been kidnapped, her marital chances would be crushed forever. Even Edward wouldn't have her after this.

Harold was perplexed. How was an English gentleman such as himself supposed to know how to deal with this type of foreign foe, one who expected matters to proceed in such an outrageous, incomprehensible manner?

His attention strayed to the center of the desk, where the other note rested—the one Penny had left in her room. The two pieces of writing were very strange. Pendleton, scoundrel that he was, obviously considered the incident to be an abduction. Penny apparently believed it to be something else entirely.

Where had they met? How had they managed to spend secret

time together? Did Penny think they were eloping? Would Pendleton have the audacity to marry her? The very idea that she might wed the brash American before Harold could find her set his heart to pounding.

Penny appeared to have gone with Pendleton of her own accord, so she must have been sweet-talked by the handsome rogue. What other explanation could there be? While Penny, no doubt, thought she'd run off for love, Pendleton had lured her away from home with false promises, the kind of which a young woman in Penny's shoes wouldn't have known how to resist.

What a calamity!

He gritted his teeth and glared across the desk. "Where is Pendleton's ship, Mr. Purdy?" he growled. "I told you I wanted it found. Yesterday!"

"We're still looking, Your Grace," the man said, bravely able to still meet his gaze.

Harold couldn't imagine where else Pendleton might have taken her, and he was certain that if they found the ship that had brought him from Virginia, they'd find her as well. And they had to find her! Before anyone learned that she was missing!

Out of patience, he ordered, "Tell me again what you've learned about him."

"He's smart, Your Grace," Purdy began. "Honest, brave, and, unfortunately for us, he instills intense loyalty in others. He's been hanging around the dockside taverns and such for weeks. Clearly everybody knows him or knows *of* him, but we can't get anyone to talk—not even with the offer of coin. People like him and trust him. They won't give him up."

"Keep trying. And increase the amount of money you're offering as bait."

"Certainly."

"Is Pendleton a violent man?"

"He can be," Purdy said, "but not unless he's provoked."

Harold winced, remembering that his earlier refusal to claim Pendleton's nephew had already been sufficient provocation for the cad to cause mayhem. "But would he hurt a woman?"

Harold asked fearfully. "More important, would he hurt Penny, do you think?" In Harold's opinion, Pendleton appeared mad, capable of carrying out any crazed deed, but no one else seemed to share the same impression.

"Doesn't seem likely, sir," Purdy said. "He's got a certain *way* with the ladies, you might say. They all adore him."

That piece of information was more daunting than any fact Purdy might have related. Would Penny fall victim to Pendleton's masculine charms? Would she come back ruined, useless in Harold's financial schemes with Edward, unmarriageable to anyone?

As quickly as the supposition had come, Harold shook it off. He couldn't worry about how all of this might affect his own plans. For a change, Penny had to come first. Her welfare was all that mattered, and surprisingly he felt good about his decision, as though a huge weight had been removed from his shoulders.

He glanced back and forth at the two notes and an idea started to take shape. It was clever and devious, but then, Pendleton was a clever and devious adversary, so Harold needed to think like him in order to succeed. Besides, in the end he wasn't going to give in to blackmail.

Once Pendleton became aware of Harold's resolve, what benefit would there be to keeping Penny in captivity?

From all the reports they'd gathered, Harold was willing to wager all—even his daughter's life and future—that Pendleton would never harm a hair on Penny's pretty head. He might posture and menace, but he wouldn't injure her.

With no extortion gain to be had, what choice would Pendleton have but to return her?

Hastily he penned a response, then handed it to Purdy. "Go to Bond Street and hang about in the crowd. Find that boy, the one who calls himself Paulie. Tell him to deliver this to Pendleton."

"Shall we nab the little blighter, sir?" Purdy asked, looking overly enthusiastic at the prospect. "I haven't had much experi-

ence with children, but I'm confident that with a minimum of
torture, we could quickly learn Pendleton's whereabouts."

"Not just yet," Harold replied.

"Shall we attempt to follow him?"

"If you can, but do not detain him in any fashion. I want
Pendleton to get my message. After he does," he said, smiling
wickedly, "I wouldn't be surprised if Penny is home in time
for tea."

"Read this!" Matthew said, jamming the note he'd brought
back from London with all possible speed into Lucas's out-
stretched hand.

"What is it?" Lucas asked.

"It's Westmoreland's reply. Paulie brought it to me," Matthew said. "You won't believe it!"

They were huddled in the woods behind the house where
Penny had lived for the past two days. They'd taken turns
spying on her and the property, lest she try to leave or someone
attempt to enter. Neither event had occurred.

In the dark, the stub of a short candle gave off a tiny glow,
and the two brothers leaned over the piece of parchment in
order to see better, as Lucas read the words Matthew already
knew by heart.

> *Pendleton,*
> *Since you have already taken her, she is completely*
> *ruined for my purposes. Thus, she no longer has any*
> *value to me whatsoever. Do what you will.*
>   *Westmoreland, Duke of Roswell*

Lucas read the words over and over, then over again. He
couldn't believe his eyes.

" 'Do what you will'?" he finally asked rhetorically, completely shocked. " 'Do what you will'? What the hell kind of
response is that?"

"I couldn't make any sense of it myself."

"It took him two days to answer," Lucas began, thinking it had been the longest forty-eight hours of his life, "and he replies with 'do what you will.' Is the man insane?"

"Perhaps," Matthew said with a shrug.

"I mean . . . doesn't he care what might happen to her? What we might do to her?"

"Apparently not."

"What kind of man is he? What kind of father?" Lucas shook his head in wonderment and disgust. "How dare he throw his only daughter to an unknown wolf like me? I might do anything to her. . . ."

"But you won't."

"He doesn't know that!"

They glared at each other, confused and disturbed. In all their fevered whisperings, it had never occurred to either of them that Westmoreland would send such a flippant reply. How could they have been so wrong? And what should they do now? They couldn't keep her, but they could never return her to such a despicable knave. Lucas would never condemn her to that horrid fate.

No wonder Westmoreland had been able to seduce Caroline and walk away without a backward glance! No wonder that learning of Harry's existence had had no effect on him at all! The man was heartless as stone and ruthless as a snake. He probably had ice water running in his veins. His own daughter had disappeared, and he remained completely unmoved.

"What should we do now?" Matthew asked. "Raise the stakes? Increase our demands?" Facetiously he added, "Cut off an ear and deliver the bloody appendage?"

"It would serve him right if we did," Lucas said, at a loss. They stood in silence for the longest time. Eventually he murmured, "I'm so exhausted, I can't decide what's best. Let me sleep on it. We'll decide in the morning."

CHAPTER TEN

Lucas took a sheltered back path to the main road in order to ride his horse in the front gate as though he'd just returned from the city. It was late, and as he approached, the house looked dark and quiet, and the occupants abed, although someone had thoughtfully left a lantern burning by the door. He supposed that it must have been Penny. Who else cared enough about him to do such a kind thing? His heart did the funny turn it always did when he recalled her.

Although he'd spent the entire day hidden in the trees, he'd still caught a few glimpses of her. As she'd played with Harry. As she'd trimmed a basket of early flowers meant to lighten the house. As she'd relaxed on a bench, taking the afternoon sun. She was captivating, more exquisite than he remembered in his constant imaginings, making him glad he'd been able to stay away. Nothing good could come from forced proximity, and the longer he could make her believe he was busy in London, the better.

She trusted him and already fancied herself half in love with him. Whenever she gazed at him so sweetly, he could see the deep emotion in her eyes. While she perceived him to be some kind of hero and savior, in reality he was little more than a cruel villain using her in the worst way. Of a morning he couldn't even look at himself in the mirror, because he couldn't stand to see the face of the despicable man who stared back.

To her dying day she'd rue the moment their paths had crossed, and he felt wretched and miserable every time he pondered how he was treating her. But it couldn't be helped, and the only way to ease their interactions was to avoid her completely. If he was absent, he didn't have to answer questions or make up stories to placate her, but most of all he wouldn't be tempted into a carnal situation from which he couldn't extricate himself.

The woman called to all his contemptible masculine appetites, and he had no method of fighting his attraction save putting as much distance as possible between her and him. If he could have avoided the house altogether, he would have, but any increase in the length of his absences would have become too suspicious.

There was a small barn across the yard from the house, and he quickly stabled his horse, then headed for the back door. As he advanced, a figure jumped out from behind a bush, causing him to reach for the pistol he always kept at his side. At the very last second he recognized Penny's maid, Colette, and managed to prevent himself from drawing the gun and pointing it at her.

He bit back a groan. She was the last person in the world to whom he wished to speak.

"I've had a long day, Mistress Colette," he said dangerously. "You might want to be more careful about approaching me in the darkness. You never know what I might do."

"Bah," she laughed scornfully, placing her hands on her hips, "as if I would be scared of one such as you."

"You should be," he warned, but he was so tired that he hardly sounded threatening. All he coveted was the opportunity to fall into his bed and get a good night's sleep so that he'd be refreshed on the morrow, when he had to decide how to respond to Harold Westmoreland, but apparently imminent rest was not to be.

Colette took a step closer, looking him up and down with her usual disdain, and he received the distinct impression that she was sniffing at him, at his clothes and person, but hoping to encounter . . . what?

"May I ask what you are doing?"

"I am trying to smell the other woman," she said baldly. "The one with whom you spend all your time."

"What?!" he gasped.

"I am curious about this American," she said pensively, tapping a finger against her lip and musing as though he weren't present. "This Pendleton, whom my lady deems so wonderful . . . why is he not here with her, eh? Where does he go? Who is he with when he is absent for so many long hours?"

"What are you babbling about?" he asked. She leaned in, searching for a female's scent or perfume against his shirt. "Stop that," he ordered, but she paid him no mind.

"At first," she said, "I am speculating that this Pendleton, perhaps he likes the men instead, *non?* For how could any *real* man resist Lady Penelope? Why would he try? Unless . . ." She shrugged and let the impolite insinuation trail off. "But *non,* Colette can tell: Pendleton is a man who likes all the women. So . . . why does this Pendleton not like my lady? This is my question."

"I like Lady Penelope just fine," he said, attempting to slip around her, but she shifted as well, completely blocking his exit.

"Then why am I wondering when this wedding will be? This one for which there was such a rush? Why does this Monsieur Pendleton say that we must hurry, *vite, vite,* that we must escape the duke, but then there is no wedding?" She shrugged again. "Perhaps it has something to do with the man in the forest who Colette sees watching the house all the days, eh?"

Lucas felt his skin crawl. The blasted woman was much too

astute. "I don't have any idea what you're talking about," he
said casually. "If you saw someone in the woods, he was
probably poaching. Now, if you'll excuse me, I'm tired, and
I'd like to go to bed." She didn't budge, so he added, "If you
don't mind?"

Colette made a contemptuous sound low in her throat. "I
am considering that something is . . . how you say . . . fishy?"

"Your imagination is running wild," he insisted.

"And I am deciding"—she continued as though he hadn't
commented—"that if my lady is not married by tomorrow
night that maybe I am leaving this place and taking her with
me."

"Good night, Colette."

He grabbed her by her forearms, picked her up, and set her
off the path, then hurried into the pantry, hanging his cloak on
the hook by the door and letting his eyes adjust to the darkness.
There was a candle burning in the kitchen, lighting his way,
and he moved toward it quickly, lest the maid enter behind
him and start her harangue once again.

In the dim glow of the kitchen light he stopped dead in his
tracks. His breath caught, his ability to speak vanished, his
heart skipped several beats.

Penny was taking a bath.

A copper basin sat in front of the hearth. A cozy fire blazed,
warming the chamber and casting intimate shadows around the
walls. There was a stool next to the tub, and a glass of wine,
a bar of soap, and a cloth rested there. She'd disrobed in the
room, and her clothes were scattered about. Her corset was
slung over the back of a chair, the laces dangling down. A pair
of finely embroidered stockings was hanging next to it. A silky
chemise and a thin, lacy pair of drawers were tossed carelessly
on the floor.

With her back to him, she was on her knees in the tiny,
uncomfortable hip tub, the water lapping at her thighs. She'd
washed her hair and brushed it out. It was damp and hung in
a blond wave to where it skimmed her bare buttocks. His eyes

traced a delectable line from the creamy width of her shoulders
to the slim taper of her waist to the swell of her hips to the
two rounded globes of her bottom.

Rising from the water as she was, she appeared to be a
mythical mermaid about whom sailors often fantasized, and he
wouldn't have been surprised in the least if she'd begun to sing
the first bars of the siren song that would lure him to his doom.
Perhaps she was already singing it. His body certainly seemed
to recognize the silent tune. His phallus hardened instantly and
ferociously, the swiftness of his erection astonishing him with
its intensity, and he could barely suppress the groan of desire.

Penny's long, slender fingers reached for the washrag, dipped
it in the water, then began sponging her stomach, running the
cloth between her thighs, across her cleft, up her abdomen to
her breasts. She raised an arm over her head, and he could just
make out the soft down of hair nestled there, the faint curve
of her breast viewed from behind.

A thousand alarm bells were ringing in his head, commanding
him to flee. Immediately! Something dangerous and uncontrollable would happen if he remained, but try as he might to force
a retreat, he couldn't move. In all his years of sensual activity
he'd never seen anything as erotic as the sight of Penny washing
herself. As though he'd suddenly turned to stone, he was rooted
to his spot and staring like a voyeur.

In agony he watched her touching all the places he longed
to touch, her hand running along the peaks and valleys. His
fingers tingled in anticipation of doing the same, his unruly
cock expanded to an aching readiness. He could smell her, all
that hot, wet skin, and he yearned to dive into the water with
her so that he could press his face between her breasts.

"Could you do my back?" she asked.

So weak did his knees become at hearing her request that
he nearly fell to the floor. Her voice was low and husky, full
of carnal intent, and she turned her head in order to glance
over her shoulder. As she migrated, he was blessed with a
spectacular view. Of a breast, perfectly rounded and just the

right size to occupy a man's hand, the nipple erect, coral-tipped, and pouting.

Upon seeing him, her eyes widened with surprise, and she gave a sharp intake of breath, but to his dismay she did nothing to cover herself. Showing not a hint of the modesty he desperately hoped she'd display, she didn't slip down into the shallow tub, grab for a towel, or fold her arms awkwardly across her chest. If anything, she squared her shoulders and stiffened her spine, as though challenging him to look his fill, which he did without hesitation.

For many long, disturbing, sexually charged moments, he gazed at her, taking in her womanly form and deciding she was the most seductive female he'd ever laid eyes upon.

Finally she smiled and said, "I wasn't expecting it to be you."

"Obviously," he said, trying to make light of the encounter, but the hazardous blaze of lust in his eyes ruined the attempt. "I just arrived."

"I heard you come in, but I thought you were Colette." Like a practiced coquette, her tongue flicked out and nervously ran across her bottom lip, wetting it so that it glistened red and inviting.

Through sheer force of will he kept his hands at his sides. He tried to speak but no sound emerged. He swallowed. Swallowed again. Cleared his throat. "Ah . . . I'll just go around to the front door," he said, but his feet had turned to granite.

"Could you help me first?" she asked. "I don't know where Colette's gone off to."

In slow motion she dipped the cloth, swirled it about, and brought it out, dripping. Like a supplicant, she offered it to him, her azure eyes begging him to reach for it. With her other hand she tugged her hair off her back and draped the long mass over her shoulder, covering the breast that had teased him so splendidly.

"I don't think so," he said, wanting nothing more in the

world than to grasp onto the washrag and run it over all that smooth, pale skin. "We'd better not . . . I mean . . . well . . ."

"But we're going to be married shortly," she said. "Surely it can't hurt at this late date."

"Probably not, but . . ." He stumbled for an excuse, then decided on the truth. "You're so ravishing, I don't think I could stop with just washing your back."

"Maybe I don't care," she said boldly. "Maybe I wouldn't want you to stop."

Dear Lord, but this was quickly becoming the most excruciating incident of his entire life. How was a mortal man supposed to resist such blatant temptation? He felt as though he'd been thrown back in time and suddenly found himself standing in the Garden of Eden, confronting Eve. "But it wouldn't be right, Penny." He gestured around the small, simply furnished room. "It wouldn't be right to take you here. To have you like this. For your first time, you deserve a soft bed and candlelight."

She recalled hearing that once before. "In that case, let's go upstairs," she suggested.

This was absolutely more than one man should have to endure. "No, not till we're wed," he said. "It's important to me that we do it right."

"Then wash my back, Mr. Pendleton," she said, growing irritated and losing patience rapidly. "I'm certain you'll find yourself up for such a trivial task."

Daring him to grab it, she laid the cloth on the edge of the tub and returned to facing the opposite wall. Her hair was still pulled over her shoulder, so he was graced with a panorama of her entire naked backside.

For a lengthy instant neither of them moved, then slowly, imperceptibly, as though she were reeling him in with a sturdy rope, he took one heavy step, and another, until he was near enough to retrieve the cloth. He dipped it into the warm water, then, careful not to let his fingers so much as brush her skin, he skimmed it from neck to waist, crossing up and down in a thrice.

Done, he tossed the cloth into the basin and promptly retreated, ready to make a run for it, if that was the only means of escape. "There," he said. "All finished."

She nodded toward the table. "Could you hand me a towel?"

Keeping his gaze averted, he lingered as far away as possible, draping the towel from his fingertips until she ripped it from his grasp with an angry yank. At the sound of sloshing water, he realized she was climbing out of the tub, and he closed his eyes in order to prevent himself from observing anything more stimulating than what he'd already witnessed. Miserable, his ears attuned to the slightest movement, he could hear her going through the motions of drying herself, briskly rubbing all her intimate spots.

Oh, how he wished he could become that towel!

She pitched it, and it landed at his feet, partially covering one of his boots, and the damning weight felt like a thousand pounds of trouble. Not brave enough to pick it up, toss it aside, or kick it away, he simply continued to stare out the window into the darkness as she puttered behind him.

Eventually her ministrations ceased, and she said, "I'm fairly decent. You may turn around."

He did so cautiously, relieved to discover that she'd slipped into a robe, that her clothes were bundled in her arms and the bulk of them shielded her from any of his untoward glances. She looked furious, spurned, hurt, and he wasn't certain what to do or say. He couldn't bear to see her unhappy.

"I'm sorry—" he began to say, but she abruptly cut him off.

"Spare me your explanations. I've listened to quite enough of them for one evening." Taking a deep breath, she held it, then let it out slowly, visibly calming herself. "If you would like to bathe, there's more hot water." Pointing toward the far wall, she said, "Cook showed me; there's a reservoir behind the stove. It heats the water when the food is cooking. So, there's more . . . if you'd like to use it."

"I believe I would," he said, smiling in acceptance of her

minor concession toward civil conversation even as he was kicking himself for handling the incident so badly. "Thank you for thinking of my comfort."

"You're welcome," she said politely. "I'm simply glad to see that you've arrived safe and sound. There's a dry towel there on the table. Would you like me to bring you down anything else?"

"I'll be fine."

"Are you hungry?" she asked. "I had Cook show me where things are. I could dish you a plate of cheese and bread."

"It's not necessary." He voiced the lie even as his empty stomach rumbled in protest, and he hoped she hadn't noticed. "I ate in town."

"Well, then," she said, and she turned to leave, "I'll bid you good night."

Now that she was departing, he couldn't bear the idea of being alone in the room without her, yet what could he say? What could he do? He'd already hurt her enough for one night. For one lifetime. Still, he said to her retreating back, "Penny?"

"Yes?" Looking over her shoulder, she looked so hopeful and so very, very young.

"Nothing." He sighed. "Nothing at all."

Without another word she went on her way. He listened to her foot on the stair, finding it soothing and joyful, and was unable to prevent himself from wondering what it would be like if all of this were real instead of a fantasy of his own creation. What if they were really married? What if this were their home? Little Harry their son?

There was something immensely pleasant about picturing her dawdling in the kitchen, feeding him and helping him with his ablutions. What if he had such a moment to look forward to at the end of each day? What if Penny were actually his?

Cursing himself for a fool, he rummaged through the shelves until he found the cook's brandy. He poured himself a stiff shot of the dreadful stuff and drank it down as he struggled to gain control of his unruly emotions. He could still detect her overhead, and the urge to rush up the stairs and join her in her bed, as she'd invited him to do, was so strong that he actually grasped the table, needing the extra restraint in order to prevent himself from going to her.

Once he was calmer, he found the bucket hanging next to the stove and scooped the last of the water into the hip bath. Hastily he removed his clothing and stepped into the unpleasant contraption, wondering why such a well-proportioned house would have such a worthless contrivance for bathing. He was a big man, and he liked to sit back and relax when he was washing.

Still, the water felt good. It was no longer hot, but it was warm enough for comfort, and it smelled like the rose oil Penny had added. With any luck, the aroma would remain on his skin all the next day, and he would feel that he was carrying a part of her with him as he went about the odious task of dealing with her father. He shifted around as much as he could, immersing as much of his body as he was able. As he did, the idea occurred to him that only seconds earlier the very same water had surrounded the nude, beautiful Penny.

The realization was outrageously erotic. A vivid portrait of her naked form flashed before his eyes once again, and another jolt of arousal surged between his legs. Hoping to clear his mind, he maneuvered around and dipped under the water, holding his breath and scrubbing his hair. He came up, blowing out air and shaking his head like a shaggy dog, all the while thinking that if the abduction began to drag on indefinitely, he was going to have to start visiting a brothel before he returned to the country house for the evening. There was no help for it! He doubted he'd live through a second rendezvous with Penny like the one he'd just survived. Such unrelieved discomfort could very likely kill a man.

Just then he heard a noise, and more jumpy than usual, he whipped around. Penny was standing in the doorway, the dark parlor at her back, haloed in the bit of light from the kitchen's dying fire. She was wearing something that was probably meant

to pass as bedtime attire, but it definitely wasn't a garment for
sleeping.

It was white and sheer, and it hugged every delicious curve,
leaving nothing to the imagination. On her shoulders were two
tiny straps, barely wide enough to hold the bodice in place—
not that it needed much assistance, for there was hardly any
fabric to support. Her flawless, spectacular bosom was on display, the neckline cut extremely low, revealing her full breasts
nearly all the way to the tips. Below, the flimsy material shielded
no secrets. He could see the pink of her erect nipples. Lower
down, the shadow of her navel. Lower still, the push of her
woman's hair.

"Penny?" he asked, gulping.

This was not the same woman who'd left several minutes
earlier, looking dejected and glum. Somehow she'd changed
herself into a beguiling vixen. There was a female confidence
about her, a seductive air that definitely had him thinking about
Eve again—and poor Adam as well. If *his* encounter with the
infamous biblical character had been anything like this, the
poor bastard hadn't stood a chance.

"I forgot something," she said, floating across the room,
heading directly for the tub.

The nightgown had a slit up the side and with each step he
could see to the top of her leg. An extra inch and he'd be
staring full-on at her mound. His cock swelled and rose in in
the water, and he frantically grabbed for the washcloth and
tented it over his privates, attempting to hide as much of himself
as he could.

"What is it?" he asked as she neared and settled her bottom
against the rim. He gripped the edges so hard that his knuckles
turned white, but he wouldn't allow himself any pleasure, not
even the simple indulgence of running a finger across her arm
or resting his palm against her thigh. If he so much as touched
her, all would be lost.

"I used most of the soap, and I wanted you to have plenty."
She leaned across to the stool and laid the bar on it. Stretching,

she took her time, letting the lacy fabric pull and tighten against her bosom. Her fabulous cleavage was directly in front of his face, her hard, raised nipples clearly visible. All he had to do was give a tug, and her breasts would be fully bared for his delectation. In the snap of his fingers he could be squeezing one of the swelled, precious nubs. He would lick it with his tongue, then suck it far inside. She'd squirm and groan. . . .

"Would you like me to bathe you?" she asked in a throaty voice filled with sensual assurance.

She reached for the washrag, which was perched so precariously over him, and he grabbed her wrist just before she whisked it aside.

This was torture!

"That won't be necessary," he said tightly.

"Are you certain?" she asked.

Her lips hovered scant inches from his. Her minted breath moved across his cheek. In animated detail he remembered the times he'd previously kissed her. He could do it again. Right then! He could lean forward, press his mouth to hers, taste and bite and sample . . .

"I'm certain," he said, barely able to speak as he denied himself the finest conceivable delight.

"Lucas?" she said, and she placed her hand on the center of his chest, her soft palm enmeshed in the scratchy hair, and she began making slow, small circles directly over his heart.

"What, love?" he asked, hardly realizing that he'd used the endearment.

Her fingers widened the circumference of the orb she traced, the tip of a manicured nail just brushing his nipple. "When are we getting married?"

"Married?" he croaked, pronouncing the word as though he'd never heard it before. Everything was spiraling out of control. All he could concentrate on was his aroused state, how he wanted to feel her finger flicking against his nipple.

"Yes, darling," she whispered, her mouth almost grazing his as her hand dipped lower and lower toward the water and what lay below, but the tantalizing stroke never went quite as far as he wished. "When will the wedding be? I find I can hardly stand"—she licked her lips, first the top one, then the bottom—"the waiting."

"I don't know, Penny. . . ." His thought faded away.

Her breasts had shifted, and the front of her gown had loosened until he could see past her cleavage to her navel. The bodice no longer covered anything, and the scoop neckline was caught against her nipples, the two tightened buds the only restraint keeping it in place.

This was an impossible torment! How could a man be expected to hold out against such obvious titillation? He leaned back, trying to force more space between them. "I haven't quite gotten everything—"

"Could we do it tomorrow?" she asked, closing the distance so there could be no escape, then went in for the kill. "Please?" she begged in that pretty manner she had that he'd already learned he couldn't resist. Her expressive sapphire eyes showed no mercy. "It would mean so much to me if we could get it out of the way."

"Tomorrow?"

"Yes . . ." she said on a breath, touching her lips to his.

"Tomorrow," he agreed, not meaning to, not wanting to, not knowing how the word had slipped out.

"Promise?" she questioned.

"Yes, I promise," he said.

"Swear it to me!"

What was to be done when she was looking at him like that? He vowed, "I swear it."

"You'll never be sorry," she said, giving him a smile that lit up the room, and his tenuous control finally snapped. He reached for her, intending to pull her into the warm water, but his arms filled with nothing but air.

She was gone, and he laid his head against the tub while he wearily tried to calculate the enormous ramifications of what he'd just sworn to.

* * *

Penny slipped into her room and turned the key in the lock. Colette, having let herself in the front door when Lucas first entered the kitchen, was waiting impatiently. She was perched on the edge of the bed and eager to hear the news of how the downstairs visit had proceeded.

"Was he there?" she whispered.

"Yes," Penny answered, suppressing a shiver. The house was cold, the hallways frigid, and the skimpy nightgown offered no protection. She walked to the chair and fetched her woolen robe, stuffing her arms in the sleeves and wrapping it tightly about her body. "He was at his bath."

"Naked?"

"Very," Penny said, and Colette chuckled.

"*Bon, très bon,*" she said. Lifting her brows suggestively, she asked, "How did he like my lady's nightdress?"

"Quite effective," Penny said. She was so glad Colette had insisted on packing it in the bag they'd brought from home. The French-styled undergarment had been part of her original trousseau, but she'd never had the chance to wear it, and she had to admit that it certainly worked wonders on a man's attention span. Lucas hadn't been able to take his eyes off her.

"So the negligee, it was a good choice?"

"A perfect choice."

She and Colette had plotted all day about how to snare Lucas into a nuptial decision, and when they'd carefully conspired to have him discover her wet and naked in the bathing tub, Penny had been sure they'd planned correctly. But Lucas had astonished them by refusing to take advantage of the intimate opportunity he'd been so shamelessly offered, and they'd been at their wits' end.

They'd hastily huddled upstairs in her room, Penny feeling unwanted and undesirable, Colette confused and irritated by the virile man's strange behavior.

Why didn't he desire Penny in a sexual fashion? What would

shatter his composure so that he'd embrace the necessary steps
from which there could be no return? What was the matter
with him?

Then Colette had remembered the nightgown.

Penny had put it on while listening to a few wise words
regarding Colette's various erotic suggestions. Her courage
bolstered, she'd returned to the kitchen, ready to do more battle
with Lucas's self-control. This time she'd succeeded. The thick-
headed man was probably still wondering what had happened,
unable to discern how she'd bewitched him.

"Did you ask him about the wedding?" Colette queried.

"Yes," she responded, hating how she'd had to go about
making her marriage an actuality, but there'd been no other
solution.

Morning would bring the third day of their elopement, but
in the time since they'd run off, she'd rarely seen Lucas, let
alone wed him. Colette insisted something odd was happening,
and they'd argued about Lucas all day, with Penny continuing to
defend him and insisting the ceremony hadn't occurred simply
because he hadn't managed to arrange it yet.

In the meantime, she was a realist and knew they couldn't
tarry forever. If the duke discovered her location and *rescued*
her before the act was done and consummated, she'd be forced
to proceed with her marriage to Edward, and she uncondition-
ally, emphatically couldn't go through with such a horrid event.

She wanted Lucas and needed him, and though he appeared
hesitant, she had to believe that it was simply a case of male
jitters over pending matrimony. It couldn't be anything else!
The thought that he might have deceived her, or that his intentions might not be entirely honorable, was too terrifying to
contemplate. Considering the precarious state of her present
and future circumstance, she had to trust Lucas implicitly, and
she declined to give credence to Colette's dire warnings.

"And this wedding," Colette asked. "When is it to be?"

"Tomorrow," she said, barely able to suppress the swell of
excitement she felt about all the changes the union would bring

to her life. She would become Lucas's wife in every way, and she couldn't wait to finally make the transformation.

"He has promised you this?"

"Yes," she responded, knowing him to be a gentleman who would never go back on his word. "The wedding will be tomorrow."

CHAPTER ELEVEN

"You're going to do what?" Matthew asked much too loudly.

"I'm going to have to marry her," Lucas replied.

At Matthew's outburst, other morning customers in the roadhouse's dining room glanced their way, which was very bad. Not knowing who might be looking for them, or where the search might be progressing, they were trying to remain extremely inconspicuous, dressed in simple clothing, and barely speaking to the serving girl, lest she notice and remember their American accents.

Lucas leaned across the table, talking softly and attempting to extinguish his brother's furious glare with one of his own. "Do you have the forgery of the marriage license completed?"

"Yes, but that doesn't mean I want us to have to use it!"

"Don't be so upset. You knew it could come to this. We discussed it."

"But I never intended for it to go this far," Matthew complained. "It makes the deception so much worse, and it's too cruel a trick to play on Miss Westmoreland."

"I know," Lucas responded. He was feeling guilty enough

without his brother rubbing it in, so he shook off his culpable thoughts, forcing himself to plunge ahead. "It can't be helped."

"Why can't it be helped?"

"Because the ladies are beginning to question my intentions."

"How could they question your intentions? They haven't even seen you in the past three days." Matthew paused, leaning closer as well, until their eyes were locked across the small table. "Or have they?"

The very last thing Lucas wanted to do was review the previous evening's double display of carnality by Penny. He'd survived the first encounter—the one where Penny was the naked person in the tub—and walked away unscathed, but the second had proved deadly. He'd been left confused, disturbed, and wondering when his engorged member had gained such powerful control over all his other faculties.

He had tossed and turned all night, working hard to persuade himself that at the sight of a wet, disrobed Penny Westmoreland freely offering her numerous charms, he hadn't reacted differently from the way any other red-blooded male would have under similar circumstances. Yet, he wasn't so sure Matthew would agree.

How could Lucas explain the need for a quiet room, the candlelight, and cozy fire? What words could he use to describe Penny's loveliness, her nudity, her seductiveness? Or, worse, how could he admit the attraction he'd felt since the moment they'd met? Best to keep all his little secrets to himself.

"Look," he said, growing irritated, "her maid stopped me outside the back door last night."

"That nosy Frenchwoman?"

"Yes. Just as I was going in," Lucas said, nodding, "and she said she thinks something fishy is going on."

"Fishy? She said that?"

Lucas nodded again. "It's because I convinced Lady Penelope to elope, but I haven't made any move to marry her."

"What's fishy about that? You two hardly know each other.

The idiotic woman should be glad you're willing to let Miss Westmoreland take some time before proceeding.''

"Apparently that's not the way she sees it."

"How does she, then?"

"It's just that ... well ... Miss Westmoreland is very pretty," Lucas said, trying to make the portrayal sound casual. In all their discussions of her, Lucas had mentioned her appearance on only one occasion, saying that because of her hair, eyes, and other facial features, she looked enough like Harry to be his mother. Lucas had never ventured more than that, worried that if he'd given a lengthy accounting, Matthew would have seen how affected he was by her poise and beauty, so he'd left it alone, and he wasn't about to go into it now either.

He changed the direction of their conversation by saying, "Although Miss Westmoreland has never mentioned it, I'm sure she has quite a dowry too. It just seems strange to the maid that I wouldn't jump through any hoop in order to snare Lady Westmoreland as quickly as possible."

"Understandable, I guess."

"Plus, I think the maid has caught us watching the house from the woods. She said she's seen a man hovering about in the trees."

"Damn ..." Matthew grumbled. "I've been so careful."

"So have I, or so I believed, but she has a keen eye, and she's very devoted to Miss Westmoreland. We can't underestimate her."

"No, I should say not."

"Anyway, she told me—in no uncertain terms, I might add—that if the wedding wasn't held today, she'd convince Miss Westmoreland to return to London."

Matthew visibly gulped in dismay. "Could she do that?"

"I think she has that kind of power. They've known each other for many years, and Miss Westmoreland respects her very much. Yes, the maid could influence her."

"Blast!"

"Before I left this morning, I had to calm their anxiety about my arrangements, so I told them we'd do it tonight. I suggested that the event needed to be completed covertly, so I'd arranged for a minister to come by the house.''

''They bought it?''

''Without a hitch,'' he said, hiding his eyes by lowering his gaze and pretending to be gravely interested in his cup of tea, though in reality he was grimacing and wishing these British would learn how to make a cup of strong coffee.

While he sipped the steaming brew, he took the opportunity to think of Penny and how she'd looked when he'd come down the stairs earlier that morning. Boots in hand, he'd been planning to sneak out again before anyone in the house was up and about. Dawn was breaking when he'd stepped into the kitchen, and there she stood, freshly scrubbed and smiling and seeming every bit the part of the new bride fixing breakfast for her husband.

Proudly she'd placed a bowl of oatmeal—no longer hot and a bit on the lumpy side—on the table, accompanied by some crusty, dark bread, fresh-churned butter, and a pot of jam. When he'd stared at the food in amazement, she'd taken his silence for dislike of the simple meal she'd created.

To his horror, tears had welled into her eyes, and she'd begun apologizing profusely, explaining how she'd not learned to cook, never imagining that she would need to know the skill when others had always been available to complete the task for her. She'd asked the hired woman to teach her about the kitchen, and she was just acquiring the first steps of culinary lore.

He'd been so touched by her willingness to please, by the fact that she would go to such lengths to ensure that she was acceptable in his eyes, he'd been unable to do anything but sit with her, eat the breakfast she'd prepared, and chat about the coming day as though they were a married couple. Through it all he hadn't been able to stop himself from reveling in the sensation of closeness they had in the quiet kitchen, or from deluding himself that their situation was real.

When she'd casually raised the topic of the pending wedding, he hadn't the heart to renege on the promise he'd made to her. He could not go back on his word.

"This is getting worse by the second," Matthew said, interrupting his daydream. He rubbed a tired hand over his eyes. "I wish we'd never heard of Harold Westmoreland."

"I agree," Lucas said, "but we've come this far. We can't quit now, not when we're so close to success." He reached out a hand and patted Matthew's arm. "And think of it this way: The ceremony won't be so bad. It's not valid, so you can skip the unimportant parts and cut to the chase. It will be over in a matter of minutes."

"I suppose," Matthew groused. They'd already decided that he would impersonate the minister, and he'd be good at it too. Over the years he'd performed a handful of weddings while captain on one of their ships. He was familiar enough with the routine to make it believable.

"Just keep telling yourself," Lucas advised, "that we're buying more time in which to bring the duke around to our point of view. That should make what you're doing easier to stomach." He blew on the tea while pondering the close quarters into which he and Penny had been forced. "You don't know what it's like at the house, trying to pretend all is well but trying to avoid her at the same time. It's been extremely difficult to carry on, so this will take some of the pressure off me. Just this morning Penny was saying that—"

"Penny?" Matthew asked, cutting him off.

"What?" Lucas asked.

"You referred to her as *Penny*. Not Miss Westmoreland. Not Lady Penelope. Not even plain old Penelope. You called her Penny!"

Lucas hesitated, then said, "So I did."

"Why did you call her Penny?"

"Because that's her name?" Lucas answered, trying to make

light of the slip, but from Matthew's outraged expression, his brother obviously wasn't buying the faltering justification. Out of patience, Lucas clarified tersely, "I'm supposed to be completely infatuated with her. I can hardly go about without calling her by her given name!"

Matthew stared long and hard, digging deep with those perceptive eyes of his, staring far down inside to where Lucas kept his direst imaginings and darkest regrets.

"Oh, Lord, don't tell me ..." Matthew breathed. "You fancy her!"

"No, I don't," Lucas insisted, shaking his head in denial, but they could both hear the lame conviction in his response.

"I don't believe this!" Matthew hissed. "You're completely smitten!"

Lucas actually blushed, his cheeks turning a bright red. "What if I am? It doesn't mean anything. It doesn't change anything."

"Like hell," Matthew muttered. "I know you. You're imagining seducing her even as we speak!"

"That doesn't mean I will. Despite all, I'd still like to think I'm an honorable man."

Matthew laughed so loudly that people's heads turned once again, and he visibly subdued himself, sitting back in his chair so that he had more distance from which to appraise his brother. "Why are you even contemplating this?" he asked, pointing an angry finger. "Are you mad?"

Lucas crumpled his napkin, wishing he could adequately explain what was happening between Penny and himself, what had been happening from the moment they'd crossed paths in her father's garden. Nothing he could come up with would work to ease Matthew's dismay or explain the strong emotions the woman stirred in Lucas's heart.

"You don't know what she's like," he finally said.

"Then, tell me," Matthew asserted quietly.

"She's different from any woman I've ever met." He

squirmed like a schoolboy who'd been caught doing something wrong.

"Oh, no . . ." Matthew sighed.

"I can't define it. . . ."

"Bloody hell, it's worse than I thought." Disgusted with the manner in which events were progressing, he shook his head indignantly. "Keep your hands off her!" he whispered harshly. When it looked as though his older brother hadn't heard, or perhaps hadn't heeded the warning, he added, "Are you listening to me?"

"I'm listening," Lucas grumbled.

"You can't risk making things worse than they already are!"

"I realize that," Lucas said, understanding that Matthew was absolutely right but wondering how he was going to comply with the command. Matthew hadn't been the one to see Penny kneeling naked at her bath. If he had, he wouldn't be so quick to give orders about how Lucas should comport himself.

He laid a handful of coins on the table, then followed his brother into the yard, where their horses were waiting. They were alternating between watching the house and going into the city, and it was Lucas's turn to head for London, but as he checked the saddle and prepared to mount, Matthew said, "Perhaps I should go to London today instead of you."

"What?"

"Well, considering what I just discovered, I don't imagine your mind will be focused on business. Who knows what kinds of mistakes you might make? They could prove deadly if you're not paying attention."

"For pity's sake, I know what I'm about!"

"Oh, spare me!" Matthew snorted. "Your concentration has shifted a bit lower than your brain. It's completely centered between your legs."

"I'm perfectly capable of carrying out my duties!"

Matthew rolled his eyes and decided to give up the argument. Lucas was a grown man who needed no assistance from his younger brother in order to get himself in and out of trouble.

Plus, he had a dreadful habit of refusing to listen to reason when Matthew was speaking truths he didn't want to hear. Still, Matthew couldn't help giving a few last admonitions. "Don't forget to stable your horse before you arrive in the heart of town."

"I won't forget," Lucas said, nodding in agreement. They'd decided in advance that they were too visible riding through the streets. Because of their size and stature, they would be recognizable to anyone who might be looking; it was easier to be swallowed up by the crowds when they were on foot.

"You know how to find Paulie?"

"He'll find me."

Matthew managed a chuckle. "Do you have the new note?"

"Yes, I've got it." Lucas patted against his shirt, where he felt the satisfying crackle of the parchment he'd stuffed there. Late in the night he'd penned the letter to Westmoreland, and the words seemed to be alive and geared to burst out. "I told the ladies I'd be late. That the wedding will be after nine."

"What if the duke refuses to comply with today's conditions?"

Lucas shrugged. "We'll deal with it when the time comes."

"If he rejects our demands again, should we still go through with tonight's ceremony?"

"We can't release Penny," Lucas said. "Not yet. So we can't postpone the wedding. It would look too suspicious. But don't worry, he'll come to terms. You'll see." Any other outcome was unthinkable.

"Make sure Harry's asleep before I get there," Matthew advised. "Even disguised as a minister, he'd recognize me."

"The women have him on a tight schedule, so don't worry. He'll be long abed before you arrive."

"How's that going? Has Miss Westmoreland spent much time with him?"

"She likes him very, very much." *Much more than is wise,* Lucas thought but didn't say so. "She thinks he's a wonderful lad."

"Well, she's right about that," Matthew said. "He is."

They both fell silent, staring, wondering if they'd acted appropriately by bringing the half brother and half sister together. Had they made things worse by engaging Penny's sentiments over the boy?

It was too late now for second thoughts or second-guessing. As though reading Matthew's mind, Lucas said, "What's done is done."

They swung onto their mounts. Matthew turned toward the village and the secluded house that lay beyond. Lucas turned toward the road that would carry him to London.

"The duke's men are everywhere. Searching. Asking questions," Matthew said just as they were about to pull away. "Be careful."

"I always am," Lucas affirmed, his usual cocky smile firmly in place. "I've no intention of giving Westmoreland the pleasure of hanging me!"

With a wink and a wave he was off.

The ornate carriage pulled into the drive of Westmoreland's home, and he barely waited for it to rattle to a stop before jumping down. The latest ransom note, which had been thrust into the hand of an unsuspecting coachman while they were stalled in traffic, was clutched tightly in his fist. He strode up the walk, ready to go to his library so he could reflect upon the current turn of circumstance—why hadn't Pendleton sent her home as Harold had expected him to do?!—when the front door opened just as he was about to enter.

Edward Simpson, the very last person Harold wanted to see, came bumbling out.

"Harold," the man said by way of greeting.

"Edward." Harold nodded, gritting his teeth while trying to make it look like a smile of welcome. He hadn't time to waste talking with the blowhard! "What brings you by?" he asked, although he hadn't needed to voice the question. Penny had been missing now for four days, but Harold had been so certain she'd be returned at any moment that he hadn't admitted the reason for her absence to anyone. Not even the duchess had been granted a meeting to discuss what was happening.

No doubt, the curious fiancé had begun to hear stories.

"I was just visiting with Her Grace," Edward said. "I had hoped to pass some time with Lady Penelope while I was here."

"Yes, well—" Harold paused, unable to add anything substantial that wasn't an out-and-out lie.

"We had a bit of a tiff last time we talked," Edward said irritably, angry that he'd have to admit such a thing. "It's been over a week since I've seen her."

"As long as all that?"

"Her Grace advises that she's gone to the country."

Though the remark sounded casual, there was a definite query behind it, so Harold kept his face carefully blank as Edward scrutinized it for the tiniest hint that what he'd been told wasn't true.

Harold responded, "Yes, I thought it best."

"Why?"

"Well, after your disagreement, she was quite upset."

Penny wouldn't tell him what had happened, and he couldn't blame her. He'd never taken any steps to have the type of relationship with her where they would feel comfortable discussing difficult topics.

He'd asked Edward the cause for her agitation, and Edward had admitted that they'd quarreled, but Harold knew it had been much more than a simple argument. With his burgeoning feelings for Penny's welfare coming to the fore, it was probably just as well that Edward had downplayed the situation, for if Harold learned that Edward had done something despicable to her, Harold might very well give the man a beating.

There were only two people in the world who knew what had occurred that night in the garden, and neither of them would say. Harold couldn't get past his suspicion that Edward's actions had been the reason for her sudden desire to run away.

Bluntly he declared, "She was no longer certain that she wanted to go through with the wedding."

"What has her opinion to do with anything?" Edward scoffed. "You and I have already agreed to move up the date. It's to be held in nine days."

"I realize that," Harold said testily.

"I thought it was all arranged."

"It is. Penny is just taking a brief respite in order to come to terms with our decision." He stepped around Edward and into the foyer, saying as he went, "Now, if you'll excuse me . . ."

He rushed down the hall before Edward could detain him further. As he passed one of the salons, he heard his wife calling out, but he didn't break his stride. He walked into his library and closed the door, knowing that no one would dare disturb him.

He paced back and forth, but the trip from one end of the room to the other was too short to give him an opportunity for adequate contemplation. Frustrated and angry, he stalked the floorboards while wishing he could get his hands on that accursed American's neck. He'd squeeze until there wasn't a breath left in the knave's long, lanky body.

A servant braved a knock, which was surprising. None of them knew what was going on except that the duke was in a state, and they were all staying clear until the current storm blew over.

"What is it?" he barked.

Jensen, the boldest of the dozens on the staff, stuck his head in. "It's the duchess, sir. Her Grace asks me to advise you that she desires an appointment." He tipped his head in that manner he had, as if he didn't care what response he was given, but Harold suspected that the old bastard was hanging on every word, ready to run to the kitchens, where he and others would pick over each juicy detail like dogs at a bone.

"I do not want to be disturbed. By *anyone*," he emphasized, letting Jensen get the message loudly and clearly that he didn't intend to talk with his wife. The capable retainer would obey, and the duchess would need an army to move past the fortifications Jensen would erect to block her entrance. "I would have thought the closed door would have told you as much."

"Very good, sir."

"However, I must speak with Purdy. Have him found and sent in immediately. Him and only him. Is that clear?"

Jensen exited, nodding, and Harold moved to his desk and laid Pendleton's missive in the center. With shaking hands he broke the seal and unfolded the note, reading quickly.

> *Westmoreland,*
> *This is your last chance. Your daughter's future lies in the balance. What say you?*
>
> *Lucas Pendleton*

With immense relief he collapsed into his chair. He'd guessed right! He'd read the scoundrel correctly! Pendleton wouldn't hurt her. For the time being she was safe, and the game could proceed while his men continued to search.

A sudden gleam entered his eye, and he took a piece of parchment, dipped his pen, and wrote his reply.

"Dearly beloved . . ." the minister began curtly.

Penny barely listened to the opening words. The pastor Lucas had found was a tall, stern man in his late twenties who probably would have been quite good-looking if he hadn't appeared so dour and grumpy. He was another American visiting in London, as Lucas was, and Lucas felt that his nationality made him a better choice than any of his English counterparts whom they could have enlisted in their scheme. Just by the fact that he was a foreigner, he was less likely to run into any of the duke's men.

Her only concern about him other than his poor attitude was that he might not be officially sanctioned by the Church to perform a marriage on English soil, and she couldn't afford to be engaged in any act that would allow others to cry foul later on. All the details about the wedding had to be on the up-and-up.

Before the man opened his prayer book, she'd had a brief second to whisper her concerns to Lucas, and he'd quickly assured her that there were no problems with credentials or authority. Lucas had the special license in his pocket, and the man was a fully vested minister, so the service could go forward. She felt obligated to agree, but that didn't mean she had to like the fellow, and she refused to let him dampen her perfect moment with his foul mood.

Instead of paying attention, she let her gaze wander around the front parlor, and she was forced to muffle a squeal of unrestrained glee. She and Colette had spent the morning gathering flowers and greenery, trimming candles, and decorating the room. It looked like an enchanted bower, a place in which a woman could wed the man of her dreams, then proceed to living happily ever after.

The afternoon had passed in a frenzy as she'd readied herself out of sight of the two serving women. They believed that she and Lucas were already married, so Penny needed to continue the ruse. In order to give them an acceptable explanation for the hurried preparations, Penny had told them that it was her first anniversary, and she was going to surprise her husband with a celebration when he arrived home for the evening. The two women had found the entire idea extremely romantic and cheerfully agreed to do their part to make the night a success.

The housemaid had played with Harry all day in order to keep him from getting underfoot, but also to tire him so he'd go to bed early.

Penny had asked Cook to try her hand at a more exotic fare than she typically fixed, and she'd created a number of interesting items before she'd left for the day. Wanting only to please, the other woman had graciously accepted Penny's simple suggestions regarding choices, and had even made a trip into the village to buy a few particular items.

Though Cook was by no means a chef, she had a good heart and had tried her best. Penny hoped the dishes would prove edible, because she intended to feed them to Lucas as his wedding supper. In her bedroom. Even now, as they huddled in the downstairs salon, saying their vows, the trays filled with food, wine decanters, and crystal goblets were discreetly situated, awaiting his enjoyment of the refreshments and much, much more.

Her stomach twinged. Finally! Finally she would discover what was whispered about behind all those fans! Finally she could put into practice all the lessons Colette had taught her over the years. Finally she would know the joy and pleasure of lying with a man who meant everything to her.

Colette had massaged her skin with fragrant oils, buffing her nails, styling her hair, and making last-minute alterations to her dress. It had nothing in common with the gaudy, elaborate gown that had been designed by a Parisian modiste for her first wedding. That dress still hung in one of the many closets in her father's home, in anticipation of the day they had all supposed she would walk down the aisle with Edward.

Although she wished Lucas could have seen her wearing it, the gown, along with its stays and petticoats, wouldn't have fit in either of the bags in which she'd packed her elopement wardrobe. Necessity had forced her to choose a simpler dress, but she'd chosen well, and it fit the country house and the event as though specially made for the modest celebration.

A light blue silk with a high waist, low neck, and puffed sleeves, it was the exact color of her eyes, the dark blue piping around the neck and skirt making them seem deeper, darker, more mysterious. The fabric had a silver thread running through it that shimmered when she walked. With each shift in the candlelight, she glowed, and the dress came alive as though it were moving about on her skin.

She'd highlighted her ensemble with a single strand of small diamonds that sparkled as well. The matching earrings dangled and swayed with each turn of her head.

Her blond hair, brushed a thousand strokes during the never-ending afternoon, glistened. Colette had wound it into dainty ringlets, then swept it up on her head, where it was held in place by a few diamond-studded combs. The long curls brushed softly across her shoulders, making her appear beautiful and desirable.

Lucas agreed, she could tell. He hadn't been able to take his eyes off her from the second she'd started down the stairs.

Suddenly the room became dreadfully quiet. She looked around. Everyone was staring at her.

"Well?" the minister asked into the daunting silence, his expression decidedly grim.

"Well, what?" she asked.

"Do you take this man," he repeated firmly, enunciating each word as though she were a simpleton, "to be your lawfully wedded husband?"

"Oh!" she exclaimed, blushing as she faced Lucas and gave him her brightest smile. "I do. I truly do."

All parties breathed a sigh of relief, as though they'd feared for one horrid instant that she'd changed her mind and wasn't going to go through with it.

As if she would walk away from this wonderful man!

He'd returned late, with barely enough time to wash up before the proceedings began, so he wasn't dressed in any finery, just his day's work clothes. Still, he was so handsome that it hurt to gaze upon him, and she lowered her eyes.

He squeezed her hand, and she squeezed his. She made a few more vows. He made a few too. Then, just like that, the ceremony was over. With Colette and the pastor watching, Lucas gave her a quick chaste peck on the lips, they signed the license, and the minister prepared to leave. Lucas followed him out, whispering to her that he needed to give the man a few coins for his coming round so late and saying the words.

Once the door closed behind the two men, she turned to Colette. "I did it!" she declared, taking what felt like her first breath in months. "I really did it!"

"*Oui, oui, mon amie,*" Colette said, huge tears of joy dripping down her face.

"What did you think?"

"*Magnifique!*" she replied. "You are the most beautiful bride I have ever seen."

"And my husband?"

"*Magnifique, aussi! Très beau. Très charmant.* What a brilliant pair you are. You will make many pretty children together." She took Penny's face in her hands and kissed both her cheeks. "This I know to be true."

The mention of children set Penny to blushing again. But though she reddened at the reference to what was coming, she couldn't wait to present Lucas with a son, and she was excited to start working on the project immediately.

"I'm going upstairs before he comes back," she said, beginning to climb even as she spoke. "I want plenty of time to get ready."

"With the way you look tonight, *Monsieur* will not be able to resist."

They stepped into her room, and Penny closed the door.

Lucas stood inside the barn, lantern in hand, while Matthew prepped his horse in order to depart. Since they'd stepped out of the house, his brother hadn't uttered a word, and Lucas couldn't bear the damning silence a moment longer. He asked, "What are you thinking?"

"What am I thinking?" Matthew gave him a vexed stare, fiddled with his saddle, then said in a low, hushed voice, "She loves you. You realize that, don't you?"

"No," Lucas insisted, shaking his head in denial. "No, you're wrong."

"She does!" he came back tersely. "Don't diminish what she's feeling by denying it."

"I don't know," Lucas said, shrugging. "Maybe . . ."

He didn't want it to be true; he hoped that it wasn't, but in his mind's eye he couldn't stop seeing Penny. How beautiful she'd looked as she'd glided down the stairs at the beginning of the ceremony. She'd shone as she'd spoken her vows, and she'd smiled so preciously when the service ended.

As for himself, he hadn't had the decency to bathe or dress for the occasion. Intentionally appearing at the last possible minute, he'd simply walked into the parlor as though nothing out of the ordinary were scheduled to occur. Despite his sloppy condition, she'd gazed up at him as though he were the most remarkable man in the world.

With the room decorations, and all of Penny's attempts to make the affair unique, the event hadn't seemed faked. As he'd repeated his vows, he pretended she would be his wife when it ended. The fact that she would *not* be burned and chafed somewhere near the region of his heart, and he couldn't chase away the dull ache.

"You lied to me," Matthew began tightly. "You said that she agreed to all this just to stymie her father. That she was going through with it simply to gain protection from his plans. That the two of you considered it to be a marriage of convenience." He shook his head in dismay. "How could you let things go this far?"

"I didn't *let* them. Things just . . . I don't know . . . she just . . . I just . . ." He cursed, kicked a stone across the floor, and it skittered against the back wall, causing Matthew's horse to shift nervously. "From the first time we met, we were attracted to each other. I haven't had to do or not do anything. The feelings are just there, and they're real."

"So what now? What about her?" Matthew stared out the open door into the night for a long, quiet moment. Finally he turned to face his brother. "We have to send her home."

"How can you say that? We haven't won what we came for."

"The price of victory has gotten too high."

"You can't think so! Not after all our planning, after all our work!"

"Lucas," he chided, struggling for calm, "you're not thinking clearly."

"What do you mean?"

"How can you expect this to come to a good end? She thinks you're her husband now. The only way you could ever make it right in the end would be to truly marry her."

"Would that be such a bad idea?" Lucas asked. The question had hung in his mind for hours. For days. Wouldn't that be the best resolution for everyone? He'd make her a fine husband—if she'd ever have him after what he'd done.

"Even if you could convince her to forgive you someday, you could never marry her."

"Why not?" Lucas argued pointlessly. He was angered to hear his brother say what he himself understood to be true.

"You're not the husband for her," Matthew said gently while resting a hand on his shoulder. "She's like . . . royalty. A princess. And what are you?" He gestured up and down, taking in all Lucas was and was not. "You're the orphaned son of a bankrupt Virginia tobacco farmer. A philanderer, a gambler, a criminal, a pirate."

"Not anymore . . ." Lamely he started to defend his character, but Matthew shot him a quelling look, and he wisely held his piece.

"This has gone too far," Matthew insisted. "She goes home! First thing in the morning."

"She can't," Lucas responded firmly. "Read this!" He handed over the duke's answer to their latest ransom demand.

Matthew read the words several times, and Lucas watched the changing emotions on his face. Shock. Disbelief. Anger.

"What is the matter with that man?" Matthew asked. "Who would say 'I don't want her back' about his own child? And this again"—he pointed to one of the lines—"this command to 'do what you will.' The man's not human. That's all I can deduce, especially now that I've seen her and discovered what a gem she is. He's either an animal or he's mad."

"Perhaps he's a little of both." Lucas sighed in frustration.

"I've been sick about it all day, and I won't send her home. Not to him. Not when he cares so little. I just can't imagine returning her."

"No, you can't."

"He might do anything to her. . . ."

"But what other option is there?" Matthew asked rhetorically, since neither brother had an answer. Silently they remained in the door of the barn, gazing numbly out at the stars.

In the house Lucas was shocked to see candles being lit in Penny's bedroom. He jumped with the realization that she was getting ready for bed, obviously anticipating that he would join her shortly. When he'd told her about the quiet, secretive wedding, it had never occurred to him that she would turn it into such an observance. Now he realized that she was counting upon a true wedding night!

With each passing hour, his list of sins was growing until it was a yoke he could hardly shoulder. What a debacle!

"Oh, Lord," he breathed, completely out of the energy necessary to continue on with their charade.

"What room is that?" Matthew nodded toward the upstairs window.

"Penny's bedroom."

Showing no mercy, he mentioned, "She's expecting you."

"I imagine so."

Looking forbidding, he asked, "What are you going to do?"

"I don't know . . ." Lucas said, casting about for a solution. "I think I'll probably wait out here for an hour or two. Until she gets tired and blows out the candles."

Matthew gave an angry nod of his head. "I realize that there is no other course of action you could possibly take," he said, sounding as worn down as Lucas felt, "but considering how much that girl loves you, I must tell you that I think that's probably the most heartless thing I've ever heard a man say."

He mounted his horse and rode off into the night.

CHAPTER TWELVE

Lucas stealthily opened the front door and tiptoed across the floor and up the stairs. His eyes scanned each dark corner, half expecting the French maid to jump him, demanding to know where he'd been. No one leapt out though, and as he reached the top unscathed, he decided that Colette was probably sleeping soundly, happily imagining that her mistress was still joyfully participating in her wedding night.

Continuing on as quietly as possible, he passed Penny's closed door, ignoring the damning silence behind it, and he moved on to Harry's room, staring for a good length of time at the blond hair sticking out from the covers, watching as his tiny breaths raised and lowered his chest.

"For you, Harry," he murmured to himself, needing the reminder to firm up his resolve. "All for you."

Harry was too young to comprehend what had happened to his mother at the hands of his father, too small to exact his own revenge, so Lucas would do it for him. When Harry was grown and the subject explained, hopefully Lucas would gain his nephew's gratitude and understanding. Perhaps then Lucas would be able to come to terms with all of it as well. Using

Penny to achieve their goal had to have been worth it in the end.

He laid a loving hand on the boy's head, then retreated, pausing outside Penny's room. Even knowing he should go to his own as he'd intended, he couldn't seem to take the steps. Before he could stop himself, he quietly turned the knob and slipped inside, thinking merely to check on Penny while he whispered a hushed apology.

Instantly he regretted his rash act, for the moonlight clearly indicated that the bed was empty, the covers not mussed. His eyes darted around and, to his chagrin, found her fully awake and leaning against the window seat while gazing blindly out into the backyard. Although he couldn't view her dazzling scarlet costume in its entirety, he saw she was dressed in another erotic ensemble. The inadequate fragment of cloth was meant barely to cover her private parts and was the perfect attire to entice the luckiest of bridegrooms. Looking at it, he felt aroused and ashamed at the same time.

She held a wine decanter in her hand. Mostly empty, the remaining contents tipped precariously as she turned.

"Oh, if it isn't my *dear* husband," she said sarcastically, running her scathing glare up and down his torso. "You've finally arrived, but I'm sorry to say that I'm quite sure I'm out of the mood."

"Penny, I—"

"Shut up, Lucas."

Now that he'd entered, he wasn't certain what to do or how to fix the situation. He thought an audible apology might be the best beginning. "I'm sorry."

"I said, shut up!" she repeated sharply with a tight, practiced control. "And go! Just leave me be!"

With the angry fire burning in her eyes, the tone of command in her voice, she looked just like her father. He wondered if she realized it. Her eyes narrowed, taking his measure, and obviously finding nary a single redeeming quality. He felt like the lowest sort of vermin.

''I can't,'' he said, wrongly assuming that they might have a rational discussion. ''Not when you're in such a state and it's all my fault.''

''If you don't depart immediately, I really don't think I can be responsible for my actions. I've still got that knife you gave me around here somewhere.'' Maliciously she eyed his crotch. ''If given the chance, I know exactly where I'll stick it first.''

The threat was so vividly conveyed that he gulped in response and fought to keep from protectively crossing his hands over his genitalia. ''Perhaps it's best if I leave, then. We'll talk in the morning, when you're feeling more calm.''

''I don't think it will help to wait until morning,'' she spit out. ''I won't be more calm in the morning. In fact, I may never be calm again.''

Over the years he'd passed through dozens of relationships, spending time with women but moving on at the first hint of an expected emotional entanglement. He hated to become embroiled in any type of amorous discord, so he always went about making the separations as pleasant as possible in order to ensure that every one of his old lovers remained a friend after their parting.

The reason for such self-preservation was that he couldn't bear to see a woman cry—tears induced him to all sorts of foolishness and always had—so he never remained once his intimate associations began to deteriorate. Consequently he had no idea how to deal with Penny when she was angry. He'd expected her to be hurt, crushed, destroyed, and weeping copious tears, as other females of his acquaintance were often wont to do.

What he hadn't planned on was a display of temper, and she seemed to be spoiling for a fight. He wasn't about to give her one, because he didn't know the rules for the type of contest in which they'd engage. Before they'd even started, he perceived that it would be a battle he had no way of winning.

Taking the coward's way out, his usual route when facing

an overwrought woman, he started for the door, but her irate bark brought him up short.

"Don't you dare move!" She swung out of the window seat and stood on wobbly legs that indicated she'd drunk about as much wine as he'd guessed. "I've changed my mind. I do believe I'd like to have this out once and for all."

"I don't think it's a good idea for us to talk right now."

"Oh, you don't, do you?" She growled and stalked toward him, looking and sounding very much like a wild animal. "Well, maybe what you want is just too damned bad, because for a change, you're not going to get it!"

His brows rose at hearing her curse. The sudden insight that she'd stoop to using such language made a frightening thought occur to him: He didn't know anything about this woman, what she might do, what she might be capable of doing. "There's no cause for us to exchange harsh words."

"Well, I disagree. I'd like nothing more than to exchange a few harsh words with you. The harsher the better!"

"What will arguing solve?" he asked, wanting only to leave the dreadful scene, while deciding that this was quickly becoming the worst moment of his life, but as soon as the thought formed, he amended it straightaway. The worst moment had been seeing Penny at her bath and not being able to join her. So, this had to be the second worst moment. "I'm not about to stand here in the middle of the night, fighting with you as though we're a pair of angry cats."

"All right, Lucas," she said, taking a deep breath and struggling to restrain her rage. "Let's be completely civil while you clarify what I have been doing up here, eagerly anticipating your appearance for the past four and a half hours." When he opened his mouth to begin, she held up a hand, effectively stopping him. "And don't lie and tell me you've finally decided to enjoy a bit of love play, because I won't believe you. I heard you sneaking to your bed, and I know that I just happened to spoil your escape by still being awake."

Running a hand through his hair, he couldn't help wishing

he'd plotted out this discussion long before it had occurred. He'd assumed it would commence hours hence, in the daylight, in the kitchen, after he'd slept, instead of then, when he was exhausted and out of ideas. "I don't know what to say. . . ."

"Why don't you begin by explaining why you refuse to consummate our marriage?"

"It's not that I don't want to," he lied.

"What is it, then?"

"It's just that . . . we hardly know each other, and I am convinced it would be a kindness to you if we wait until we are more familiar with one another."

"That's it? That's your reasoning?" She rolled her eyes and ran a hand across her front. "That's priceless. I'm standing here, dressed in nothing"—her words made her realize how much skin she was exposing for his appraisal, and she stalked to the bed, grabbed a slinky red robe that did little to rectify her condition, and put it on—"and you think we should wait until we're better acquainted. What the bloody hell is the matter with you?"

Lamely he offered, "It's better this way."

"Better for whom?" she snarled.

"You'll see," he promised. Magnanimously he added, "I know you're upset, but in time you'll agree that I was right for us to put it off."

"Oh, what a pompous ass you are," she sizzled, "thinking you know best! Do you happen to remember who my father is? Do you have any idea of his power and reach? Have you even a glimmer of a notion of what will befall you—and me— if he catches up with us before we're wed in every way that matters?"

Uneasy, he admitted, "I know all about your father, Penny. I'm aware of what could happen."

"Then why aren't we in that bed?" She pointed to it as she asked the question in a near shout. "I thought you wanted to help me! That you cared about me!"

"I did. I do!"

"Then you must grasp that unless we establish ourselves in marriage by proceeding to the point of no return, the duke could find me and take me back. With his authority he could probably have our annulment pushed through in a matter of hours, and I would be deposited at Edward's doorstep."

"I realize all the ramifications," he said gently, seeing her fear, understanding that it was valid and real, and softening because of it.

"So, just what is it, exactly, that you've done for me besides whisk me away from my life and family?" She poked an angry finger at his chest. "What have I gained by being here with you other than the increase of my father's wrath?"

"You've obtained many important things. Time. Distance."

"What bloody good are they if the duke can simply snatch me away?" Seeming to run out of steam, her shoulders sagged. Quietly, accusingly she said, "I thought you wanted this marriage." She swallowed, adding, "I thought you wanted me."

"I do, Penny."

"Prove to me that you mean it!"

"What would you have me do?" he asked, growing angry too. "Throw you down on the bed and have my way with you?"

"Yes." She nodded curtly, not appearing afraid, and definitely not suffering from the least bit of virginal trepidation. "Yes, that's what I wish. Do it right now. Show me that you desire to have me as your wife."

All he had to do was take one step. One tiny step, and he could grab her around the waist and fling her down on the soft mattress. Their bodies would sink in, and he would stretch out on top of her, covering her with his weight and presence. Finally he'd be able to feel her pressed against him from head to toe, as he'd fantasized for so long.

The temptation was extreme. Her costume was incredibly arousing; he'd never seen the likes of it on another woman, not even the most expensive prostitutes. The top was a bright red chemise-looking thing that didn't reach her navel. The lace and silk from which it was created was completely sheer, the neckline low, the outline of her breasts and nipples not disguised in the least. A mere swatch of scarlet crafted from the same material comprised the bottom half. On her legs she wore thin stockings. They were crimson too, as were her garters and heeled slippers. The robe she'd hastily donned did little to cover the outfit; it matched the set and was as gauzy as the rest.

Now that he'd gotten a close look at her apparel, he wanted her more than ever, but he didn't want her out of it. He imagined it a rather nice scenario to make love to her while she was still inside it, with all that red silk rubbing smoothly and coolly against his fevered skin. But as quickly as the vision formed, it was pushed aside by others. Of Caroline and Harry and the duke. Of his brother, Matthew, and the disappointment that would shine in his eyes if he learned that Lucas had seduced her. But most of all, he saw Penny—hurt and betrayed.

In agony, hating how much his answer would disappoint her, he shook his head and said, "I can't do as you ask."

"Bastard," she spit at him. "Answer one question for me."

"If I'm able."

"Why did you marry me?"

"There are so many reasons, and I'm tired and worn out, and I can't abide us bickering like this. Can't it wait?"

"Until when?" she asked furiously. "Tomorrow? The next day? The next one after that?"

"Well, I will be extremely busy on the morrow. I need to leave early for London."

"I'll just bet you do!"

When she began to move, he initially thought she was advancing on him, but at the last moment she veered to the door. The key was in the lock, and before he could stop her, she turned it, then rushed to the window of the second-story room and tossed it out into the bushes below.

"There, now," she said as she rounded on him, a smile of triumph on her face. "I'd say we have plenty of time to talk it out."

"Are you mad?" He stomped after her, elbowing her aside so that he could lean into the window seat and peer out toward the dark ground. Foolishly he extended his hand as though hoping he might be able to will the key to magically float back up. As he knelt there, accepting that his opportunity for a graceful exit was gone, that he was dangerously trapped with her for the remainder of the night, he took several seconds to recall that this was exactly why he didn't engage in fights with women.

There was no telling what outrageous emotional act a hysterical female might commit. And this one . . . oh, this one . . .

He was beginning to grasp why a man might come to beat a woman. Right this instant he was so angry that he'd relish the chance to give her what-for! If she'd been a male, he wouldn't have hesitated, but he remained completely still, for if he moved a muscle, he'd very likely take her over his knee and give her the thorough paddling she deserved. Oh, my, but he was sorely tempted!

Once he felt he could control himself, he turned toward her. She was standing several feet away, next to a small table, casually nibbling at food on a tray as though nothing untoward had just occurred.

How dare she look so calm and composed after committing such an improvident exploit. His temper started roiling on a slow boil.

His eyes glittered menacingly as he admonished her. "You're going to regret doing that."

"I doubt it," she said saucily.

He took one step toward her, then another. Since the occasion when they'd first met, she'd seemed docile and complacent, a woman who was happy, easily pleased, and effortlessly manipulated. When had she turned into this confrontational, confident, truculent virago? He didn't know who this woman was, but he needed to exercise some authority over her. She required a reminder of who was in charge.

Through gritted teeth, intending to cow her into submission, he said, "I am your husband."

"No, you aren't," she said nastily. "We may have spoken the vows, but until you lie down with me, we remain two separate people."

"I am your husband!" he repeated as though he hadn't heard her. Moving forward like a predator, he brought them toe to toe, but to his dismay, she stood her ground, unmoved and unintimidated. "If I say that we will talk in the morning, that's when we will speak! And if I say we'll postpone our marital joining, then it's going to happen later!"

"If you don't bed me tonight," she threatened, "I'll pack my belongings and go home in the morning."

The possibility of her attempting to leave, of his having to prevent her, gave him pause. If she proceeded, how would he respond? Would he have the temerity to keep her and her maid bound and gagged for the duration? "You will not go anywhere unless I say that you may."

"I'd like to see you try to stop me."

"I can, and I will."

"Well, aren't I just terrified?" she asked smartly, having the audacity to bat her eyelashes.

How he'd like to wring her pretty neck! "You should be!"

"What will you do if I refuse to come to heel when you order me about? Beat me? Lock me in my room? Make me go without supper?"

"I'll . . . I'll . . . I'll . . ." He sputtered for a chastisement that would sound plausible. Embarrassingly enough, he couldn't conceive of a single one. Evil treatment of women simply wasn't in his nature. Besides, he liked her too much to consider the possibility of doing something nefarious. Any remark he might make was an empty threat. He knew it; she did too.

"That's what I thought," she said, shaking her head in disgust. "I've been ordered about by more brutal men than you, so if you hope to exercise some husbandly dominion over me, you'd better figure out what it will be in a hurry. Otherwise,

I will be gone like that"—she snapped her fingers—"with the sunrise."

"Is that truly what you want?" he queried. He had to squelch any desire to leave, so he struck at her most vulnerable spot. "Would you return to your father's care, where he can foist you off on that drunken sot you call fiancé?"

"I'd rather be back in the duke's house, than living here like this. Where I'm an . . . an invisible person who has no claim on you, no ties to you."

"The duke might do anything to you!"

"Then, I will escape again." Viciously she added, "I found you to help me the first time, didn't I? I shall find another, and if I'm lucky, he will be a man who enjoys my company."

At the mention of the prospect that she might seek out another, Lucas became furious. She was his! In some buried section of his heart he suspected that she had been his forever, and the time had finally come to claim her for his own. No one else could ever have her.

"You are mine!" he contended. "You belong to me and with me."

"Then, show me your regard is genuine!"

Penny held her breath, waiting, then waiting some more, to see what he would do.

The night had been the longest, most horrible of her life. She'd been forced once more to examine herself and wonder, as she had continually for the past three years, why she was so unlovable.

Why didn't anyone want her?

As a girl she'd been so vainly proud. About her beauty. About her family's exalted status. About her role in society. About her marital prospects.

Because of her arrogance, she'd been petty, overbearing, rude, and insensitive. She'd believed that every boon was exactly what she deserved. Her attitude had caused hurt and jealousy wherever she went, and she hadn't noticed what kinds of reactions her contemptible behavior stirred in others.

When her first engagement had ended so hideously, it had come as an enormous shock when reality began to rain down. No one liked her! She had no true friends! Those people who'd fluttered on the fringes, pretending camaraderie and affection, had merely put up with her, enduring her with a jaundiced eye. They had delighted in her downfall, and in retaliation they gleefully jabbed at her with hateful words and actions whenever they had the chance.

In the lonely aftermath of abandonment by her acquaintances, she'd molded herself into a different woman from the one she'd been raised to be. She tried to exemplify every positive characteristic her peers did not. She'd grown attentive, concerned, involved. Loyal. Trustworthy. Likable. The kind of woman anyone would call friend.

By the time she'd met Lucas, she'd evolved completely— or so she'd thought—and it had never occurred to her that she would still be so unappreciated. At his decision not to come to her bed, she felt as if all the soul searching, alterations, and personal changes had been for naught.

How could he not love her?

The first hour had passed in breathless anticipation, and she'd jumped at every noise, hearing his foot on the stair. The second hour she'd spent pacing to the window and looking out, trying to catch a glimpse of where he'd gone. The third hour had left her unbearably angry, and the fourth, miserably despondent.

But with Lucas's reluctant appearance, and her opening to vent her frustrations, she was no longer despairing, for her words and his had totally focused her mind: She wanted Lucas; she had from the first night she'd laid eyes on him.

A fierce battle was raging inside him. He coveted her, but some unknown factor kept him from admitting it and following through on his natural inclinations. She didn't know what was driving him to behave as he was, and she didn't want to know. Whatever the reason, she simply needed him to move beyond it, so that they could clear up her past and begin their future.

The internal war continued unabated. His fists were clenched, an angry muscle ticked in his jaw, and he was breathing hard, as though he'd just run a long race. Unfortunately for him, she was tired of tarrying while his mind came to terms with what his body so obviously craved.

Deliberately she reached out and laid her hand on the lower part of his abdomen, and she was delighted to feel him instantly begin to swell against her palm. Clearly taunting him, she asked, "Are you a man or aren't you?"

"What did you say?" he rasped as he snatched her hand away from his enlarging erection.

"Colette and I were merely wondering. . . ."

She never had the occasion to finish her insult. With her crude gibe, she'd finally destroyed whatever personal dam had been restraining his wave of desire. His arms came around her, holding her tautly, so that their fronts intimately merged. Her breasts were mashed against his chest. His muscled legs cradled her thighs. Against her stomach he was boldly aroused, and his hands lowered to her bottom. He pulled her closer still, so that she could experience every throbbing inch of his erect male member. It seemed alive, and it strained ferociously to be released from his trousers.

He stared her down, his dark eyes glittering angrily, daring her to virginally shrink away. With a resolve that easily matched his own, she returned his stare while she flexed forward, letting her hips meet the unyielding ridge of manly flesh.

At her immodest gesture he tightened his grip and brazenly stroked his length across her, giving her a first clear hint of what was coming. "I am going to have you," he declared. "In every way that counts. Before the night is finished, you'll be begging me to stop."

"I challenge you to try your best."

"I don't want to hear any complaints after. Not one!"

"No complaints. No regrets."

With that, his mouth covered hers in a dangerous kiss. His fingers fisted in her long hair, using it as leverage to tip her head back, and he nipped, tasted, and sucked her, learning her flavor and texture. His tongue came inside without hesitating, asking, or letting her become accustomed to the new sensation. He manipulated it back and forth in a carnal rhythm, making her stomach tickle and her breasts ache.

As his lips and tongue worked savagely against her own, his hands were busy as well, caressing her back from her shoulders down to her hips, then up again, tracing the bumps on her spine, the width, the nip of her waist. He slipped inside the lapels of her robe, parting the front and pushing it away. The belt at the waist was knotted, so the fabric caught at her elbows, effectively trapping her arms. She wanted them free so that she could explore just as he was doing, but she couldn't get loose.

While he had her partially immobilized, he took full advantage, roaming across her arms, her shoulders, her upper back. He abandoned her mouth in order to place kisses across her cheek, under her chin, to the sensitive area where her neck met her chest. In the exact spot where her pulse pounded so ominously, he sucked greedily, forcefully enough to leave marks on her creamy skin.

Her body whirled with sensation. She felt hot and cold, ready to burst with laughter because she was so ecstatically happy. At the same time, she needed a few minutes of separation to calm her shattered nerves. The entire world had been reduced to this moment and this man. All she could hear, feel, taste, see, was him, but it wasn't enough. She wanted to touch every inch of him until there wasn't a speck she didn't know. If she could have figured out how, she'd have climbed beneath his skin to get so close that she could no longer tell where she ended and he began, but the binding at her waist kept her from going to all the places she truly wished to be.

Ineffectively she fought to free her arms, the skirmish causing her mound to writhe against his swollen phallus, and the movement inflamed his already raging desire. No longer able to delay, he circled her small waist and lifted her off the floor, twirling her around and swinging her to the bed so fast that she became dizzy from the sudden rush. She landed hard enough to bounce, and then he was on her, covering her. With his body. His hands. His mouth.

His weight pushed her into the mattress, and her untutored body's first instinct was to move out from under the strange heaviness, but even as she attempted to escape, she endeavored to get nearer. Pinned down as she was by his legs and chest, the unusual confinement was one she hadn't known before, but her body instantly recognized it as something desperately essential.

His lips were everywhere. Her forehead, eyes, hair. They dipped to her chest but never dropped as low as she craved them to go. Her breasts were screaming for attention, her nipples full and throbbing, and she perceived that he could ease some of the ache if he would only suck them, but he did not. He kept coming closer and closer, never quite stroking, grazing then moving on, biting and squeezing, hurting but not.

A thigh wedged between her legs, applying pressure to her center, and suddenly she was riding him as though mounted on a horse. He drove against her, over and over in a maddening tempo, causing her interior parts to stretch and spread. She was light-headed, overheated, uncertain. Unable to continue. Unable to stop.

Gradually the relentless ride eased, and he came over her until both his legs were between hers. She was splayed wide open. The sides of her robe did nothing to shield her tender inner thighs, and the rough fabric of his trousers rubbed erotically, making her raw and sore and overly sensitized to his slightest motion.

"Please, Lucas," she whimpered in a voice that sounded nothing like her own. "Please," she said again, and she wasn't certain for what she was begging. Her body was on fire, a teeming cauldron of unrelieved agony. Her skin felt too hot and too extended, her breasts swollen nearly to bursting, her fingers and toes tingled, her heart raced, and between her legs she was wet and dripping, the moisture soaking the fragile scrap of lace that covered her woman's core.

He toyed with the knot on her belt, pulled it apart, then yanked the robe off her arms. They were finally free and ready to explore every inch of his torso, but he wouldn't allow her movement, continuing to hold her down with his size and strength. He tugged at the straps of her chemise, baring her breasts. For the longest time he stared, his gaze so intent that she felt as though he were touching her with his eyes. The heat caused her nipples to inflate further, until they were hard, erect, and excruciatingly inflamed.

With thumb and forefinger he reached for both breasts and pinched the raised nubs, and she hissed out a breath of shock and surprise. He growled low in his throat as he squeezed, shaped, and molded them. The application of pressure caused her to wriggle, seeking escape, but she was trapped, thighs spread, and she couldn't get away from the immeasurable torture.

Leaning down, he licked her with his tongue. Licked again, then sucked the roughened tip far back into his mouth, causing her to rise up off the bed. He pushed her down, keeping her in place and working at her until she felt she just might go mad if he didn't end her distress.

Just as she decided she couldn't bear another moment of the delicious misery, he pulled his lips away, but he continued to massage the rounded globes. Her nipples were wet, pouting, and she sighed with regret over the loss of his mouth.

His eyes bright with lust, he said, "I am a big man. Bigger than most." He flexed at the V between her legs, and the ridge of his phallus lay balanced against her cleft. "I'm going to take you hard."

"I don't care," she said mindlessly, shaking her head, panting, out of breath.

"I'm going to mount you, then ride you until I have you squirming and pleading for mercy."

"I'll never ask you to stop," she insisted.

"It's going to hurt," he said. "The first time."

"It doesn't matter."

His hand left her breast and drifted down her stomach, low, lower, and he pressed the heel against her, massaging it in a deep rhythm and causing her hips to respond. He dipped below the line of lace, his fingers spread out across her sex. She was dripping with want, his hand slippery with the flood of her desire.

"God, you are so ready for me." He pushed one finger up inside, then another and another, until three fingers were exploring and stretching. Not gentle or cautious, neither taking his time nor giving her ease, he learned his route through the secret cavity, and she closed her eyes against the invasion, intrigued and repelled at being manipulated in such a strange fashion.

"Why are you doing that?" she asked.

"I'm preparing my way."

"It's painful," she said.

"It will get worse," he said bluntly.

Needing more room with which to maneuver, he grabbed the sheer panties in his fist and ripped them off, exposing her to his hot, steady gaze.

Before she knew what he intended, he leaned down and burrowed his face in her woman's hair, sniffing, smelling, then tasting. Startling her, his tongue parted the hair and found her slick, sizzling center. He flicked against her, then began sucking. The fingers of one hand were still buried deep inside and stroking back and forth. The fingers of the other hand were at a breast and pressing a rigid nipple.

The pleasure was so intense that she felt she just might burst into flames if something didn't happen soon. With a vague sort of cognition she discerned what was coming in her direction. Colette had been a frank and explicit teacher regarding the pleasurable side of joining with a man, but how could mere words have possibly prepared her?

Surely this sensation was more than one human body could tolerate.

She was spiraling higher, out of control, and finally, blessedly he shoved her over the edge, and she shattered into a million pieces and flew across the universe. Time and reality had no meaning, and the agitation continued until she began to believe it would never cease.

Gradually sanity returned. Her eyes fluttered open, and Lucas was hovering above her, his weight braced on one hand. The other fumbled with the front of his trousers, and then his phallus was between her legs, burning and insistent. She felt finished, sated, and couldn't imagine how there could possibly be more, although she knew there would be. From the tension in his shoulders, the sweat on his brow, the intensity of his regard, she understood he was ready in a manner she couldn't have understood before they'd started.

A thrill of excitement coursed through her as she amply realized the feminine power she possessed that enabled her to bring him to such a frenzied state. She gazed up at him, and the realization surged over her that she'd been prepared her entire life, since the day she'd been born, to share this milestone with Lucas. He would take her; she would be his. Until the end of time.

"Open your eyes," he said fiercely. "Look at me while I make you mine." He pushed into her with the heated crown of his erection. "Look at me! Know that I am the first. That I am the only one."

"Yours," she said as he pushed again, coming in farther, her body extending and adjusting to his enormous size, the fear of the unknown causing her to bite her bottom lip.

"Always and forever," he promised.

With that he steadied himself and plunged inside. Her body tensed, and she had the irrational urge to flee from the intrusion, but she wanted to be united with him more than anything. She was astonished when he leaned down and tenderly rested his forehead against hers. His eyes were tightly closed, his frame rigid with pressure, his breathing fast and labored.

"God, don't move," he whispered, his hands at her waist, holding her.

"It hurts . . ." she whispered in return.

"It will pass," he asserted, sounding like a lover, a friend, a confidant, and even as he gave the assurance, he was proved right. The pain began to abate, and her body started the physical process of accommodating him.

"You're so tight. So hot and wet." As suddenly as it had come upon them, the period of calm passed, and he was once again overtaken by his spiraling drive for completion. "I'm sorry," he said, "I can't wait."

Slowly at first, then faster and faster, he drove deeper than she ever imagined a man could go. There was a primal madness to it, of having no control over their bodies or where their animalistic dispositions were precipitously leading them.

It was so . . . wild. So uncivilized. His palms rested on either side of her head, the muscles of his arms defined and straining, and she gripped her hands around them, holding on with an untamed abandon, not daring to let go, and perfectly content to follow him to wherever the turbulent journey would take them.

Without warning he stopped, and he clutched her hips and thrust as far as he was able, keeping her motionless while he reached his peak. He snarled fiercely and emptied himself, and she felt a delectable tingle low in her stomach as his warm seed spilled against her womb. The sensation was so unexpectedly wonderful that she didn't notice he had collapsed onto her. She was finally able to enfold him with her arms, as she'd been attempting to do through the entire encounter. She wrapped her legs around him as well, surrounding him with her body, her mind, and her soul.

Their hearts pounded together in a constant rhythm, and she held him to her breast, his breath passing across her chest as his respiration eventually slowed. The intense physical gratification gradually passed and was languidly replaced by something bordering on serene affection. She ran her fingers though his hair and across his shoulders as she placed light kisses against his skin.

When he made an effort to pull away, she wound her legs more tightly, locking them behind his back so that he couldn't leave her. And he didn't. He started growing hard inside her, and they began again, with Lucas thrusting at his magical pace. Shifting, he looked her in the eye, an unreadable, unknowable expression on his face. It wasn't love she was seeing, but proprietorship, and that would have to be enough. For now.

As he was still fully clothed, she tugged at his shirt, dragging it over his head and tossing it on the floor. She ran her hands across his chest, learning every bump and ridge, sifting her fingers through the thick mat of dark hair, plucking and toying with his nipples as he had done to hers.

The coupling was different, slower and more gentle but no less dramatic for the changes. The initial joining had burned away much of the savage determination with which he'd taken her, and it had been replaced by a changed sort of driving force. The kisses lasted longer, the touches were more tender, and the speed of their climb back to the apex of desire was much more slow-paced. But soon they both approached the pinnacle again, and as her body struggled toward the release she knew she'd find in his arms, he amazed her further by hugging her tightly and holding her close.

"Come with me this time," he urged. He covered her mouth with his and kissed her thoroughly. She lost herself in delight as he swallowed her cries of ecstasy.

The wave crested and receded, seeming more concentrated because they'd shared it. As it ebbed and normalcy returned, still she did not let him leave her, though he tried his damnedest. Finally he gave in, and before long he was hard once more and riding her.

She gave herself over to the reckless madness, letting him go and traveling along. They did not speak as he took her. Hard and fast. Slow and sweet. He turned her and moved her, and made love to her in every possible manner, until her muscles cramped, her mind became numb, and her legs shook with fatigue. Her thighs were bruised, bite marks and whisker burns covered her in the most shocking locations, her woman's spot was sore and abused. Yet, she felt miraculously alive, energized, and ready to explode with rapture.

Five times during the night, she let him have his way with her. When he finally drifted into an exhausted slumber, the sun was rising and the morning chorus of birds was singing outside the window. But Penny didn't hear any of the commotion. She fell asleep immediately, smiling and content to be lying in her husband's arms.

CHAPTER THIRTEEN

"So, is Penny my mother now?" Harry asked.

"No. Your mother is in heaven," Lucas said from across the supper table.

"But she's not here. I want a real mother here on earth. Can it be Penny?"

"Certainly," he said. *And I'll pretend she's my wife.*

"Good," Harry said, "because I like her very much."

"I'm glad," Lucas said distractedly, feeling more heartsick with each word that came out of the boy's mouth.

This was an unmitigated disaster, and it had been from the very beginning. Everyone was going to be hurt by his rash act—the one that had seemed so logical and justified at the start. No one had immunity from harm, including himself.

He kept thinking of Penny, of how open and giving she was during their nightly sexual rompings. Initially he'd wanted to scare her into backing down from any type of carnal relationship, but she wouldn't be intimidated.

When frightening her hadn't worked, he'd hoped to sensually torture her so that she would be overwhelmed and thus walk away from further couplings. But that plan hadn't succeeded either. She welcomed their bed play, the more erotic, the better.

He'd now taken her many, many times, on each occasion believing that spilling his seed would rid him of the greedy lust that raged in his veins. Instead, his hunger had grown with every joining, and now his need for her was a living, breathing ache in the center of his heart. He didn't know how he could go about the rest of his life without having her by his side.

That first day after their purported wedding, the light of early afternoon had found him still snuggled in her bed, with his arm around her and her cheek pressed against his chest. He had lain, staring at her, then staring at the ceiling, while he contemplated all the failures that had led him to that moment. Surprisingly, with the smell of her lingering on his skin, hands, and tongue, and her warm, lush body cuddled intimately next to his, he couldn't find the necessary forbearance to be sorry for anything that had happened.

When she'd awakened and stirred, stretching and purring like a contented kitten, he'd instantly lost his head and taken her again, though he did so slowly and cautiously because she was sore and tender from the previous hours of acrobatics. Since then his entire world had been turned upside down. All he could think about was having her. His body was constantly primed and ready for copulation as though he was a young lad eager to empty himself at the drop of a hat.

His hunger for her had become insatiable, his desire so strong that he could hardly converse with Harry. Concentration was impossible, completely shot to hell, and he could focus only on her and what he wanted to do to her the next time he managed to get her alone. Even though he'd just bathed, carefully washing away all traces of the swift frolic they'd enjoyed just before supper, he couldn't remove her scent from his head, and her special musk had become a permanent part of his consciousness.

Despite his best intentions, he was entirely thunderstruck. To his dismay, the days and nights of sexual combat had done nothing to abate his rampant cravings, and he had no idea how to subdue his powerful urges, thus causing him to realize that his problems had been multiplied a thousandfold.

What a mess!

"Is she going to live with us?" Harry, with his continual chatter, unknowingly persisted in rubbing salt in Lucas's wounds.

"Of course," Lucas said carefully, already plotting the lies and reasonings he would have to use on the boy after Penny was gone.

"Forever?"

"Yes," he said tightly. "Now, why don't you finish up. It's past your bedtime."

"Oh, Uncle Luke . . . I'm not tired."

He offered a bribe. "I'll tell you a story once you're settled under the covers."

Harry glared at his uncle for a moment, then asked, "The one about the pirates? When they boarded your ship, and you were just a boy? Like me?"

"Yes," Lucas promised, knowing it was a favorite. "I'll tell that one. If you hurry."

"I guess that would be all right with me," he said imperiously, as though he were a king granting a boon.

Or a duke, Lucas thought. It was amazing how paternity affected a fellow. Even though they'd never met, Harry had so many of his father's characteristics. Many of his half sister's too. Would she ever learn the truth? If she did, what would she think?

Just then his personal tormentor, in the form of Penny Westmoreland, entered the kitchen. She was attired in a simple housedress, an apron covering most of her front, but it did little to hide her luscious curves. He knew the tantalizing secrets hidden beneath the clothes, and he could barely prevent himself from reaching for her. As it was, his cock stirred just from gazing upon her, just from smelling her and having her stand so near.

She stopped behind his chair and casually rested a hand on

his shoulder as if she'd been touching him in such a regular, offhand fashion for years. Though he tried to ignore how wonderful the gesture felt, he couldn't, and he had to force himself to remain facing toward the table lest he shift around and pull her onto his lap. Which he absolutely, positively, dare not do! He was a man full grown. He could and would master his riotous masculine appetites.

Every morning he swore he'd exercise some restraint, that he wasn't about to allow his behavior to lead them back under the covers. He'd already discovered that the slightest inappropriate step carried them directly to the bedroom. Each episode was too memorable, as his tormented body was shouting loudly and clearly. If Penny gave the slightest hint that she'd like a repeat performance, he'd be dropping his trousers as quickly as he was able. So, there was no reason to tempt fate.

Penny leaned closer, lovingly sifting her fingers through his hair, and the move brought her torso in contact with his upper back. Her breasts, those two perfect globes of womanly splendor, were pressed against him. Her nipples were poking against her apron.

How much suffering, he wondered, could one man tolerate and still manage to survive?

"What are you about, Master Harry?" she asked, smiling at the boy. "Are you finished?"

"Yes, ma'am."

"Then, it's off to bed with you."

"Just a few more minutes?" he asked, looking so sweet that he might have been one of those cherubs painted on a church ceiling.

"I already let you stay up longer than I should have."

Harry looked to Lucas, his big blue eyes begging silently for an ally. "I already gave you my opinion," Lucas said. "You're off to bed."

"Don't even *think* about forgetting your promise," Harry ordered haughtily as he slipped off the chair.

Penny patted his head, saying to Lucas, "He sounds just like my father when he talks like that," and Lucas nearly choked on the ale he was attempting to swallow.

"Lead on, my lord duke," she said to Harry, holding out her hand, and the lad trustingly slipped his small one into hers.

"Don't forget," Harry repeated, and Penny glanced at Lucas, raising a questioning brow.

"I said I'd tell him a story," Lucas explained while struggling frantically to keep his wits from fraying like a worn rope.

"A true one," Harry offered. "That means it really happened."

"Is that so?" She talked to him as though she'd interacted with four-year-old children all her life. "What sorts of stories do you enjoy?"

"I like the ones about when Lucas was a boy like me. And about my mother," he added. "I like those too."

"I'll bet you do," she said. "I'd like to hear some stories about Lucas and your mother too."

"He's very good at telling them. Especially about the pirates ..." And their voices trailed off as they climbed the stairs.

Lucas leaned forward and miserably rested his head in his hands. She appeared so contented in the little home Matthew had found for them, she'd taken to Harry like a mother hen to a chick, and she'd become Lucas's pretend wife in the most passionate ways imaginable. Good Lord, but in a matter of days they'd begun to carry on like an actual family, and at the sudden insight he could barely keep from groaning aloud.

Just that very morning they'd risen from their bower of bliss, and she'd taken a bath, so he seized the opportunity to slip away, hoping to meet with Matthew at their rendezvous spot in order to learn the latest ransom news from London. But his brother hadn't been there, and Lucas spent the time in the quiet woods, trying to clear his mind in order to come to terms with what was happening and how he felt about it.

When he finally returned to the house, Penny welcomed him sweetly with hugs and kisses and not a hint of embarrassment over their dawn escapade. Worried about her and her condition after his rough handling, he managed to whisper, "Are you feeling all right?"

"Just a little sore," she said, giving him a saucy wink that had made his pulse increase and blood rush to his groin.

Then Harry had begun tugging at his pant leg, yammering on about the coming day, and they played together in the yard while Penny watched and laughed. Lucas spent the afternoon engaged in all manner of husbandly chores, even helping her move some heavy furniture. Later, supper had been warming on the stove, and he and the boy sat together at the kitchen table while Penny dished up their meal. She fed her men, as she referred to them, hesitantly asking about the thick stew and shyly admitting that she'd fixed it herself. Just for the two of them.

Without warning they'd become a unit, a cohesive group instead of separate individuals.

What was he going to do?

A voice sounded behind him, the French accent unmistakable. "For a new husband who is having the most fabulous of nightly pleasure," Colette said, "you do not look so delighted, eh?"

He growled and turned to face her. "Don't start with me, Mistress Colette."

"You have much manly gratification these days, so you should be content, relaxed, and able to talk of difficult topics." Looking overly sly and wise, she said, "So, you are not distressed? You are very satisfied, *oui?*"

"Yes," he said through gritted teeth. "I'm ecstatic."

"I am glad to hear that my lady has served you well."

The woman had an incredible amount of gall to speak of the subject of his and Penny's supposed marital couplings, and he caught himself blushing at the picture of her lying awake belowstairs, and perhaps hearing all the racket coming from the upper bedroom. "I hardly think that how we pass our private hours is any of your business, and I don't intend to discuss it with you.''

''Not my business?'' she asked, scoffing as though he were a dolt, then narrowing her eyes menacingly. ''Everything about my lady is my business.''

He was tired of bandying words with her. ''If you're so worried about my intentions,'' he said irritably, ''why didn't you take her back to the duke like you threatened?''

''We remain for one reason and one reason only!''

''That being?''

''Because my lady is filled with joy, and she still believes you will bring her much happiness.''

''And if at some point she changes her mind?''

''Then we will be gone''—she clapped her hands loudly— ''like that!''

''Well, then,'' he said softly, dangerously, ''I don't plan to ever make her unhappy, so we don't have a thing to worry about, do we?''

She gave a French curse. ''I do not know what you are about, but if you hurt my lady when you are finished,'' she warned, her voice full of venom, ''I will hunt you down and kill you like a dog!''

''Oh, for pity's sake,'' he grumbled, exasperated. Would the woman's rampant speculation never end? ''I don't have to listen to this.'' Pushing the chair back, he walked to the stairs. Behind him, he could hear Colette muttering in French. He didn't understand what she was saying, but he caught the general drift, and he was fairly certain she'd have his head on a pike if she ever had half a chance.

Ignoring her diatribe, he climbed to Harry's room, finding him scrubbed and in his nightclothes, already abed. Lucas sat on the edge of the bed and related the tale about the pirates' boarding.

The boy never tired of hearing how Lucas had been hiding behind a barrel when one of the brigands reached for him. He'd escaped by stabbing the cutthroat in the hand. A gruesome narrative, to say the least, but it always kept the boy enthralled, and Lucas had omitted the truly terrifying sections about what had actually transpired, instead making it sound as though evading murderous pirates was full of fun and adventure.

At the end he blew out the candle, then waited while Harry's breathing slowed and became deep and regular. He leaned over and kissed the boy, then stepped into the hall, only to discover Penny standing there. Obviously she'd been eavesdropping on their whispered words of love and good-night, and she blushed prettily at having been blatantly caught.

"I couldn't help listening," she said.

"It's all right," he insisted. "I don't mind."

"Was that account really true? Did that really happen to you?"

"Yes," he answered casually, shrugging off those horrid, lonely years, hating to talk about them, hating to think about them. "It's water under the bridge."

"But you must have been little more than a child!"

"I was eight," he surprised himself by admitting.

"Hardly older than Harry," she murmured.

"By a few years."

The more she thought about it, the more she became incensed. "Why, that's outrageous. How did you come to be in such a place?"

"I was kidnapped off the docks in Virginia."

"Oh, Lucas . . ." she said with such genuine concern that it caused a sudden wave of powerful emotion to sweep over him. He'd never felt anything like it before. All the memories he thought he'd carefully buried—the desperate yearnings, the fear, the hunger and cold and whippings—were unexpectedly close to the surface, scratching and clawing and trying to see the light of day.

Barely able to speak through the lump in his throat, he commented, "It took me a long time to find my way home."

"How old were you when you were stolen?"

"Five," he said. "I was five."

"And your parents? Did they search for you?"

"They wouldn't have had the means, I don't expect." He gazed down the hall, past the compassion and worry registering in her eyes. "But I don't know. They died of illness shortly after I disappeared."

"Oh, my dear husband," she said, and she did the very worst thing he could possibly imagine, she wrapped her arms around his waist and hugged him tightly. "What became of your sister, Caroline? And Harry told me you have a brother as well?"

"Matthew." He murmured his brother's name.

He wanted to resist her comforting, but no one had ever offered any before, and he realized that it was something he'd never known he was missing. Overwhelmed, he returned her embrace, draping his arms across her shoulders and resting his chin on the top of her head. "They were just babies. They were farmed out. It was bad . . . for all of us. . . ." He left it at that and was relieved that she didn't press for more information.

"How old were you when you returned?"

"I was nearly fifteen. I found them, and we became a family again." Closing his eyes, he crushed her to his chest, desperately trying to impart comprehension of some of the intense emotion that had been driving him these past years. "When I was still on the ship, I spent every moment conjuring up methods of making my way back to them; it's all that kept me going. After we were reunited, I would have gladly given my life for either one of them. When Caroline died . . . it was as though someone had snatched out my very heart."

"Yes, I imagine that's exactly how it felt." She pulled back slightly so that she could gaze up into his face. "Who is Harry's father? He didn't marry Caroline, did he?"

"No," Lucas said, shaking his head.

At her question he wanted to be angry, but she'd asked it so delicately that he couldn't be. For the first time, he was able to think about Caroline's death without becoming blinded by rage. "She went visiting, and she was away from home. Even though she was fully grown, she was impressionable, and, apparently, easily tempted and swayed. If I hadn't allowed her to go, I always wonder if it might have ended differently.''

"You feel as though it's your fault, don't you?"

"Well . . . perhaps."

"Oh, darling, you mustn't." She gave him a slight shake to emphasize her point. "Do you know who the cad is?"

"Yes, I learned just recently."

"Harry is such a wonderful boy, and knowing both of you as I now do, I can surmise what Caroline must have been like. What kind of man would behave so badly toward the two of them?" She gazed up imploringly. "Now that you've detected his identity, what are your plans?"

"I haven't decided," Lucas fibbed.

"Is he an Englishman?"

"Yes," he said carefully. "That's one of the reasons I'm in the country, but I'm not certain what steps to take."

"Perhaps I could help you. I'm acquainted with many people, and my family has extensive connections. . . ."

"Perhaps you could," he agreed, wanting to forestall any further discussion of the topic. "I'm still contemplating what I'd like to do."

"You will let me know if I can help, won't you?"

Without answering, he pulled her close unable to stare into those sapphire eyes. "I loved my sister beyond imagining. You can understand that, can't you? I might go to any length to see her avenged."

"Of course I understand." Her words were a mere rumble against the center of his chest. She held him for a few moments, then said, "It's been such a long day. Let's go to bed."

"Oh, Penny . . ." he breathed, hating what was occurring, hating himself. He released her from the circle of his arms and set her away. Pulling himself together, he said gently, "I need to go out for a few hours."

"Truly?" She regarded him, taking his measure, looking inside to the private, solitary places he never let anyone see. "You know, Lucas," she ultimately said, "whatever it is, whatever is worrying you, you can tell me about it. We can get through it together. That's what I'm here for."

"There's nothing wrong, Penny," he lied, wishing it weren't so.

"All right," she sighed.

"Don't wait up for me."

His statement brought a crushing look of disappointment to her eyes, but she quickly concealed it. "I won't, then."

"Good night."

He took a step back, wanting only to reach the safety of the stairs, when her quiet voice stopped him. "Lucas?"

"Yes?"

"If you ever get swept away from home again, I'll spend the rest of my life trying to find you. I'll never quit searching. And Harry and I will always keep a candle burning in the window to light your way back to us."

He left her standing there and went to the barn, waiting in the shadows. Eventually he saw a light in her room, and with a painful urgency he thought about how she would appear as she prepared to retire. Her arm would bend and flex as she pulled a brush through her long hair. Her breasts would shift and move as she washed. The muscles in her back and legs would stretch as she tugged her nightrail over her head. Those long, slender fingers would smooth the fabric down her front and thighs. Her rosy lips would pucker as she leaned over to blow out the candle.

Quietly she would lie in the bed with her knees curled up to her chest, gazing out the window into the night, wondering where he had gone and when he might return.

She deserved so much more than the pittance of emotion he'd given her. All he'd done was compromise her and ruin her for any other man. While some part of him reveled in the knowledge, his more rational self felt only an extreme burning shame.

How was he any different from Harold Westmoreland?

Westmoreland had seduced Caroline when she was alone

and away from the protection of her family. She'd fallen for his smooth talk and charms, and thus ended up offering him the most precious part of herself, and he'd gladly accepted without hesitation or consideration of the consequences.

Wasn't that exactly what he himself had done to Penny?

As he pondered the similarities between his situation and the duke's, he couldn't help ruminating over the most horrifying possibility of all: What if he'd gotten Penny with child? In light of how quickly sexual events had spiraled out of control, he had yet to spend any length of time calculating the probable aftereffects of his incautious behavior, but he knew better than anyone that a disastrous conception could be the result. His conduct was so outlandish that it almost made him think he wanted her pregnant.

People always said a babe couldn't be created from a handful of joinings, but what if they were wrong? And when did a handful turn into numerous opportunity? Certainly, they'd passed any safe limits. What if his child were already growing in her?

He'd need to marry her straightaway.

But how can you marry her? a small voice warned. *She believes you're already married!*

If a babe became a reality, he'd need to wed her legally and truly, which would mean confessing his sins, telling her all.

What would she do?

Without having to consider very extensively, he decided she'd leave him and never return. For wasn't this false marriage the ultimate betrayal of her faith in him? Probably she'd be willing to forgive many sins, but not deceitful vows. If she learned that she couldn't believe him when he promised to love and honor her till death parted them, how could she ever trust him again?

There would be no absolution. She would vanish, only to be reabsorbed into the sheltered, wealthy world from which he'd taken her. The Westmorelands would banish her to a secluded country property where no one from Polite Society would ever hear from her again. Or perhaps they'd marry her secretly to another, falsifying the date of her wedding, in order to hide her disgrace.

Some other man would have Penny and raise Lucas's child, and Lucas would never learn the outcome. He'd never know if it was a boy or a girl, if it was healthy, what name Penny had selected. The child would remain a vast open hole in his life that he would never be able to fill, a continuing disgrace to his personal honor, one that he would never be able to make right no matter how long he tried.

There was no distinction that could be made between himself and his nemesis, Harold Westmoreland. He and the duke were two of a kind, so why persevere with his search for vengeance?

For years he'd yearned to locate the person who had ruined Caroline and to make him pay. Now he had the rogue within his grasp, was a hairsbreadth from winning what he'd come so far to receive, but the contemplation of victory was hollow. It was definitely a sobering thought to realize that he was no different from the man he hated, and that the rationalizations for his intense dislike no longer applied.

How was he to find the animosity necessary to continue on with the plan? Being enraged at Westmoreland was like being angry with himself.

Disgusted, dismayed, confused, he stood in place long after the light was extinguished in Penny's room, then he walked through the woods to the secret meeting place he'd arranged with Matthew. He gave the bird's whistle that signaled his approach, and he encountered Matthew sitting against a tree, resting patiently.

Without preamble his brother asked, "How did the day go at the house?"

"It was extremely difficult. How did it go in town?"

"No better."

Matthew rose, dusting the dirt and leaves off his trousers. Of a same height, they faced each other under the spreading limbs of an ancient oak.

"What was Westmoreland's response to my last note?"

"Much the same diatribe. He doesn't want her back."

Lucas blew out a harsh breath. "Did you hear any rumors running about yet that she might be missing?"

"No."

"Why hasn't he told anyone?"

"I wouldn't even venture a guess."

"Before she left with me, he'd pushed up the date of her wedding. It's to be held in a week. How is he explaining her absence from the preparations?"

"Maybe he's not." Matthew shrugged. "Perhaps a man in his position doesn't feel he owes explanations to anyone."

"Perhaps," Lucas agreed.

"But I've been thinking," Matthew said, "that if the wedding date passes by and she doesn't appear, there truly is no value in keeping her. We'll have no continuing leverage with which to bargain."

"So . . . we need to finish it," Lucas said, giving voice to what he'd been contemplating without realizing it.

"Yes."

"In the next day or two. One way or the other."

"My conclusion exactly."

"We tell him we're going to kill her," Lucas said harshly. "I'll write the note and see it delivered on the morrow."

Matthew nodded his accord, and they parted.

Lucas returned to the house, and it was late when he arrived. Luckily he wasn't accosted by Colette, although he almost wished she'd caught him sneaking in. He fantasized about telling all and letting her carry out one of her numerous threats. His untimely death would certainly end his misery without further ado.

Tiptoeing, he hurried to his room, disrobed, and lay down under the bedcovers, the cool linens brisk against his bare skin. Unable to sleep, he was staring at the ceiling, when, many minutes later, he heard the soft fall of footsteps coming across the hall. Penny slipped in unannounced and uninvited. Sighing, he should have realized she'd appear as she had each night so far.

What courage it took for her to traverse the small distance that separated them. He never did anything to make her feel welcome. Despite his pretended disinterest, she always came. It seemed there was no avoiding her, for how could he command her to her bed? He understood enough about her to know that even if he tried, she wouldn't obey.

At seeing him awake, her eyes widened, but she didn't speak, instead stepping to the edge of the bed. She reached for the bottom of her nightgown, pulled it over her head, and tossed it on the floor. Gloriously naked, she stood with her blond hair shimmering around her shoulders and down her back, her breasts swelled and full, the nipples puckered from the cold.

"My parents always slept apart," she explained, "and they were never happy. I don't want it to be that way for us." She lifted the covers and slipped underneath, and he tensed as she stretched out against him. "Don't tell me to leave," she whispered. "I won't go."

He chuckled. "I was just imagining it wouldn't do any good to order you about."

"No, it wouldn't," she said, smiling, then sobering. "You're distressed, Lucas; I can feel it." He started to deny her observation, but she placed a finger to his lips, silencing him. "You'd be surprised at how well I understand you. Let me ease your worries. That's what I'm here for."

With that, she moved over him. Her two perfect breasts dangled in front of his lips, her thighs spread wide across his abdomen, and her sex rested directly against his phallus, which was long, hard, and achingly erect.

He did nothing to further the encounter, neither moving nor touching, and he thought he was succeeding well until she shattered his resolve by stroking her hips across him in the sexual rhythm he'd taught her.

Dear Lord, but did she have to prove to be such an apt pupil?

"Take me to that place again," she begged. "Where we go in the night." She kissed him, and he was lost.

He pulled her forward, just that last inch, and her breasts were in his face, her nipple in his mouth. Greedily he sucked, taking her far inside, and as she was obviously still tender from his prior ministrations, she hissed out a breath, but he didn't care. He didn't care about anything. Except her and this.

Caressing her breasts until she was wet and squirming, he anchored her hips just so and eased her down. Then she was riding him. With her head thrown back and her hair tumbling about, she looked like a goddess. The tempo increased, and he let her revel in the power she held over him, encouraging her in her movements, loving the way she manipulated him with skill and confidence.

One hand drifted between her legs, toying with her sexual nub, making her tense with anticipation. The other rose to her nipple, twisting it roughly, giving her all the sensation she could possibly stand. When she shattered, so did he, holding her through the mutual pleasure. Finally, blessedly the moment ended, and she collapsed onto his chest with a lusty laugh that made him feel virile and experienced and so very fortunate.

Their breathing slowed, but she didn't shift away. Nor did he. He held her, feeling her heart beating against his own as her body relaxed and her weight increased. He caressed her, comforting her and cherishing her presence.

Perceptions tried to intrude into the sweet hiatus—that he was weak and unprincipled for what he'd just done to her again—but he refused to pay attention to them. Considering what was coming in the next few days, this precious tryst might never be repeated, and he intended to enjoy every second while their time together lasted.

Tomorrow, he told himself. *I'll chastise myself tomorrow. But not now. Not tonight.*

She probably thought he was asleep, because she whispered, "I love you so. I always will," and she placed a gentle kiss against his neck.

Remaining completely still, he closed his eyes and inhaled her words, letting them sink like a balm into his troubled heart and soul, where they could ever reside. Though he loved her more than life, he dared not repeat the sentiment. What purpose would a declaration of emotion serve? He adored her, he worshipped her. But instead of telling her, he kept the words to himself, speaking them to her silently, then he let them drift away on the falling tide of slumber.

CHAPTER FOURTEEN

"Are you certain this is the one?"

Westmoreland turned to Purdy, giving him the eye, then looking back at the sleek three-masted schooner tied off before them.

Time had run out. After the message he'd received earlier, there could be no more blundering, and no more waiting for the opportunity to stumble into a successful conclusion. They had to find Penny. Today!

"Certain as I can be," Purdy answered. "We've been watching it for two days now."

"I thought his ship was the *Sea Wind*."

"This is it. It's just recently gotten a new name is all," Purdy explained, pointing to a section of stain and paint that didn't quite match the old.

"Any sign of Pendleton?"

"No, Your Grace." Purdy shifted uncomfortably. "An old sailor seems to be the only one aboard."

"Is he one of Pendleton's men?" Harold asked hopefully.

"Don't rightly know," Purdy answered, "and, just in case he is, we didn't ask. We didn't want him to suspect we were on to him."

"How is he passing his days?"

"He appears to be readying the ship for a lengthy voyage."

To take Penny away from England? To aid Pendleton in his escape? "Do you think Penny might be stowed away below?"

"Perhaps," Purdy said, shrugging. "Anything is possible."

"Is the sailor there now?"

"Yes."

Harold regarded the sailing ship for a few minutes. He didn't want to make a wrong move, but with the most drastic threat of all staring him in the face, he was doubting his ability to discern the best course. Finally he said, "Let's do it."

On Purdy's nod, several armed men materialized out of the crowd and converged on the ship, rushing up the gangplank and swarming across the deck. By the time Harold stepped aboard, they'd located the sailor and brought him to his knees.

"What's your name?"

"Fogarty," he said gruffly, bravely staring Harold down. "Theodore Fogarty. What do you bloody bastards think you're doing on my ship?"

"Show some respect for your betters, old man," Purdy said, stepping forward and slapping him hard across the face, but the wizened elder didn't flinch.

"Where's Pendleton?" Harold asked.

"Who?"

"Lucas Pendleton."

"Oh, Cap'n Pendleton. The American."

"Yes."

"How would I know?"

Purdy raised a hand, ready to strike again, but Harold stayed him when he saw that the clenched fist caused no fear. "This is his ship."

"Not anymore. I bought it from him several weeks ago. Got the papers in my cabin, if'n you don't believe me."

That would certainly explain why the old sailor was there all alone, with no crew as of yet. Harold fumed and stewed.

"When you had your business dealings, did he say why he was selling?"

"He said he'd contracted for a brand-new ship. Built by the Fitzsimmonses, down in Portsmouth. He didn't need this one anymore."

Harold's heart sank; he had limited contacts in the distant city. Was Penny being held there? He'd need to send men, divert his resources. If Harold had calculated incorrectly, and Pendleton was truly crazed, he could be on his new ship and sailing away before anyone could stop him. As for Penny, it wouldn't matter where she was or wasn't being kept in captivity. She'd be dead.

Just then Purdy's men burst back on deck. "No sign of anyone below, sir," one of them said to Purdy. "Except the old codger."

The man handed some papers to Purdy. Purdy scanned them, then passed them to the duke. They were a bill of sale, just as Fogarty had explained. "Do you know where Pendleton was staying?" Harold asked. "Where he might be? Where his men might be?"

"I don't know anything about him really," Fogarty responded. "I just heard the vessel was for sale, and I needed it. Never had no contact with him other than to make the purchase transactions."

Harold continued to fire questions, but Fogarty answered each with a shake of his head. Finally the duke could think of nothing further, and in the pause Purdy leaned close and said, "He might be lying. Do you want us to find out? We could take him below and learn the truth right quick. . . ."

Harold glared at the stooping sailor, wondering if he was bluffing, but he continued to glare back with the same steely gaze he'd shown since they'd come on board. He was either a complete fool or stupidly brave. Harold contemplated what Purdy might do to the elderly man behind closed doors and decided he hadn't the stomach for it. Besides, Fogarty's tale rang true: Pendleton was nowhere around, and the seasoned sailor hadn't any idea where he might be.

"Let's go."

As quickly as they'd come, they returned to the docks. Purdy's men dispersed, but Purdy and Harold huddled beside his coach.

"What now?" Purdy asked.

"We need to send some men to Portsmouth."

"I don't think she's there. . . ."

"What if you're mistaken?" Harold barked.

"It's just that . . ." Purdy began cautiously, "Pendleton is close by. We know that."

"That doesn't mean *she* is."

"You're right, of course," he said deferentially.

"Locate their messenger boy," Harold said. "Seize him. He and I need to have a long, long talk."

"Will do!" Purdy declared, fairly skipping away at the prospect of finally getting his hands on the lad.

Harold hadn't shown Purdy the disturbing note that had just arrived from the American. Lucas Pendleton had played his trump card, promising to slay Penny if Harold didn't give in to his demands. While Harold persisted in assuming that Pendleton wouldn't hurt her, the message had definitely been chilling, and he couldn't help asking: what if he'd pushed Pendleton too far? What if the information they had on the scoundrel was erroneous and they'd misjudged his resolve or his lethal intent?

If Pendleton killed Penny, Harold would have no one to blame but himself. The foolish game of cat and mouse in which he'd engaged would all have been for naught, a poorly planned, ill-advised scheme based on incomplete facts. So he hadn't told Purdy about the murder threat. If the ending went awry, he didn't want Purdy to know how badly he'd allowed his own pride and misjudgment to foul the entire situation. He didn't want *anyone* to ever know.

"I'm not wrong though," he muttered vehemently to himself.

"I can't be!" Pendleton wouldn't maltreat her, and they would rescue her by sticking to the course they'd laid out from the very first. He had to believe his initial assessment was correct.

Wearily he climbed into the carriage, ready to head for home, to where he knew Edward was waiting. What was he supposed to say to the man? And what about the duchess? There was no way he could continue to avoid their inquiries. The wedding was drawing near, like a runaway horse, and they were both loudly demanding answers as to where Penny was and when she would return.

"Bugger Edward," he grumbled. "Bugger them all."

He wasn't about to start making excuses, and they wouldn't dare question his word. All he needed was a few more days. He'd see her home before the ceremony, in plenty of time for final alterations on her dress and whatever else the duchess felt were the last-minute emergencies.

If the predicament wasn't resolved in an expeditious fashion, he'd simply postpone the wedding, saying she was ill or giving some other pretext as to why she hadn't been able to return from her stay in the country.

He had to keep a lid on things for just a bit longer, but he couldn't help worrying that at any moment someone might ascertain the truth. If rumors circulated that Penny had gone off by herself with Pendleton, there'd be no containing the gossip and innuendo, and there'd be no reparations he could make that would be sufficient to fix the debacle. The consequences would be so horrid that she'd probably wish Pendleton had never brought her back.

How well he remembered the snide castigations and beratings she'd suffered after her first two arrangements had fallen through. No one should have to endure such an experience once, let alone twice, and the third occasion would be worse still. He didn't know if she could survive such an ordeal again.

Edward would vocally cry off, stirring up another hornet's nest, and the derogatory insinuations about Penny's personal problems would flare anew, burning a swath through Polite

Society that very likely could never be stamped out. Duke or no, there were only so many of her matrimonial disasters he could smooth over. He had too many enemies who loved nothing more than to see both him and his daughter brought down a peg or two, and he'd not be able to convince anybody to have her.

As it was now, they'd already scraped the bottom of the barrel with Edward; they couldn't possibly sink any lower. Penny was out of options, and she would be forced to pass the remainder of her days as a lonely spinster, without ever having the chance for children and a family—the things a woman needed to make her life complete—and Harold would have failed totally in his duties to her as her father.

All because of Pendleton.

Well, none of that calumny was going to happen to his girl. He intended to resolve the disaster favorably, and he refused to accept any finale other than the one that would see her safe and under his protection again. He gave a tap on the roof, and the driver started toward Mayfair.

Fogarty waited on the deck, scanning the docks but not seeing anyone watching. Still, a man could never be too careful, and the exalted gentleman who'd just visited might have men hovering about. Then again, maybe not. Considering how readily the regal-looking fellow had bought his fabricated story, perhaps they had all moved on.

"Bloody fool," Fogarty grumbled, and he couldn't help wondering if the wealthy bloke had been part of the royal family. Now, wouldn't that be something? A lowly sailor such as himself having words with a man who sat about drinking his port with kings and princes!

Captain Pendleton had prepared him carefully, telling him what could transpire and exactly what he was to say if the worst occurred. Fogarty felt elated to have performed his part so well, the entire scene playing out just as the captain had explained. Fogarty didn't know what sort of dubious activity Captain Pendleton was involved in, and he didn't care either. It was enough that the man had asked for assistance, plus there was the added fun of giving it to the likes of the blowhard who was just aboard.

He walked down the gangplank and let himself be swallowed up by the crowd as he strolled casually toward the alehouse where he'd made a habit of taking his midday meal. Passing the alley on the way, he slowed but didn't turn his head; he could see the boy out of the corner of his eye.

"Tell the cap'n," he said softly, "that they've found his ship. Tell him everything went just as he'd expected." Then he continued on without stopping.

Paulie sneaked up to the tavern and peeked in the window. Lucas was sitting at a table near the back. His brother, Matthew, was with him, and Paulie was surprised to observe them together. Usually they came to London separately, one remaining in the country while the other carried out the business of the day by sending and receiving the notes that Paulie so skillfully delivered.

They were deep in conversation, leaning forward, and glaring at each other, furious expressions on their faces. Inspecting them silently, he imitated Lucas's hand gestures and facial movements. When he grew up, he wanted to be exactly like Lucas Pendleton. During the dreary hours he passed on the city's streets, he constantly fantasized about the dashing American sea captain who had filled his young life with excitement and intrigue.

With the money Lucas was paying him, he could have rented a bed and found himself shelter, but he hadn't. He kept sleeping under the deserted stairway with the other boys he considered his family. The nights passed safely enough in their tiny hovel, and he felt secure there. He didn't desire to have the others thinking he'd taken on airs with his stroke of financial luck.

As he lay on his pallet of smelly straw, covered with a ragged blanket—the only place he could ever remember slumbering—he would listen to the sounds of his friends shifting about during their dreams, of an occasional carriage passing by, and he would stare out at the sky and wonder where Lucas was, what he was doing at that very moment.

Long and often he thought about the house in the country—the one he wasn't supposed to know about, or ever have seen, lest the duke's men catch him and force him to tell—but he hadn't been able to stop himself from following Lucas home in order to see how the man lived. Surprisingly the beautiful princess, Miss Penelope, lived there too.

He'd often imagined sitting down at the table in the kitchen that he saw whenever he peeked in the windows while sneaking around secretly to visit Harry. In his reveries Miss Penelope would feed him supper. His stomach growled every time he conjured the tranquil scene.

Sometimes, but not too regularly, he'd close his eyes and pretend he was Harry's older brother, that he resided in the grand house with the boy, and that Lucas and Miss Penelope were his parents. The vision was painful and always left him feeling sick afterward, although he didn't understand why. If he'd been older or more mature, he might have recognized the sensation as a desperate yearning for a type of love and affection he'd never encountered.

Since that pretty view was too difficult to contemplate, he would quickly switch to another, more masculine setting. In this Lucas was ready to leave England. He would pat Paulie on the back, telling him how brave he was, how smart, and he'd insist Paulie was such an invaluable partner that he couldn't be left behind. Paulie could easily picture the two of them out on the middle of the ocean, standing on the deck of the *Sea Wind,* bracing their feet as the ship crested and dipped with each roll of the waves. They would sail the seas and fight pirates and find treasure and rescue beautiful women who were in danger. . . .

His gaze moved from Lucas to scan the other patrons. They were a rough-looking group of characters, deep in their cups, sitting in twos and threes and passing the time with ribald chatter. However, one man was by himself and regarding the two brothers with more interest than he should have. Paulie had to admit that it was difficult *not* to notice the two Americans. Their size and looks definitely made them stand out in a crowd, but this man was paying much more attention than casual curiosity demanded.

He finished off his mug of dark brew, slipped a coin onto the table, then exited, but not before pausing to take one last glance over his shoulder at the two brothers. As he walked out the door, Paulie melted against the wall, becoming invisible.

The man strode to the corner, where another man was just coming out of an eating establishment. The two talked quietly but animatedly, the first one pointing toward the tavern where Lucas and Matthew believed themselves to be shielded from prying eyes. The second man nodded, whispered something, then hurried away. The first leaned against the front of the restaurant, much as Paulie was doing, and he kept shifting back and forth so that he could keep a clear view of the tavern's door.

Paulie didn't like the looks of this suspicious circumstance one bit.

Turning to the window, he peered inside again. Whatever topic Lucas and Matthew were discussing was causing both of them to proceed past caution and restraint. Paulie looked at them, then looked down the street to where the man continued to wait. The brothers' argument grew more vehement; the man on the corner was joined by several others. They were tough, rugged men wearing bulging coats that no doubt shielded clubs and pistols. Making plans, they huddled together for a few moments, then the one who appeared to be the leader gave a nod, and they headed toward the tavern.

* * *

Matthew glared across the table, keeping his voice low. "Which room are you sleeping in? Isn't it the upstairs one on the left?"

"Yes," Lucas answered. "Why?"

It was dangerous for them to be seen together, but matters were coming to a head with Westmoreland, and they had decided that the affair could be resolved more quickly if they were both in town during this last flurry of notes and responses. Although they'd come to the city separately and arrived individually at the tavern, Lucas still couldn't get past the impression that every eye in the place was upon them, even though he knew it wasn't so.

On the handful of occasions when he'd glanced about, no one was paying them any mind. He and Matthew appeared to be two workingmen who were enjoying some afternoon refreshment. If any of the other customers were perusing the crowd, it was because the establishment was filled with cut-throats and ruthless characters, the kind you couldn't turn your back on. His fellow troublemakers were occasionally curious, but it didn't have anything to do with Lucas personally. Elevated observation on everyone's part was the reality of the place.

Very likely his perception of a heightened scrutiny was caused by the increasing pressures of the furtive endeavor in which they were engaged, and he would be heartily glad when it was all completed. His patience was at an end, his tolerance for nonsense—never high—completely gone, his mind exhausted by the hours he'd spent trying to come up with an acceptable conclusion.

Factor in his lack of sleep due to his nighttime antics with Penny, and he was like a vicious dog on a short leash, ready to bark and bite at whoever came near. Mix in some guilt and remorse, some lies and continued deception, some joy and heartache, and all told he was a bubbling inferno of irritation and exasperation, and he pitied any man who dared approach too closely.

Apparently Matthew was preoccupied enough with their situation that he didn't have the good sense to notice Lucas's volatile condition and to back off because of it.

"I stopped by the barn last night," Matthew said, his teeth clenched, his fists curled, "in order to grab some braiding to repair my saddle, and guess what I saw?"

"What?" Lucas said, worn down, and not in the mood for any kind of game his brother wanted to play.

"I saw Miss Westmoreland standing at the window. The top one," he said tightly. "On the left." He leaned closer, whispering harshly, "Of course, it may have been just the shadows, but I don't believe she was wearing any clothes!"

Lucas regarded him with a deadly calm. "And your point is?"

"My point is," he hissed, "that I would like to know why the bloody hell she was naked in your room!"

"Why do you think she was there?" he asked crudely.

"You mad bastard!" Matthew taunted. "What have you done?"

"What do you think I've done?" Lucas asked caustically. "I didn't have any choice about it!"

"No choice? No choice?" he asked, the volume rising with each exchange. Others were starting to notice them. "How are old are you? Fifteen? Sixteen?"

"She believes we are married," Lucas responded, voicing the inadequate lie, and even as he spoke it aloud, he knew how unsatisfactory his explanation sounded. "She expected me to act accordingly."

Matthew assessed him, finally shaking his head in disgust. "When she came into our care, she was a maiden. We agreed we would send her home unharmed."

"Well, it didn't work out that way, did it?"

"We can't fix this! Not ever!"

"Don't you think I realize that?"

Matthew leaned closer still, his angry gaze like a visible slap. "What if you've given her a child?"

"Leave it, Matthew. I'm warning you," Lucas said dangerously. "Leave it be!"

"I won't," his brother said, pushing an irritating finger into Lucas's chest. "You're going to make this right. You're going to marry her! Tomorrow, if I can arrange it by then!"

"My, aren't we quick to change our tune?" Lucas swatted Matthew's hand away. At the acrimonious motion, more men stared, and a few, sensing impending fisticuffs, grabbed their mugs and moved out of reach. "I thought you felt I was a lowly commoner, too far beneath her lofty status to become her husband."

"Considering your behavior, I'd say it's far too late to worry about the details." Matthew nodded gravely, his mind made up. "You're going to marry her. I'll try to get one of those special licenses I've heard about, but if I can't, we will bring her on board the ship, sail out onto the river, and I'll perform the blasted ceremony myself. I'll make it real this time, and it will serve you right!"

"How are we going to accomplish such a feat? Am I to bind her, then carry her, kicking and screaming, down to the docks?"

"Just get her there. I don't care how you go about it."

"Well, you should. She thinks we're already married. I could never rationalize the situation so that she would peacefully agree to go along."

"Then you'll have to explain it to her so that she understands and agrees. And explain it you shall!"

"And you deem that marrying her a second time is the answer? That another wedding will finish it?" Lucas shook his head at Matthew's naïveté, at his obtuseness that all could be remedied so simply. "It will never be over! If I could convince her to go through with the ceremony again—which I have to tell you, from knowing her as I do, such an event is highly unlikely—her father will demand my head for it, and he'll chase us to the ends of the earth to have his revenge."

"If we send her home ruined, you don't anticipate he'll do the same? Although it's clear the man despises her, there are some indignities that even the worst father won't tolerate. This has to be one of them."

Lucas drummed his fingers against the table, a muscle in his jaw twitching perilously. He craved nothing more than to lash out, and Matthew was precariously close to pushing him past his limits. "All right," he finally said tersely. "It's over. We'll put in a call to the crew, we'll sail away, and we'll take her with us. We'll figure out what to do with her later."

"No," Matthew said, deadly calm. "You are the one who's wrecked this girl's life, and you are going to repair it."

"There is no valid atonement I can make!"

"That's what you think!" Matthew insisted. "Through all this, I felt justified by the fact that we are honorable men trying to rectify a grave wrong. But you're no better than Westmoreland."

"Take it back!" Lucas shouted, beyond the point of worrying about who was listening or observing. He might have decided on his own that he and the duke were two of a kind, but he was too angry to allow someone else to utter the same condemnation.

"I shall not! It's the bloody truth!"

They rose to their feet. The table between them went flying, and mugs of ale sloshed against Lucas, spilling down his front and soaking his clothing, but he didn't notice. As the liquid splashed, he was throwing the first punch. Bone connected squarely with bone, and it felt grand to vent the frustration that had been building for weeks. Matthew's head snapped to the side, but he didn't so much as stagger before swinging with a hard right of his own.

None of the patrons knew either man, so no one joined in. All stepped out of range, happy to watch as the two skilled combatants had at each other, landing one stunning blow after the next. Both were so enraged by their argument that they hardly appeared to feel them. Sweat flew, blood fell, cloth tore.

The bartender made a single attempt to intervene, slamming a club on the bar with an imposing *whack,* but when neither man paid him any attention, he turned his efforts to moving furniture, trying to save as many tables as possible.

Lucas circled with his brother, all the while cogitating that it had been years since he'd gone the rounds with Matthew. Perhaps it was Lucas's age, but it certainly seemed as though Matthew had gotten to be a much better fighter. He'd received numerous solid jabs but wasn't slowing in the least, and Lucas couldn't help wondering how long they'd keep at it. How long would it take for their rage to be completely spent?

Would they kill each other before it was over?

Matthew sagged, and Lucas surged forward to take advantage, when suddenly his weight shifted and he couldn't lift his arm. A hand went about his throat; he felt himself losing his air.

"What the devil?" he muttered, spinning and struggling. There appeared to be a monkey on his back, someone small, and the spectators had begun laughing at the sight. He took his focus off Matthew and twirled as Paulie slid to the floor.

"The duke's men!" Paulie warned, his eyes wide, his breathing labored. "Someone spotted you. They're outside."

Lucas had to pause for several moments to allow his head to clear so that he could make out the import of what the boy was saying. As it was, he could barely see the lad; an eye was swelling shut, and a deep gash on his forehead spilled blood down his face.

Gathering his wits, he managed to ask, "How many?"

"Half a dozen."

"Armed?"

"Yes."

His regard settled on the bartender. "Is there another way out of here?"

The bartender didn't respond until Lucas pulled out a bag heavy with coin and tossed it. The man caught it in a tight fist.

"Aye," he said, jerking his head toward the back.

Lucas asked Paulie, "Can you help me through the alleys?"

"Yes," he nodded confidently, "but we've got to go. We can't dally."

Lucas looked around the room, taking in as many of the desperate characters as he could. "It's the law, gentlemen," he announced, which caused many of them to murmur with agitation, "and they'll be stretching my neck if given the chance. I'd appreciate any head start you can offer me."

A few of the more quick-thinking among them started pushing tables and chairs back into place and relaxing as though nothing untoward had just occurred.

His furious gaze rested on Matthew, and his brother vowed, "This isn't finished between us."

"No, it isn't," Lucas agreed.

"Now, off with you!" Matthew wiped blood from his face while gesturing toward the escape route provided by the bartender. "Before it's too late."

Lucas nodded, then turned to Paulie. The boy grabbed his hand and pulled him along. A serving girl held the door open.

"Good luck," she called as they rushed into the alley, and they were two blocks away when Westmoreland's men burst into the room in a tight pack. But there was no sign that Lucas Pendleton had been there, no sign of a recent brawl, no sign of the man with whom Pendleton had allegedly been talking. The table where he'd supposedly been spotted had two customers sitting at it, their glasses half full, and neither of them looked anything like the man for whom they were searching.

They tried asking a few questions, but the stormy attitudes and stony silences with which they were greeted quickly convinced them that either Pendleton had escaped or he'd never been there in the first place. Greatly outmatched by the lawless bunch, they left as quickly as they'd come, so they didn't see Matthew hiding underneath the bar with a dirty towel pressed to his wounds, or the handful of broken table legs and chairs that had been hastily pushed along the wall and shielded from view by the customers' feet and trousers.

As the duke's men departed, milling about in the street and trying to decide where they should proceed next, further pursuit would have proved futile, for Lucas and Paulie were no longer in the neighborhood. They'd twisted through the maze of narrow streets and alleys, moving more and more slowly. Lucas's energy was spent, a few ribs cracked, his wrist sprained, blood still running freely and dripping onto his shirt and pants. Paulie urged him on until he could hardly keep the older man going.

Although they were passing through the roughest parts of London, they still turned heads, and Paulie was worried about being remembered or the possibility that others would notice what direction they'd been traveling. He led Lucas to an abandoned building and sat him on the filthy floor, out of sight, behind the door.

A small pistol was stuck in Lucas's boot, and Paulie removed it and steadied it in Lucas's hand. When the man couldn't do more on his own, Paulie wrapped Lucas's fingers around the trigger, then ran off, his mind on his mission, trying not to fret over the likelihood that Lucas would be discovered before he could return.

Thirty minutes later he breathed a sigh of relief as he slipped into the shadows and found Lucas still propped against the wall, just where he'd been deposited.

The barrel of the gun came up as Paulie stepped inside, telling him that Lucas wasn't quite as bad off as he outwardly appeared.

"That you, Paulie boy?" Lucas asked.

"Yes, sir," Paulie answered.

"Did you find what you needed?"

"I did," he said, and he came forward, but not before taking a quick peek down the alley to see if anyone had detected him entering. There was one cluster of boys at the other end, but they paid no attention. He laid the pilfered items on the squalid planking, pleased when Lucas attempted a smile, though he quickly squelched it when his lip started bleeding again.

"A veritable treasure trove," Lucas said.

"I'm a handy fellow to have about," Paulie replied prudently.

"I beginning to see that."

"You have to help me," Paulie remarked.

Lucas leaned forward, and they eased his ruined shirt over his head. His ribs were swollen and blue, the skin cut and oozing blood in numerous spots. The sight brought tears to Paulie's eyes, which made him feel like a baby, so he was careful not to let Lucas see his distress. A considerate stranger had been foolish enough to leave a clean shirt hanging on a line, so Paulie had stolen it without a thought. It was tight on Lucas's broad frame, but it served its purpose, and Paulie hastily pulled the bottom down, hiding Lucas's injuries so he wouldn't have to witness them.

"You're a crazy man, you are," Paulie mused.

"Not the first time I've heard that," Lucas admitted. He shifted, the pain in his side intense, and he grimaced, running a bruised hand over the damage. "My brother hits a lot harder than I remember. . . ."

Paulie didn't respond but set about his work, holding a cloth against the scalp laceration and wiping Lucas's hands. Once the bleeding had slowed to a minimum, he tugged a purloined hat over Lucas's head, dropping the brim, and it did a fair job of hiding his face and its injuries.

"Why were you fighting?" He hadn't meant to ask, but he'd never seen the likes.

"Over a woman, Paulie. Don't ever do anything so absurd."

"I won't," he vowed. There were many topics over which he might come to blows, but a female was hardly one of them, though he had to admit he might engage in a brawl for a woman like Miss Penelope. He couldn't help wondering if that's who had been the cause of the altercation. From the eavesdropping he'd managed, he suspected she was the reason for everything that was happening. He knew Lucas was keeping her at the house, but he didn't comprehend all the circumstances, nor did he understand the ramifications, so he said nothing.

"I need to get out of the city," Lucas said, "but after that run I'm turned around. I need to find my horse."

"I know where you keep him," Paulie blurted out. The past few days he had followed Lucas everywhere, unable to prevent himself from discreetly tailing the man, so the location of the public stable was another fact Paulie wasn't supposed to have gleaned. Lucas gave him a telling look, one of those that made you shiver down to your bones, but he didn't comment on the information Paulie wrongly possessed.

"Let's be off, then, my little champion," Lucas said, coming unsteadily to his feet and groaning in agony as he attempted a deep breath.

In a matter of minutes they were at the livery, the horse retrieved. Deciding that he couldn't let the man go off by himself, Paulie helped Lucas to mount, then climbed on behind. Somebody needed to protect his back and stay with him in case he couldn't complete the journey.

The trip was slow going. Each clop of the horse's hooves jarred Lucas's aching body. They talked little, with Paulie occasionally breaking the silence simply to ensure that Lucas was awake. By the time they rode into the drive of the country house, it was evening. The sun had set, and the last hint of daylight remained in the sky. The house and garden were quiet. Lucas brought the horse up to the front stoop, and Paulie slid off, waiting while Lucas swung out of the saddle, and his feet steadied on the ground.

"Can you make it in?" Paulie asked.

"Yes," he said, swaying toward the door, "but you beat it. If Penny catches a glimpse of you, there's no telling what might come to pass."

"I know what I'm about," Paulie said cockily. "She'll never lay eyes on me."

"I like the way your mind works, Paulie." Lucas smiled, and Paulie smiled in return. "Go now. To the barn and sleep. In the morning I'll see you make it to town."

"You don't need to help me," Paulie assured him, wanting to look capable and mature. "I can find my own way."

Lucas assessed him for a long while, then ordered, "No. You wait for me. Do you understand?"

"Yes, Captain."

Lucas patted him on the shoulder. "You did well, lad. I'm proud of you."

Paulie beamed with pride. He tried to respond, but there was such a large lump in his throat that he couldn't speak. Instead, he banged the knocker. When he heard footsteps, he gave Lucas a confident wink, then slipped off into the night, where he silently watched the unfolding scene from the corner of the barn.

The door opened, and Miss Penelope was standing there. Light from the front room surrounded her, making her look like a golden angel.

"Lucas?" She inhaled a sharp breath as she realized his condition.

"Hello, my pretty Penny," he said in his American accent. "It seems that I'm a bit of a mess."

"Lucas! What have you been about? Colette!" she called over her shoulder, then she turned to him once again. Scolding and fear were in her voice, but there was a hint of amusement as well. "Brawling, Lucas? You've been brawling?"

"Yes, love. Forgive me?"

"Oh, and you stink like a brewery." She waved a hand in front of her nose. "I didn't realize you were a drinking man, Mr. Pendleton."

"I'm not. Not usually anyway."

"Shame on you! Drinking and fighting!" she reprimanded him, but even as she did, she rose up and kissed him on the cheek. "You look like a pugilist I saw once at a fair. My goodness!"

"Did he win?" Lucas asked archly.

"No, he lost, and he emerged better than you! Colette!" she called again, then to Lucas: "Get yourself in here!" With her tender concern obvious, she wrapped her arms around his waist and helped him inside. The door closed.

Paulie spied on them for a long time. A lamp went on in the kitchen, and he imagined the warm room, the soft murmuring of the women's voices, the clucking and prattling as they lectured and fussed. Once, he dared approach and took a peek through the kitchen window. Lucas was soaking in a tub of water, and Miss Penelope was holding cloths against his chin and his swollen fingers. Much later a candle was lit in one of the upstairs rooms, and he managed a quick glimpse of Miss Penelope through the curtains before the flame was extinguished and the house grew still.

No one had remembered Lucas's horse, so Paulie did the best he could by taking the animal into the barn, removing its trappings, and spreading some hay. He thought about trying to sleep, but his stomach kept growling with hunger, so he crept to the house, entered through a window, and found some bread and cheese. Back in the barn, he chewed idly until all the food was gone. Then he took several saddle blankets to the loft and made himself a comfortable bed. He snuggled down, warm and cozy in the sweet-smelling hay.

Even though he was exhausted after the eventful day, it took many hours for sleep to come. He kept thinking about Lucas. And Miss Penelope. And Harry. All three were asleep inside the house, and he pretended he was there with them as he finally drifted into dreamland.

CHAPTER FIFTEEN

Penny strolled along the stream, pausing occasionally to look toward the house. She was alone on the property but didn't mind. In spite of her protestations, Lucas had gone to town. Harry, Colette, and the two serving women had walked into the village. They'd invited Penny to come along, but she'd declined, wanting some time to herself when she could saunter through the empty rooms and around the grounds without anyone interrupting.

After the excitement of the previous evening, Lucas had admitted that they might not be staying much longer, so she'd needed the opportunity for quiet reflection. Because of the hasty circumstances under which they'd married, she'd never considered the small manor to be any type of permanent lodging, but despite the temporary surroundings, she carried a fond attachment to the house and hoped to remember it always as a happy place.

She'd become a wife here, a woman too. She'd fallen in love with her husband, started learning to cook and tend to her very own family. God willing, perhaps they'd already created a babe.

Thinking about her husband caused her to smile. What a

man he'd turned out to be! He was the complete opposite of the staid, stuffy gentlemen around whom she'd been raised, and how she cherished the excitement he brought into her day-to-day existence. No telling what mad caper he might engage in next.

He was the wild type, who drank and brawled and returned home full of mischief and devilry, spewing tall tales and making a general nuisance of himself. Through it all, Penny had held her tongue but gave him mild reproofs so that he would understand that she believed nary a word of the yarn he was spinning.

The simple act of caring for him had been wonderful. She'd savored being needed and wanted, and it was grand to discover that when he'd been injured and aching, he could have gone anywhere for help, but he'd come to her.

If it hurt that he hadn't chosen to divulge the truth about the actual particulars of his negligent encounter, she refused to dwell on that fact. When the opportunity presented itself, she was certain he would, and she was determined to let it go at that. Their life together was too new, they were still becoming familiar with each other, and she didn't want to start off the third week of her marriage by nagging at him about where he'd been and what he'd been doing. He'd come home after it ended—whatever *it* was—and that was sufficient. It had to be. For now anyway.

She'd covered her disappointment by washing his cuts, kissing his wounds, and tucking him in, finding herself rewarded for her efforts by being allowed to tend to his carnal needs as well, and he hadn't even done his usual grousing when she'd slipped into his bed. Because of the amount of pain in his ribs and hands, the joining had been different from many of the riotous others they'd endured. Perhaps it was due to his level of fatigue, his impairment, or the fervent aftermath of his disastrous skirmish, but whatever the reason, his loving of her had been slow and gentle and nothing like any of the prior occasions.

The affection he'd shown her was so poignant that if she weren't careful, she might start presuming he harbored deep feelings for her. While she chose to remain guardedly optimistic regarding his growing emotional attachment, she knew without a doubt that he lusted after her with a reckless abandon. Just remembering some of their antics set her to blushing.

The man had unleashed an earthy side to her character of which she'd previously been unaware She adored the dark, naughty pleasures they enjoyed in the quiet of the night, so much so that she could concentrate on little else. Constantly she found herself checking the clock, and counting the hours until she could romp with her handsome husband once again.

To think that they'd stumbled on each other in her father's garden, and all this gladness had been the result!

"Meant to be," she said to herself, because that's exactly how she felt. She and Lucas were a perfect match, and he made her so contented and gay, she couldn't help but conclude that the crossing of their paths had been predestined.

Through the trees she could just see their house. The flowers in the window boxes were ready to open, and Cook had said they would be tulips. Penny wasn't well versed in gardening, so she couldn't know if Cook was right or not, but she suspected she'd begin seeing tulips before long. The country woman was right about so many things, and surprisingly she made Penny yearn for a greater knowledge of the real world.

Her upbringing had been so sheltered, with every chore in it accomplished by servants, it had never occurred to Penny that she might wish to learn the rudiments of something as simple as the growing of flowers. There were many useful skills she didn't possess: how to cook, how to mend, how to grow food, how to shop for household necessities, how to barter for goods and services. She felt like a total imbecile, one who perceived nothing about the ways in which an adult woman was supposed to carry on in life.

Well, there was plenty of time to improve at the tasks she needed to accomplish. She was dedicated to her role as Lucas's wife; she was determined, a hard worker, and an apt pupil who readily absorbed the tidbits taught to her by the other females in the small lodging. By the time they arrived in Virginia, Lucas would be so proud of her!

As her eye wandered to her timepiece, she told herself it wasn't an attempt to determine the length of time Lucas had been gone, or to try to guess when he might return. Though he'd awakened bruised and out of sorts, looking like he'd met with the flat end of a battering ram, he'd insisted on going to London, saying that he had pressing business that couldn't be delayed. No matter what arguments Penny had used, she hadn't been able to dissuade him, but she hadn't let him leave until he'd sworn that he would stay out of trouble.

The sweet promise and kiss he'd given her at the moment of his departure had almost made her decide he'd do as she'd requested, but she had her doubts. The man had too many secrets and was prone to finding the difficulty in any situation, so she could only tarry and wonder what his condition would be when he came home. That being the case, she put her worries aside, knowing she needed to keep busy so she wouldn't fret.

Back at the house, her bread dough was probably finished rising, and she turned from the brook and started toward the garden, contemplating the sense of satisfaction she would enjoy later when one of the loaves was sliced and fed to Harry and Lucas with their supper.

"Who would have thought it?" she reflected, grinning. Who would ever have thought that spoiled, fussy, demanding Lady Penelope Westmoreland would love to bake bread? Or that her incompetent hands would so quickly adapt to the routine?

As she'd observed Cook on the first occasion, she'd been fascinated by the manner in which the older woman's knuckles worked into the thick dough, by the yeasty smell that filled the kitchen, by the delicious aroma that drifted through the entire house.

After the cook had shown her the procedure, she'd been pleasantly surprised to ascertain that she treasured the newfound skill. There was something pleasing about the simple steps of kneading and shaping, waiting and watching. The process was

timeless and made her feel ancient and wise. Remarkably all
of her unease and apprehension vanished by the time she popped
the first loaf into the oven.

Greatly anticipating the next hour or so, she moved through
the garden. As she approached the back door, she was shocked
to see it open a crack. No one was supposed to be about, and
before she had time to wonder who it could be, a dark-haired
boy hastened out, cradling several items under the flap of his
short coat.

The little scamp! He was stealing! Right from her house!

He was a small, thin fellow who looked as though he hardly
ever had a bite to eat, so although she was alone, she wasn't
frightened. Without devising a plan of action, she tiptoed until
she was directly behind him. She was standing an arm's length
away as he pulled the door closed very softly, obviously assuming he'd escaped.

"Hold it right there, my good lad," she said, and he froze.

"Oh, no," he breathed. He hesitated for a mere instant, then
bolted to the right, pushing past her and losing his hidden
valuables as he went.

Penny came to the quick realization that the pilfered pile
was food before she took two swift leaps and grabbed him by
the collar, bringing him up short and yanking him around.

She blinked once, then again, staring till recognition gradually dawned. "I know you!" she said.

"Yes, ma'am," he said dejectedly.

For a moment she paused, trying to place him. "Paulie. Your
name is Paulie."

"Yes, ma'am," he repeated.

"We met on the street in London."

"Aye," he said miserably. "We did at that."

"You crashed into me." She narrowed her eyes in speculation, attempting to make sense of who she was seeing. "Whatever are you doing way out here in the country?"

He nervously wet his lips. "I can't rightly say, Miss Penelope."

"You can't? Now, that's a fine response." She pointed to

the ground where he'd dropped his stolen victuals. "You burglarize my house and take my food, and you don't think you can tell me what you're about?" Giving him the ducal look she'd learned from her father, the one that brought grown men to their knees, she added, "You'd better try to do a bit better than that, young man."

"It's not that I *can't* say. It's just that . . . I don't believe I want to."

"Oh, I see," she said, though she didn't. "Well, you certainly look hungry. Let's go in, and I'll feed you a proper meal. Perhaps a spot of dinner might loosen your tongue." Keeping a tight grip on his jacket, for she knew he'd try to flee if provided with the slightest opportunity, she reached for the door with her free hand and pulled it open, but he didn't move.

"I don't think I'd better," he said, shaking his head.

Leaning down, she pushed her face directly in front of his own. "This is *not* a request, Paulie," she said sternly. "Now . . . in!" He was light as a feather, and she lifted him off the ground and carried him much like a mother cat transporting her kittens. She deposited him in a corner chair behind the table, ensuring that there was an entire kitchen full of furniture and clutter between him and the door. If she had to block an attempted exit, she wanted every extra advantage, so she positioned herself directly in his path as well, as she ladled a dish of warm soup, buttered a few slices of bread, and set the lot in front of him.

Taking the chair next to him, she sat intimidatingly close. He glanced up once, then at the food, mumbling, "Thank you, ma'am."

"You're welcome," she answered. His stomach complained loudly, and she heard its rumblings. When he wavered, she picked up the spoon and placed it in his hand. "Eat!" she ordered softly but firmly.

He took one bite, then another. The food was consumed in a flash, so she dished a second helping, and he gobbled that too. Through it all she remained quiet, wearing him down with the force of her gaze. She'd had two weeks now of practicing the expression on Harry; she was getting good at it.

Finally he appeared to be sated, and he dropped the spoon into the empty bowl. As he continued to stare at the table, she let the silence linger on and on until it became oppressive. Eventually he cleared his throat, pushed the chair back, and started to rise, saying bravely, "Thank you again, ma'am, but I should be going now."

She laid her hand on his shoulder and easily pushed him into the seat. "I don't think so," she said, giving him a nasty smile. "We haven't had our little chat."

"Oh, ma'am," he sighed.

"Just tell me what you're doing here, and I'll let you go," she said, although her promise was a lie. She wouldn't allow him to leave. Not without talking to Lucas first anyway. The boy was obviously on his own, and she couldn't bear the idea of sending him back to London's streets.

"Perhaps it would be best," he remarked, "if you asked the captain about me."

"The captain?" she asked, not understanding.

"You know," he said, and his hand went to his side, rubbing distractedly against it in a small circle.

"No, I don't."

"Cap'n Pendleton."

"Oh, *that* captain." The title *Captain* was a dashing way by which to refer to Lucas. Is that what others called him? Perhaps she'd use it on him herself, on any occasion when she was sorely vexed by his conduct, which caused her to decide that she'd probably end up using it rather often. "So you're acquainted with my husband, are you?"

"Yes, ma'am," Paulie admitted grudgingly. "I'm not much for talking though, and he'd probably explain things more clearly." He asked hopefully, "Is he here?"

"No, he's gone into the city."

"Well, then——" He paused, pondering, then tried to stand a second time. "Perhaps you can ask him when he——"

''Sit!'' she commanded in a near shout, and the emphasis had the desired effect. He collapsed onto his bottom. ''You know, Paulie,'' she said, perching close by once again and giving him a feral leer that had him shifting and squirming and rubbing his side more ferociously, ''I'm beginning to regard this as the strangest coincidence.''

''Really?'' he asked, his voice coming out in a croak. ''Why would you say that?''

''Well, I met you in London. Now I've met you here. You're acquainted with my husband when it seems very odd to me that you would be.'' A sudden thought occurred to her. ''You know Harry too, don't you? My stepson? You're his friend.''

''I suppose,'' he said, kicking one foot back and forth under the table and rubbing his side.

She felt like a fool, recalling her first day with Harry when he'd been yammering on about his friend Paulie, and Penny had assumed that the lonely boy had an imaginary friend, never supposing in a thousand years that the two Paulies were one and the same. But Harry's companion wasn't illusory; he was very real and sitting in her kitchen.

What did it all mean?

Clearly Paulie was familiar with all of them, with where they lived and how they went about their business. Lucas and Harry knew him and about him, but obviously they didn't want her to know about him in return.

Why?

Dreadful details began to play at the edges of her consciousness. A small voice called out that there were dangerous events at work, events she didn't understand, events she didn't want to understand. With a frightening conviction she heard the voice growing louder, but she knew she dared not listen, for if she did, she would hear of critical particulars and secrets. Circumstances involving Lucas. Involving herself.

Colette's insistence that all was not as it appeared came rushing to the fore. Though the wedding had quieted her recitation of misgivings, she remained wary, eavesdropping on private conversations, skulking about out-of-doors after dark, finding excuses to go into Lucas's room to help the cleaning woman to tidy up and put his clothes in the drawers and wardrobe.

Always Penny had ended up chuckling over Colette's obsession regarding Lucas's intentions. The other woman couldn't let go of her opinion that Lucas was hiding something, although what it might be, Penny hadn't a clue. She'd found humor in the situation, blaming it all on the fact that Colette's exceedingly distrustful mind was working overtime.

Even if Penny had shared some of Colette's unbridled skepticism, she would never have examined her own doubts too rigorously. Of late she'd been so happy, so consumed with adjusting to her new status as a wife, and so overwhelmed by the physical delights of marriage, she refused to gaze closely at what was happening around her. Perhaps her strident inner voice had always been whispering in the background, but Penny had refused to heed its call. There were some pitfalls about which she didn't want to be warned.

Still, when a person least expects it, bad news has a way of creeping up, and she couldn't prevent herself from questioning Paulie further. "Do you come to visit Harry often?"

"No, I wouldn't say often."

"You meet him in the woods, don't you?"

"Aye," he breathed, in agony at having to admit his behavior.

"When you come, why don't you simply bang the knocker?"

"I don't suppose the captain would like it."

What was afoot? "Then, why are you here today?"

"Well, I helped the cap'n make it home last night, and—"

"You came with him last night?"

"I slept in the barn. I was hoping to catch a ride—" He stopped, offering nothing more.

After a long, deadly interlude she said, "So you know what happened in town—"

"Yes . . ." he responded cautiously.

''Tell me.'' His gaze darted around the room as though seeking help from some unseen person, so she grabbed his chin and held his head steady, forcing him to look her in the eye. ''What transpired?''

''Didn't the cap'n tell you?''

''Yes, he did.''

''Whatever he said,'' Paulie insisted, ''that's what occurred.''

''You wouldn't have anything to add?''

''No, I wouldn't.''

''No matter what?''

''No matter what!''

''How exactly is it that you know Captain Pendleton?''

''I work for him.''

''In what capacity?''

''I deliver messages,'' he said quickly.

''What kinds of messages?'' she asked.

''Don't rightly know,'' he said, shrugging. ''Can't read.''

''Were you working for him the day you crashed into me?''

''I believe I might have been,'' he answered slowly.

''But when we met, you were running from my father. His men were chasing you.'' Her heart began to pound furiously. The truth was hovering right at this very spot, and it was so precarious and so foul that she couldn't begin to fathom how she would develop the fortitude to proceed. Struggling for control, she asked, ''Who are some of the people to whom you make your deliveries?''

''The people?'' He started absently stroking his side again.

''Yes, who are the people!'' she snapped, out of patience. He didn't answer, but the massage of his torso became more frantic, and she inquired, ''Are you injured?''

''What?'' Seeing her gaze fixed on his rib cage, he dropped his hand and stuffed it under his leg, where he could sit on it and keep it out of trouble. ''No, I'm perfectly fine.''

She reached out and pulled back the corner of his jacket. There was no wound, but there was an envelope stuffed into the band of his trousers, and she yanked it away before he could stop her. He leapt for it, nearly retrieved it, but she jumped to her feet and held it high over her head, and he slumped down in his seat, looking aghast and defeated.

The parchment was heavy, obviously of the finest quality, and, therefore, expensive. The single word *Pendleton* was carefully printed on the front. "What is this?"

"I was supposed to give it to Captain Pendleton yesterday, but with all the ruckus, I forgot." He bent forward, his shoulders sagging, and the disturbing story came tumbling out. "That's why I came into the house. I didn't see his horse in the barn, but I was hoping he'd still be here so I could deliver the message to him, and Master Fogarty asked me to tell him that they found the ship too, but the fight with his brother popped up so fast, and it was so terrible—"

"With his brother?"

He continued on as though she hadn't interrupted. "—and they were almost caught, and the cap'n was hurt so we barely got away, and we were in such a hurry. I didn't remember that I had any of his messages, so I was going to talk with him this morning, because he needed to have them before he went back to the city, only he's already gone, and I don't know what to do now, and last night I couldn't go to sleep for the longest time. Out in the barn, I was, and I kept worrying about the incident in town, and hoping Lucas was all right, and I figure he must have left for London without me hearing him because I was so tired and I slept too late, so it's all my fault he didn't receive it"—he waved at the envelope—"and it's really important, and he was waiting for it to come all day yesterday, and he'll be waiting for it to come today too, only it won't because I've got it here with me, and I saw all the food on the counter, and I was so terribly hungry, and I didn't think you'd miss any, and I didn't mean to steal it because I would never do anything to upset you, and I—"

"It's all right, Paulie," she said wearily, sliding back into her chair and patting him on the arm, and he quieted.

She was torn by the spill of words and disturbed to recollect that he was just a boy. A child who had been lured into one of Lucas's schemes! He had obviously been extremely upset by the course of the previous day, where incomprehensible mishaps had swirled about the grown-ups in his life. Worst of all, the poor lad thought the adults' misfortunes were his fault.

The parchment lay in her hand, feeling like a malignant object, and they both stared at it. Finally she flipped it over and looked at the seal on the back, and she recognized it instantly. "This is from my father," she whispered.

"Don't open it, Miss Penny," Paulie said, begging with his eyes. "Please don't."

"Do you know what's in it?"

"No," he said, shaking his head. "And you don't want to know either, do you?" He rested his hand on hers and said kindly yet vehemently, "Let's pretend you never saw it. I'll just take it and make my way to town, and I'll give it to Captain Pendleton as I was supposed to yesterday." She sat stone still, so he declared, "Better yet, let's just burn it. We can toss it into the stove—the fire's going—and it will be as though it never existed."

"I can't," she said, still staring and wishing she could peer past the outer wrapping to what was inside. "I have to know."

With that she slipped her finger under the flap and broke through the glob of wax meant to shield the contents from prying eyes. A single sheet lay inside, and she pulled it out. It had been folded in half, and she placed it on the table and smoothed it flat. Her father's handwriting was distinctive, and although she didn't want ever to know what he'd penned, she couldn't stop herself from reading the words on the page.

Pendleton,

I've said it before, and I say it again. I have no intention of paying any ransom to bring Penny home. Her return is not worth a farthing to me. As she has been alone with you for some time now, she has no reputation remaining,

therefore she no longer has any value to me whatsoever.
You hold nothing I am interested in paying to retrieve.
Kill her. Don't. It matters not to me.

                                                    Westmoreland

At reading the last, she gasped aloud, and she covered her mouth with her fingertips, wondering if she might be ill. "Oh, my . . ."

"What is it, Miss Penny?" Paulie asked. "Is it something horrid? If they've hurt you, I'll . . . I'll . . ."

Penny glanced across the table at her young defender. He appeared so earnest in his offer, and she couldn't help speculating what in his youthful fantasies he might risk to do on her behalf, and she needed to quell any notions before they could form. Still, she had to swallow three times before she could speak.

"It's nothing, Paulie," she contended, appreciating that she hardly sounded as though the note were trivial, but she was too confused and agitated to speak about it.

"I don't believe you. . . ." Just then they heard voices coming up the drive, and Paulie peeked out the window, asking, "Who is that?"

"It's Harry and our serving women." Paulie jumped up, ready to run out the other door, but she didn't want him to go. Not when so much remained unresolved. She prevented his leaving with a simple shake of her head. "I want you to stay. Harry will enjoy the company."

"I don't think Captain Pendleton will like it."

"At the moment I don't really care what he likes or doesn't."

"If you're sure, then . . ."

"I am."

The women were approaching the back door. In a matter of moments they'd be inside, but she couldn't face any of them. Not now. Perhaps not ever. Especially Colette. What could she possibly say to the woman that would dampen the sting of this . . . this . . .

Betrayal, her internal voice proclaimed loudly. *Betrayal.* By her father. By Lucas. She needed time. Time to think. Time to understand. Time to come to terms with what she'd just learned.

The two men had been playing some unfathomable game, and she'd been caught in the middle. Of what? Apparently her elopement was merely part of some distorted plot for blackmail. Her father didn't want her back. Wouldn't take her back. And Lucas ... Evidently his affection had all been feigned, and with a shudder she questioned if they were truly married.

Had no one ever cared about her? Not her father? Not even her husband?

Lucas had obviously told the duke that he would *kill* her if his unknown demands went unmet. Would he? Could he contemplate such a heartless act after their numerous intimacies? Was she in danger even now, sitting unsuspectingly in her own kitchen?

Grabbing a towel off the counter, she wiped her eyes while looking at Paulie. "Please, don't say anything to them about all of this." She gestured toward the envelope and note as she scooped them together and slipped them under her apron.

"I won't," he vowed.

He tried to continue the discussion, but the door opened and Harry burst in, running with his usual spurt of energy. At seeing who was sitting at the table, he pulled to a halt.

"Paulie? Paulie! It's you! You're here, you're here." He danced around Penny. "He's my friend. I told you about him. I told you!"

"Yes, you did, Harry."

"This is so grand! Isn't it, Penny?"

"It certainly is." She forced a smile to her lips, but it didn't reach her eyes, and she hoped the other women were too involved in their arrival to notice the bleak look of despair lurking in their depths.

"Can you stay?" Harry asked Paulie, then he turned to Penny. "Can he?"

"For as long as he likes."

She glanced toward Colette, making certain her gaze didn't settle, and keeping her focus somewhere past the other woman's shoulder. "Colette"—her speech seemed quite steady, considering—"this is Paulie. He works for Mr. Pendleton, and he's a friend of Harry's. . . ."

"He is!" Harry declared. "He's my best friend."

"He's going to be staying with us."

"Can he sleep with me?" Harry asked excitedly.

"Of course," she agreed. "He'll need a bath. . . ."

"A bath!" Paulie exclaimed with such a degree of horror that Penny pondered whether he'd ever had one.

"Penny's big on baths," Harry explained to his stricken friend, "but don't worry. They're quite pleasant once you get used to them."

"And perhaps," Penny continued absently, "we could give his clothes a laundering so they'll dry during the night."

Colette appeared to sense that something was amiss, and Penny was thankful when she replied easily, "I'm sure we can find him some sort of nightshirt."

"Thank you," Penny breathed. She came to her feet, swaying slightly and stumbling blindly past the table, knowing she had to depart before she utterly succumbed to desperation. As it was, everyone but Harry was staring, her distress obvious to anyone older than four years.

"Miss Penny?" Paulie started to say hesitantly. "Is there anything—"

"We'll talk on the morrow," she replied curtly, rubbing the area between her eyes, where a headache was beginning to pound. "Don't you dare leave before we've had the chance."

"I'll be here," he promised.

"Now, if you'll excuse me," she said, hurriedly making her way out of the kitchen and through the front room, "I'm not feeling well. I don't wish to be disturbed."

"Would you like me to send up a tray for supper?" Colette asked to her back. The crowd behind her was absolutely silent and apprehensively awaiting her response.

"No," she answered, not turning around, not stopping, needing to flee the eyes cutting into her back. "I won't be able to eat. Just . . . just let me be."

She climbed the stairs to her room and closed and locked the door.

CHAPTER SIXTEEN

Lucas stabled his horse, taking much longer than necessary to feed him, rub him down, and make him comfortable for the night. He hoped the few extra minutes would help him locate the perspective for which he'd been searching, although he doubted it. He'd had plenty of opportunity to ponder during the long hours he'd passed in London and on the ride back, and he was no closer to finding answers than he'd been when the day had started. All he'd deduced was that his problems had grown to be insurmountable, and he had no idea what to do about fixing any of them.

How could such a simple plan have gone so wrong?

In the beginning it had seemed straightforward. Harold Westmoreland had committed a grave injustice against Lucas's family. Lucas wanted to rectify it. Harold's daughter had dropped into Lucas's lap, providing him with an easy method for achieving an acceptable resolution: He'd lure her away, hide her in the country for a few days, and use threats and intimidation regarding her welfare in order to win the concessions he sought from the duke.

Instead, the days had turned to weeks. The duke had refused to pay, not caring what nefarious thing might happen to his daughter as a result. Lucas had fallen madly in love with Penny but didn't dare tell her. Penny thought they were married, which couldn't be further from the truth. Harry believed she was his new mother, though she'd soon be leaving forever. Paulie had mysteriously vanished without a trace. And Matthew was, at that very moment, helping Fogarty prepare the *Sea Wind* for its return voyage to America which, Matthew had furiously stated in no uncertain terms, he intended to undertake whether Lucas joined him or not.

He'd always perceived himself as a strong, capable, intelligent fellow. How had it happened that he'd run up against the Westmorelands and, no matter what he did or what he tried, he ended up looking like an impotent fool?

With no more reason to linger over the horse, he patted the animal on the rump, then stood in the door of the barn, gazing across at the house. It seemed dark and quiet, but he knew appearances could be deceptive. Colette might be lurking in the shadows, ready to accost him. Penny was probably in his bed, awaiting his return, and like the worst sort of cad, he'd couple with her again because he was too weak to prevent himself from partaking of the delights she offered. She'd be hot, naked, and willing, and when he climbed under the covers, she'd smell so damned good, and she'd reach for him so sweetly, he wouldn't be able to resist.

While he knew he shouldn't enter the house at all, that he should stay far away, he also knew, without pausing to consider, that he'd do no such thing. He would throw caution to the wind and plunge recklessly ahead. Where Penny was concerned, he couldn't chart any other course. He wanted her. He had to have her often and thoroughly, and he couldn't contemplate passing a single minute of the night without holding her in his arms.

In his entire miserable life he'd never felt a similar connection before. He hadn't even realized that such an affinity with a female was possible, always imagining that it was the nonsense of romantic dreamers and poets. But their bond was firmly

established. It was real and overwhelming, and his heart ached
with how much he loved her.

And what man wouldn't?

In an extremely short period she'd changed into a new person,
one whose only goal was to please him in every fashion. She
had shucked off the stuffy yoke of her upbringing, easily and
joyfully adapting to her reduced circumstance as she went about
learning how to be ordinary instead of affluent and privileged.
She performed every act with an eye toward making Lucas
happy, and there was no question that she carried out her duties
good-naturedly and willingly merely because she was devoted
to him and wanted her presence to make his world more comfortable.

Combined with her ardor and concern was the fact that
she was a rare beauty, the most stunning woman he'd ever
encountered. Although she'd been sheltered in her contacts
with men and might have shied away from the steamier aspects
of male-female liaisons, she'd heartily embraced the physical
side of their relationship. She'd eagerly learned all he showed
her, taking the time to discover what he liked best and applying
her ministrations with a zesty delight, teaching him a few things
about loving in the process.

From the first, he'd asked her to be kind to Harry, and she'd
honored his request, going far beyond what anyone could have
expected. Effortlessly she'd slid into the role of friend and
companion to where Harry could hardly remember when she
hadn't been there. She considered them both to be her men,
and she watched over them with the ferocity of a dog guarding
her pups. Her gentle tending was extremely welcome in their
bachelor environment, and he and Harry had become so
attached to her, Lucas wasn't certain how either of them had
ever gotten along without her.

He was the luckiest of men. Or the unluckiest, depending
on one's point of view.

"What am I going to do?" he groaned aloud. The question
had been circulating relentlessly. Unfortunately despite how

many times he raised it, no answer was forthcoming, and he felt more wretched than ever.

And where the hell was Paulie? That morning Lucas had searched high and low around the small property, finally deciding the boy must have made his way back to town alone, so Lucas had gone on by himself. But Paulie couldn't be located in London. He hadn't been to any of his usual haunts; no one had seen him or had the slightest inkling of where he might be.

Lucas had selfishly exploited and endangered the lad, enticing him with money and camaraderie in order to convince him to help Lucas carry out his rash scheme, and if he'd suffered an injury, the damage was Lucas's fault.

Paulie's use and abuse was simply another sin to add to the lengthy list Lucas had accumulated since arriving in England. Very likely he could spend the rest of his life in church and on his knees, begging the Lord's forgiveness, and he'd still not find enough hours to confess all the wrongs he'd committed against those about whom he cared so deeply.

His own brother had thrown up his hands in disgust, declining to assist in whatever course Lucas chose in order to bring the affair to a satisfactory conclusion. Matthew had insisted Lucas bring Penny to town so that Matthew could marry them properly on the ship; Lucas had refused. He'd then demanded that Lucas return her to the duke's; Lucas had refused again, arguing that they had relayed a note to the man, saying they intended to kill his daughter, and the despicable swine hadn't bothered to respond. Lucas wasn't sending her back.

As far as Matthew was concerned, Paulie's disappearance was the final straw. After hours of exploring and meeting hastily to exchange information, it had become obvious that the boy was missing, and Matthew had determined that he'd had enough. He was sailing to Virginia with or without Lucas, and he intended to take Harry with him too, no matter what Lucas decided to do. He'd said that Lucas could scurry around England, casting about for his petty revenge and worthless retribution, and trying to salvage his wounded pride, until the sky turned green and the ocean ran to red.

In the meantime Matthew and Harry—the family members he loved so dearly and for whom he'd undertaken the entire senseless ordeal—would be gone.

With a heavy heart and his lagging spirits as low as they'd been in a good long while, Lucas left the barn and walked to the back door, only to be intercepted by Colette.

" 'Allo, mon ami," she said maliciously.

"Oh, no . . ." he grumbled in dismay, though he should have known she'd show her face before he could make it to the safety of his room. Didn't she always manage to turn up at the very worst moment?

"I see that you are finally home," she groused.

"What is it now, Colette?"

She laughed meanly. "I suppose you are thinking that you are on your way to my lady's bed, eh?"

"I've told you before, madam," he said sternly, "that my intimate moments with Lady Penelope are none of your business."

"Well, I am sorry to say"—Colette continued as though he hadn't spoken—"that she will not have you. Not tonight. Probably not ever again."

"What?" he asked, hating the wicked gleam in her eye. "What are you rambling about?" He glanced toward the house, recalling how from his view in the barn all had appeared calm, but as he paid closer attention, the silence seemed unnatural, and his senses flared to readiness.

Slyly she said, "Your friend, Paulie. He is a sweet, sweet boy. . . ."

"Paulie?"

"A little—how you say—*rough* around the edges, but . . ."

"Paulie is here?"

He turned to rush inside, but she grabbed his arm and stopped him in his tracks, surprising him with the strength of her grasp. "The boys are sleeping," she said. "Paulie is proud to be wearing one of his captain's shirts as his nightdress. He thinks his Captain Pendleton is a great man." She spat dramatically into the dirt. "But what I am wondering is this: What could this boy know about his beloved captain that would break my lady's heart?" Pensively she tapped a finger against her lip. "What could it be that this American has brought crashing down upon all of us?"

Lucas's pulse began to pound. "Is Penny awake?"

Colette leaned near, muttering remarks in French that sounded as though he and the future generations of his family had just been cursed throughout eternity. "I warned you, *mon capitan*."

There was a flash in the dim light, and he noticed that she was wielding a knife. It looked dreadfully familiar. "Give me that," he ordered, reaching for her hand and trying to wrench it away before she could hurt either one of them, but she was quicker than he suspected, and she stepped back, holding the sharp blade low, where any man would hate to have it aimed.

"I will find out what you have done," Colette promised, "and when I determine the depth of your duplicity, I will cut you open and scatter your entrails for the scavengers."

The woman was mad!

Shaking his head, he walked past without responding to her drivel. He crept through the door and into the pantry, and he paused. Then, nearly on tiptoe, he moved toward the kitchen, wondering at the absolute silence until he saw Penny. She was still dressed, sitting at the table with her back to the wall, a location from where she could easily view both doors. Though the room was dark, a sliver of moonlight shone through the window and ignited her hair in a shimmer of white. She looked ethereal, ghostly, and cold. Very, very cold.

The length of the table suddenly seemed huge, the expanse of wood looming between them large and unnavigable. She was turned sideways in the chair and absently staring out the window into the yard. Probably she had been watching as he'd ridden in, as he'd lingered in the barn door, contemplating all the ways he'd failed her, as he'd sneaked across the yard and exchanged insults with Colette.

"Penny?" he asked cautiously. "What are you doing up?" She didn't turn. Didn't speak. Didn't so much as appear to heed him. "I'm going to light a lamp." He thought she shrugged at the suggestion but couldn't be certain. Moments later a small flame caught, doing its best to bring cheer to the pervasive gloom, but it did nothing to warm the chill in the air or melt the icy fear clawing at the core of his being.

She continued to look out the window, toying with the edge of the lace curtain, and he wanted to implore her to speak, though he knew beyond reason that he didn't wish to hear whatever comments would eventually tumble out.

Just when he'd concluded she would never begin, she said, "I was thinking about Adam St. Clair."

"Adam?" He didn't recognize the name. "Who is that?"

"He was my first fiancé." She sighed, lost in painful memories. "From the time I was a girl I was advised that I would grow up to marry him. When we became engaged I was only seventeen. I thought he loved me madly, passionately. I was such a fool."

"Why would you say that?" he asked kindly. He had heard parts of this heart-wrenching story but never in its entirety, and he repeated what he always did when she'd shared a few of the details. "Who can understand the correct path at such a young age? You can't blame yourself for anything that happened back then."

"Do you remember . . . I've recounted how he resolved to marry someone else."

"Yes," he said.

"Someone he truly loved. Not me."

"His loss," Lucas insisted quietly, hating this waiting, this skirting of the issue. A vile topic was lurking and ready to be discussed aloud, and all he could do was brace himself for the pain she would inflict once it was mentioned.

"I never revealed all of it." She paused, still staring outside.

"He married my sister. Well, not really my *sister*. My half sister, I guess she'd be. She is my father's by-blow from an affair he had many years ago."

She waved a hand meant to encompass all of Harold's numerous affairs, and Lucas cringed at the implication that there were uncounted numbers of his abandoned children scattered about the countryside. How many were there? How many other siblings did Harry have about whom he would never know? How many would be thrown up in Penny's face in order to shame and embarrass her? And what about Harold's wife? Gad, no wonder the poor woman hardly went out in society. Who knew what she might encounter?

Penny continued. "After Adam and I parted, you can't imagine how many people delighted in announcing the fact that she was really my sister. They loved to recite how my father and her mother had supposedly shared a grand amour. They relished the opportunity to rub salt in my wounds and laugh because I was so horrid that Adam would choose a bastard girl over me. I heard it all. Every cutting, snide observation."

"I'm sure his preference didn't have anything to do with you personally," he said, realizing that any commiseration was inadequate.

"I saw them once, you know? Just last year." Her eyes narrowed as she gazed to a distant time. "I was at a garden party. The hostess was Italian, so I guess she wasn't aware of all the circumstances surrounding us, because we'd all been invited. Fortunately I noticed them before I went outside. They were with their baby daughter, and"—Penny swallowed a surge of emotion—"they were so happy. I was hidden from the other guests, so I spied on them for as long as I dared, and it was painfully obvious how much Adam loved them both. I couldn't help thinking that I was glad for him. I was glad that he'd found such meaning in his life, and that he'd been wise enough to have the good sense to pass me by. It helped to understand that he was truly fond of her. The realization tempered some of the sting."

"I'm sure it did. . . ."

"And I thought how lucky I had been to have escaped a loveless marriage to him—one like my mother's to my father— because I would still have a chance to experience joy with another. You see . . . all I've ever wanted is to find a man who loves me the way Adam loves my sister." Finally she turned and stared him down. "Do you love me, Lucas?"

He'd never admitted the sentiment, had avoided the strong emotion all his days, and the utterance was lodged so far inside his throat that he couldn't bring it out even though he loved her beyond imagining. What good would it do for her to know anyway? It didn't change anything. It didn't fix anything.

"Do you?" she repeated sharply into the embarrassing silence.

He flinched, understanding that he would have to muster the courage to confess what she meant to him, although before he'd even started, he figured he'd bungle it like everything else he'd attempted lately.

"Yes, I do, Penny. I love you."

"How bloody convenient." She tossed his declaration back in his face. Then, shocking him to the limit, she asked, "Are you armed, Lucas?"

"What?!"

"Are you carrying a weapon?"

"I have a pistol," he admitted. Astonishing him again, her hand came out from under the table, and he saw that she possessed one of her own, and it was aimed very much as Colette's knife had been.

Was he to pass the remainder of the night being waylaid by irate armed women?

"Where did you get that thing?" He fought the urge to leap across the table and wrestle it away from her, because her fingers were gripping the stock so tautly that her knuckles were white.

"It's amazing what sorts of useful items are hidden in this house," she said. "A woman can find just about any object she needs to get her hands on. Would it surprise you to learn that I can load this? That I can fire it?''

''No,'' he said, realizing that although she was fraught with tension, she was holding the pistol correctly.

''My brother likes to shoot. He showed me.'' She gestured in front of her with the tip of the barrel. ''Your pistol . . . I'd appreciate it if you'd place it on the table. Carefully, please.''

''What are you about, Penny?'' he asked, shaking his head in consternation. ''First Colette accosts me outside and threatens me with a knife. Now this!''

''Just do as I ask,'' she commanded shortly.

He didn't believe she'd shoot him intentionally, but accidents happened all the time, and he didn't want to see that tense finger squeezing the trigger any more tightly than it already was. ''I have to reach behind my back.''

''Fine. Do it slowly.''

He retrieved the gun, gently resting it on the wood and shoving it across.

''Anything else?'' she asked. ''Perhaps in a pocket or up your sleeve?''

''No,'' he lied. ''Nothing else.'' He wasn't about to part with the small pistol—his last resort—kept in his boot. Apparently she'd decided to accept his untruthful admission, and she pushed both her weapon and his own off to the side, though she kept hers within range. At least she'd lowered the blasted thing, so he felt encouraged enough to ask, ''May I sit?''

She nodded to a chair, and he tentatively pushed it back. As he settled down, she advised, ''Keep your hands where I can see them.''

''For heaven's sake, Penny! What's going on? What's happened?''

From under her apron she retrieved an envelope and tossed it across the table. ''I presume this is yours.''

His eyes widened. The note! Westmoreland's note from the previous day. It had to be. A thousand questions swirled through his head. How had she come to have it? What did it say? What had she discovered?

Obviously nothing good. He chanced a glance in her direction. The joyous, playful woman to whom he'd grown so affectionately attached had vanished, only to be replaced by this ruthless, dangerous adversary. She looked like one of those ice carvings he'd seen occasionally at fancy suppers.

The envelope lay between them, an inanimate object filled with prevarications and deceptions, and it seemed to swirl in confusing circles, making him dizzy just from gazing upon it. His hand ached to snatch it up, but he couldn't move. He knew Westmoreland; knew his style and his opinion of Penny, so whatever was written inside would be blunt and brutal.

"Read it!" she ordered, and the frantic inflection underlying her tone gave him the tenacity he needed to pick it up and turn it over.

The seal was already broken, and he pulled the parchment out and hastily scanned the text. Although it was nothing more or less than he expected, reading such a barbaric response made him feel as though he'd just received a physical blow. Penny had obviously read it too. What must she have thought!

He reread the last line. *Kill her. Don't. It matters not to me.* Severe, merciless sentiments from a severe, merciless man, but at least Lucas had had weeks to come to terms with the manner in which Westmoreland's mind worked. Penny had just acquired the cold, hard facts about her father, and it had to be a bitter dose of reality. Yet, at the same time, he couldn't help believing that maybe it was just as well that she'd finally discovered what type of person he actually was. She'd always suspected that he was a cold-blooded bastard intent on his intrigues and outcomes, but surely, this went beyond even her crystal-clear imaginings.

Let her have no illusions, he thought. He met her gaze with a steady one of his own as he tried to discern the best way of explaining why he hadn't, why he couldn't, send her home.

"I'm going to give you one chance," she said harshly, "and

one chance only, to clarify what has been going on, so I suggest
you use your time wisely." He opened his mouth to begin, but
she held up a hand, stopping him before any words could come
forth. "It's amazing, really, how accurately I've come to know
you. For you see, I can tell that your mind is already conjuring
a half-dozen stories that you imagine might placate me. So, I
warn you now: My patience is at an end, and I will not listen
a second time. I have cared for you, and therefore I am willing
to give you one occasion to justify your actions before I leave
you forever. If you choose to use this opportunity to spout lies,
so be it."

Giving a swift nod of agreement, he was stunned and frightened by how fast she'd made her decision to go. He had to
alter it.

"It's not what you think," he started, and instantly realized
that he sounded like an idiot.

"Which part?" She snorted in distaste. "You haven't kidnapped me? You're not blackmailing my father? My father
will not pay to have me returned? You're not going to murder
me?" She leaned forward and whispered, "Which part is not
what I believe it to be?"

"I would never hurt you, Penny."

"Too late! You already have!" She tapped her fingers angrily
on the table, her loathing clear and excruciating to witness.
"So . . . it's all true?"

"Yes," he admitted, his shoulders slumping with defeat.

"Did you inform my father that you were going to kill me?"

"I did," he said into the damning void, "but I didn't mean
it."

"How terribly lucky for me!" She stood. "That's all I need
to know. Good-bye, Lucas."

She rounded the corner of the table, and he grabbed her arm.
Though she didn't physically shake off his grip, her eyes were
like a pair of pliers, pressuring his fingers with her steely regard,
but he refused to let go. He couldn't allow her to depart, not

without hashing out the whole affair to its unbearable conclusion.

"You told me you'd listen," he asserted.

"So I did, but I find that there is no longer anything you could possibly say that would be worth hearing."

"Wouldn't you like to know the truth? I'll tell you every bit. I swear it."

"And now—*now?*—I should give credence to whatever crazed tale you choose to relate? What an incredible amount of gall you have! You must assume that I am the greatest dimwit who ever lived."

He swallowed, visibly unnerved by the anger that was flowing from her in waves. She'd left both pistols on the table, which was good, because if she'd still been clutching one of them, she might have shot him through the middle of his black heart. He'd have deserved nothing less.

"I've wanted to tell you," he said, "from the very beginning, but I didn't know how—"

"Answer me this! Are we married?"

"No, we're not." The admission came out more abruptly than he'd intended, and its effect was overwhelming. Her knees buckled, and he had to guide her into a chair lest she slide to the floor. Once she was safely reclined, he added, "But I want us to be!"

"Oh, God, please be quiet!"

"I won't!" he said. "I wish to be married to you more than anything in the world. I've been dying to repair the mess I've created, but how could I confess to you that . . . that . . ."

". . . that the ceremony was false?" she finished for him.

"Yes."

Tears welled into her eyes and began to fall. "How could you be so heartless? Didn't you have any respect for my feelings? Have you enjoyed one minute of genuine tenderness toward me?"

"Always! Always, Penny," he insisted. "You know it's

true. From the very first there was a special relationship between us. You felt it too! I know you did.''

"I felt it. You're right. *I* did. But what about you? You've been happy enough to drop your trousers at a moment's notice, but it was never more than that for you, was it?'' She shook her head in distaste, in despair. ''For you to sit here now, after luring me away from my home and family . . . For you to say to me that—on your part—it was love after all . . . That is absolutely beyond what I can bear!''

''I didn't intend it to happen this way!''

''Stop it!'' She placed her hands over her ears as though his comments were hurting her physically. ''Just stop it! I can't tolerate your alibis and justifications.''

''But I need you to understand all the circumstances.'' He paused. ''Please, Penny!''

''Who was the minister?'' she asked, struggling for breath.

''My brother, Matthew.''

''Ah, yes, your sparring partner.'' She laid her face on her palms, the tears coming harder, dripping through her fingers and down her wrists. ''Lord, but I am such a bloody imbecile.''

''No, Penny, no!'' he soothed, rubbing his hand along her back, but she shook it off. ''This is all my fault. Mine alone! You didn't know. You couldn't have known!''

He couldn't stand to see her cry, to see her distressed or unhappy. Spreading his arms, he tried to scoop her onto his lap, where he could cuddle her until the worst of the emotional storm had passed, but even though she was distraught, she realized what he calculated and fought her way out of his grasp.

Rising again, she took one step, then another, moving a chair in between them. Using it as a barrier. Using it as protection. ''You have the audacity to attempt to comfort me? After all you've brought about?'' His touch had become repugnant, and her entire body shuddered.

Would this be the way it would end? Would she depart hating and detesting him? No, he couldn't let it happen! He studied her as she trembled, and he said quietly, "It started as an argument between your father and myself."

"What could my father ever have done to you that would make it acceptable for you to commit so many wicked offenses against me in return?"

There was no hope for it; he was going to have to disclose all. Perhaps he'd always wanted to. He gestured toward the chair. In her condition this was definitely news she should hear while seated. Reluctantly she complied.

He commenced with "Do you remember that night . . . when we talked about Harry and his mother?"

"Yes," she said, still wary, watching his every move. "You told me you had just learned who had fathered her child. That he was an Englishman, and you were trying to—"

She stopped, and he could almost see the wheels spinning inside her head. When comprehension began to dawn, he finished her sentence for her. "I said I was trying to figure out how to handle the situation. Well, I had decided how to proceed, but I couldn't quite get the scoundrel to agree to my terms." He waited, letting the weighty admission sink in. "It's your father, Penny. The duke seduced Caroline while she was in England, and she came home a few months later and gave birth to Harry."

If he'd imagined she might perform some thoroughly feminine act such as fainting, swooning, or vehemently denying his charges against her father, he'd been absolutely wrong.

Laughing wearily, she said, "So . . . another of Harold's children comes home to roost." She stared down at the table for a very long time. "And that makes Harry my brother." The simple statement hung in the air, and she worked it over, pondering the implications and finally asking, "What was the purpose of having me befriend him when you knew we would grow attached but never be able to see each other again? Was I to be the mother for the week? Or did you surmise, perhaps, that I would have such an insignificant impact that he'd be able to quickly forget I was ever here?"

"No, it wasn't like that. Not at all. I was excited for you to meet him. I hoped—and I realize it was selfish—but I hoped if you ever discovered my scheme, that knowing Harry would lessen some of the bite. I supposed that meeting him would help you to understand."

"Well, I regret to inform you that Harry or no, I shall never understand."

"I love my family, Penny."

"*Love,*" she said, letting the word swirl on the tip of her tongue as though checking its flavor. "Of a sudden, you're certainly ready to throw it around, aren't you? You seem to think it excuses whatever insane havoc you want to wreak, but I have to tell you: It doesn't. I doubt that you even know what it means."

"I know exactly what it means!" he said fervently. "It's what I savor with you. I didn't fancy loving you. I admit it! I didn't want to suffer any tenderness for you at all. My goals would have been much easier to accomplish that way. But I love you, Penny. I love you more than my life. And I can't imagine what would ever become of me if I had to live one day without you by my side."

"You're very good at this," she mused without a single hint of emotion, completely unmoved by his heartfelt avowal. "Colette has always insisted you were some type of confidence artist. I didn't want to believe her, but I see that she was correct. You have an interesting ability to use just the right words at just the right time in order to further your purposes, but you can relax. There's no need to keep laboring so diligently. My eyes are open wide, so your gibberish no longer has any effect. You don't have to keep up the ruse."

"It's not a ruse! I don't want the duke's blasted money! I don't want his recognition of Harry! I'm no longer concerned about any of my demands." Not daring to touch her, he implored with his eyes, but it was clear they'd moved far beyond the relationship they'd once relished. She'd become a stranger, but he couldn't give up. Pleading now, he explained,

"I'm going back to America, Penny. In a few days. With Harry and Matthew. Marry me. Come with us. We love you and need you. Come . . . be part of our family."

He waited an eternity, his entire future hanging in the balance. Finally she responded, "I'm leaving in the morning."

"To go where?"

"Back to my father's house. Where do you think I would go? There is nowhere else."

"I can't let you. Don't you understand what he's like? How little you matter to him?"

"I understand. More than you could ever fathom," she said, "but I would rather pass the remainder of my days there, with people who have always and openly shown me their disregard, than to spend another moment here with you, where it's all been lies. At least in my father's home I know where I stand. I have no illusions."

She rose, and he rose as well. "Penny, don't leave it like this. . . ."

"Do you want to know the most ironic part of all this?" She didn't expect an answer or care what he might choose to respond with. "You did all this for money."

"No, no," he protested. "It wasn't just the money."

"Oh, spare me!" she jeered. "In the end it was all about money. And I'm going to have so much! My trust and my dowry. I would gladly have given you every last pound to my name. All you had to do was ask me for it."

"I failed in every possible way," he said, feeling angry now as well. At himself. At her. At her father. At his brother. At poor, deceased Caroline. At the entire bloody world. "I've made a mess of everything. I accept it! I agree completely! I'm a fool! An ass! A despicable excuse for a man!" He realized it was too late to make amends, but he professed his mistakes anyway. "There! That's what you desired to hear from me, isn't it? Are you happy now?"

"No," she said, staring at him as though he hadn't understood a single comment she'd spoken. "Actually I don't believe I shall ever be happy again."

The back door opened, and Colette entered. The maid was obviously a servant with many years' experience, because she didn't so much as raise a brow when her mistress picked up two loaded pistols from the kitchen table.

Penny handed one to Colette and kept one for herself as she said to her maid, "I'm going to sleep in your room." Then she returned her attention to Lucas. "I really can't trust anything you say. I know you've contended that you won't hurt me, but just in case you haven't told me all your intentions, we'll be barricading the door. One of us will remain awake through the night to keep watch, so it won't do you any good to attempt an entrance."

"Penny ..." he breathed, holding out a hand to her in supplication.

"One other thing," she said. "I hope, after all you've accomplished, that you'll watch over Paulie. That you'll get him off the streets and take him with you to Virginia. You owe him that much, don't you think?"

"I had always planned to do exactly that," he asserted, but he could see that she didn't accept his assurance.

"And I hope"—tears welled into her eyes again, but this time she refused to let them fall—"I hope ..." she began again, but she couldn't finish whatever she'd meant to say, and she marched by him and into Colette's bedchamber. The maid sent him one ferocious glare, then followed.

He stood in the kitchen, listening to the noises coming from the other room. They moved a large piece of furniture in front of the door. There was whispering. Then silence. Finally he walked outside to the dark night, where he could be alone with his tortured thoughts.

CHAPTER SEVENTEEN

Penny walked down the hall to Harry's room. She could hear him talking to Paulie about a horse Lucas owned at their farm in Virginia, how pretty it was, how fast it ran, how it had won a race at a fair. Lucas had let Harry sit on the animal's back while it was paraded in front of the crowd. For several minutes she lingered unnoticed, outside the door, listening to his tale as his young voice washed over her.

Although he spoke in his four-year-old manner of only the memories that had directly affected him, in her mind she vividly depicted the beautiful country day in America: the brown clay of the track, the green of the common in the middle, the owners' box seats with colorful red and blue bunting draped across the front.

It would probably have been a hot summer afternoon, the people casually dressed, the men in shirtsleeves, and ladies perfectly turned out in their party dresses, their skin shielded from the scorching sun by straw bonnets and lacy parasols. Lucas and Harry would have been in the middle of it all, stroking the winded horse while accepting congratulations from their friends and neighbors.

If she momentarily saw herself standing proudly next to them with a hand slipped through Lucas's arm, rounding out the portrait of a handsome, happy family, that was only to be expected. After all, that was the type of vision she'd often imagined for herself from practically the first time she'd laid eyes on Lucas Pendleton. The Virginia fair was the type of bliss-filled occasion about which she'd often fantasized, and as she tarried in the corridor, the image overwhelmed her senses until it became so real that she was certain she could smell the fresh-cut grass and the sweat of the tired animals.

Madness, she whispered to herself. *This is madness.*

None of her dreams was ever going to come true, and it didn't do any good to torture herself over what would never be. Her wishes for the three of them had been those of a foolish, silly female who insisted on believing in romance and grand passions, when she had been shown over and over again that such impossible notions do not exist. The girlish illusions that had sustained her needed to be put aside.

Reality was a bitter tonic to swallow, but swallow it she must while she forced herself to face facts: Her life would never be filled with the great ardor for which she'd always yearned. Where she was concerned, it simply wasn't meant to be.

Time to get on with the business at hand, dreadful though it was. She shook off the depressing picture in her head. There would be no trip to America. No home in Virginia. All that was left now was for her to say her good-byes and take her leave.

Pausing a moment, she was smoothing the creases of despair and worry from her brow and stepped toward Harry's door, when she realized that Paulie was speaking. From the questions he asked, and the topics he mentioned, she could tell that he was enjoying a fantasy much like her own. He could imagine himself in Virginia with Lucas and Harry, and she allowed one more brief interlude where she saw Lucas with both boys, and she couldn't help but hope that one good ending would come from all this misery. Paulie would find a family, and Harry an older brother.

Calming herself, she waited for a lull in their conversation, then she entered. She wanted to smile but couldn't. The agony in her heart was too vast, and she couldn't put on a false front. Not even for the two of them, whom she liked so much.

"Hello, boys," she said.

"Hello, Penny," they said in return. They were as subdued as everyone else in the house and had played quietly all morning as Penny had huddled in her room with Colette, initiating the plans for her departure. Neither of them knew what had happened, but they understood that something terrible had occurred. From the looks of it, they were both obviously braced for bad news.

Paulie, being the elder of the two, was more observant. He stepped forward and said, "What is it?"

"I need to chat with Harry. Could you give us a few minutes?" At being cut off from the important discussion, he gave her such a sad stare that her composure nearly shattered, and she rested a hand on his shoulder. "I need to speak with you as well. Privately." The reassurance appeased him, and she motioned toward the door. "You go on downstairs. I'll join you shortly."

He hesitated, then left. She stood before Harry, taking him in, tracing his features with her eyes so that she wouldn't forget anything about him, and so that she would always remember exactly how he'd appeared on this last, hideous day.

In the short time they'd been together, she'd come to think of him as her son. On the handful of occasions when she'd pondered why their relationship had deepened so quickly, she'd told herself that her affection for Lucas made it easy to love the boy. But when she added in the fact that they were closely related by blood, it made their connection completely comprehensible. To learn that he was her brother was actually quite thrilling.

Would he remember her in years to come? Or would his

four-year-old cognition quickly let her go? She hoped he'd recall her kindly, fondly, and often, even if it was a vague recollection, and when he was older, she wished Lucas would tell him that Penny was his sister. Lucas could explain how much Penny had cared, the reasons she'd left, and why she hadn't been able to return.

Uncertain as to how a young child processed grave events, she didn't want him thinking badly of her, or—heaven forbid!—believing that it was something he had done that had caused her to go.

She had to assume that when the time was right, Lucas would handle the accounting gently and tactfully, and that a more mature Harry would come away with a valid grasp of past history. But what would actually occur was anyone's guess. She was far beyond the place where she understood anything about Lucas and how he might or might not act. The riddle of how his mind worked remained one of the world's greatest mysteries.

Thankfully he'd left her in peace during the long night, a fact she knew for certain because she hadn't slept a wink, so she was aware that he'd left the kitchen shortly after she had, and he hadn't returned. When she'd heard the two serving women strolling up the drive shortly after dawn, ready to begin their chores, she'd slipped out of Colette's room and cautiously went to her own, with Colette following close behind.

Once the day was under way, she'd sent Colette to check the barn, and the maid had reported that there was no sign of Lucas or his horse. To where he'd ridden or why, Penny hadn't a clue, but it was typical of him to vanish, knowing she would be gone when he finally appeared. They would never have another opportunity to converse, she'd never see him again, and her last memory would always be of the angry words they'd exchanged that had brought about their parting.

The notion lay like a heavy ball of lead inside her stomach, weighing her down with the sadness of all that was lost, and it seemed to have sharp edges, poking at her with the most inopportune reminders of the asinine dreams she'd brought with her to the small country house.

Had it been only three weeks? How could one woman so completely immerse herself in a new life in such a short time?

She'd been a different sort of person before she'd gotten the chance to mother Harry, before she'd passed so many hours with Lucas. She had been so in love with him, and that spot— the one where she kept all her powerful feelings for him so carefully hidden and tended—that spot was empty, the overwhelming emotions she'd harbored replaced by remorse and bitter regret.

How was she to go to London and carry on as if nothing had happened? She was no longer the girl her parents had raised. She was no longer the young woman her father had manipulated and exploited. In all actuality, she felt no connection to those dreadful people. After meeting Lucas, the tether that had bound her to them had been efficiently snapped, and she had no inclination to see it reattached.

Her life was here. Her future too. She still felt like Lucas's wife and Harry's mother, but she wasn't either of those things.

Who was she now, and where did she belong?

When the boys had awakened and descended the stairs full of mischief and appetite, she'd fed them Cook's morning concoction of eggs and ham while she listened to their chatter, but even though she tried to display her usual enthusiasm, it was abundantly clear that something was amiss. A pall hung in the air, as though someone had died. The acrimonious comments she'd exchanged with Lucas hovered in the kitchen, and the boys were conscious of the tension. It was too overwhelming for them not to notice, so they did their best to cheer her, but nothing they did or said could coax a smile.

If they'd had any doubts about the seriousness of the situation, they vanished once Penny had given Cook a few coins and sent her into the village to hire a carriage and driver who could make the trip to London on short notice. To rent the conveyance, she'd paid with her own money, using the coins

Colette had sewn into her cloak on the night she'd thought she was eloping, and she was heartily glad that her maid had had such foresight. Her only other option for getting to London was to tarry so that she could ask Lucas for assistance, and she'd have walked to town before she'd have allowed him to aid her in any manner whatsoever.

Without question she was the biggest idiot who'd ever lived, the proof being that she still experienced such a surge of emotion every time she thought about Lucas. Despite all, she still wished she could see him one last time. Talk with him one last time. Touch him one last time. Lie with him in his bed, one last time. Her desperate longings pressed in on her, making her heart ache with a strain so enormous that she truly wondered if it might quit beating altogether.

How could she continue to desire him so badly? How did the rogue hold such power over her? Without a doubt, if she spent a second in his company, she'd be deposited right in the middle of one of his duplicitous schemes.

How could she still love him after all he'd done?

Fool! Fool! she chastised herself, shaking her head. She didn't have any valid reason to speak with him ever again. Nor was there any sane purpose for frantically needing to hear his low, melodic voice calling her name in good-bye. It was best that he was away, so there'd be no unpleasant scene in front of the boys or the servants. She'd be able to finish her packing and make her final farewells without interruption. As soon as Cook returned with a coach, she'd be ready to depart.

"What is it, Penny?" Harry asked, cutting into her reverie by echoing Paulie's question.

"May I sit down?"

He patted the bed, and she nearly sat next to him, but at the last moment she chose the chair instead, scooting it up so that they were face-to-face with their knees touching, and she was able to gaze into his blue eyes.

"I heard Colette say that you're going to town."

"Yes, I am."

"How long will you be gone?"

Tears worked their way to the surface of her eyes, but she tamped them down. She was not going to let him see her cry. "I'm afraid that it might be quite a while."

"Will you be back in time for supper?" he inquired.

His question made her realize that rationalizations regarding her decision were going to be much more difficult than she'd imagined. "No, I won't be back for supper. In fact, I've come to say good-bye."

"What do you mean—good-bye?" His face furrowed into lines as he tried to understand.

"I mean that I'm going away and I won't be returning."

"But where are you going? You belong here with us."

I thought I did. "No, actually I have my own home. With my own mother and father. They've been missing me." Funny how such a bald lie could slip out. Perhaps some of Lucas's deceitful methods had rubbed off on her.

From what Lucas had told her, and what she'd read in her father's note, she didn't know what type of reception her family would offer. But it hardly mattered; she didn't intend to stay with them long anyway. She required just a few days of shelter, where she could rest her weary, broken heart and settle her confused mind. Then, once she was feeling more herself again, she would decide what to do next.

"I don't like this at all," he declared. "You're to be my new mother. Isn't that what you promised?"

Had she really made such a vow?

She thought back and realized no, she hadn't, but that's how he'd perceived their friendship. Lord, what a reckless scoundrel Lucas was, bringing her into the boy's life for an abrupt encounter. "No, Harry. Your mother is in heaven, remember? I could never take her place."

"Who's going to watch over me if you go?"

"Well, your two uncles. Cook. There will be plenty of people ready to take my place," she said, hating that it was true.

They'd adjusted to her presence so rapidly; they would easily readapt to her absence. But how it hurt to think it was so!

"What about Uncle Lucas?" he asked. "He needs you. What will become of him if you're not here?"

"Lucas will be fine," she responded, although she couldn't help wondering what would become of him. She had no idea and refused to ponder his future. Whatever came his way was certainly disaster of his own invention. "He and I have talked it all out," she lied again, "and we decided this is for the best. My mother would simply be too lonely if I sailed off to America with you."

"I don't believe this is a good idea at all," he said firmly, playing the part of the little duke so well. His manner was so like their father's, and she winced when he said regally, "I should like to talk with your mother. I'll set her straight quickly enough."

What would her mother think of this boy? This love child of Harold's and Caroline's who looked and acted so much like the duke? Harry was the spitting image of Penny's legitimate brother and the duchess's only son, William. How would her poor mother take this walking, breathing specimen of her spouse's continual infidelity?

"Oh, Harry . . ." she murmured, smiling. "You are such a grand lad. I will miss you so." She gave him a long, tight hug. "I want you to promise me something."

"What?"

"I want you to promise me that you'll take care of Paulie. He doesn't have a family. Did you know that?"

"I did," Harry responded, sounding so grown-up.

"I hope that you will let him be part of your family."

"He can be my big brother," Harry said. "I already told him."

"I'm glad, Harry. I'm so glad for you. . . ." Then, because she couldn't say any more past the lump of emotion clogging her throat, she stood. "I need to be going."

"Not so soon, Penny," he said. "I'm hungry. Can you fix

me something to eat? It's dinnertime; I can tell from the smells
in the kitchen. And I want to show you a rock I found out by
the stream.''

Penny shook her head in dismay. He was too young to grasp
the concept of forever, and she couldn't decipher any method
of adequately defining it. Time would do that for him, she
supposed. Once the days and weeks began to pass and she
didn't return, he'd start to realize what she'd meant. ''Would
you come downstairs with me?''

He nodded, and she held out her hand, and he slipped his
small one into it. They reached the bottom as a wagon rolled
into the yard and stopped outside the front door. Through the
window Penny could see Cook climbing down. A weathered
older man sat on the wagon's bench, the reins balanced across
his knee. Cook spoke to him, then came around to the back of
the house. Once Penny heard her in the kitchen, she sent Harry
scurrying off in his search for food.

Paulie regarded the same scene, his twelve-year-old maturity
giving him better insight into what was transpiring. ''You're
leaving?'' he asked once they were alone.

''Yes, Paulie, I am,'' she answered softly.

''Permanently?''

''Yes.''

''But where will you go?''

''Back to my father's house.'' A look of terrible consternation crossed his face. She saw worry and fear, and she was
moved to realize that she could be held in such high esteem
by one so young.

''Oh, Miss Penny,'' he said seriously, ''I can't think that's
a good plan.''

''Why would you say that?'' she said, wanting to ease his
concern. ''He's my father. I'll be fine.''

''I've met your father, miss, and I have to admit that I don't
like him very much. He doesn't deserve to have the care of
someone as wonderful as you.''

''Oh, Paulie, what a sweet thing to say. . . .'' She ruffled her fingers through his hair, pleased that he allowed it. "You'll see . . . everything will work out for the best. My father's house is where I belong," she insisted without conviction, because she knew it wasn't so. Perhaps she'd never belonged there. Even as a child she'd yearned for so much more than the empty, emotionless life she'd endured.

"Does the captain know you're going?" he asked.

"Yes."

"And he doesn't mind?"

"It's not for him to say."

He glanced out the window at the wagon, where the driver waited patiently. "Would you like me to come with you to town? I could help you. . . ."

"No, thank you. I need something else from you."

"Anything, Miss Penny!" he vowed earnestly. "You may ask me anything."

"I'd like you to stay here and watch over Harry for me. He doesn't realize what's happening. I tried explaining it, but he doesn't understand, and I imagine he will be quite upset once he discovers I'm not coming back."

"He's very young," Paulie said sagely.

"Yes, he is, and he will need you. It would make me feel ever so much better if you are here to keep an eye on him."

"I've always taken care of the littlest boys," Paulie explained, "the ones who have no one else to watch over them. I'm very good at it."

"I'll bet you are," she said kindly, pondering whether his experience was one of the reasons he seemed so mature, but she didn't inquire about his life on the streets, or about the other children who shared it with him. There were some matters about which she didn't want to become enlightened, and in her current condition, excess information would bring more unwanted upheaval.

She simply breathed a sigh of relief that he'd now have a secure home and no longer be forced to pass his youth as a hungry, outcast child raising other orphans.

"I will care for Harry, Miss Penny. Always. I swear it." He paused, then asked, "Are you certain you're doing the right thing?"

"I'm certain," she answered, though she wasn't sure of anything. She knew only that she had to go before she completely lost the strength to leave, and she swallowed down a flood of unruly sentiment. "There's one other subject I need you to bear in mind: Captain Pendleton has decided to let you sail with him when he leaves for Virginia. He promised me. So if he attempts to go back on his word, you must be brave and speak up for yourself by reminding him of his vow. Can you do it?"

"Yes, I can. I'll see to it." His eyes shone with joy at the prospect of traveling off with his hero.

"And I hope you'll bother the captain so that he will teach you to read and write. When you've learned, I want you to send me a letter someday, to let me know what's become of you. I shall always wonder. . . ."

"I'll do that, Miss Penny," he said quietly. "Just for you, I'll do exactly that."

She left with barely a good-bye to any of them. The two serving women appeared upset and confused, the boys mystified by the goings-on of the adults. While she would have liked to give them hugs, kisses, thank-yous, and assurances with respect to the future, the well of fortitude she needed to see her through the morning had run dry, and she hardly had sufficient energy to climb into the wagon.

As it was, her knees failed her at the last, and Colette had to grab hold and lift her, sharing her strength as she had so many times.

"I've got you, *mon amie,*" she said compassionately.

"*Merci,*" Penny answered as Colette settled her on the hard bench next to the driver.

Colette tossed their two bags in the back and climbed up as well, and Penny couldn't help being relieved that Colette was not the type to ask questions or point fingers or crow with pleasure at being proved right. She'd silently accepted that Lucas had done something horrific, that Penny hadn't the stamina to articulate his terrible deed, and Colette was content simply to remain at Penny's side, the constant stalwart companion she had always been through the years.

The driver flicked the reins, and the two horses pulled away with a lurch. Penny looked over her shoulder once at the pretty house and green garden, at the quartet of servants and boys waving solemnly from the stoop. She didn't wave back, for she hadn't the mettle to raise her arm.

It started to rain, and Colette retrieved Penny's sable cloak from the back and hooked it under her chin. The driver turned the cart onto the road, headed for London.

Edward Simpson paced across the floor of the drawing room in the duke's home, eyeing the furnishings and knickknacks, assessing worth, and attempting to place pound values on each item. While his own fortune was substantial, his town house didn't look anything like this one, like a museum dedicated to wealth and privilege. He wasn't certain why his own residence didn't appear nearly so resplendent. His three previous wives had always been given free rein to enhance and entertain.

It was a question of style, he supposed, thinking that the Duchess of Roswell had it in spades while his spouses had not. Hopefully Lady Penelope had inherited some of her mother's abilities with decoration and decor. He wouldn't mind opening his door to guests if he knew they'd end up enviously surveying the surroundings much as he was currently doing in the Westmorelands's parlor.

"Penny, Penny . . ." he mused aloud as he drained his glass and poured another. He had many plans for how the girl was going to improve his life, but the manner in which she might eventually refurbish his abode was very low on his list of priorities. Other, more pressing matters would require her initial attention.

His third wife had been dead now for over four years, and
he was acutely anticipating the opportunity to enjoy once again
a nightly dalliance without seeking out a whore at one of the
brothels. He detested those places, even the nicer ones with
the prettier girls, and he wanted to luxuriate in regular sexual
congress in the privacy of his own bedroom with an attractive
female of his own choosing.

Certainly Penny came with some baggage and some problems, and Westmoreland believed he'd had the upper hand in
pushing the engagement. When the duke had first broached the
idea, Edward had even pretended disinterest, playing as though
Penny would be a great burden, when in truth she was exactly
the type of female for whom he'd been searching.

He favored carnal partners who were fetching and young—
especially young—but a man in his position couldn't go about
seducing adolescent maids without serious repercussions, so
he'd always rectified the situation by marrying girls who were
fresh out of the schoolroom, unspoiled, and completely naive
as to their marital obligations. While Penny was a few years
older than he liked, he could barely stand the wait for the
ultimate adventure he'd relish with her as his bed mate. She
was pleasing to the eye, and she was also overly full of sass
and uncontrollable attitude. But he knew how to temper that
sort of behavior through appropriate training, so marrying her
wouldn't cause him any undue distress.

He'd been thirty years old when he'd taken his first bride.
She'd been sixteen. At age forty he'd selected wife number
two, still in her teens also. At age fifty he'd managed to snag
a seventeen-year-old. All three occasions he'd chosen an untried
virgin. Their families, and the girls themselves, had been only
too eager to join their names to his, wanting the affluence and
title that came with the union.

Conveniently they'd all obliged by dying off about the time
their looks were starting to go, allowing him to bring another
nubile body to his bed, so he'd had plenty of practice at breaking
undeveloped brides to their duties.

Now, at age sixty-three, he'd have Penelope Westmoreland, by far the richest, most beautiful of the lot, but she had numerous bad habits, mainly talking back and making snide comments and rude insinuations. He intended to cure her of those tendencies straightaway. There were many things she could do with her mouth besides talking, and he planned to see to it that she thoroughly learned her lessons.

Footsteps sounded in the hall. A moment later the duchess, Patricia Westmoreland, entered the room in a swirl of blue silk, her matching slippers skimming across the floor, the expensive fabric of her skirt crackling as she passed. She had been a typical English beauty in her day, blond and blue-eyed, carefully raised and tutored in order to join herself effectively to Harold Westmoreland. Their fathers had arranged the match when the pair were children.

She'd stoically endured a great deal of nonsense as Harold's wife, and it was well known that Harold had never cared for her, had wed her out of duty and for the assets the alliance brought, but his penchant for illicit sexual gratification and his ongoing peccadilloes had tried even her unlimited patience. Although Harold went to immense lengths to keep his affairs quiet, everyone followed them and delighted in informing her of all the juicy details. The marital discord had now fallen to such a state that the duke and duchess never passed time together and hadn't for years.

The effects of the strained marriage were definitely taking their toll, although she did her best to disguise the changes with facial paints, hair rinses, and other feminine concoctions. Still, her fading blond hair was dull, her face well lined, and she was thin as a rail, as though food never crossed her lips. Edward could smell alcohol on her breath, and it was bandied about that she spent her days secluded in her rooms, where she could imbibe freely.

While he often did the same, he couldn't tolerate such comportment in a woman, particularly one in such a lofty position, and he wondered why Harold didn't get control of the situation.

''Well, Your Grace?'' he asked as she entered. ''What did he say?''

''I wasn't able to speak with the duke. Jensen informs me that my husband is out of the house.''

''Jensen?''

''Our butler,'' she said, flashing him a restrained smile.

The blasted woman had to ask the butler if her husband was home! If she couldn't keep track of her wayward spouse, how could Edward expect that she'd know where her daughter had gone?

''Your Grace,'' he started, trying to remain polite, but his impatience was beginning to rumble to the surface. He'd been striving to ascertain Penelope's location for the past two weeks, but he had to hand it to this family. They were frightfully good at keeping a man from discovering what he truly wanted to know. ''May I remind you that the wedding is in three days.''

''No, you may not, Edward,'' she responded shortly. ''I'm perfectly aware of the date of my daughter's wedding.''

''Well, I certainly feel that someone should point out how rapidly time is progressing.''

The comment was rude, but he was glad he'd made it. Something was afoot, and he was trying to figure out what. There were scores of rumors floating about regarding her disappearance. The most widely circulated held that the bride-to-be was unwilling to go through with the ceremony, and due to her refusal, Harold had beaten her so badly that they'd had to hide her away until the bruises faded.

While the scenario was indeed possible, Edward didn't believe it. He intensely feared that Harold had received a better offer. If he thought to force Edward into backing out of their agreement, he was in for a surprise. Edward had every intention of marrying Lady Penelope in three days. If Westmoreland thought to hide her until the date had passed, they'd simply set another, then another, then another, until the girl was produced and the event completed.

The papers were signed, the deeds drafted. Initial preparations for the wedding breakfast were proceeding, and nothing would change his mind. All was in readiness—except for the bride, but he didn't care whether or not she was balking. In fact, the idea of her being reticent made the deal all the more exciting. How marvelous his wedding night would be if she didn't want to go through with it. The more reluctant, the better.

Speaking of the devil himself, they heard the front door opening, and from the fawning attitude of the doorman it was obvious the exalted man had arrived. Without saying a word to the duchess, Edward rushed into the hall before Harold could make his getaway. Patricia was hot on his heels. Harold had pulled a vanishing act on the two of them numerous times now, and once he escaped to the inner regions of his private rooms, an explosive device would be required to move his efficient personal staff out of the way in order to gain an audience.

"I say, Harold!" Edward began before the duke had the opportunity to remove his cloak.

"Not now, Edward," Harold said, eyeing the man with disinterest. Although the duke's stare was impolite and impertinent, Edward fared better than the duchess; Harold didn't even spare her a glance.

"Right now, Harold!" Edward said emphatically, causing the duke to pause.

"As you wish," the duke responded testily, "but I'm extremely busy today, so state your piece and be done with it."

"I've come to call on Lady Penelope."

"And I've told you she's not here."

"Yes, you have," Edward said, "and I find her absence to be quite odd." Harold went very still, and a cold, calculating look came into his gaze. Lesser men would have been terrified, but not Edward. Harold didn't frighten him in the least. Well . . . not much anyway.

"Just what exactly do you find odd about the fact that my daughter isn't in the house at the moment?" Harold took a step closer.

''Well, there have been numerous rumors going around
and—''

''Rumors, Edward? You're listening to rumors?''

''I can't help it. They're rampant and vile. Perhaps if I knew
the truth . . .''

''The truth?'' Harold asked, suddenly appearing very much
like a dangerous predator. ''Are you hinting at something?
Questioning my veracity, perhaps? Impugning my motives?''

''No, Harold. Not at all.''

''Then what, precisely, are you trying to say?''

Westmoreland took a second step, then a third, until they
were toe to toe. The duke was bristling, as though he were
itching for a fight and the two of them might break into fisticuffs
at any second. Had the man gone completely mad?

''I'm not trying to say anything,'' Edward insisted. ''I'm
merely curious.''

''Curious as to what?'' Harold queried shortly. ''If you have
some valid comment to share, be out with it, otherwise I suggest
you remain silent. I won't have you standing here in my foyer,
making spurious insinuations about me or my daughter.''

Patricia came forward, attempting to intervene. ''Perhaps,
Your Grace,'' she said to her husband, ''it would be best if we
took Lord Simpson into the parlor so that we might discuss
this privately.'' With a quick glance about the room, she silently
indicated the excessive number of lurking servants, all of whom
seemed to have their ears stretched in the direction of the two
noblemen, hoping to overhear every word.

''We don't need to take it 'into the parlor,' my lady wife,''
Harold said. ''I've told both of you where Penny is. She's in the
country, and she'll be back tomorrow. Perhaps the next day.
Now,'' he added, turning toward his rooms, ''if you'll excuse
me . . .''

''I don't excuse you!'' the duchess said sharply, surprising
everyone, her husband most of all. ''I would speak with you.
Now! In the parlor!'' She didn't raise her voice, but the hint

of steel in her tone had all of them straightening. Even Edward came to attention.

Whirling briskly, she stamped away, each forceful tread accentuating her fit of pique. She didn't glance back to see if the duke and the earl were following, but then, she didn't need to. Her command had been so shockingly pronounced that neither of them thought to refuse. The two men were unused to any display of emotion from Patricia, let alone an outburst of temper, so they didn't know how to do anything but obey.

Harold shot Edward a glare that could have set the curtains afire. Edward shriveled from the malevolence in the duke's gaze, thinking that once he had the ring on Penelope's finger, his reasons for calling on the Westmorelands would come to an end, and he'd never have to suffer through another visit to this asylum of lunatics.

He tentatively walked into the parlor and headed directly to the glass of brandy he'd left sitting on a table. As he sipped, both the duke and the duchess gave him such rancorous looks that Edward couldn't help wishing he'd never raised the accursed inquiry into Penelope's whereabouts. Who the hell cared where she was as long as she was home in time for the ceremony?

"All right, Harold, we're alone," the duchess began. "Where is she?"

"You're questioning me, Patricia?"

Edward rolled his eyes, his stomach determinedly undulating with upset. If they were calling each other by their given names, a nasty family brawl was brewing, and he didn't want any part of it. "Perhaps we should discuss the matter at a later—"

"Be quiet, Edward," Patricia Westmoreland barked.

"Of course, Your Grace," he mumbled, and his meager response caused her to convey the full impetus of her venom to her husband.

"Answer me, Harold! This minute. You're not leaving this room until you tell me where she is."

"She's gone to our country house," he responded much too smoothly. "In Sussex."

"So . . . if I send a messenger with a letter, he'll find her there?"

"Absolutely," Harold said, gesturing magnanimously toward a small writing table by the window. "Go ahead."

"Liar!" she exclaimed.

"Oh, Lord," Edward breathed. A marital spat! And he was caught right in the middle of the dreadful scene. This was definitely more than he should have to endure, future in-laws or no.

"You always were such a horrid liar!" she hissed. "Now, tell me where she's gone, or I'll . . . I'll . . ."

"You'll what?" Harold asked wickedly. "Take to your room and drink the rest of the day away? Have at it, dearest."

"Oooh . . . you hateful man! If anything's happened to her . . . If you've done anything to her . . ."

Just then, more noise came from the hall. There were hasty salutations and running from the servants. Edward peered over his shoulder just as the butler knocked, then opened the door without waiting for a summons.

"Your Grace," he said to the duke as though nothing at all were amiss, as though the lord and lady of the manor hadn't just been engaged in a shouting match that could be heard all over the house, "Lady Penelope has arrived home."

Was Edward imagining things, or did Harold's knees buckle upon learning the news? He was certainly grasping the back of that chair with all his strength. Before any of them could move, Jensen bowed, and Penny entered. She was wrapped in her dark fur, her hair wet from being out in the rain, her nose red from the cold, but otherwise seeming none the worse for wear.

"Hello, Father," she said, a malicious gleam in her eye. "Are you surprised to see me still alive? Or were you expecting that I was already dead and buried in the ground?"

Upon hearing Penny's words, the duchess swooned. Luckily there was a small sofa directly behind her, so she was able to obtain dramatic effect without having to fall all the way to the floor. "Penny . . ." she wailed. "Penny, darling . . ."

"Don't overdo it, Mother," Penny said harshly.

The duke took a step toward Penny, but she took a step back. "Don't come near me, Your Grace," she ordered. "With the mood I'm in, I really can't be responsible for what I might do."

"Penny," he said, holding out a hand, "I've been so worried."

"Oh, spare me," she said, rolling her eyes in disgust. "Mr. Pendleton saved me from the indignity of reading your early responses to his blackmail attempts—"

"Blackmail!" Patricia and Edward burst out at the same time.

"—but I saw the last one," Penny continued without giving them a chance to interrupt. "How did you so delicately phrase it? 'Kill her or don't'! As if I could ever forget such a coarse remark." She shook her head in dismay. "Really, Father, how could you?"

"It's not what you think—" Harold started to say, but she rudely cut him off.

"You know, Your Grace, it's the funniest thing," she said, "but when I discovered the little game you two were playing, I confronted Mr. Pendleton with the facts, and that's exactly how he started out himself when he was trying to explain it to me." She placed her hands on her hips, prompting them all to jump as she shouted, "Spare me your justifications! I wouldn't listen to them coming from him, so I assuredly won't listen to them coming from you!"

"Who is Mr. Pendleton?" Edward interjected, a sick feeling coursing through his stomach.

"Hello, Edward," she said, noticing him for the first time and speaking to him as though he were a bug on the floor. "Didn't Father inform you?"

"Inform me of what?" He narrowed his eyes at the duke, but the import was lost on Harold because the man wouldn't take his gaze off Penny.

"I've been off with another man. For three weeks," she announced, apparently glad and happy about the whole affair.

"What?!" Edward and Patricia chirped together, beginning

to sound like a pair of trained tropical birds. Edward added, "Harold said you were in the country."

"I was in the country all right. With Lucas Pendleton. He's a dashing, handsome American. And, Edward, I'm relieved to be able to admit that I was *with* him in every way that matters."

"Oh, no . . ." Harold groaned, looking stricken. "He's a dead man! I will kill him myself!"

"Say it isn't true!" Patricia proclaimed at the same moment.

"What is the meaning of this?" Edward asked, aghast.

A soiled dove? Harold had sent her away for two weeks, and she'd come home ruined? When the nuptials were so close? He didn't want to marry her now. No sane man would! How could she have spoiled all his plans, and how dare she look so desperately happy about having done so? "Explain yourself!" he said.

"I was kidnapped."

"No . . ." Patricia gasped. "All this time . . . we thought—"

"Thought what, Mother?" Penny gazed around at their shocked faces. "Didn't Father apprise you of my circumstances?"

"No," Patricia responded, glaring furiously at the duke.

"Why am I not surprised?" Penny glared at Harold as well. "What was your excuse going to be when I was found dead, Father? Or hadn't you thought that far ahead?"

"Penny, hear me out . . ." the duke implored, using a gentle tone none of them had ever heard before. "I was positive he'd never kill you."

"How? How could you be so confident?" she demanded. "He might have done anything to me for all you cared!"

"I did care. I've had my men searching everywhere. I didn't mean what I wrote to Pendleton. I was just stringing him along, buying time until I could locate you. I knew he would never hurt you. . . ."

"Well, you were wrong about that," she said, tears welling into her eyes. "He hurt me in more ways than I can ever undertake to describe."

"What did the bastard do to you?" Harold ground out between clenched teeth. "I'll have him swinging from a short rope—"

"Oh, just let it be," she breathed. "I'm sick to death of both of you, with all your insidious male machinations and manipulations. I've come home just long enough to announce that I'm leaving."

"No, you're not," Harold said, endeavoring to sound authoritative, but his voice kept breaking, ruining the effect. "Where do you think I'd let you go?"

"I plan to purchase a small house. As payment for what you've put me through, you'll buy it for me now, and I'll pay you back when I turn twenty-one next year."

"I absolutely will not!"

"I'm not asking you, Father," she shouted, a whirling virago of uncontrolled female wrath. "I'm telling you! It's out of your hands. From this day forward I intend to live on my own, and I'll answer to no man ever again. If you refuse to assist me, I'll find a method of accomplishing it by myself. I'm sure someone will lend me the money against my trust." She looked over at Patricia. "You're welcome to leave with me, Mother. You don't have to stay with him any longer."

"Me?" Patricia stared around the room as though Penny might have been talking to someone else. "Why, I would never leave your father. Such things simply aren't done," her mother said, struggling for calm. "What's come over you? You can't mean what you're saying. What would people think if you tried something so outrageous? Now . . . you've just arrived home; you're tired and distraught from whatever has happened. Your wedding is in three days and—"

"Get this through your head, Mother: I'm never marrying, and I don't choose to discuss it further."

"What about me?" Edward interjected angrily.

Although he no longer desired her, he refused to become a laughingstock because of her antics, or—heaven forbid—be painted the fool because he'd gotten tied up with the insane girl when everyone had warned him off. Sadly he'd been so enamored of her physical charms that he'd refused to heed the advice of others. Why . . . she was hardly more than a common strumpet! And he'd almost made her his countess! He shuddered at the thought.

Caustically he asked, "What am I to say publicly?"

"I really don't care," Penny responded. "You may say anything you wish. It matters not to me in the least." She added ominously, "You shall have your version, and I shall have mine!"

The scurrilous child! Shrugging off their marital intentions as though they'd never existed. How dare she treat him this way! "See here, you little Jezebel—"

The affront brought Harold swinging around. "Watch your mouth, you filthy dog! I lay most of this catastrophe at your door"—he stomped toward Edward, grabbed him by the lapels, and gave him a vicious shake—"and if you utter one more word, I will personally rip your tongue out with my bare hands!"

"My door? My door?" Edward slapped the duke's hands away. "You let her trot off with some American, and she comes home crowing with pride over the fact that she's compromised, and you—"

"Me?" the duke growled in return, clutching Edward's jacket again. "You think this is my fault, you drunken sot?"

"I should have realized you couldn't be trusted, you bloody rat!"

They started to tussle. Furniture tumbled while they cursed and hurled insults, each seeking more and better reasons that the debacle was the other's responsibility. Suddenly there was a loud crash, and they paused, glaring over their shoulders at the new commotion.

Penny had lifted a priceless Chinese vase off its stand and smashed it onto the floor. Water, flowers, and shards of porcelain were scattered everywhere. Patricia sat still as a statue, her fingers against her mouth as though she might be ill all over

the floor. Jensen remained in the doorway, a brow raised in
amusement and surprise, one of the few times in his life he'd
witnessed behavior by members of the Quality that was outrageous enough to bring a hint of emotion to his face.

"Stop it!" Penny commanded, shaking with fury. "I matter
so little to both of you that I can hardly understand where you
find the energy to argue about me."

"That's not true!" Harold proclaimed. "I tried everything . . . I
did everything imaginable to bring you home safe and sound—"

"Stop it, Father," she spit out at him. "Mr. Pendleton confessed all. Save your lies for someone who is gullible enough
to believe them." She glowered at Patricia till there was no
doubt about whom she was referring, then she whipped her
angry attention back to her father. "Now, I've had a rather
arduous day, and I'm off to my rooms. Do *not* disturb me. I'll
be down once I decide where I want my new house to be
situated. Until then, leave me be! All of you. Just leave me
be!"

Edward couldn't accept that her parents were going to let
her storm out of the room after the trouble she'd created. If
nothing else, she ought to have a good beating right then and
there! He was still officially her betrothed. If they wouldn't
exercise any control over her, he intended to. "Hold it, miss!"
he ordered. "We're not through with you!"

"Away with you, you inebriated swine," she said crudely.
"Go ensnare some other unsuspecting child to inflict yourself
upon!" She stalked to the door but stopped in front of Jensen.
"Show Simpson out." Scowling at Edward, her malice was
clear, her resolve unmistakable. "Don't let him back in. Ever!"

She left the room, leaving them standing there in a bewildered
silence. As she headed for the stairs, they could hear her muttering, "Men! Hate the lot of them . . ."

CHAPTER EIGHTEEN

"So . . . that's it?" Matthew asked. "That's your plan?"

"That's it," Lucas answered, leaning against the rail of the *Sea Wind* and staring at his brother, looking dispassionate and unconcerned.

"We disappear"—Matthew snapped his fingers—"like illusionists at a circus."

"Yes."

"After all we've been through, this is how you want it to end?" Matthew shook his head in disbelief. "When the tide turns tomorrow afternoon, we simply hoist some canvas and we're down the Thames."

"I know of no other route to the ocean."

"We're off to America," Matthew tried again, "without so much as a bloody by-your-leave? Is that what you're telling me?"

"What would you have me do?" Lucas inquired irritably, tired of going around and around.

At his wits' end, Matthew threw up his hands in defeat. They'd been through this a hundred times, and talking to Lucas was like arguing with a stone. "Go to that fancy mansion of which they're so proud." He pointed off toward the heart of

London. "Ride up the drive, bang the knocker, and demand an audience with his royal assness. If that bumhole butler won't let you in, kick in the door and search till you find Westmoreland. Hold him down if you have to, but make him listen. Ask for her hand. Insist that you're going to bring her along whether she desires to come or no."

"You sound so certain that he won't throw me in jail," Lucas said with feigned disinterest. "I've become rather partial to having my head attached to my shoulders. I plan to keep it there."

"Westmoreland will do nothing of the sort."

"Of a sudden you definitely seem to think you know exactly how he'll act."

"What other resolution could he want for her? He's still her father. You're the man who compromised her. He has to know that this is the best conclusion for all concerned."

"I rather suppose he imagines that my untimely death would be the best conclusion."

"If he preferred that outcome, he'd have had you seized," Matthew insisted. "No, at this very moment he's probably sitting behind that grand desk of his, wondering what to do with her. You'd be giving him an easy way out."

"Taking an unpleasant burden off his hands, so to speak?"

"Exactly."

"I think you're forgetting a small detail."

"Which one?"

"Lady Penelope." He sighed as he spoke her name aloud.

"What about her?" Matthew asked. "She loves you; I saw how much with my own eyes. Just now she's upset, angry, and hurting, and she has every right to be. But we'll get her on the open sea, where there's no escaping, and you'll have weeks to work on her. She'll come around, mark my words. . . ."

"I wouldn't be too certain if I were you."

Lucas turned from his brother and the deck of their ship, gazing across the docks. Dusk was nigh, and the frantic commerce of the day was grinding to a halt. The traffic had thinned, the noise and commotion had quieted, people had finished their business and retired to their rooms. The busy carters and longshoremen were clogging the taverns, eagerly drinking away their day's wages. Sailors were beginning to stroll, looking for trouble. Prostitutes were calling out, hoping for business.

He watched with a curious disinterest, not really paying attention, thinking instead of Matthew and how quick he was to give his opinions on what Lucas should do. But his brother hadn't been present that last night, when Penny had discovered the truth. He hadn't been the one who caused her despair, listened to the words of anguish pouring from her mouth, endured the cruel sting of her wrath, or felt the bitter stab of her rejection. Mostly Matthew hadn't been there while her heart was breaking, while the fire of her love had been slowly extinguished, so he couldn't know how terrible it had been.

Lucas had viewed her from a distance that final, horrible day as she'd made her farewells to the boys and the house she had liked so much. When she'd traveled to town, he'd followed at a discreet distance, ensuring she arrived safely. Through much of the journey she'd wept uncontrollably, resting her weary head on Colette's shoulder. Her gait slow, her countenance despondent, he'd secretly observed her climbing down from the farmer's wagon and walking up the steps to her father's house, looking as though her life were over.

Matthew hadn't witnessed any of it, but Lucas had.

He'd seen her bleak expression of hopelessness. She had given him all—her love, her friendship, her care, herself—and he had foolishly squandered all her precious gifts. Heart and soul she had adored him, and like the inept cad he was, he'd casually tossed it all away, refusing to accept her devotion for the treasure it was. His idiotic pride and sense of familial duty had blinded him to what truly mattered, and now it was too late to do anything to rectify the circumstances.

Some sins were too grave to be forgiven.

Penny wasn't coming back. Despite how fervently Matthew wished it, or how long or often Paulie and Harry asked about her potential return, they all had to face the fact that Lucas had hurt her in every despicable manner a man could possibly hurt a woman. There was no reason to hope that he could ever be pardoned for using and abusing her so deplorably, and he was too ashamed of his behavior to ask for absolution. For all his offenses, he deserved to lose her.

"You're overlooking something important," his brother asserted, bringing him out of his reverie.

"What?"

"Suppose she's with child."

"She's not," Lucas contended, though he had no method of knowing whether his statement was true.

"How can you be so confident?" Matthew queried. "What if she's increasing? If you've committed such a heinous deed, will your honor allow you to leave her here in her ruined state? Is that how you hope to be remembered among these dreadful people? I know you well, brother. You couldn't run off without ever seeing your child." He twisted the knife into Lucas's most vulnerable spot. "And what if it's a boy? Another man would be his father. With the way your luck is running, Miss Westmoreland will probably remain at home with her parents, so the duke would raise your son. Is that your choice of outcome?"

Lucas couldn't admit that creating a babe with Penny had been his greatest aspiration. Even now, after all that had occurred, he yearned to discover that his child was growing in her belly. Only a miracle would bring Penny back, the kind of miracle a child would be.

In the dismal hours of the night, as he lay on the narrow bed in his tiny cabin, he closed his eyes and pretended her pregnancy was a reality, that Penny had relented and Westmoreland sought him out. But he knew without a doubt that the dream was just that—a dream—and it would never be anything more than a fantasy best left to his dark, midnight imaginings.

"Stop it!" Lucas seethed, refusing to contemplate his boy in the hands of the uncaring duke, not able to acknowledge what a hideous consequence he would consider it to be. "There is no babe."

"You can't be certain," Matthew insisted, "and the only way you can prevent such a debacle is by marrying her. Now. Before we leave. Bring her with us, Lucas. It's the only acceptable solution. You know I'm right!"

"No, I don't," he responded. "I don't know that you're right at all." He shifted uncomfortably, unable to further discuss the emotional topic. God, that he could do as Matthew suggested. That he could just walk up to their front door and ask to speak with her.

There was a terrible pain pushing at the center of his chest, and he felt as though his heart were shattering in two. He rubbed a hand across the distressing torment, but he couldn't ease the ache. Only wanting the agonizing subject closed once and for all, he said, "I understand her, Matthew. I realize what she's like and how she views the world. She would never grant me pardon, and she would never have me back in a thousand years."

"But you love her, Lucas. I'm sure you do!"

"So?" he said shortly. Matthew's statement was the truth. Lucas wouldn't even try to deny it, but love mattered so little. It didn't mend anything; it didn't change anything.

"Your level of regard for her has to count for something," Matthew said, sounding like a genuine romantic.

"No," Lucas said harshly, "it counts for nothing." He hated to see the dismay in Matthew's eyes, and he truly didn't want to hurt any of them, or further disrupt their lives, so he continued more gently. "My only motivation is to do what is best for her. Staying here, attempting to see her, would only inflict additional damage, and I can't bear the thought of committing yet another nefarious act where she is concerned. She deserves to have me gone. To have some peace." He patted his brother on the shoulder. "You once told me that I was not worthy of her."

"I didn't mean it!"

"Yes, you did, and you were right." He gazed up at the first visible stars, then around the ship—at the empty masts, the sails tidily wrapped and ready to be put to use. Soon he would be spirited away from this vile place of deception and woe.

"It was never meant to be, Matthew," he said quietly. "Let it go."

Suddenly the ship seemed too small. With the crew returned to duty, there was no corner where he could be alone. He required time away, to clear his mind and dissemble privately, while he made his own special good-byes to her. After they left England, he would have many long weeks on the deck to grieve in view of the others. For now, during these last few hours on the foreign shore, he needed to be secluded with only his memories.

He stepped to the gangplank. Halfway down, he turned and looked at his brother, standing on the deck, so solitary and forlorn. "You'll see," he asserted a final time. "My decision is for the best."

Strolling quickly, he jumped onto the dock and hurried off into the night, so he did not hear his brother respond, "The best for whom, you silly man?"

Penny sat at the dining table, pushing the food around with her fork. She had so little appetite, and she couldn't work up the energy required to become hungry. Abstinence from nutrition had caused her to drop a few more pounds, until her dresses hung loose on her slender frame. Although her health was in a perilous state, she couldn't muster the stamina to take better care of herself.

Nothing seemed worthwhile. She filled her days as she had before she'd ever had the misfortune to cross paths with Lucas Pendleton, keeping to her rooms, declining social invitations, and quietly going about a tedious routine of boring pursuits.

She couldn't find any purpose to getting up in the morning when she didn't have Lucas to love or Harry to fuss over. There was no bread that needed baking or garden that needed tending or child that needed watching. Most of all, there was no husband who needed a joyful coupling with his wife, a soft scrub of his back while he was at his bath, a kiss good-bye as he left for work.

As always, she couldn't get beyond the fact that she had spent such a small amount of time in their company, and yet they had managed to completely dominate the picture she had of her life and who she was. She couldn't remember how she used to pass day after month after year in this stifling house with her unhappy parents and frivolous brother. Sometimes the stillness became so intense that she caught herself listening for footsteps, a cough, laughter—any sign that real people occupied the drafty abode.

She didn't have anything to do! No tasks that required minding, no schedules to heed. Hadn't she always been someone's wife and mother, jobs that brought with them a myriad of duties and responsibilities?

No, came the surprising answer, and it was difficult to realize that she was not, had never been, either of those things, and that she had no useful activity to keep her busy. She felt unencumbered, unattached, and floating free of whatever cords had once bound her to her parents' world.

Upon returning that first night, she'd been brimming with righteous indignation, spouting plans for a home of her own. She'd craved a personal space where she could go and lick her wounds in private. How she'd wanted to simply collect her mother, and the two of them go to live in a spot where men couldn't hurt them. The duke could still have his women and his affairs, his schemes and intrigues, and they would never have to hear about or suffer from any of it.

But her mother obviously considered the concept to be preposterous, and Penny hadn't pressed her father on the idea. She couldn't abide the thought of meeting with him, talking with him, haggling over terms and costs. She was hurting too much to have a civil conversation, so she'd left things be.

Her plan remained a viable abstraction, rolling around on the edge of her consciousness, but she couldn't put it into action. Any discourse with the duke would require some referral to her episode with Lucas, and she wasn't ready to describe what had happened. So far her parents had been blessedly silent on asking about her ordeal, tiptoeing around her emotional state and physical presence as though she were ill and they must take extra care not to disturb her. After all, discussion would require that some of their feelings be aired, and who wanted that?

Don't talk about it.

The hidden message ran through the hollow halls of the Westmoreland home, and for once she embraced the overwhelming necessity for avoidance of any authentic emotional outbursts. If she sat down with her father, he would expect her to talk about Lucas, he'd demand to know the details, and she simply couldn't confess what was in her heart to someone who held her in such low esteem.

Although she'd never imagined that the duke fostered much affection for her, she'd always believed he possessed some. But he had no regard for her whatsoever, caring so little that she could have been murdered by a stranger and he wouldn't have minded. The knowledge was a greater burden than any daughter should have to bear.

Lucas was impossible to explain, as was their time together, so she couldn't speak of it. Not to anyone, not even to Colette, who had been there with her, who had seen how joyous Penny was at having encountered Lucas and how devastated she was by losing him. Colette had stayed by her side, pensive and helpful and worried, but supportive of Penny in her grief. For Penny understood why she was overwhelmed by such melancholy.

She was grieving. For the loss of her great love for Lucas. For the loss of the life she might have had with him and Harry. For the loss of her marriage and the happiness she assumed she'd found with her handsome, exciting new husband. Yet, all of those losses paled in comparison to the terrible discovery that no baby had resulted from their brief union. Two weeks after returning to London, she'd learned of her barren condition, and the news had seemed to be the greatest sorrow of all.

Although she tried to tell herself that a babe would have been the least desirable ending and that no pregnancy was the best for all concerned, in her heart she couldn't accept the wise counsel. A baby would have provided her with a piece of Lucas she could have always cherished.

Sadly she'd brought nothing of Lucas home from the country. No slip of clothing, no miniature portrait lovingly kept in a necklace charm, no lock of hair or other memento to smell and trail through her fingers. A child would have helped her to remember that handful of wonderful, thrilling days before she'd had the opportunity to learn what Lucas was really like.

Gradually her grand adventure would fade, her memories growing less vibrant, until it would seem as though none of it had ever happened. Her recollection of events would languish and decline, and she would look back and wouldn't be able to say for certain if it had really occurred or not. What a pathetic, sorry statement about the only truly extraordinary thing that had ever transpired in her long, boring life!

Down the length of the table she saw her father sitting at one end, her mother at the other. Both were chatting with their respective dinner partners about various inane topics. They appeared and sounded extremely gracious, the perfect host and hostess, while carrying on as though the other spouse weren't in the room. They could keep it up for hours, days. Their mutual disdain had been developed to an art form, and it might have been funny to witness if it hadn't been so pathetically tragic.

The gathering was an intimate one of only ten people, just family and a few extremely close friends, and much different from those her mother usually hosted every night this time of year. After the split with Edward had been announced, the gossipmongers had begun circling, and everyone was fishing for an invitation to one of Patricia Westmoreland's famous suppers.

As Penny no longer made the rounds in Polite Society, her peers were dying to find a route into the Westmoreland mansion, where they could feast their eyes upon her and decide if any of the wild stories they'd heard had the slightest basis in fact. Thankfully her mother had immediately shut down the flow of people coming into the house, a surprising move considering that it was now mid-April, the Season upon them once again, and all of the beau monde arrived for the festivities.

The dearth of celebrations had been her mother's only concession toward acknowledging that something out of the ordinary had befallen her only daughter. Yet, Penny had no misconceptions about what had prompted the change. The lack of parties had nothing to do with Penny's period of personal distress and everything to do with her mother's hating to have their name connected with any sort of scandal. The entertainments would remain modestly unpretentious until the members of the *ton* found something else upon which to focus their attention.

Just then her father's voice cut through the din of table noise, surprising her into alertness.

"A small shipping dispute . . ." he was explaining.

"With an American, you say?" asked the man with whom he was conversing.

"Pendleton," the duke said casually. "Lucas Pendleton is his name. He's trying to leave the country, but I've asked to have his ship detained. Possibly seized."

"Cargo and all?"

"Yes," the duke answered. "The man trifled with something precious that belongs to me. I intend to see that he pays, and pays dearly, for his rash act."

Penny looked up from her plate to notice her father watching her intensely, as though he'd hoped she'd overhear the snippet of information. In the three weeks she'd been home, it was the first and only occasion any mention had been made of Lucas or what had ensued while she'd been away.

She hadn't realized the Pendleton brothers were still in England, having assumed that they had fled the moment the blackmail attempt had fallen apart. In her floundering state of private despair, it had never occurred to her that her father had sought Lucas out, had harassed him in some fashion, maintaining ulterior plans with regard to his person and property.

Didn't the duke understand that she just wanted Lucas out of their lives? She had no desire to run into him or talk with him or pass him on the street. The pain that any type of encounter would bring was beyond imagining.

All eyes were upon her as she spoke for the first time during the meal. "What will you do with this American once you've gotten your hands on him?"

"I haven't decided what punishment will be severe enough."

Does he think he's doing this for me? she wondered as she stared him down. Was he acting out of the misguided impression that revenge must be taken on her behalf? Or was he proceeding for the same reason he always used to justify his behavior: that he was a wealthy, powerful peer of the realm who hated being bested by anyone?

Was it so important that he have the final say as to who would be hurt the most? And who would be the victims? Lucas's brother? Harry? Paulie? Perhaps it would be Lucas himself. Would the duke have him publicly whipped? Transported? Hanged? She couldn't suffer to imagine any of those punishments meted out to the man she had once loved so desperately.

Clearing her throat, she asked, "May I be excused?"

"Certainly, darling," her mother said, barely sparing her a glance.

Penny rose and hurried from the dining room to the back of the house, passing through the family's sunroom. It was dark, and she cautiously wound a path through the collection of plants and foliage and out onto the terrace, where a few lamps were lighting the pathways into the garden. Gazing up at the sky, she couldn't help wondering where Lucas might be. Was he at that very moment looking at the same stars? Was he contemplating all the damage he'd accomplished? Did he ever think of her as she thought of him every minute of every day?

Footsteps sounded, and her father stepped out of the house behind her. He had her trapped. Quite effectively too, but maybe he had the right of it. It was long past time they had it out.

He said, "You seemed quite upset at the mention of Captain Pendleton."

She shrugged, pretending disinterest. "No more than I am upset by any topic you might raise."

"I should like to know your opinion before I continue," he said. "What would be a valid outcome for the man?"

"I don't wish you to do anything to him. Or to his family. Both of you have already done more than enough." Unable to tolerate his unwavering scrutiny, she turned her attention out across the quiet yard. "Just leave him alone. Allow him to take his family and his crew and sail away from here. Away from me."

Startling her, he moved next to her and rested a gentle hand on her shoulder. In all the years of her life she couldn't recall him touching her in a loving manner. She closed her eyes to stave off the wave of tears the gentle contact induced.

"Penny," he sighed, "I can't stand having you so distressed. It's been weeks now. His ship is ready to sail, but how can I let him depart when you are in such a state?"

"It's easy, Father," she answered. "Pay no attention to him. Let him sail away."

"You never told me—" he started delicately, then stopped, paused, then started again. "In the beginning, when you left with him, you wrote me a note. It sounded as though you went willingly."

"Aye, Father, I did. Fool that I was."

"But I've never asked you what happened when the two of you were together. . . ." Easing closer, he rested a hip on the balustrade and looked into her eyes. His hand slipped into hers. A shocking development, indeed! "Can you tell me?"

"No. I will never speak of it."

"That is why I must prevent his departure. He's hurt you so terribly, but I don't know what sin it is of which he's guilty."

"Nothing as nefarious as you're imagining," she said carefully. "They are sins of the heart and no more. Hardly worth torturing a man over."

"Did he promise to marry you?"

"I thought we—" she began to admit, then shook her head. "It doesn't matter what I thought."

"I could force him to live up to the vows he made you. If you fancy him for a husband, just say so. If that's what is needed to bring a smile back to your beautiful face, I'll see to it that the nuptials are accomplished immediately."

"I don't wish to marry him," she said, pronouncing, "I shall never wed."

"Is there a babe?" he asked quietly.

"Don't worry, Father. There is no babe." The duke hissed out such a breath of relief that she felt compelled to add, "But I wish with all my heart that there had been one."

"Oh, Penny, my dear—"

She cut him off by breaking the link of his hand holding hers. It was too late for any type of comfort he chose to offer. Twenty years too late. "As far as I'm concerned, it's over, Father, and I never intend to see Lucas Pendleton again. Let him go so that he is away. Perhaps then my personal torment will cease." Tears flooded into her eyes, sparkling like diamonds in the lamplight. "I've not asked anything of you in a very, very long time. So, I'm asking you this: Let him be away."

"I don't know if I can agree, darling."

"Please!" she begged stubbornly, then, unable to continue, she ran into the house, leaving the duke standing alone and staring desolately at the night sky.

* * *

Lucas hid in the Westmorelands' garden, along the rear wall, where he'd first encountered Penny. He hadn't meant to come, but after leaving the ship he'd begun walking and hadn't been able to stop until his legs took him to this very place. For some reason, the images were more concentrated here, where she'd always lived with her family, where they'd first met and begun to fall in love.

How far they'd ventured from that precipitous moment!

Across the way Penny stood on the terrace, the lights on the poles casting her in shadows. She appeared so dejected and unhappy, and even in the semidarkness he could see how much weight she'd lost in the past few weeks. It took every ounce of fortitude he possessed to keep from sprinting across the yard and taking her in his arms.

During his restless stroll toward their property, he hadn't imagined that he might actually set eyes upon her, and he watched silently as she searched the night sky, looking for some type of message written in the stars. He'd tensed as the duke joined her but relaxed upon seeing the manner in which they talked. Her father held her hand and tipped his head close to her own, listening intently, as though the words she spoke were the most important he'd ever heard.

Before Lucas knew what had happened, Penny vanished. As she disappeared, he could hardly keep from calling out, from running after her. But he remained rooted to the spot, telling himself over and over that she would never forgive him, so asking again was futile. She didn't deserve the upset that would ensue if he inflicted his presence on her. To what purpose would he? The only reason would be an attempt to salvage a last bit of his pride in one final effort to explain away his deceptions, but the doing would be at her expense.

He refused to hurt her anew.

After she departed, her father remained on the terrace. He

seemed different from how Lucas remembered him. It was as though the last two months had aged him, leaving him older, weary, less dynamic. He gazed out at the sky much as his daughter had done, seeking answers but not finding them. Finally, on a sigh that Lucas could hear clear across the expanse of lawn, he went back inside.

Lucas stayed where he was, and he couldn't prevent the wave of profound memories that swept him away. Of Penny, and how special she was, compared to the woman he had imagined her to be in the beginning. Funny and enthusiastic, she'd been openly ready for whatever came her way. She'd taken to Harry like a mother with her own. In their small kitchen she'd puttered about, clucking and fussing and seeing to their happiness and comfort. Shyly she'd presented them with the bread she'd baked, the meals she'd cooked, trying to please them in every manner.

And she had. Oh, how she had!

Mostly he remembered how beautiful she was. On the night she believed they were marrying, she'd been a stunning sight. The candlelight had glowed in her hair and the love she'd carried for him had shone in her eyes. Willingly and eagerly she'd learned the ways of their marital bed, and she'd joined in their encounters with a wild abandon. She had delivered unmitigated joy into his life—when he had deserved so little.

His visions of her were so extreme that he was aware of little else, so that was perhaps the reason he didn't notice the quiet footsteps approaching from his right. Only when he heard the distinctive female voice, the one with the soft French accent, did he realize that he was not alone.

" '*Allo, mon ami,*" Colette growled.

Lucas tensed, then spun around. "Mistress Colette," he welcomed her, giving her a mocking bow. "I see we meet again."

"*Monsieur,*" she responded coldly in return.

"What are you doing out here?"

"I might ask you the same, *mon capitan,* but I must say I am not surprised to find you lurking in the dark, once again sneaking about like a thief in the night!'' Her angry eyes narrowed. ''I have been watching for you—each and every night!—because I suspected that this was how you would come. You are a coward, afraid to face my lady in the light of day!''

He looked down at her hands, relieved to see nary a weapon in sight. ''What? No knife? No pistol? You're slipping.''

''Hah! As if I would waste good ammunition on a dirty dog like you!''

''As always, mistress, I am stimulated by your stellar opinion of me.''

''I have been patient, because I knew you would eventually show your true colors.''

''And what are they?'' he asked, almost amused by her level of disdain.

''There is just one: yellow. You are a spineless animal. They should hold you down and paint the yellow stripe down your back!''

He blew out a heavy breath. London was an enormous city, yet he couldn't locate a single corner where he could nurse his wounds in private. Was there to be a chiding, good-intentioned busybody no matter the direction in which he traveled? ''Let it be, Colette,'' he said, too tired to fight with her. ''I'm in no mood to hear your criticism, and,'' he added, ''no matter how you would chastise me, the words are no more than I have already said to myself.''

''So . . . you have finally shown your despicable face in this place where you have caused so much grief and heartache,'' she said as though he hadn't spoken. ''What will you do now? Will you tuck your tail between your legs and scurry back to your America—like the rat you are?''

''I'm not running away,'' he insisted.

''Aren't you?'' Gesturing furiously toward the house, she asked, ''Will you leave her like this? Is that the kind of man you are?''

''Leave her like what?''

''My lady cries herself to sleep each night. She believes I

do not know, but I hear the ocean of tears she has wept for you. She lies in her bed all the day, without eating, without resting . . . wondering about you! Longing for you!''

"That's not true," Lucas said, shaking his head. It couldn't be!

"And she has informed her father that she will never marry. That she will never have a family of her own. All because of you! Because you have hurt her so terribly!''

"She won't forgive me, Colette. If I thought there was any chance . . .''

"Bah!" Her entire body shuddered with disgust. "You are not a man, Lucas Pendleton. You are a boy playing at a man's games. You and her father both are children! The two of you, you compete at your hateful boys' games, but it has all been at her expense!''

"I never meant to hurt her!''

"Oh, how you lie! You lie like a dog! And in the meantime my lady wastes away. Loving you! Missing you!" She started to retreat into the shrubbery. "You do not deserve the regard of such a fine woman.''

"What would you have me do?'' he asked, frantic to find an answer he could understand.

"If I would have to explain the course you should follow, then it is as I have always suspected: You are not man enough for her." Furiously she waved her hands toward the garden wall. "Begone, Lucas Pendleton, we do not need you here. Be off to America and leave us in peace.''

He waited in the dark, listening as she retreated as quickly and quietly as she'd come. Long after she'd retreated, he remained, rolling her comments in his head. She seemed convinced that deep down Penny still harbored sufficient affection to heal their rift.

Was Colette right? Was his brother?

Determinedly, as he pondered the past and the future, he began to understand what he had been working so hard to suppress in the weeks they'd been apart.

He still considered Penny to be his wife! Even though they weren't lawfully married, he deemed himself wed to her in his heart—where it mattered, where God would give his blessing. The legalities could be rectified later.

Was there a possibility she still felt the same? Given the opportunity, would she come around to loving him again as Matthew believed? Was there a chance?

Despite how he'd hurt her, she was his. She belonged with him, and not in her father's house and living under the duke's protection, for she had a husband who loved her more than life itself. If he quit England's shores without having her by his side, he didn't know how he'd manage to survive the remainder of his years.

She was coming with him! He could not let her go. He would not let her go!

CHAPTER NINETEEN

Lucas Pendleton hurried quietly down the long corridor of the extravagant mansion, counting doors as he passed. With his senses fully engaged in his stealthy endeavor, his eyes constantly scanned the area ahead, looking for movement and checking for hiding spots in case a servant came wandering down the abandoned hallway. Luckily he'd not seen another living soul.

Laughter whispered past from somewhere far off in the grand house. A handful of silver clanged on china, and he paused, listening for footsteps, but none came in his direction. He took a deep breath, let it out, then boldly started off again. His dispute with the Duke of Roswell was a family matter, and where Lucas's family was concerned, he would take any risk, shoulder any task, carry any burden in his efforts to protect them.

Stopping short, he glanced up and down the hall, then slipped into the library. A hasty scan of the room indicated that it was empty of human occupation. A fire burned in the grate, a brandy had been poured by an efficient servant and awaited the duke's pleasure. On tiptoe he walked to the end of the room to hide himself behind one of the heavy velvet drapes.

His wait was not a long one. In a matter of minutes, the library door opened, and someone crossed the floor, coming around the desk. Lucas peeked out just in time to view the back of the duke's head as he settled himself in the large chair. He appeared weary, very much as he had a few minutes earlier out on the terrace, and he leaned against the soft leather, relaxing for a moment before reaching for the glass of liquor.

With a silent step Lucas was away from the curtain and behind him, the barrel of a pistol dug deep into the duke's neck. "Don't move," he warned.

Westmoreland sighed tiredly, then asked, "Captain Pendleton, I presume?"

"Yes, 'tis I."

"What do you want? And please be quick about it."

"Place your hands where I can see them," Lucas said.

"Oh, for God's sake, man!" he said. "At least have the decency to come around the desk and look me in the eye!"

Lucas hesitated, assessing the area, searching for hidden weapons, rechecking his escape route. Satisfied that all was secure, he removed the pistol but kept it gripped in his hand as he skirted the heavy piece of furniture, and they were face-to-face.

Westmoreland dubiously regarded the gun. "Put that thing aside before you hurt one of us. And don't you dare shoot at that portrait," he said, pointing over the fireplace to where a new painting of the duchess had been substituted for the one Lucas had ruined on his previous visit. "If you wreck another one of my wife, I'll never have any peace for the remainder of my days."

"I'll try to control myself," Lucas said, tamping down a smile as he relented and tucked the pistol into the band of his trousers.

"I appreciate it."

"I'm here to talk about Penny."

"What a surprise." The duke gestured to a chair, and Lucas

pulled it closer and sat down. "State your case, and be done with it."

Without preamble Lucas said, "I'm asking you for her hand in marriage."

"Goodness, but haven't we turned into the polite swain all of a sudden?"

"I didn't ask before, so I'm asking now." He refused to let his temper flare over the duke's acerbic remark. "I want to marry her."

"As if she'd have you!" the duke scoffed. "Besides, from the way she tells it, you already had the chance to marry her and didn't. Why should I wish her to go through such heartache a second time?"

"Because she might be with child."

"She's not," he said curtly.

"She's not?" Lucas was completely deflated. He'd been earnestly hoping that a babe would be the link that would force Westmoreland to agree. "How can you be positive?"

"Because I asked her, and she told me." He leaned nearer. "Which is fortuitous for you, or I might very well come across this desk and kill you with my bare hands."

"I would not blame you," Lucas said humbly, obviously surprising the duke with his candor. "I apologize for using her in my scheme. She had no part in the quarrel between you and me, and I shouldn't have involved her. I did it badly."

"Yes," Harold said, nodding in agreement. His tone softened when he charged, "You've wronged her terribly."

"I know."

"And my family as well."

"I realize that."

"My, my," Harold said sarcastically, "aren't we the epitome of decorum? When did you become so bloody agreeable?"

"I see no reason to downplay my actions, and I'm here to rectify the situation . . . if you'll allow me."

"On what grounds could you ever convince me to let you repair the mess you've made of my daughter's life?"

"I love her."

"Well, she doesn't love you back—"

Lucas cut him off. "I wouldn't be too certain if I were you."

"Not thirty minutes ago she told me she hoped you would take your ship and flee the country." Harold shrugged. "She never desires to see you again. I'd hardly call those the sentiments of a woman in love."

"I was having my own conversation thirty minutes ago. With her maid."

"The Frenchwoman?"

"Yes," Lucas said, thinking that Harold appreciated so little about Penny that he didn't know the name of the maid who had served her for years. At least Lucas was ahead on that count. Who could ever forget Colette? "She related a much different story."

"I'll just bet she did," Harold grumbled. "So, what would you have me believe? That you and my daughter are a love match? That you're destined to be together, and I should permit the two of you to sail off into the sunset?"

"Something like that," Lucas admitted.

"You expect me to accept that Penny's level of distress is so great"—Harold's entire body oozed skepticism and incredulity—"because of her attachment to you?"

"Yes."

"She's merely suffering from a broken heart."

"Yes."

"She'd throw her lot in with you in an instant if given the chance."

"Well ..." Lucas prevaricated, "I wouldn't go that far. She's quite piqued with me."

"Sorry, Pendleton, but whatever you're selling, I'm not buying. I understand you too well, and there must be something else up your sleeve." He sipped his brandy and eyed Lucas carefully. "Tell me the real reason you've come."

"It is for Penny and no other purpose."

"You swear this?"

"I swear it."

"What of your demands for Caroline's boy?"

It hurt to hear Westmoreland refer to Harry as though he'd been immaculately conceived, but Lucas let it slide away with so much of his other outrage. Penny was all that mattered. "I make no demands. Harry has an exemplary home and a family who loves him. We don't need anything from you in order for him to have a happy life."

"I see," the duke said, pondering, while he toyed with the boundless implications of Lucas's announcement. "Explain something to me."

"If I'm able."

"How did you keep her there with you? And what caused her to return to my home?"

"I led her to believe we were eloping and that we would be married straightaway." Lucas blushed with shame. "We conducted a false ceremony; she thought it was authentic. Then she found that last note."

"The one from me?"

"Yes, and she easily deduced that it had all been a lie."

Harold steepled his fingers, then said pensively, "Hence, she has been your wife in every way that matters."

"Yes, sir," Lucas said, hastily adding, "but I won't apologize for what happened between us. It was a wonderful, joyful time, and she was incredibly content." He stood and started to pace. Westmoreland was a cool customer, and it was difficult to see what he was contemplating. Lucas didn't feel as though he was making any headway with his arguments. "I realize you don't know me, and what you do know isn't good—"

"Very true," the duke interjected.

"But I'm a good man. I'm hardworking, I'm honest, and loyal. I'm devoted to my family, and as Penny would become part of it, I would be devoted to her as well. I have a solid business and a beautiful home in Virginia. We raise tobacco and horses, and along with the shipping, they furnish me with a fair income. Not what she's used to here by any means," he said, looking around at the opulent ornamentation, "but she'd never go without. I have many long-term servants who would graciously give her first-rate attention. And it's a good place to raise children. I could give her the many, many children she craves and provide sufficiently for all of them."

"Penny wants a big family?"

"Yes."

"I didn't realize that about her . . ." the duke said wistfully, sad and perplexed at what had been lost over the years.

"She would be happy," Lucas vowed. "I would love her all my days. I swear it to you."

"I should take your word for it?" the duke asked chidingly. "Just like that?"

"Yes," Lucas nodded. "Just like that."

"After everything you've done, you barge in here, declare your suit, expect me to go along like a sheep to the slaughter. . . ." He sat back, assessing. "You're a bold son of a gun, aren't you, Pendleton?"

"I've always had to be, or I'd never have gotten to where I am today."

"Too true," the duke said, and at Lucas's questioning look, he clarified, "Actually I've learned quite a bit about you. You'd be surprised." He downed his drink, walked to the sideboard, and poured himself another—and one for Lucas too. When he returned to his seat, he handed the glass across, and Lucas couldn't help but be encouraged by the gesture. If he was about to be run off, laughed out of the room, or, worse yet, arrested and hauled away in chains, he didn't suppose Westmoreland would offer him a brandy first.

"Why did you go to the trouble of unearthing my past?" Lucas asked.

"Because it was imperative that I determine what kind of man had taken my Penny."

"So, you realized I wouldn't hurt her."

"I realized it from the beginning."

"I was convinced that you didn't care about her."

"I always have," Harold asserted indignantly. "Maybe I didn't show it as clearly as I should have, but what father wouldn't love her? She's a fine young woman. Very fine."

"Yes, she is," Lucas agreed, relieved to discover that he'd been wrong, to see the tenderness burning in her father's eyes.

"And from the details I've gleaned," Harold continued, "I'm certain you'd make her a worthy husband. But there's just one small problem."

"What's that?"

"She's so furious with both of us that we couldn't convince her to do anything. Not in a thousand years."

"Well, I have this idea," Lucas said, a confident grin slowly spreading across his face.

"I was afraid you were going to say something like that." Harold sighed. "All right, let's hear it. . . ."

"What is your surprise?" Penny asked her father while fanning her face in an unsuccessful attempt to move some of the overheated air in the stifling coach. They hit a rough bump in the street, and she lurched sideways, falling onto Colette, who sat beside her.

"All right, I'll tell you," Harold said, "although I had hoped to wait until we pulled up in front."

"Pulled up where?"

"I've found you a house that might be suitable. I thought you might like to take a look at it."

"Really, Father? You'd truly do this for me?"

"I'm not the beast you believe me to be, Penny," he said. "I ask that you try to remember that in the days to come. I desire only what's best for you, and I pray you will be happy and content with your life. That's all I've ever wanted."

"If you say so," she grumbled.

Her ungracious response was rude, and she hadn't meant it to be, but the Duke was behaving strangely, and the heat was taking its toll, causing her patience to wear thin. With his strange words his eyes were suddenly blazing with an intensity she'd never witnessed in him before. The effect was unsettling, and she couldn't help wondering what had brought about this sudden change of heart. Guilt? A desire to be rid of her once and for all? A father's love?

On pondering the last, she shook her head. It couldn't be anything that outrageous. Whatever the reason he was proceeding with his kind deed, she intended to remain cautiously optimistic.

Gradually she began to realize that they weren't heading out of the city at all. From the smell of rotten fish and putrid water, coupled with the level of noise outside the closed coach, she could discern that they were nearing the river. She lifted the curtain and hazarded a glance. As she'd suspected, they were approaching the docks.

"You said we were going to look at a house," she remarked irritably. "What are we doing here?"

"I have a quick appointment to keep first. It will take only a moment." With that, the carriage rumbled to a halt, and they sat in silence while the coachmen hustled about, lowering the step and preparing the door.

When it opened, Harold stepped down, and Penny peered after him, her view filled with a beautiful sailing ship, its paint newly applied, its varnish and brass fittings shining in the afternoon sun. It occurred to her that she'd never been on a ship before, and it was a beautiful vessel to see up close. She leaned out, looking up and down the wharf where they'd stopped. There were ships tied off as far as she could see in both directions, but the one directly in front held her attention.

"What ship is that, Father?" she asked, pointing to it.

"It's the *Sea Wind*. Part of the Pendleton line." He took a step away from the carriage. "I've finally decided what I shall do with your Mr. Pendleton, so I must talk with his brother. He's probably concerned that Lucas hasn't returned to the ship, and he'll need to be apprised of the details before he sails today." Not trying to hide a guilty smile, he added, "Unfortunately Lucas Pendleton won't be joining his brother for the voyage home. In fact, he won't be going anywhere for a very, very long time."

"What, Father?" she called, but he was already moving through the bustling crowd and toward the gangplank. "What have you done?" she shouted more loudly, but he was already away and couldn't hear her question.

Where was Lucas? He wasn't leaving for Virginia? Had the duke had him thrown in jail? What other reason could be serious enough that they would journey to this foul place in order to inform Matthew?

She was furious. Hadn't the blasted man listened to a word she'd said? He wasn't supposed to do anything to Lucas! Or to his family! Did Penny have to hit the duke over the head to make her point?

Just then Colette leaned close and peeked out the door. "That is the captain's ship, *non?*"

"Yes, Colette."

"You don't suppose—" She paused, then gasped.

"What?" Penny queried, startled by Colette's reaction.

"I was just curious. . . . What if *mon petit* Harry is on the boat? In the very moment your father may come face-to-face with his boy. I cannot think this is such a good idea."

"Oh, no," Penny groaned, distressed. She didn't think it was a good idea either. Not for father or son. Before taking the opportunity to reconsider, she was out of the coach and scurrying after the duke, hailing him, but he was already on board. From what she could observe, the ship appeared deserted; no one was about, so she followed her father with Colette close on her heels.

As she stepped onto the deck, her worst fear was realized as Harry burst out of the hatch, crying, "Penny! Penny! It's you! You're here!"

Paulie accompanied him, and the two boys raced to her side, unable to contain their excitement. She hugged them fiercely, powerless to hide the joy she felt at seeing them again. Harry began chattering a mile a minute, trying to describe every mishap that had occurred in his life in the past three weeks. She couldn't bear his happy babbling; she truly couldn't, and a few tears worked their way down her cheek.

"Miss Penny!" Paulie exclaimed, looking aghast. "We've made you cry."

"Oh, no," Harry breathed. "We didn't mean to."

"You haven't done anything," she said, forcing herself to regain control. "I'm just so very glad to see both of you."

"Have you been well?" Paulie asked.

"Well enough," she lied. "How about you?"

"We've been so grand," Harry answered. "We're going home, and Paulie is coming with us. We're going to turn him into a sailor; that's what Uncle Lucas says. Just see if we don't."

"That's very nice," Penny murmured, immensely relieved to hear that Lucas had kept at least one promise. "And look at you," she said to the older boy, grasping him at arm's length and shifting him back and forth. "You've grown a foot."

"What are you doing here?" Paulie inquired. "Have you decided to travel with us after all?"

"Please say you will," Harry interjected. "Please!"

The encounter turned awkward. Staring into their hopeful faces was too painful, and she struggled to take a deep breath as she said softly, "I haven't changed my mind. I'm just visiting with my father. He needs to speak with your uncle Matthew," she said, daring a glimpse at the duke for the first time since Harry had rushed up.

When she would chance to recall the incident later in life, she would always remember it as the only occasion she'd ever seen her Father rendered completely speechless. He'd turned white as a ghost, and Penny wondered if he might faint.

"Are you all right, Father?" she asked gently, moving to his side. Apparently the meeting was just as shocking for him as she'd imagined it might be when she'd initially seen him climbing up the gangplank.

"I need to sit down" was all he could manage to say.

"Here you are," she said, easing him against a pile of rope. Penny glanced over at the two boys. They were staring at the adult man who was acting so oddly. She said to Paulie, "Could you go find Matthew for us?"

"Certainly, miss," he said, eager as always to do her bidding, and he hurried off.

She turned back to her father, noting the emotions that passed over his face as he regarded his son for the first time. The blond hair and the high cheekbones. The blue eyes and sharp intelligence. They were exact copies, one of the other, although Harry's hair was a shade darker. Even their bodies responded in the same fashion. They held their hands in a loose fist, tipped their heads just so while they carefully assessed each other, committing face and countenance to memory.

"My," Harold choked out, barely able to talk, "what a fine-looking lad."

"He is, Father. He's a wonderful boy."

"Would you introduce me?" He rubbed distractedly at the center of his chest as though his heart were aching.

"Yes," she said, reaching for Harry and urging him closer. With the duke perched on the stack of ropes, father and son were nearly eye to eye. "Harry," she began, "this is my father, Harold Westmoreland. Father," she added, "this is my good friend, Harry Pendleton."

"Hello, Harry," the duke said, pride and amazement shining in his eyes.

"How do you do, sir?" Harry said in impeccable tones, not sounding like the young child he was. "Are you the king?"

"No, Harry, I'm not." The duke smiled warmly.

"You look like you might be the king."

Harold reached out as though he wished to hug the boy, but at the last second his hand dropped to his lap. Stunned beyond measure, he simply stared and stared, then stared some more and finally said, "I knew your mother."

"Were you a friend of hers?" Harry asked.

"I suppose you could say that," he replied cautiously.

Out of the blue, the boy inquired, "Were you kind to her?"

"No, Harry," the duke admitted frankly. "I wasn't kind to her."

"Then, I hate you," he spit out, and he stepped forward and kicked the duke in the leg so hard that he had the man bent over and gasping in pain and shock.

"Oh, my Lord . . ." Penny breathed, embarrassed but amused as she grabbed the lad and pulled him away.

But Harry wasn't finished with his father. Standing rigid and tall, appearing every bit like the gentleman who had sired him, he pronounced angrily, "How could you have been cruel to my mother? She's an angel in heaven. How could you not love her?"

His authoritative voice rang across the deck, and Penny was surprised to notice that the duke actually had tears in his eyes. "I'm sorry, Father," she said, wincing while trying to decide how a person could possibly fix a moment such as this. "I never imagined he'd . . ." But her voice trailed off.

Rubbing his leg and surveying the boy with a brutal respect, Harold stated somberly, "I suppose I deserved that."

Just then Matthew Pendleton walked into the middle of the dreadful scene. Penny took a quick assessment of him, but she refused to be civil to the scoundrel who had so adeptly helped Lucas to break her heart, so she used Harry to escape, saying, "Harry, my father wishes to talk privately with your uncle. Perhaps you could show me your quarters while they're busy. I've never been on a ship before."

"Really?"

"Really," she answered. "Would you like to give me a tour?"

"I'd like that, Penny," he said decisively. "I should like that very much." He moved away, a wary eye cast in the duke's direction.

"Lead on, my little duke," she murmured, speculating on how long it would take for her father to recover from the

emotional strain of the rendezvous. She left the two men to
their business, and she was distracted by events, so she failed
to notice the keen look of triumph that Colette flashed to them
before attending Penny, offering assistance in descending the
ladder.

Penny disappeared from view, and Lucas slipped onto the
deck and walked up to Harold. "Our plan worked well," he
said, displaying an impudent grin that exhibited much more
bravado than he was feeling. Facetiously he added, "We didn't
even have to tie her up to get her here."

"I'd better be away," Harold mumbled, surprisingly having
to pause and wipe his eyes with the back of his hand.

At seeing his obvious distress, Lucas asked, "Is something
amiss?"

"I hadn't imagined . . . that is, I hadn't realized the boy
would be on board. It never occurred to me."

The duke appeared stricken, and Lucas glanced at his brother,
seeking an explanation. Out of the corner of his mouth he
asked, "What happened?"

With raised brows Matthew said, "The duke and Harry just
met." He leaned closer and whispered, "I don't think Harry
liked him very much."

Harold was quickly regaining control of his swirling sentiments. He stood, though he was shaking and his knees were
weak. He asserted, "She's going to be extremely angry in the
beginning." He smiled halfheartedly. "I don't envy you the
first few days."

"Neither do I, but she'll come around. I'm not worried. It's
a long, long way to Virginia."

Reaching to the inside of his coat, Harold extracted an envelope and gave it to Lucas. "Show this to her when the time is
right, will you?" he asked. "It clarifies why I agreed to help

you. It's important to me that she understand my reasoning. Hopefully someday she'll forgive me.''

Lucas patted him comfortingly on the shoulder and insisted, ''I'm sure she will in time. Don't fret.''

Harold fumbled around and produced another envelope. ''This one is for you. It's the information about her dowry accounts, her trusts.''

''I'll handle them well.''

''I don't care about the accursed money!'' Harold proclaimed vehemently. ''I care about her! Be kind to her, or you'll be dealing with me. Make her happy.''

''I intend to,'' Lucas vowed.

Harold took a step to go. Paused. Turned. For a telling moment he frowned at Lucas, struggling with an inner torment. ''Write to me about the boy,'' he finally declared. ''Tell me about him and about his mother. Explain what it is you'd like me to do. I'll consider it.''

''Thank you,'' Lucas said, surprised and dazed by this bizarre, sudden change of heart. ''You'll never be sorry.''

''No,'' Harold admitted, ''I don't imagine so. Watch over them both.''

''I will,'' Lucas promised. ''Good-bye.''

Lucas held out his hand in farewell, and Harold clasped his tightly in Lucas's own. They shared the bonding handshake for as long as they dared—partners in crime, cohorts, accomplices, two men who were hoping to soon be in-laws—then, without another word, Harold hastened down the plank to the dock.

Lucas looked at his brother and issued the command. ''Cast off.''

Matthew gave a quiet order. From out of nowhere sailors emerged and efficiently went about their tasks. Slowly, imperceptibly the ship left the land and found itself caught by the river's strong current.

Harold Westmoreland waited impassively next to his carriage until the ship disappeared from sight.

Penny was fascinated by the *Sea Wind*. She lingered much longer than she'd intended, encouraging Harry and Paulie to show her every nook and cranny.

In all the romantic stories she'd read as a girl about pirates and sailing heroes, none of them had ever mentioned how cramped the quarters were. Or how dark and dreary. The galley was the only area of any significant size, being where the food was cooked and eaten, but it was also where the sailors slumbered in shifts, hanging from hammocks in the corner. There were no portholes to welcome daylight, and the ceiling was terribly low. In several spots she was forced to crawl on her knees in order to move from one section to the next.

She couldn't imagine how a person remained in such a place for weeks or months at a time, though to be fair, she forced herself to remember that the *Sea Wind* was a working vessel, not a pleasure craft.

Toward the rear of the ship there was a handful of cabins where the officers slept, tucked along either side of the curve of the stern. Peeking in, she could see that they contained only enough space for a narrow cot and small trunk. The center hallway ended at the captain's chamber. It, too, was small and cramped, and nothing at all like the rooms of her imagination. She'd always envisioned a ship's captain as living a life of luxury whenever he came belowdecks.

The cabin was austere in its furnishings, with another low ceiling that provided a claustrophobic ambiance. A desk sat in the middle, covered with maps and logbooks. There were bookshelves lining the walls, filled with volumes on science and ocean travel. There wasn't even a bed! Paulie showed her the roped hammocks, the same as those used by the older sailors, that were pulled out at night and hung for the boys to sleep in.

From the looks and sounds of it, the entire affair of sea voyaging was some sort of fantastic male adventure, where they were constantly forced to rough it, and she decided that was why so many men were drawn to be sailors. They could play at the type of hard life men seemed to enjoy without any women hanging about and ordering them to bathe, dress, or eat better. By its very condition, the boat wouldn't permit them to engage in hygienic habits.

Lucas's presence in the cabin was strong, the very essence of his spirit ingrained into the planking. She sensed him overwhelmingly, so she was unable to prevent herself from dawdling. It was the last occasion when she would be near him or his belongings, and she suffered from an irresistible impulse to make a final good-bye. She couldn't prevent herself from committing everything to memory.

Much longer than was wise she tarried, reading the titles of his books, running her finger across his handwriting in the ship's log, looking through one of his trunks. When she realized that the clothing so carefully folded inside was the same that she had lovingly touched in his armoire during the short time they'd lived together, she hastily closed the lid.

Her heart pounding, her face unexpectedly hot, she had to get out of the stuffy, confined enclosure and into the fresh air. Immediately! But a quick escape was no easy task. From the manner in which they'd come down, winding and crawling through the stacks of provisions, storage, and supplies, it would take several minutes to accomplish an exit. As she requested that the boys show her the route back to the top, she took slow, measured breaths, trying to calm her shattered nerves.

Why, oh, why, had she ever been so foolish as to come on board?

The trip out of the narrow, dimly lit passage seemed more difficult than it had been when she'd first begun exploring. There was a slight sway now underfoot, making it harder to find purchase. Finally she espied the base of the ladder near the bow, the bright swatch of sunlight shining in, and she eagerly rushed to it.

She stepped to the bottom rung and began to climb. As she neared the top, a hand extended down through the hatch to help her navigate her ascent. Glad for the offer of assistance, her eyes on her feet and her full skirts, she grasped it tightly. Her foot reached the last rung, and she maneuvered onto the deck, blinking in the bright daylight as she readjusted from the darkness of the hold.

The helping hand still held hers, and she gazed around, trying to make out images while her vision cleared. Finally she was able to see the face of her attendant.

"Hello, my pretty Penny," Lucas said, smiling, his eyes full of love and desire.

Unable to believe what she was witnessing, she blinked numerous additional times before managing to convince herself that she was truly seeing Lucas. He wasn't an illusion, and for a moment, a single one, the same look of love and desire shone through her own eyes.

Although she didn't want it to be so, he was just as tall, just as sturdy and broad as she recalled. Her vivid imagination hadn't embellished reality. If anything, he was more handsome than her memories. The hopeless attraction she always felt for him was alive and well. Her pulse beat a trifle faster at finding him so near, her skin tingled, her cheeks flushed, and she breathed a bit more rapidly, needing to fill her lungs with the scent of his skin and clothes.

With a wifelike attention to detail, she noticed that he'd trimmed his hair. It was several inches shorter but as thick and dark as ever, and she caught herself wishing she could run her fingers through it, then lay her open palm against his beard-stubbled cheek.

Lord, but it was so good to see him again. The day seemed more cheerful, the sky bluer, the ache in her heart a little less severe, but as quickly as the potent feelings rose to the surface and swept over her, she tossed them down into the absurd pit from which they'd sprung.

Because along with the love and longing he instilled, she also remembered everything else. The betrayal, the loss of trust, the failure of love.

She hated him!

"You!" she said, yanking her hand away and taking a step back, but her legs were unreliable, and she swayed precariously.

"Easy," Lucas cautioned, grabbing her elbow and steadying her.

"Don't you dare touch me!" she declared, shaking him away and balancing herself by grabbing hold of a barrel.

Frantic for rescue, she cast about from side to side, but nothing looked familiar. For one dizzying moment she questioned whether reality had slipped and she had entered some sort of altered dimension. Her entire surroundings were different, and her mind couldn't process what she was beholding.

The busy docks were gone, the long line of tall ships a speck off in the distance, and London was briskly disappearing. She could barely make out her father's extravagant coach. He was standing next to it, unmoving. If he also saw her, he didn't wave or give any indication.

And she was encircled by water stretching in every direction. Ahead, the Thames grew wider and wider, awaiting its chance to sweep her out into the vast, huge ocean.

"What have you done now?" she wailed, running to the rail and glancing about agitatedly while calling, "Father! Father!" even though he was far away.

He couldn't have agreed to this! He wouldn't have!

She whirled on Lucas, and he was standing there, looking so serene and content, he was lucky she wasn't holding a loaded pistol. She'd have shot him in the chest without a second thought or moment of regret. For the first time in her life, she understood what circumstance would reduce a person to commit murder. The desire was so overpowering that she could feel the steel of the trigger in her hand.

As she stared him down, a clear picture of duplicity began
to form, one that only fueled her anger. Lucas and the duke
had met secretly, plotting how the duke would lure her to the
ship; Lucas would be allowed to steal off with her.

Fuming, she speculated as to when and where they'd completed their clandestine discussions, what sorts of bargaining
they'd resolved in order to arrive at their decision. Had the
boys and Colette offered assistance? Was no one in the entire
world her true friend?

What would they all have done if she hadn't been so atro-
ciously gullible and walked aboard on her own two feet. What
then? To what lengths would they have stooped? Would they
have bound and gagged her, then dragged her onto the ship
kicking and screaming?

Why had the duke proceeded in this fashion? Did he care
so little? Despise her so much? She thought of her home in
London, and the life she'd passed there with her parents. How
unhappy she'd been! How lonely! How desperate for some
scrap of attention that never came her way. Yet, twenty years
later, she was still pining away and wondering why he'd never
been fond of her.

What a pathetic creature she was!

Harold Westmoreland was a man who would abandon his
daughter to the likes of Lucas Pendleton! who would entice
her and trick her so that Pendleton could abscond with her
anew. He'd delivered her, then walked away. To Lucas! To
the man who might as well have ripped her chest open and
torn her heart out with his bare hands! He was to have her
now, after everything.

Her father was all despicable characters rolled into one, yet
she mourned this most recent betrayal as though it were the
first.

Fool!

Over her shoulder the water was rushing by, gradually moving faster. A sail was hoisted, then another as they gained
speed, each knot taking her away from England and her father,

stranding her with Lucas. For a brief moment she considered jumping the rail and letting the river swallow her up so that she'd never have to set eyes on either one of these detestable men again.

As quickly as the notion arose, however, she realized she'd never commit such a cowardly act. She was too angry, and she intended to live to a ripe old age in order to spend the rest of her days planning and taking her revenge against both of them. It would take decades to sufficiently vent her wrath!

The nerve of them, imagining they knew best! After all their games and manipulations! For the two of them to decide what the future course of her life should be! The gall! The arrogance!

"Turn this ship around, Mr. Pendleton," she commanded. "Right now!"

"Sorry, but I can't."

"Why?" she asked bitterly across the expanse of deck. "Why would you do this to me?"

He took one step toward her, then another. "I wanted you to come with me. I always did."

"I hate you!" she insisted as he advanced.

"No, you don't."

"I do!" Another step. "I really do!"

"I saw how you looked at me just a moment ago."

"How?" Another.

"You were ecstatic."

"And you are a dreamer!" He was only a step away, so close that she could see the gold flecks in his dark eyes, the spot where he'd nicked himself shaving.

Softly he asserted, "You're glad you're here with me."

"I'm not. I swear, if I had a pistol, I'd shoot you right through your black heart."

"No, you wouldn't," he said, smiling brazenly.

"I would," she said, nodding vehemently. "You're a swine, a bug, a gnat—"

"You're mad about me."

"No! Oh, no! I think you are the most contemptuous, conceited, overbearing, pompous—"

He cut off her tirade with a kiss. It was light as a butterfly, so fleetly begun, she hadn't time to prevent it, and so promptly concluded that she almost couldn't tell if it had truly happened.

"Don't be angry," he said good-naturedly. "This is for the best. You'll see."

He looked so smug, so self-assured, so presumptuous, and his confidence in his ability to judge her wishes made her so indescribably furious that she moved back, wound up, and slapped him just as hard as she could.

Without another word she pushed past and went below. As she settled in her cabin for a nap, he was still rubbing his sore jaw.

CHAPTER TWENTY

Penny stayed in her cabin for six days. At least she thought it had been six days. Being down in the hold with no window, she could only guess at the hour. One dark, dreary moment seemed very much like the next. The only change was in the level of noise, although even that was minimal. Occasionally sounds would drift in her direction from the galley located at the other end of the ship, making her suppose the sailors were eating or their work shift changing.

Her cabin was one of the tiny hovels along the stern. Nothing about the small enclosed space offered comfort. It was stuffy, hot, dismal, and she languished, minute after dragging minute, on the miniature cot, feeling the sway of the hull and listening to the creak of the ship's timbers as it glided through the water.

Twice a day Colette laid a tray of bland lukewarm food outside her door, along with a tiny basin of water for washing. She'd give a quick knock and ask if Penny needed assistance, to which Penny always advised her to depart immediately. The boys stopped by sporadically, speaking softly and trying to cajole her to emerge. Since they were children, she could hardly blame them for the scheme that had landed her on the *Sea*

Wind, so her answers were more polite but still the same: Go away. Leave me alone.

Her door didn't have a lock, and there didn't appear to be any method of securing it. To keep others out, she'd heaved one of her two large trunks in front, using it as a barricade against anyone who might try to enter. No one had. If they'd wanted, they could have simply shoved hard enough against the door to move it aside, but apparently they'd all decided to permit her to suffer in solitude while she came to terms with what had happened.

They had all conspired to bring her to this unbearable juncture, and as she rested on the lumpy mattress, her gaze shifting from the low ceiling to the narrow walls, then back again, she endeavored to find one positive point, but nothing came to her. She was trapped for the duration, and she wasn't certain what to do about it.

The space on the vessel was too limited to allow for any privacy. If she walked into the corridor, she'd instantly be elbow-to-elbow with a group of people she detested, none of whom she wished ever to set eyes on again. There was nowhere to take a unaccompanied afternoon stroll, no place where she could sit quietly and read a book or look out at the rolling waves. So she remained where she was, flat on her back in her cabin.

From where she lay the view was extremely depressing, mostly because the only objects she had to look at were the two trunks containing her clothing. They'd been stuffed full of her belongings and delivered to the ship without her knowledge, and already stowed away by the time she'd arrived. Somebody had gone to a great deal of trouble to prepare the luggage, and to ensure that it contained exactly the items she would require for comfort during the lengthy voyage.

After reviewing the contents, she decided that Colette had done the packing, and the realization of how her maid had connived with the others to bring her on board was shattering. She must have secretly toiled away, right under Penny's nose, in order to have the lot ready on time. For years Penny had felt as though Colette were her only friend, and the betrayal hurt, although she couldn't lay the entire blame at her servant's feet.

There was no doubt that Lucas had a hand in the arrangements. The dresses were all in shades and styles he liked. They were simple, lightweight, and easily laundered, as though he'd taken time explaining what would be best for Penny to wear. When she imagined him giving Colette instructions and wardrobe suggestions, her temper flared anew.

No one was safe from Lucas once he started in on them with that silver tongue of his. Lies and falsehoods swirled out of his mouth with ease, and even suspicious, reticent Colette hadn't stood a chance. Wholeheartedly she'd jumped into the middle of this latest scheme, playing her part well and doing everything she could, along with the rest of Lucas's accomplices, to guarantee that Penny would be at Lucas's mercy.

And hadn't they all succeeded beyond their wildest dreams? For what was she to do?

The crossing to America would take many weeks, so she could hardly stay locked in her cabin. Lunacy would overtake her if she tried. On occasion she would need to find the necessary fortitude to leave the cabin in order to enjoy some exercise and fresh air. There had to be some method she could use for moving about on the deck, while at the same time managing to keep her anger sufficiently contained so that she didn't murder anyone on sight.

However, so far the prospect of peaceful interaction with her shipmates was out of the question, chiefly because she'd had such a lengthy opportunity to ponder the quandary into which they'd forced her, and she couldn't figure out how to fix the situation they'd taken such care to create.

After they arrived in America, then what? She didn't know anyone who lived in Virginia or anywhere else on that continent. One casual acquaintance resided in Jamaica, but even without checking a map she was certain that the island was quite a distance from the Pendleton home. If she'd felt comfortable sending a letter to the friend—which she didn't—and asking for assistance, she had no money with which to mail it.

Going back to England was absolutely out of the question. She had no funds in order to book passage. But even if she returned, to where would she travel? She wouldn't dare once again to place herself under the duke's protection. Talk about walking back into the lion's den! Bearing in mind what he'd accomplished so far during the two decades she'd lived in his home, she wasn't about to let him take another stab at orchestrating her future. She'd suffered through an abundance of his attempts at guardianship and was ready to risk it on her own.

Which meant she had no options at all. Other than to stay with Lucas. But stay as what? She refused to put her tender heart at his mercy by marrying him a second time. As far as she was concerned, the knave had had one shot at her affection, and he wasn't going to get another.

The alternatives were to convince him either to pay her way back to England or to find her the means to live on her own in America. However, after all the trouble he'd gone to in abducting her, she doubted he would agree to any idea she proposed. Actually she questioned whether they could even have a rational discussion regarding a resolution. Focusing on her plight would require conversation, and she enthusiastically intended never to speak with him again.

The only other course of action she could determine was to linger in his home until she became a permanent houseguest. Perhaps she could simply while away the years in one of his upstairs rooms until she began to putter around and mutter to herself like some crazed old auntie!

The vision of herself, aged, mad and alone, and still dangling after Lucas Pendleton, caused a hysterical swell of giggles to burst to the surface, and she lay there in the confines of her cabin, laughing so long and so hard that she began to suspect that insanity was already settling in.

She had to get out! The enclosed space was confining and stuffy, and she could hardly take a breath. It was hot too. With each passing day, as they sailed farther from her homeland, the air was getting warmer, until it lay heavy and moist on her skin. While resting on her cot without stirring or doing any chores, she'd broken out into a sweat, so she'd changed into the skimpiest of her nightwear, but perspiration continued to pool between her breasts and under her arms.

Once upon a time, when she'd still loved Lucas, she remembered him saying that the way home was south from England, toward Africa, and then across the Atlantic Ocean on the temperate tradewinds. When she closed her eyes, she could imagine what it must be like on the deck at the moment. The atmosphere would be bracing and humid, the sky clear, the wind strong and stimulating and pushing the beautiful white sails as the ship raced along the crest of the waves.

Outside was exactly where she needed to be, because the ship was rocking back and forth like a wild bucking horse. How was a person supposed to find serenity with this constant motion? She had to see the out-of-doors! She had to get out of the stifling room, or she just might become deranged.

From the lack of bustle she was fairly certain it was the dead of night, although with the length of time she'd kept herself locked away, it was difficult to know. Surely all of her nemeses would be asleep, and the only people she might encounter were the handful of sailors who had the misfortune of manning the canvas in the dark.

Hastily she shrugged off her nightgown and tugged on a dress, doing nothing to her hair or person, not even putting slippers on her feet. Then she nudged aside the trunk and opened the door, needing to be away.

Observing no one, she tiptoed out. A few feet from where she stood, there was a ladder ascending through an open hatch. It hadn't been there on the first occasion when she'd been lured into the hold and become trapped. Obviously Lucas had closed it in order to make her escape more difficult, but she was glad to see it now. She could pop up onto the deck, take a quick walk about, inhale the sultry air, and be sheltered in her cabin before anyone knew she'd been out of it.

Pell-mell she climbed the ladder, frantically kicking at her skirt as she went. Without any petticoats it was too long, and the bottom kept getting tangled about her feet. Then, blessedly, she was at the top, and as she stepped out onto the rolling deck, raindrops splashed on her face. They were warm and fat and big, and they showered down on her hair and skin, drenching her from head to toe.

Off in the distance, lightning flashed against the horizon in all directions; thunder rumbled past, appearing so close that she could feel it pressing down. The sky was black and gray, and through the occasional displays of light she could see rough, roiling clouds passing by. The world was entirely new and full of unleashed power, unlike anything she'd ever experienced before. She could smell salt and wind even though she'd never before realized that they held such enticing aromas. Her surroundings were invigorating and clean, and she couldn't pull enough air into her lungs.

She walked to the rail and leaned against it, her legs easily balancing against the roll of the waves. The rain washed down, wetting her face and the backs of her hands, saturating the fabric of her dress until it clung to her form like a second skin. The stout breeze pushed it against her torso, outlining her breasts, her taut nipples, her flat stomach.

Relishing the relief she felt after days of being stowed away, she raised her arms to the heavens, welcoming the freedom and joy of being part of the storm. It was raging and wild, and she absorbed its energy with a fervent, almost carnal animation, as though it had connected with her soul and she'd become one of the elements in the heaving, turbulent tempest.

The ship dipped into a huge wave, sending water splashing up over the bow and dousing her anew. Lightning flared over her shoulder, and she glanced around. Off to her right stood Lucas, not a dozen feet away. As though rapidly drawn to the

deck as she had been, he wore only a pair of his tight-fitting
trousers. They were soaked through and molded to his muscular
thighs and calves. Involuntarily she shuddered as she remembered those strong limbs entangled with her own, and how
forcefully and deftly he'd used them to maneuver her about
his bed.

His broad shoulders narrowed to his chest, which was bare,
the mat of dark hair wet and plastered against his fevered skin.
Not wanting to, she recalled the special musk hovering about
him, how he'd tasted on her tongue. She could just imagine
running her hands across all that brawn and bone, rubbing her
nose in the thick pile of hair, flicking at his nipple while it
pebbled and tightened with desire.

Between his legs his male parts were fully outlined. He was
aroused! His male member was engorged and straining to be
free of its confines. The two sacs dangled, swollen and ready
for the massage of her hand. In vivid detail she remembered
when he'd shown her how to pleasure him with her mouth,
how erotic it had been to fall to her knees in front of that
mighty erection. When he was just entering the bedroom, she
had liked to push his trousers off his hips and wantonly suck
him far inside. He'd always hissed out his breath, his stomach
muscles clenching at the rush of sensation provided by her lips
and teeth.

He'd tasted fiery and salty, his cock demanding and insatiable, and she'd reveled in the authority she held over him while
indulging him in such a shocking manner.

Perhaps it was the violence in the storm clouds or an intensity
on the wind, but, dear Lord, how she wanted to do the same
right at that moment. To fall to her knees and have the reckless
rogue at her mercy once again. She longed to luxuriate in one
of those savage rides of gratification in which they'd once so
impulsively engaged.

Though it was dark, she saw his eyes were glittering with
lust, his gaze like a torrid caress against her lips, her nipples,
the curve at the center of her thighs. Obviously unsettled by

his own incorrigible need for a vigorous coupling, he hastened toward her and held out a hand. She caught herself extending hers in his direction, so she turned and ran to the hatch as fast as her legs could carry her.

"Penny!" he bellowed at her back, but it might have been a rumble of thunder.

Racing, she hurried down the ladder to the safety of her cabin, where she lit the lamp with shaking hands. As the dim glow permeated to the corners, she grabbed for a towel and dried her face and hair, then stripped off her soaked dress, stepping out of it as it pooled about her ankles. Naked, she shivered, but not from the cold. As she briskly rubbed herself, her skin rippled with goose bumps, and her nipples pebbled to a painful ache.

At her back, the door squeaked, and she realized too late that in her alacrity she'd forgotten to return one of the trunks to its position as a barrier. Lucas was outlined in the shadows, water dripping off his hair and trousers, his enormous bulk occupying the diminutive space to capacity. She was thoroughly trapped by his entering; there were no extra inches that would allow her to skirt around him in order to flee. One footfall brought them toe to toe, and her nostrils flared at his smell, at the awareness she held of him as a virile, sensual man.

She did nothing to cover herself, remaining motionless, her back straight, her shoulders squared and braced for battle, while he looked his fill. As had happened on the deck, she endured his assessment like a physical embrace, and her body yearned for him with a devastating ache. Without asking he laid his fingers to her breast, his thumb manipulating the nipple. Instantly moisture flowed between her legs as her traitorous body welcomed his wicked touch.

"I've missed you," he said, his eyes burning fiercely as they meandered down her nude form.

"I've not missed you," she fibbed, glaring disdainfully. "Not for a moment."

"Liar," he said softly. "You're more beautiful than I recalled," he declared, then he fell to his knees, his palms on her buttocks. He shifted so that the hair of her mound was mingled with those on his naked chest. His lips closed around her receptive nipple, and he sucked it far back into his mouth, playing sweet games with the sensitive nub.

"No," she insisted, "I don't want this from you." But even as she spoke the words, her hand was at the back of his neck, imploring him to continue.

He moved to her other breast, giving it the same attention, then he squeezed the two full-sized globes together, the nipples only inches apart, and began swinging back and forth until she could barely tell on which one he sucked. All the while he was pinching and squeezing the raised tips until, against her will, her hips began to writhe and squirm against his chest.

Wrapping an arm across her backside, he urged her toward the cot. She encountered the slat of the frame, and he eased her down. Though in her mind she refused to obey his silent command, her body complied immediately. Her thighs spread the moment her back hit the uncomfortable ticking.

His concentration shifted from her breasts as he kissed a path past her ribs, her navel, her abdomen, until he finally placed himself where she most craved his attention. He began kissing her cleft, his tongue working its delectable rhythm into her secret cavity, and she couldn't resist flexing against the pressure of his mouth.

His arms gripped behind her knees, settling them over his shoulders as his hands rose to her breasts and began fondling her. She was open and splayed and completely at his mercy, and, without protest, she allowed him to drive her to a furiously intoxicating excitement. When his lips closed around the intimate protuberance that provided her with such rapture, she willingly jumped over the edge without pausing to contemplate the consequences.

Then he was over her and on her—exactly where she needed him to be—and their mouths melded, their tongues plunging and straining to be together. The taste of her sex was on his lips, an arousing erotic tang that made her desire him more than ever before.

His fingers went to the fly of his trousers, and then the weight of his swollen phallus demanded entrance at her core. He reared back, hovering precariously, his hand at the crown, ready to guide himself inside . . . when she reached between them and slipped her hand under his, encircling his hot, hard shaft with her palm.

At her gesture, an acceptance of the inevitable, his eyes broadened in satisfaction, and she centered him and extended her hips to receive his eager thrust. She braced for a frenzied joining, but he didn't comply. Once he had penetrated, he halted his movements, taking a slow, deep breath. Steadied on one hand, he ran the other over her face, neck, and bosom, tracing the lines and ridges of her features as though he were a blind man who could suddenly see again.

"Penny . . ." He smiled down at her with such love and affection that a sob caught in her throat. "Penny," he repeated softly, "I've missed you so. I never thought I'd feel you like this again. Tell me that you've missed me too." He leaned down, gracing her with a sweet kiss. "Say it."

"No," she responded as tears welled into her eyes. "I can't."

"Yes, you can," he persuaded her. "Tell me how much you want this. How much you want me."

"I won't," she said, shaking her head in dismay.

"Say it, love," he coaxed, "say it just for me." Then he began a tender, gentle exploration of her inner depths.

The ride was soothing and careful, a captivating combination of intense physical sensation and monumental emotional regard. With each press of his hips, she could detect her resolve slipping, her anger fading, and her common sense flying straight out the window. How did he manage to overwhelm her defenses so quickly and easily? All he had to do was gaze at her a certain way, give her an assured look, and her good judgment vanished as though she'd never had any in the first place.

If he kept at it much longer, she'd be completely enmeshed

in his life once more, as though she'd never succeeded in extricating herself. Being near him was breathtaking; he was a human whirlpool sucking her down into his torrent against her will, his current too strong to withstand.

But do you truly want to resist? her internal voice asked. Did she?

The steady tempo of their mating increased, and she let herself be swept up in the delight. Her hands went to his arms, holding on as the joining became more intense. He was stroking her with his entire length, propelling himself all the way in, then receding to the tip, then plunging in again. Sweat beaded on his brow, and the cords of muscles in his neck grew thick and marked with tension.

"I'm going to love you so hard and so deep"—he spoke through clenched teeth—"that I plant a babe in your womb. I want to make a baby with you, Penny. I need to know that my child is sheltered inside you."

"Oh . . . Lucas . . ." she breathed, unable to form an adequate reply. A child was the very entity he could give her to which she couldn't say no, the one true thing she had always craved. A child of his. A boy with dark hair and eyes who would act just like him, and who would grow to be an exotic, handsome man just like his father.

"Will you allow me to try, love?" He pushed in, pushed again. Deeper, deeper, each surge bringing her closer to her heart's desire. "Tell me that you want a babe as well, that my child is what you desire more than anything in the world. Or tell me to stop." He hesitated imperceptibly. "The choice is yours. What is your answer? You must decide, so we may know how to finish it."

She gazed up into the beautiful brown eyes that beheld her with such glowing devotion. Though he had hurt her terribly and she'd tried to convince herself that he was the worst sort of monster who had preyed on her unmercifully, she realized it wasn't so. The bad memories had vanished, along with her animosity and torment. In their place was a sensation of finally ending up where she'd always belonged from the very start.

Gone were the heartache and pain of the past weeks. All she could remember were those heady days they had shared at the country house, where she had been happy and inundated with joy. He had never been anything but attentive and amiable to her. He'd made her feel necessary, adored, and so very, very loved.

Of their own accord her legs circled his thighs, and she locked them behind his back, holding him close, providing him with his answer. His smile spread in exultation, and he steadied his hands on her hips.

"You'll never regret your decision," he vowed. "Not a single day of your life."

After considering his statement for a long while, she asserted, "No, I don't suppose I ever will."

"You'll have to marry me a second time. My brother will insist, I'm afraid."

"Your blasted brother . . ." she grumbled.

"Oh . . . he's not such a bad fellow once you get to know him." Looking chastened, he shrugged and added, "If it's any consolation, he thinks I'm a cad and a scoundrel. He kicked my ahh . . . behind quite effectively, on your behalf, in an attempt to explain his low opinion of me."

"Is that what you two were fighting about?"

"Yes."

"Well, then . . . maybe you're right: Maybe he's not such a bad fellow."

"He'll be so relieved if you say yes. So will Colette and the boys." He brushed a precious kiss across her lips. "So will I. Will you have me, Penny?" She vacillated, parts of her terribly leery, and he jumped into the void, hopefully striving to convince her. "Let us become a family, love. We'll proceed correctly this time, so I may proudly proclaim to the world that you are mine. Allow me the honor of being your husband. I swear that I will always be kind to you, that I will care for you and watch over you. And I promise that I will love you and shower you with affection for the rest of my days.''

What woman on the whole of the earth could have said no to such a stirring declaration? She sighed, realizing it was pointless to pretend that she didn't want what he was offering, that it was senseless to try to avoid a destiny written in the stars against which it was useless to struggle.

Many responses came to mind, each more logical and resourceful than the next, but she refused to spend much time pondering whether she was about to make the correct decision. And what was the correct decision anyway? If she didn't accept his overture, she gained nothing but a lifetime of wondering what might have been. She would pass by the gladness he gave her every minute and never again know this undiluted bliss.

''Yes, I will,'' she whispered.

''Oh . . . my true love,'' he said gently, and he leaned down and pressed his lips to hers.

Tears were stinging at her eyes, and she cursed herself a thousand times for a fool, but then he was urgent and eager inside her, his long, thick shaft massaging her mysterious passage, and suddenly none of her reservations mattered. There was only him, and their joined bodies, and the possibility that this amazing moment might bring them a babe to cherish.

She moved with him, her hips elatedly matching each penetration, until by the end, all she could do was hold on as the glorious waves of ecstasy washed over them with a stunning force.

The exhilarating encounter gradually concluded, and she was relieved to discover herself safely sheltered in his arms. He cradled her tightly until his erection finally began to wane, then he rolled to his side and held her so that her bottom was spooned against his front. Lazily he rubbed his hand in slow circles across her stomach, and she drifted off, thinking that there was nowhere else she'd rather be.

''I'll make you a great wife, Lucas Pendleton,'' she pledged quietly, just as she had on the night he'd first proposed in her father's garden. "Just see if I don't."

"I know you will," he said, sounding smug.

She elbowed him in the ribs. Hard. Then fell asleep with a smile on her face.